# The
# SUMMER
# OF '98

## Tay Marley

wattpad books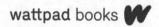

wattpad books **W**

Copyright © 2020 Tayler Marley. All rights reserved.

Published in Canada by Wattpad Books, a division of Wattpad Corp.
36 Wellington Street E., Toronto, ON M5E 1C7

*www.wattpad.com*

First Wattpad Books edition: July 2020

ISBN 978-1-98936-567-0 (Trade Paper original)
ISBN 978-1-98936-568-7 (eBook edition)

Library and Archives Canada Cataloguing in Publication
information is available upon request.

Printed and bound in Canada

1 3 5 7 9 10 8 6 4 2

Cover design by Ysabel Enverga
Images © yanlev
Typesetting by Sarah Salomon

*The*
# SUMMER OF '98

*Also by Tay Marley*

The QB Bad Boy and Me

To the readers. This book wouldn't have happened without you.

# MAY 28, 1998

## *Ellie*

There were rules when it came to attending an open frat party. I'd seen them in *Teen Cosmo* while at the nurse's office waiting room when my mom had an allergy shot a few weeks ago. I read the article as a way to pass the time. But now that I was at an actual frat party for the first time, I was reciting those rules in my head—I wanted to follow every step.

Alpha Theta Phi was one of the biggest frat houses in Waco, Texas. It belonged to Baylor and was along the same road as the several other fraternities and sororities. It smelled like stale beer and it looked like someone emptied a thousand trash bags and scattered garbage across the house. Nothing was broken. It was just a mess of beer bottles, solo cups, and glow sticks. It might be a nice place in between parties, but from what I'd heard, there was never much of a breather.

My best friend Amber managed to convince her sister, Sasha,

to let us come along tonight. Sasha's boyfriend is in the frat, and he, along with the rest of the house members, decided to throw the doors open to whoever wanted in as long as we paid a twenty-dollar entrance fee. They were trying to save so that they could fund a summer vacation in Mexico.

The first rule was obvious: *Don't leave your drink unattended.* No issue there. *Don't take your shoes off.* Looking at the floor, that one made sense. *Don't steal.* Who would do that? *Don't eat from the fridge. Don't break house items. Don't wear anything you care too much about.* That last one was harder. I wanted to look cute and all my clothes were treasures, considering I didn't have a huge wardrobe. *Don't go to the bathroom alone.* Again, another rule that made sense.

"Amber!" I shouted over "I Love Rock 'n' Roll." It was a shame that I was so desperate to pee—I loved this song. "Amber! I need to go to the bathroom!"

It was useless. She couldn't hear me. Or if she could, she was too drunk to respond. I reached out to give her a quick tap because her eyes were closed as she danced to the music with some cutie named Eric. He was from Colorado; he was here with a friend. That was all I'd acquired so far. When my fingers lightly connected with Amber's cheek, she startled and snapped her eyes open.

"I'm bursting! Can you come with?"

Making our way off the dance floor, we headed to the staircase to find the bathroom. I wasn't inexperienced with drinking or parties, but I hadn't been to one like this before. If Momma found out I was here, she'd blow a fuse. But Amber convinced me that it was the perfect way to celebrate our graduation.

We pushed our way through the crowd.

"Eric is so hot, right?" Amber slurred, we held onto each other—well, she held onto me—as we stumbled up the staircase. "He reminds me of Will Smith. But with more hair and a sharper jaw. He's so funny and sweet. Do we look good together?"

"You look perfect together."

"Am I being a bad friend? I shouldn't be chilling with a boy, should I? I've ditched you."

"No, it's fine! You came out to have fun. It's good. I'm fine."

And I was. Amber was always there for me when I needed her. She was one of those friends that was so familiar, she felt more like a sister. We could go three weeks without talking and fall right back into a routine when we saw each other again. Or we could spend three weeks straight together and never get sick of it. I loved her and I'd never stand in the way of her meeting a cute boy.

"Okay, good," she said. "You know I told him that as soon as school is out, I'm getting this 'fro twisted into locs and he said that I would look super cute and he approves and I said, I didn't ask for approval! But thanks, and then he said he loves a confident woman and I don't think a boy has ever called me a woman before, but damn do I feel sophisticated."

I laughed. "Make sure you get his number. He sounds like a total babe."

"Right?!"

As soon as we hit the landing upstairs, Amber was intercepted by a friend of Sasha's—Aliyah was her name. There was no way that I was going to wait while she had her drunk cuddles-and-catch-up. Normally the two had nothing to do with each other, but with the way they carried on, you'd think they were best friends.

I told Amber that I'd be back in a minute and dashed up the corridor where the bathroom was open. I slammed the door shut and locked it, breathing a sigh of relief when I finally got to sit down. There was something so uncomfortable about getting blackout drunk in a huge house of strangers, so I'd opted for being the sober friend tonight. There had to be one. But in place of beer, I'd downed a fair amount of soda.

When I was done, I gave my outfit a quick once-over in the mirror. Summer had barely started but I was a sun-kissed olive due to the weather we had almost year-round. My strapless crop top and denim midrise jeans were free of alcohol spillage and I was thoroughly impressed with how well the double-sided tape had kept my top from slipping down while we danced. The rules might have been to wear something dark and cheap, but I was proud of how well I was keeping free of spills. Perhaps it helped that I was sober.

When I opened the door, I froze—a group of guys had gathered in the hall. Ducking and weaving through them, I awkwardly made my way toward the staircase; luckily, they weren't paying any attention to me at all. But there was one boy who watched me with his deep-brown eyes. His dark, unkempt hair was effortlessly wavy in a tidy mess and his fitted T-shirt accentuated what appeared to be an incredible physique.

When I stole a glance behind me on the way to find Amber, he was still looking at me with a small, curious smile that made my heart hammer.

When a hand gently touched my shoulder, the beautiful boy was there behind me. "Hey," he said.

"Hey."

"I'm Leroy Lahey."

"I'm—"

"Stunning," he interrupted, and I couldn't help but laugh. He shook his head and almost looked as though he was blushing. "Sorry, go on."

"I'm Ellie Livingston."

"That's a beautiful name for a beautiful girl."

I laughed and folded my arms across my chest. "Do these lines usually work for you?"

"Lines?" he said. "Why would I use cheesy pick-up lines when the truth is so much more accurate?"

"Like I haven't heard that one before," I teased.

He slid his hands into his pockets. "Believe me, Ellie. The fact that my heart almost leaped out of my chest when I saw you is not something I could make up."

Okay, that rendered me a little speechless. I'd been hit on tonight, offered a drink here and there, grinded on. But no one had ever said something like that to me before.

"Single?" he asked.

"Yep."

"You gonna ask if I am?"

"You'd better be after *those* lines," I joked.

He laughed and the song coming from downstairs changed to "Summer of '69" and I heard a collective cheer before the words were being drunkenly sung. "I love this song. The music is so good here. I need to find out who made this CD."

"You know the theme is All-Out '80s, right?"

My face fell. "There's a theme?"

Leroy stepped closer when a group of girls ran past us toward the bathroom. "You didn't know?"

"Of course not. I have the perfect outfit at home for an '80s theme."

"Don't worry," he said. "Only the frat and sororities dress up. Most people are just here for the open party. Besides, the outfit you're wearing is perfect."

His gaze swept over me. He tousled his hair and a strand fell onto his forehead. I could feel my cheeks warming, but before I could even think of a response, a series of voices and clattering sounded behind me and I turned around to find Amber in a heap on the floor.

"Amber!" I ran forward to crouch down beside her. "What happened?"

"She's super drunk," Aliyah slurred. "I'll take her home."

"Ah, wait," I said as she lifted Amber off the ground. My friend blubbered and mumbled something completely incoherent, which relieved me a little. At least she wasn't dead. "You're drunk as well. You can't drive."

"I'm the designated drunk driver," she laughed and practically dragged Amber down the staircase. A few of her friends hollered in agreement, but I wasn't about to have it.

"No way," I said, bumping shoulders with people stumbling up and down the staircase as I chased her. Leroy trailed behind me. "You cannot drive her!"

"How did you two get here?"

"We took the last bus."

"How were you planning to get home?"

"A cab."

"I can drive her," Leroy said. By this point we were beside the front door, where dozens of people were coming and going, but no one found it unusual to see Amber in the state that she was in. "I have a friend's car keys. I'm the designated driver. I'll take her home."

"Who are you?" Aliyah asked.

"He's my friend," I answered. "Leroy."

Aliyah seemed satisfied and before long, Amber was laid across the backseat of a sedan while I sat in the passenger seat and gave directions.

"By the way," I watched the streetlights illuminate his features as I slipped a palm-sized canister out of my pocket. "I have pepper spray. And the will to live. So—don't be weird."

He burst out laughing and my heart skipped a beat at the sweet sound. "I was planning to kidnap you and lock you in my basement. But you've convinced me otherwise."

"You're not from here, are you?"

"Colorado," he answered. "I'm going to Baylor at the end of August. I'm here to finalize a few things."

"What are you studying?"

"Is it this one?" he asked, the car slowing down.

"Sorry. Yeah." I'd been staring at him instead of the road. "This one. Just pull over beside the curb, and if you don't mind, help me get her through the window?"

"How old are you two?" He switched the car off and stared at me with incredulity.

I was tempted to tell him that we were fifteen as a joke, but I thought better of it. "Eighteen. And yes, we're allowed some freedom. But drinking at a frat party? She'd be in trouble and so would I."

It was an effort to get Amber conscious enough that she could help herself out of the car. With some maneuvering, we managed to get her out and push her through the window where she landed on her bed. I leaned through and asked if she was all right.

"Mmhmm," she mumbled.

"You're a good friend," Leroy whispered. I appreciated him taking our sneaking about seriously. "I'm guessing that you're supposed to be staying here tonight as well?"

I chewed on my lip, replied yes, and peeked through the window again to the bright red digits of Amber's clock that said 10:30, and I sighed with frustration that she'd gotten so wasted so freaking early.

"I can drop you off again later if you want to come back to the party?" Leroy said.

"Really? Do you . . . do you want me to come back?"

"Yes," he said, "I need more time to get to know you."

The frat house was still pumping when we got back. Leroy put his hand at the base of my spine and steered me through the crowded entrance, where groups were gathered on the stairs, cheering as people slid down on cardboard and collided with the wall. There was a group of boys leaning over the railing around the top floor, throwing darts at a dartboard that was on the living room wall on the bottom floor.

"I was going to suggest that we sit in here," Leroy said, looking up at the half-drunk college kids flinging darts around. "But I don't really feel like getting stabbed in the head tonight."

He had a point. I looked at all the people gathered in the living area, all of the heads that could be the victim of a stray dart.

"Let's go out back," he said, leaning in close and taking my hand. "You feel like dancing?"

"I'd love to."

We went through to the kitchen and passed a game of suck and blow. I laughed as a girl hollered in protest when the guy beside her dropped the card from his lips and kissed her. Guys were making a tower of solo cups on the table and someone was throwing up in the trash can. Outside, the antics were much the same, but the air was easier to breathe and there were dozens of couples dancing together, which made it easier to insert ourselves into the crowd and do the same.

Leroy and I danced to "Tell It to My Heart" by Taylor Dane. His hands rested on my waist, tugging me in close as my heart fluttered, painfully so.

"So," Leroy said, staring down at me. "What brings you here tonight?"

"An invitation," I said and tried to steady my voice when it came out with a hitch. It was hard to be calm when his thumbs were circling the bare skin on my waist. "And Amber and I are celebrating graduation. How about you?"

"I know someone in the frat too. He's a family friend. His dad knows my dad sort of thing. I'm sure glad I decided to come along. I almost passed."

My chest squeezed. "I'm glad you didn't."

A light breeze ruffled his brown waves of hair, tousling it so that it fell across his face. He quickly swept his fingers through it and pushed it back, looking amazing as he did. I tried not to salivate at his bicep that expanded when his arm was in the air, but wow. Surely, he couldn't be sweet *and* drop dead gorgeous.

"I like your accent," he said, putting his hand back on my waist. "Southern belle."

"Ooh, no," I said, wincing. "Nope. So, the Antebellum era is where the idealization of the Southern belle originated. And as you know from your history class," he chuckled, "that era was defined by slavery and its profitable gain. Southern belles were often from high society plantation-owning families. I'd never want to be associated with someone who was in favor of slavery."

"Wow," Leroy said, "I feel terrible not knowing that. I mean, I knew about plantations and stuff. Just not the Southernbelle part. Thanks for telling me."

It was a relief that he wasn't like some of the scrubs at school who refused to hear about anything that might educate them.

"Yo." We both looked at a guy standing beside us, drunk and wobbling, his cap on sideways. "Me and my babe need someone to double with us in beer pong. Want to join?"

I looked at Leroy, searching for his thoughts on the invitation, but he was looking at me for the same thing. "I'm not drinking tonight."

"I have to drive," Leroy added.

"Aw man," the guy slurred. "No one's down for beer pong. Bummer."

"We could have one game," I gave in. "I'll just take a sip. Not the whole cup."

The guy's excitement was obvious as he jumped, almost dropping his loose baggy jeans from their place around his butt. He held onto them and ran over to the table that had been set up, where his girlfriend was waiting, smacking her gum.

"You don't have to drink at all," Leroy said beside my ear as we walked over to the table hand in hand. "We can tip it on the grass."

"I'm sure a few sips won't hurt."

"All right," he said when we stopped at the other end of the table. "Go easy, though. If you get too drunk, I won't be able to kiss you later."

My stomach did an abundance of somersaults and I missed the round of introductions that were made with our opponents, entirely too focused on his words and the tingling that was running rampant through my veins.

It turned out that I didn't need to be concerned—the ping-pong ball almost never landed in our cups, and between a sober Leroy and me, we sunk most of our shots. The drunk couple congratulated us and hollered for the next contenders to step up as Leroy and I wandered off.

"That was fun," I said, stepping over a discarded keg on the ground. Leroy held my hand to steady me, and before we could go back inside, a tall, lean college student intercepted us, a little redhead clinging onto his arm.

"What's up, man," Leroy said as the two of them clapped hands. "Ellie, this is Preston, the family friend I mentioned."

"Hello," I said, and he gave me a chin nod, his gaze moving between us before he pointed with enthusiasm.

"You wanna room tonight, bro?" he asked Leroy, who suddenly turned crimson red. It was endearing. Leroy opened his mouth to answer but was cut off. "I'm leaving with Shellie. You can take mine, man. I won't be back tonight. Saves some random slob jerking off in there. Just chuck the sheets in the hamper after. Have a good night, dude."

He left, tugging a giggling Shellie behind him. Leroy and I stood on the back doorstep as they walked away, and he was unable to make eye contact with me. As mortified as I was, it was amusing all the same.

"I'm not expecting . . . *that*," Leroy finally said, still not looking directly at me. "We can—"

"It could be a quiet place to talk?"

His shoulders relaxed and the fact that he was such a gentle-man was a major comfort. He'd already alluded to the fact that he wouldn't kiss me if I was drunk and now it was clear that whatever we did, was up to me. I felt totally safe with him.

✦

The bedroom was tidy, thank goodness. I leaned back against the headboard and spent hours talking to this gorgeous stranger who had stumbled into my life, and somehow, after such a short time together, I felt like I couldn't remember what life was like before I knew him.

"What about college?" he asked, sitting against the wall with his legs outstretched, mine crossed on top of his. "You going?"

My cheeks warmed. "Can't afford it. Mom was in high school when I was born and I never knew my dad. He took off, which is fine—I'm not hung up on it at all. But it's been a struggle for Momma ever since. It's no big deal; I'm going to do a small business course. I want to run a skincare line when I'm grown."

"You don't need some sort of beauty diploma or something for that?"

"Nope. I'm a bit of a guru, to be honest. I do a lot of research at home. It's science of the skin and I know a thing or two."

"Is that why your skin is so perfect?"

I touched my cheek, my stomach twisting. "I know what products work for it, so, maybe?" The tremble in my tone exposed how nervous he was making me.

"What about your mom? What does she do?"

"Manages a small sporting goods store for her uncle. She's waiting for him to retire and hand it over and then she'll sell it when she takes ownership, but I have no idea what else she would do. She started working there when she got pregnant with me."

"You get along with her?"

"I guess," I admitted. "She can be a bit overbearing."

"How so?" Leroy asked, watching me while his hand reached out and his fingers ran along the top of mine, as if he was completely unaware that he was doing it. It made it hard to focus on the answer I wanted to give him.

"Amber calls her a helicopter mom. She's got a way that she likes things to be. You know? She's big on respect and if she doesn't feel respected, she gets . . . frustrated. But she's okay. She wants the best for me and she's all I've got."

I didn't want to tell him that my momma wouldn't let me out of her sight without knowing where I was going, but when I was home, she was emotionally distant. It was a weird combination, a lonely one. As if she didn't particularly want me around, but she didn't want me out having a life either.

"Do you get along with your parents?" I asked.

"I do," he said. "They were opposite in the age department when they settled down to have kids. Did the career thing first. Mom was forty-five when I was born. Forty-seven when she had my brother, Noah."

Wow, that makes his mom . . . sixty-three. I decided not to point out the obvious.

"What's he like? Your brother."

"He's a bit hard to mesh with."

"How come?"

"He's a bit arrogant, defensive," Leroy said. "Makes it hard to have conversations with him that don't end with him acting the victim. He likes to tell me that I'm the favorite son, too, which is bullshit. I just decided to follow the family career tradition and he didn't. Somehow, he's conjured up this idea that dad is disappointed in him. No matter how often Dad tells him that he's not."

"Sounds like he needs more hugs." I tapped his hand when I remembered an earlier question. "Oh, you never did tell me what you're doing at Baylor?"

"College football," he said. "I'm aiming for the NFL."

I grinned. "That explains the bod."

"The bod?"

"I know that you know I've been staring at your arms all night."

He laughed, and with a quick shift of position, he was on his hands and knees, hovering in front of me, so close that I felt his breath fanning my face. "You should know," he murmured, his gaze moving between my mouth and eyes, "that I've been staring at all of you. All night."

My heart thumped. It was almost painful how fast it was beating as he moved in closer. I was sure that he was going to kiss me. I wanted him to kiss me. But being me, my mind went into overdrive.

"You're leaving tomorrow," I said, causing him to pause. "I mean, you'll be back. But—"

"We don't have to do this, Ellie." He started to distance himself, but before he could move away, I wrapped my hand around the back of his neck, holding him in place as I fought through rapid breaths.

And then I pushed our mouths together before I could talk myself out of it and I was so glad I did because this kiss felt like no other. His response was immediate. His mouth pushed mine open as his hand came up and wound in the strands of my hair. Every lap of his tongue, each gentle caress of his fingertips against my waist or neck, it was all igniting.

We made out for . . . a while. I was sure that I'd end up with a make-out rash, but nothing else seemed important. I'd ended up underneath him and his hands explored every inch of me. I was beyond wound up with need. I was still a virgin because I hadn't found someone who made me feel enough to want to take that step. But with Leroy, I felt it all. I felt so much need that I couldn't imagine stopping him when his fingers popped open the button of my jeans.

"Leroy," I gave him a gentle push and smiled when he gave me an apologetic glance. "I'm—I'm a virgin."

His brows raised but he tried to hide his surprise. "I'm sorry. I should have asked."

He tried to sit up and move away but I held him in place, wrapping my legs around his waist. "No, no. I just. I just wanted to tell you that. Full disclosure. But that doesn't mean that I don't want to . . . do it . . ."

He cupped my face and his eyes locked with mine. "I don't want to do anything that you don't want to do. We can stop right now."

I leaned up and kissed his soft, sweet lips. "I want you, Leroy."

# ONE MONTH LATER

## LEROY

My leg bounced under the table while I ate a bowl of oatmeal with so much speed that I barely tasted it. In fact, I half-expected to choke. That'd be just how my summer with the woman of my world begins, dying at the breakfast table, being found facedown in a bowl of breakfast mush that doesn't even have sugar on it because my nerves are so damn fried as it is, sugar would have made it worse.

"Where's the fire, son?" Dad wandered into the kitchen, still half-asleep, in his boxer shorts and a tank top. The alarm on the coffee machine had been blaring but the noise was nothing but a hum in the background until the world came back into focus. He switched it off and poured himself a brew.

"Ellie's plane lands in two hours."

"Ah, Miss Ellie." Dad dragged his feet until he was sitting at the table, steam rose from his mug and he inhaled, staring out of the kitchen sliding door. The morning sun reflected off the pool surface, still and flat like glass. "You sure you didn't deposit that letter in the wrong mailbox the morning after that party?"

"Dad," I groaned, same joke, different day. After I'd told Dad that I had hand delivered a letter, addressed to Ellie, in her friend's mailbox after our night together, he came up with the joke that I'd put it in the wrong mailbox. *So* hilarious.

"Maybe you've been talking to some other girl all month, huh?" he roared with laughter. "You'll show up at the airport and there'll be some stranger running into your arms."

It was ongoing. Every other day when he knew that I'd been on the phone with Els, he said, "How's Ellie *Maybe*ston?" It made me laugh, but I didn't show him that. Instead, I waited until I was alone so that he didn't get a big head.

"Good morning," Mom smiled, her hair done, makeup on, and her clothes immaculate. She kissed Dad and me on the head and went to pour a coffee.

Dad's exhaustion was intensified next to Mom who was, in every sense, a morning person. That had to do with the fact that she was still working as a news anchor. Dad had retired a while ago and he'd adjusted to sleeping in. There was once a time when both were up at four a.m. But after Dad retired from coaching in the NFL, he was at home a lot more. He did the school runs. He helped with the homework and, of course, the weekend football practice in the back garden. Truth is, I knew I'd miss having breakfast together when I was off at college in a few months.

"The spare room is organized for Ellie," Mom said, coming to join us at the table. "Fresh sheets and the drawers are empty. I can't wait to meet her."

"You're acting like the boy has never had a girl around here before," Dad said as he ran a hand over his tired face.

"This is different, I know it is. She sounds like an absolute sweetheart. It's serious. Isn't it, darling?" Mom looked at me, cup in front of her chin. "It's serious. I can tell."

"I care about her a lot," I admitted.

Noah came wandering in, his dark-brown hair standing up. All he wore was a pair of boxer shorts. The conversation continued.

"See," Mom nodded. "None of his other girlfriends lasted more than a couple of weeks."

Noah scoffed from where he stood with the fridge door wide open. "Let's see how long it lasts when she's here and has to put up with him."

Noah hadn't been quiet about the fact that he thought my relationship with Ellie was a joke. He assumed that we'd lose interest in the phone calls and I'd forget about her. When I told him that she'd be spending the next seven weeks with us, he almost blew a fuse. Noah being jealous wasn't new, though. He couldn't stand it when I had girlfriends because it meant that I wasn't available to jaunt around to parties with him whenever he snapped his fingers.

He snatched a bottle of water and let the fridge door shut again, starting toward the door. "See you in seven weeks, whipped bitch," he mumbled.

"Noah—" Dad said.

But I stood up and faced Noah myself. "What's that supposed to mean?"

Noah glared. "It means that nothing else exists when you've got a girl. Oh, that's right, then it's off to college. It's been a fun run," he saluted. "Nice knowing you. Later."

I watched him leave the room, listened to the sound of his heavy footsteps padding upstairs, and then I sat down again.

"He loves spending time with you, honey," Mom said.

"He's being bloody ridiculous," Dad grumbled and finished the last of his coffee. "Damn dramatic."

"What am I supposed to do?" I shrugged. "Never have a relationship because Noah feels abandoned? Not my fault he bounces from one girl to another and doesn't understand commitment."

"He can do that right now. He's seventeen," Mom said, "No need for him to settle down at the moment. You're both very different. It's just the way that it is. How about making some time for him over the summer? It'd mean a lot to him."

"Yeah, sure. Can do."

"You're a good boy." She leaned across the table and patted the top of my hand. "Now, do we need to go over house rules again before Ellie gets here?"

"Nope."

"No sharing a bed," she continued, as if I hadn't declined her suggestion. "Ten p.m. curfew—"

"Door open," Dad added.

"Yep, door open. No sex."

"Mom," I groaned.

"Eleanor," Dad spoke with amusement, "the boy has been wrapped around this girl's finger for a month. The no-sex ship has sailed."

I buried my head in my hands. The lingering silence prompted me to peer up and I found Mom glaring at Dad. "Are you telling me that our son needs sex in order to remain interested in a girl?"

Dad cleared his throat and shook his head. "No. 'Course not."

"Regardless of whether you're sexually active," my mom said, "these are the rules that her mother required when I spoke to her on the phone. I have to respect rules when it comes to someone else's child."

"I get it, Mom," I said.

"You do use protection, right?" she asked.

Even though talking sex with Mom and Dad was high on my list of things I aim to avoid, the discomfort was only mild. We'd always kept an open line of communication, which is how they knew that I had been sexually active for a couple of years now.

"Most of the time."

Dad leaned forward with a stern expression. "The answer is *all* of the bloody time."

"Yes, all right, all right, all of the bloody time."

He shook his head and turned a light shade of red. "Boy, I swear. Don't be acting stupid."

"I get it, Dad, chill out."

Upstairs, I went to brush my teeth and found Noah coming out of the bathroom in a towel. He looked more awake than he had before. No less pissed off, though.

"You seeing Cass tonight?" I asked.

Cass was a mutual friend that we'd known since middle school. She and Noah were in the same grade, he'd introduced her to me, and we'd gotten along well for the simple fact that she had no issue filling in the quiet that I provided. Noah and I ran in different circles and the only time that he socialized with my friends, was if I was there too. However, Cass could bounce from group to group and show up wherever she wanted, whenever she wanted. That was Cass. She got along with almost everyone. Although, Noah's friendship with her was a little different than mine.

"Maybe," he shrugged. "Why?"

"Could you introduce her to Ellie? They'll probably get along."

"So Cass can ditch me for the new girl as well? Cool as. Does she wanna steal anyone else from me too?"

"Shut up," I said. If he gave a real damn about Cass, I might have apologized for the suggestion. But she was nothing more than someone he slept with and tossed aside on a regular basis. "You wanna come for a drive to the airport?"

He flinched with surprise. "No," he said and left it at that, stalking down the hall to his bedroom, where he slammed the door. His attitude was getting old.

My fist pounded on his door until he opened it and stared at me.

"I like this girl," I said, keeping calm so that I didn't set off his short fuse. Noah was hard to understand at the best of times. Mom was right: we were different. He was noncommittal, I wasn't. He preferred academics, I didn't. He didn't know how to communicate his shit, I did. Most of the time. "Can you just not be a dick about it? She's nice. You'll like her, honest. Just chill out, man, okay? We'll still have time to hang out."

"Whatever, man. I need to get dressed. I'll see you later, when you get back."

It's hard to say when things became distant between Noah and me. Beginning of high school perhaps. Our interests shifted; our friend groups changed. There are only sixteen months between us—we were best friends as kids. We did everything together and then we stepped out of our home, out of our comfort zones, and the way that we handled the shift was different. We stopped navigating life together and we did it on our own. I suppose that's when we lost who we were as a brotherhood.

Denver International Airport was a rush of tourists, traveling locals, and tired children. It was never quiet during summer peak. The white, pitched ceilings reminded me of circus tents. When Noah and I traveled with Mom and Dad for football coaching as children, I used to imagine that was what it was: a circus. The sheer size of the airport compared to my three-foot self was enough to leave me in awe. But there was a novelty about the shape of the ceiling—it was mesmerizing, the sort of fascination that only a child can feel. It's nostalgic to think back on an emotion that no longer exists apart from the ghost of a feeling that's tucked away for safekeeping.

My heart was beating hard as I read the board of flights. Flight 998 from Dallas to Denver had landed. She was here. It sent a chill right through me to know that she'd be walking through those electric sliding doors any minute now. The last month had felt like forever. But I couldn't complain; it was a blessing that she could come at all. I would have waited, though. Waited until I was in Waco at college, close to her again.

It happened then; she wandered out with her shoulder-length blond hair in a disheveled bun, a pair of shorts, and a Red Hot Chili Peppers T-shirt on. I grinned. She had insisted that I listen to them a few weeks ago, so passionate about her love of music. I was a fan. She had great taste. She looked around but couldn't see me. So I took the time to watch her, to admire her teeth worrying on her bottom lip, her gaze moving from left to right as she walked closer to the exit, a small bounce in her step that made my heart thump. She had this adorable light sprinkle of freckles across her button nose, and round cheeks. Her green eyes flicked up like a feline at the outer edge and made her look insanely sexy. Her beauty was impossible not to notice, but who she was, *that* was the real prize.

# Ellie

*Dearest Ellie,*

*I hope this doesn't startle you. I sat outside and wrote this in the car after our incredible night together. I should have asked for a phone number, but I didn't think about it until you had dashed that pretty behind inside. You see, I'm a little senseless when you're in my presence. You're such a stunning vision, a whisper of perfection, a blossomed beauty. I hope that we can keep in touch. If you're interested, perhaps phone me? I don't want to lose touch with the girl who has stolen my heart. It may come across as strong, but I feel more than I ever believed I was capable of feeling when I'm with you. You're an embodiment of an angel, and I'm counting down the days until I'm in Waco and close to you again, Ellie Livingston.*

*Sincerely,*
*Leroy*

At the bottom of the letter that Leroy wrote me was a phone number. A jumble of digits that set us on the course to a whirl-wind romance. We spent hours on the telephone. We got to know each other through conversation that may have been long-distance, but the smoothness of his voice and the gentle tone of his sweet nothings made me feel so close to him. Now, a month later, the paper was wrinkled and tearing at the corner from how often I reread it because the feeling that it gave me was the same as it had been the first time. Butterfly central.

By some miracle, my mother allowed me to spend the rest of summer in Castle Rock, on a strict set of conditions, of course. More miraculous still was that I could spend it with Leroy, in his home. Our mothers had spoken on the phone and agreed that as long as we were in separate bedrooms and had a ten o'clock curfew, it was fine.

However, there was still the small matter of being accepted by his upper-class parents. Mom's salary wouldn't have been a quarter of what his parents made, and I was nervous to think that I might not fit in or be the sort of woman that they want their son to date. What if they thought I was a gold digger? I'd expressed these concerns to him on the phone and he'd said that it was ridiculous to think like that, but still, I couldn't help but worry.

"You sure you've got everything?" Momma asked as I bounced on the spot, watching the boarding chart and waiting for my flight number to be called. "You didn't pack a lot."

"Momma, I've got a secure system set up," I assured her, still not one hundred percent focused on her face or words. "As long as I can use the washing machine, and I'm sure that I can, I've got all that I need."

I was nothing if not organized. I had a rotation of outfits that I could mix and match. Accessories to spice them up and seven different lipstick colors to ensure that I could pop a perfect pout no matter what the occasion.

"Be safe, and I'd really appreciate it if you could give your future some thought," Momma pointed an authoritative finger at me. "I know that I can't afford to put you through college, but—"

"Come on, Momma," I cut her off. "I'm going to take a small business course when I've got enough cash. And one day, I'll own a skincare line. I've told you all of this. There's no chance that I could work as a measly employee for the rest of my life—no offense."

Momma smiled, although it wasn't convincing. "I know that you don't want to end up like me but be realistic. And don't base your future on this boy because these things can be fleeting."

I frowned at the pessimistic woman who'd raised me. "I'm not basing anything off Leroy. I've wanted to run a business since I was a freshman. I'll do it with or without him. And what we have isn't fleeting. He loves me, Momma."

"Whatever you say," she said. "Look, I mean it, behaving. His mother assured me that she'd phone and have you sent home if there was even a hint of acting up. You don't be alone with that boy in his room, you keep your hands to yourselves, and don't even think about touching alcohol. You hear?"

"Yes Momma," I said, holding back a restless sigh. It wasn't as if I hadn't heard it all before. "I promise. Besides, I've only met him in person once. It's not like we know each other well enough to . . . you know . . ."

Fortunately, I'd become quite talented in the art of lying. She didn't know that I'd given him a piece of me that I could never get back—and she never would. She didn't know that I was in love with him. I hadn't given it away on a whim. I'd felt something for him that I couldn't explain, and I knew that even if he hadn't kept in touch, I wouldn't have regretted it.

After a few more "words of wisdom" from Momma, we said goodbye at the gate, and I went through security to wait. The call for my flight came over the PA, and I squealed through a clenched jaw as I slung my backpack on and adjusted my T-shirt, the summer sun making me sweat like crazy.

The flight wasn't long, just over two hours, but it was my first, and I tried to appreciate it. I had saved every last dollar that I'd made from working at the local pharmacy after school and on weekends. The funds were going toward the business course that I planned on taking. But I withdrew a small amount for the tickets and spending money. I wanted to appreciate what I had paid for, but my mind was spinning with the knowledge that I would soon be seeing Leroy after an entire month of nothing but hearing his voice. It had kept me going, that's for sure.

When the flight landed, I ran a hand through my frazzled mess of hair and pulled it into a bun. My palms had become damp and I vigorously wiped them on my high-waisted shorts before I stood and joined the line to get off the plane. What would it be like to see him again? Would we slide into familiarity with ease? Would the nerves make it awkward? It felt like every traveler was moving at a snail's pace, but eventually we made it off the plane.

After I'd gone through customs and collected my luggage, I stood to the side of the gate, searching for him, my thoughts still a shambles of uncertain excitement. A voice that I'd become so familiar with purred from behind me. I could feel his presence, feel an electric hum settling around me, a result of my heart working overtime.

"Hello, Ellie."

His voice was like butter. Soft and smooth, sliding over me and seeping into my skin. It was what I had come to know. I had made love to this man, cried his name in a night of passion, and touched every surface of his magnificent body. But his soul, his deep voice, his poetic words, those were what I had fallen in love with.

I turned around and laid a gaze on his gorgeous grin. He stood tall, hands in his jean pockets, his hair swept over in an unkempt mess. He screamed confidence. And why wouldn't he? He was irresistible. His charm and presence couldn't be missed, even when he didn't utter a word. I drank in his appearance. His jeans rolled up at the ankles, his white Chuck Taylors, and the fitted white muscle shirt that allowed a view of his sinfully delicious arms.

He stepped forward and drew me in with his large hand wrapped around my waist.

"I have missed you a whole damn lot, Ellie Livingston," he smiled before he crashed his lips against mine and I was lost to the world. Gone. Only existing with the life that he breathed into me with that unbelievable kiss.

I didn't want it to end. I could have kissed him until the sun set and the stars birthed a new night. But his mouth parted from mine and we both sighed with relief. "I missed you too," I finally managed to tell him.

"Mom's excited to meet you," he said as he dropped an arm around my shoulder and took my bag.

Perhaps I had jumped the gun a little. I knew a lot of the families in my hometown had a stuck-up mindset. That didn't mean every single rich person was a snob and a half. There's a good chance that *I* was the snob for making such assumptions.

During the journey home, he drove us in a black 1996 Mercedes-Benz. The seats were made of soft leather and the ride was smooth. Our pickup back home was reliable, but she was old, that's for sure. I'd never been in such a new vehicle. But still, as exciting as that was, nothing could compare to the butterflies that I felt when Leroy's hand held mine. We spent the two-hour journey talking. We never exhausted topics, and every time he turned to smile at me, my heart would flutter, threatening to fly right out of my chest. Compared to home, Colorado—or what I was seeing of it—was a lot of vast space, and the Rockies were every bit as stunning as I thought they'd be. There were large meadows, small plants, shrubs, and scattered trees. It was so open and a refreshing change from the suburban city that I was used to.

Leroy's home was at the top of a hill, surrounded by big Douglas and white fir trees, no doubt it would have been gorgeous in the winter, the needles coated in snow. Right now, the branches provided decent shade from the sun. The two-story brick mansion faced the street, climbing vines were assisted by trellises, and thick green shrubs lined the path that led from the double driveway to the front door.

We parked in front of the garage and Leroy fetched the luggage from the trunk. I glanced up at him, squinting to avoid the sun that created a halo around his dark-brown locks. His face had the ability to make my heart race and I hoped that Momma was wrong. I hoped that this wasn't fleeting.

"Ready?" he asked. "They're going to love you."

Inside, it was as exquisite as I had imagined. There was a small space in the foyer that was tiled, but after that, a cream carpet lined the corridors and living room, which was down a simple two steps. A staircase in the corridor led upstairs and beyond that was the kitchen.

Leroy dropped my bag beside the staircase and then steered us back into the living room where his parents were sitting within the gloriously air-conditioned house. I felt a little sheepish as the two of them stood up with inspecting gazes.

"Mom, Dad," his grin was proud, "this is Ellie Livingston."

"Jacob," his father outstretched his aged hand with a gentle smile. I could see Leroy in his father's face. His eyes were blue, though, rather than brown, his shoulders and chest a little wider. But there was a definite likeness.

"I'm Eleanor," the woman greeted next with a kind and welcoming smile.

"Ha!" Jacob gestured between Eleanor and me. "Ellie . . . Eleanor. Similar names. How's that going for you, Leroy?"

Leroy grimaced. "Do we have to?"

"It's obvious that I'm his hero and inspiration for all things in life," Eleanor gave her shoulder-length greying waves a sassy sweep. "How was your flight, dear?"

"It was awesome," I said. "I've never flown before. I liked it."

Leroy pulled me closer, his hand resting on the curve of my waist as he leaned down and murmured in a hushed tone, wondering if we should go upstairs. That idea was abruptly interrupted when the sound of footsteps came thudding down the staircase, causing us to turn our attention over our shoulders.

A boy appeared at the entrance to the living room. He

had a tall, leaner build and darker hair, but he bore that same mesmerizing attractiveness that his brother did. Leroy had given me a basic rundown on Noah. He was a year younger than Leroy, about to become a senior in high school. He was more business-savvy than athletic, though. He stuffed his hands into his shorts and made no subtleties about running his gaze over me at a slow and deliberate pace. Leroy's hand tightened around mine and I leaned into him.

"Ellie, this is my brother Noah. Noah, this is Ellie."

"*You're* the girl that has him whipped as hell," Noah tsked with disappointment. Leroy stiffened beside me.

"Noah, please," Eleanor scolded her son with a tiresome tone. She smoothed her button-up blouse and politely excused herself to get started on dinner preparations.

"Watch it," Jacob glared at his youngest son before he followed his wife, leaving the three of us in an awkward silence. It didn't last long.

"Do we get to share this one?" Noah gestured at me with a devious grin.

"Don't go there, Noah," Leroy warned. The brothers differed in height, Noah being taller, but Leroy was built with muscle and he was intimidating, to say the least. "We talked about this. Stop being fucking rude."

Noah rolled his eyes and shifted his weight, putting a little distance between the two of them. He gave me another once-over. "She's not good enough for this family," he muttered before his long legs carried him out of the room.

"Ignore him," Leroy said. He pressed a soft kiss on the top of my head before he led us back toward the staircase. "He's salty because he's got no one to drive him to and from his one-night stands and parties now. He's been sulking about it for the last month."

"You don't have to stop going to parties because of me," I told him as he picked up the suitcase we'd left before. He shot me a puzzled glance as we made tracks upstairs. "I mean, I wouldn't stop you from doing that."

"Would you go with me?"

"Sure," I said.

"Good. Because I want to show you off."

## Ellie

I followed Leroy upstairs and explored the framed family por-
traits lining the wall. There were some gorgeous vintage photos
of Eleanor as a young woman in tailored suits and slim sheath
dresses, capri pants, and Peter Pan-collared blouses.

"Your mom has spectacular style," I said, pausing on the
staircase. Leroy waited a step above me.

"So she's told me," he said.

There were also photos of Jacob in his old school football
gear, wedding photos, and baby pictures of Noah and Leroy.

"You were such a cute baby," I said, my finger tracing the frame.

"Nothing's changed then," Leroy teased as we continued
upstairs, knowing that I'd be back for a longer look at their photo-
graphic timeline later. We went to the left when we hit the top
floor and rounded the railing.

"That's my room over there." He pointed over at the other
side of the staircase where there were three doors, his being the
first. "Mom and Dad are at the far end on that side. Noah is at

the far end on this side. The bathroom is between you, and this is the bedroom that you'll be using."

Leroy set down my suitcase inside the first bedroom on the left side of the staircase. The floral comforter on the double bed looked plush, the frilled edges of the throw pillows looked delicate and intricate. The patterned wallpaper looked like the décor from the home catalogs that Momma pored over, coveting all the things she could never afford.

"Sorry that we can't share," Leroy's deep voice startled me from thoughts, and I turned around, noticing that he was leaning against the wall beside the door.

His gaze had become a little darker, longing.

"It's okay," I tucked a piece of hair behind my ear. It felt strange to behave as though I was shy around him. We'd shared the most intimate act that two people could share. But I still became so wound up under the heat of his stare. Unable to think, almost unable to breathe.

He leaned off the wall, kicking the door shut before he sauntered toward me. The back of my legs hit the bed and I went down, propping myself on my elbows as he placed a hand on either side of me, the mattress dipping a little under his weight. The air grew impossibly thick as he hovered mere inches from my face, inspecting every inch of it as though he was memorizing it. I understood, though. It had been months of wishing to see each other and having to settle for the sound of his voice instead. Which was something that I had come to adore. But now, I kind of wanted to just—not talk.

"You're so beautiful," he murmured, the back of his hand sweeping my cheek. Overwhelming emotions sent me into a state of bliss.

"Ellie," he murmured, as though my name were an ode.

He leaned in and his lips feathered mine. My eyes fluttered closed and under some cruel twist of fate, the door swung open behind us and hit the wall. Leroy didn't move, instead leaning his forehead on mine and taking a deep breath as his brother whistled a scandalous tune.

"Dad doesn't want the door shut up here, Lee."

I stole a peek around the side of the firm arms that had me encased and spied Noah leaning against the doorframe. It almost sounded like Leroy was counting to ten before he reluctantly stood up.

"Grow the hell up, Noah," he said, turning around to face the younger Lahey.

"Hostile," Noah said scornfully. He acted cool and unfazed but his cheeks had a dusting of red blooming in his cheeks. "She's here for five minutes and you're already wiggin' out?"

"You're being rude," Leroy snapped. "A simple tap on the door would have been enough."

"Whatever," he straightened up and shot me an indecipherable glance before he focused his attention back on Leroy. "Are we going to Eric's tonight? Oh wait, no. Saturdays have turned into bitch night, right?"

"I'm going," Leroy said. "Ellie's coming with me."

Noah's shoulders slumped but he didn't continue the conversation. What did he expect? If Leroy was going, he'd just leave me here alone? Noah left the room, not closing the door behind him. I didn't think that we'd get our moment or our privacy back, but we had all summer to steal moments alone.

"I'm sorry about him—again," Leroy said.

I shrugged, not wanting to make a fuss about it. "So, we're going out tonight?"

"To be honest, I'd rather not spend our first night together, out," he sat beside me. "But Eric will be moving out of state for college in a couple of weeks and he's been a good friend of mine for a long time. I hope you don't mind?"

"Not at all," I assured him. "We might even find the chance to be alone?"

The way that he sunk his teeth into his bottom lip and stared up at the ceiling was erotic. I stared at him, almost feeling ashamed for the thoughts that were shouting at me.

"Come on," he stood up, offering me his hand. "We'll go and help Mom with dinner and then go out later. That gives you a chance to get to know her."

I had so much appreciation for the respect and care that he showed his mother. It was clear that she meant a lot to him, and it was important that she and I spent time together.

Downstairs, the kitchen was filled with the aroma of delicious home-cooked food. I was no chef. I could boil an egg and make toast so I was quietly hoping that she wouldn't ask too much of me.

"Hey, Mom," Leroy said. The countertop surface ran along the far wall and came out in an L-shape, cutting the large room in half to create a small dining space. There was a larger dining room between the living room and kitchen, used for more formal occasions, I assumed. "Can we help?"

She smiled and gave out directions on what he could do for her. But I lost focus on her words as I spotted the pile of Post-its, scattered pens, and stacked books that were underneath the wall phone at the end of the countertop. I moved over to the clutter and started organizing it.

I stacked the books from biggest to smallest and set them against the wall. The Post-it notes were soon placed in a small pile, and the pens were dropped into the cup where a lone permanent marker was housed. It looked so much tidier in a matter of moments and when I glanced up with a satisfied sigh, I was met with two pairs of eyes, watching me with curious fascination.

"Oh, I'm sorry, I just—"

I stammered for an excuse but there wasn't one. My mild obsession for things being in their place caused me to be scolded by Momma on more than one occasion for touching things that didn't belong to me.

"You can do my Tupperware cupboard next if you want," Eleanor broke the silence with amusement. Leroy laughed and continued cutting up vegetables and potatoes beside his mother.

I admired how his biceps flexed with each stroke of the knife. How delicate he was with his large hands and how the tip of his tongue peeked from between his lips as he concentrated.

"Oh—ar—are you sure?" I turned my attention to Eleanor, rather than the drool-worthy boy beside her. I didn't want to just start going through her cabinets in case she was kidding. But I wouldn't mind stacking plastic instead of cooking.

"I'm dead serious," she said, stirring what looked like breadcrumbs and eggs in a bowl. "That cupboard is a nightmare. It's a sport to put things away now. We just open the door, throw things in, and attempt to close it before a Tupperware avalanche takes over the kitchen."

I laughed with her childish giggle and moved around the countertop, heading toward the cabinet on the other side of the kitchen. I realized that perhaps I should have watched a couple of her news broadcasts to become more familiar with this woman. She wasn't what I had been expecting at all, and it was refreshing to know that money didn't equal snobbery.

"Ellie," Eleanor said over her shoulder as I knelt in front of the cabinet. "What do you want to do now that you've graduated?"

"I want to—"

As I opened the door, just as she'd warned, dozens and dozens of containers, lids, cups, and every variety of plastic that you could imagine came loudly tumbling out of the cupboard.

At least we'd have plenty of time for conversation.

*N*

The meal was delicious. A stuffed roast chicken with all the extras. Vegetables, potatoes, gravies, and sauces. I had expected that the atmosphere might have been a bit tense with Noah but he didn't talk a lot during the meal and Eleanor kept the conversation moving enough to expel any awkward lulls.

Leroy's dad seemed nice. He didn't talk a whole lot, either, but what he did add to the conversation was pleasant enough. As it was Saturday, and we had plans to go out for the evening, Leroy negotiated with his mom about pushing back the curfew until one in the morning. It seemed a waste of time to only go out until ten. She agreed that it was fine with her, but I would have to clear it with Momma over the phone.

I was offered a little bit of privacy in the dining area so that I could use the phone while Leroy went to get ready. The phone rang while I twirled the cord around my finger, hoping that Momma would be in a gracious mood. *Maybe I could always lie if she says no?*

"Hello, Sandra speaking?"

"Hi, Momma."

"Ellie!" Momma all but shouted down the phone line. "I've been waiting to hear from you all afternoon. How was the flight? How's Castle Rock and all that? Having a good time?"

"It's great here." I couldn't help but smile when I thought about Leroy. "Listen, I called to ask something." The phone crackled. "Could I perhaps extend the curfew this evening? Leroy and I are going to a little gathering with some of his high school friends. It's a sort of farewell for one of them going off to school."

There was a brief pause, silence came through the receiver, and I felt as though I was holding my breath in anticipation.

"Will there be alcohol?"

"No," I lied. "His parents are going to be there. It's a family-friendly event."

"What time would y'all be in?"

"One in the morning."

Again, there was a pregnant pause until she sighed, the tell-tale sign of a win. "All right. Be good though. Hear me? Don't do something stupid."

"I promise, Momma, thank you."

"Is that it? You just wanted to call to get a curfew extension, not catch up with me?"

I had been gone for less than twenty-four hours. Did I really need to go into a detailed conversation about the brief afternoon?

"How about we recap at the end of one week, Momma?" I suggested, tapping my foot with impatience. "I need to get dressed. I love you."

"All right, then. Love you."

The phone base quietly clicked when I hung up. Jacob and

Eleanor were in the living room talking over the television, gently arguing about what to watch. I tiptoed out of the kitchen and crept up the staircase.

The shower was running as I walked past the bathroom door upstairs. My steps faltered for a moment, listening to the sound of Leroy's upbeat humming. My imagination built up the sight behind this door. His built torso dripping wet, his hair damp and unkempt. Heat filled my cheeks at the images and I forced my eyes to the floor to hide the shame, although there was no one to see it.

Fleeing to the spare bedroom and shutting the door behind me, I leaned against it and giggled, placing my flat palms on either side of my warm cheeks before fanning myself. I had never thought about sex this much before. Ever. But since we shared that night together, May 28, 1998—a night I would never forget—I hadn't been able to rid myself of the constant hot flushes or the sinful thoughts that plagued me without mercy.

I shook it off and changed into a yellow spaghetti-strapped dress with a white T-shirt on underneath it. An old pair of black Docs that I'd found dumpster diving completed the look. Next came mascara, lip gloss, and a spritz of hairspray to tame my natural waves, and I felt as ready as I ever would. I hadn't felt nervous about the night before us, but I did get a little onslaught of butterflies when I thought about the fact that I'd be meeting Leroy's friends. Would I make a good impression? He said he was looking forward to showing me off and it excited me to know that he felt I was worth showing off.

Just as I finished folding the clothes up that I'd chosen and organized to wear tomorrow after a shower, there was a light tap on the door.

"Come in." Leroy came in and paused at the threshold. "Ellie, you look—stunning," he said, his stare lingering on my bare legs.

"You look great too," I returned the compliment, because he did. His fitted faded-blue jeans flirted with the top of his black Chuck Taylors. The color of his shoes coordinated with the loose black T-shirt that was tucked at the belt of his jeans.

"I suppose we should head downstairs," Leroy murmured as he gazed to the left. I couldn't see whatever it was that held his attention in the corridor, but his attention moved between myself and the outside of the bedroom, repeatedly, in a matter of seconds. "Noah is coming with us. I'm driving."

"That's fine," I smiled and waited for him to suggest that we leave. But once again, he stared off in the direction of the staircase and then back at me. His expression turned to desire as he gave me another once-over and in a fast moment, too quick to prepare for, he stepped over the threshold and tucked his hand behind my neck.

"I need to do this before we leave," he mumbled, not giving me a lot of time to be confused before his mouth was moving against mine. I melted into his embrace, wrapping my hands around his back and reveling in the sheer perfection that came with his touch.

His breath was minty fresh and the scent of cologne invaded the last sense I was aware of. All else had fallen victim to his presence, to his kiss, to his hold. He was gentle, but from the light tug that he gave my hair, it was obvious that he was in charge and I was more than willing to allow it. Just as I had been the first time.

His tongue slid against my own, and although I had done

this before, I still worried that I wasn't good at it. But when a low groan of approval sounded at the back of Leroy's throat, I felt a little more confident. His hands slid down my back, his warm fingertips brushing the exposed skin before they settled on my butt.

When we parted—reluctantly—he stared at me with a longing and desire that I had never experienced with a boy before. He had assured me on more than one occasion that this wasn't something brief or non-committal. He'd unequivocally assured me that what he felt for me was pure and true. And I believed him without a doubt. I know because I felt it too.

A voice startled us from the bottom of the staircase, and I jumped with the unwanted interruption. "Hurry up! I wanna bounce!"

"Fine, asshole!" Leroy shouted over his shoulder; his hands still rested on my lower back. "We're coming!"

"So is fucking Christmas!"

He turned back to me, rolling his eyes with a frustrated sigh. But the moment that our gazes met, his entire expression and demeanor softened. "Ready then?"

I took his hand, our fingers lacing together. "Let's go."

# Ellie

We arrived at the house that was located at the end of a cul-de-sac full of other beautiful, large homes. I wasn't expecting anything less, though—the rich mingle with the rich. A wave of unease rolled over me as we parked a few houses down and walked toward the rave. I didn't belong around such high-society teenagers. I worried they'd be able to smell my barely-there bank balance. The people hanging out on the front lawn and large wind-around patio were all wearing expensive dresses, leather platform shoes and boots, bomber jackets, and brand jeans.

My outfit wasn't poorly put together; I knew how to dress. But it was purchased from the thrift store and I was sure that it was obvious. Especially from the judgmental once-overs that I received as I walked hand in hand with Leroy. Of course, there could have been another reason for the subtle scowls: to these girls, some outsider was on the arm of the school's quarterback.

We walked through the home and into the large backyard where people were spread out, talking, drinking, doing keg stands, and dancing. A few people were in the large pool—which wasn't surprising considering the heat. Leroy was greeted continuously. He was brief with his exchanges—he spoke few words and moved on as fast as he could after introducing me. I reminded him that I didn't need to be introduced to every person that we passed, but he insisted that he wanted everyone to know that he was dating the most beautiful girl there.

We stopped beside a group of people who sat in a circle on outdoor garden sofas, passing a few joints between each other. A familiar lean boy with golden-brown skin and black, curly hair stood from the couch with an inviting and kind smile. "You made it," he exhaled a cloud of smoke and offered the joint to Leroy, who declined.

"Wouldn't have missed it," Leroy said. "Ellie, you remember Eric from our weekend in Waco."

"Nice to see you again, gorgeous," he winked and I noticed that, even though his jaw was a bit uneven, he had the most charming and charismatic smile. He waved off someone's offer for another drag on the joint. "Where's Noah?"

"Probably balls-deep in his own ego," a girl with light-brown ringlets said from the sofa below us. She glanced up and flashed an innocent grin. "Don't roll your eyes at me, Lee. Your brother is an absolute self-obsessed knob jockey dickhead."

"Ellie, this is Cass," Leroy explained. "Cass, this is Ellie."

"Ahh, the famous Ellie," she stood up with an energetic spring, causing the ringlets on her head to bounce. "I've heard a lot about you. Leroy here won't shut up about his girl, which is a miracle—he's a man of few words."

Leroy was watching me with that same soft gaze, and I wondered how it was possible that he was the same man with whom

I had spent hours every single day on the phone. Paranoia set in, wondering if I'd been the one doing all the talking during our phone calls. That seemed impossible, though—I wouldn't feel like I knew Leroy as well as I did if that had been the case.

"I love that dress," Cass reclaimed the conversation. "Where's it from?"

Now-familiar anxiety flared up. I didn't want to lie about who I was, but I was already feeling out of place and it felt like this would cement that I didn't belong. She raised her brows. "It's from a thrift store back in Waco."

"Score!" She clapped her hands together. "I love thrift shopping. That's an amazing find."

Relief flooded through me. Her outfit didn't look like it was from the thrift store. She was dressed in a sheer blouse, tucked into the waist of a black leather skirt. But even if she was exaggerating to make me feel better, it worked, and I appreciated it.

"Do you two want a drink?" Eric asked.

Leroy looked to me for an answer and I gave a quick nod, not wanting to seem reserved and quiet all night when it was apparent that he knew most of these people and we'd be faced with ongoing conversation all night. At least liquid courage would assist in bringing me out of my shell and I could *seem* more confident.

⚡

Cass and I were out of breath, dancing around the small fire pit on the concrete patio, screaming our lungs out to Nirvana's "Heart-Shaped Box" while we refueled on the unidentifiable liquid in our cups. We'd been at the party for about three hours, and three drinks in, I had found the courage I'd been looking for. The umpteen amount of drinks after that were just for thirst.

Leroy and Eric sat on the couches, each with a beverage in hand while they chatted with other friends around them. Occasionally I'd catch Leroy watching me, one side of his mouth turned up in amusement. I was sure that I looked ridiculous, but I was having fun, so I didn't care.

When the song changed, Cass and I squealed, and I downed the remainder of my drink. I threw the paper cup into the fire and bounced up and down with Cass, our hands in the air as we belted out the chorus to Rage Against the Machine's "Killing in the Name Of." There were a few other people doing the same around the yard, shouting the words, getting hyped up as the outro neared.

Cass was on form as Noah came sauntering around the corner with a sway in his step. He eyed her greedily as he leaned against the back of the couch, sipping his beer. She wasn't oblivious to him and she directed the lyrics at him, emphasizing the "fuck you" part.

She spun around in a circle that almost seemed . . . flirtatious. I wasn't a big fan of cursing, so I just continued to dance, mouthing over the words that she so vehemently aimed at the younger Lahey brother.

He didn't seem bothered, more amused than anything, and I wondered if there was more than just hostility between the two. It was as though their sexual tension was being masked by anger and insults. Noah stood up and walked toward her. She carried on dancing beside me, shouting the lyrics as he got closer and closer. When he came to a standstill in front of her, she laid a solid slap across his cheek that no one seemed the least bit surprised or concerned about, least of all him. He smirked at her before he wrapped a hand around the back of her neck and kissed her with obvious aggression.

What the hell was I watching? *There's no* way *this is healthy.* Eric and Leroy were engrossed in a conversation, and when my attention turned back to Cass, she was very much into the kiss, the two of them having at each other as they backed toward the house. Should I follow Cass and tell her that she might regret that in the morning? She might not. Who was I to judge the situation? Not that I'd have been able to find them considering there were now two back doors, and both were blurred and moving, and the ground beneath me was no longer stable.

## LEROY

Ellie was standing beside the fire pit, watching Cass and Noah retreat into the house. She looked adorable—all dumbfounded and confused. She wasn't alone in her confusion—who knew why the hell Cass kept going back for more? We both knew Noah wouldn't be interested in the morning.

"I better go and get that one," I said to Eric, gesturing at Els, who was suddenly looking wobbly on her own two feet. A couple of quiet drinks had turned into a half dozen and it was clear that it had gone straight to her head. Still, she was having a good time, couldn't argue with that.

"Where did Cass go?" Eric threw his empty cup at a trash can and missed.

"Noah," I explained.

"Got it."

He gave me a quick nod as I stood up and walked toward Ellie. She spun around and collided with my chest. Startled, she stumbled backward but I wrapped a hand around her waist and kept her from falling over. The music was still blaring, loud and hard to hear over, so I leaned in close and watched her unfocused gaze trying to watch my face.

"Should we get out of here?"

She looked over her shoulder. "But . . . Cass and—"

"That's just them," I explained. "They hate each other so much that they regularly fuck. No one gets it. No one tries. We just leave them to it. Should we dip?"

"If you want."

"We can stay if you'd prefer?"

"Na-uh," she slurred and fell into my chest. Shit, she was worse than I realized. "Lesgo."

"You want me to carry you?"

"No," she said, but there wasn't a lot of effort on her part to get moving. Eric watched us from the sofa, a couple of the cheerleaders flanking him now, and he gave me a questioning thumbs-up.

"I've got it," I called back and put an arm around Ellie.

Finally, we were headed toward the back gate. The concrete was scattered with solo cups and bottles and even a few teammates who had decided to pass out where they stood. It was times like these where I was tempted to hold a random Sunday football practice just to watch them all suffer for the hell of it. But as entertaining as that would be, I knew it wouldn't be fair considering all of them put one hundred percent into their game. The weekends were for blowing off steam and they deserved that.

Getting Ellie into the car was like a game of Tetris. First, she slid right off the seat and into the gutter, and then her leg ended up over the center console, and then her laughter was so hysterical that she couldn't keep her body from going limp and she was no help at all. I exhaled and shut the door when she was finally seated and buckled. There was no way that I could take her home in this condition. Not if Mom and Dad were awake. It was midnight, but there was a good chance that they would be waiting up. We had an hour to get her as sober as possible and the only idea I had for that was food.

"Ellie," I gave her a gentle shove when we arrived at Rocky Ryan's diner. The owner kept it open late on weekends because of how much business the students brought through during the late nights. Ellie had her forehead on the car window, eyes closed, shoulders slouched. I gave her another shake and she snorted awake, blinking. "You want something to eat?"

Her eyes were narrow, glaring at the storefront that was illuminated with neon signage and flashing string lights.

She smacked her lips and stretched, "A burger sounds dope. Damn, did we fly here?"

I laughed and opened the car door. "Yeah. We did."

She met me on the other side and straightened her dress, combed her fingers through her hair, and bumped into my wing mirror while she watched her feet moving forward. "Shit, my bad."

She was amusing the hell out of me—her demeanor was so different from its usual timidness. We held hands and I opened the door so that she could head in first. The diner wasn't packed but there were a few different groups of people spread out, in the booths, ordering. Anna, Murray, and Kevin, who had been at the party tonight, were at a table near the counter.

"What's doin' bro?" Kevin hollered and leaned over the table so that we could slap hands while I stood in line with Ellie tucked into my side. Her arms were wound tight around my waist, head on my chest. Kevin gestured at her. "She straight?"

"She's just a little drunk," I said, not loving the way that Murray was staring at her bare legs. Anna leaned back in her seat, her long pink hair falling behind her. She gave my girl a slow once-over and I didn't like it one bit. Anna was notorious for her bitchy attitude to everyone—not just people she didn't like, but people she did. Just a classic mean girl. She and Noah had dated for about six months in his sophomore year, but one day I noticed that I hadn't seen her in a while and my brother said they'd broken up. He wouldn't tell me what had gone wrong, just that it was over. It surprised me at the time; from what I could tell, he really cared about her. But then again, she was not a nice person to be around.

"Hey, chick," she said, and Ellie raised her head a little.

"Hey, I love your hair!" Ellie straightened right up with excitement and stepped away from me, stumbling a little. "It's so pretty!"

Anna ran her fingers through it and wore a smug look. "Thanks," her lips pursed. "I like your . . . T-shirt. Walmart, right?"

Ellie flinched, but she still smiled.

I bit the inside of my cheek with frustration and slipped a hand into my pocket. "Hey, Anna, how's summer school going?"

Her mouth fell open, Kevin and Murray sniggered, and that was all the attention that we gave her. The line moved forward, and it was our turn to order. We got a burger and drink each and sat in a booth at the front of the diner, out of sight so that we could eat in peace. Ellie seemed a bit more put together by the time she was done. She was still drunk, but not to the point that she couldn't keep herself upright. We went back out to the car at quarter to one and I drove home to Ellie singing "Ray of Light" by Madonna, which was on the radio at full volume. It amazed me how she seemed to know the words to every single song that she heard. No matter how old or new it was, how popular or fast or slow, she knew every lyric.

I parked the car in the drive, and as feared, the living room lights were still on. "Shit," I said and looked at Ellie, who was blinking so slowly that I thought she was about to fall asleep right where she sat.

"Els?"

She swiveled toward me so fast that her forehead almost collided with mine. I gripped her shoulders and looked into her unfocused, wandering eyes.

"Listen, when we go inside, head straight upstairs. You follow? Straight upstairs. The last thing we need is Mom calling your mom and telling her that you got smashed."

"M'kay!" She nodded so forcefully that all I could do was hope like hell that Mom didn't want to talk to her tonight. I probably shouldn't have let this happen.

When we got out of the car, I held her hand, led her up the footpath, and shoved her inside as fast as I could. "Upstairs," I whispered. "Go."

Her eyes grew wide and she nodded, spinning around and taking off with so much speed that she put her foot, with force, straight into the leg of the hall table and knocked the vase off. It shattered on the tile, ear piercingly loud. My blood ran cold at the sight of shattered vase fragments and a frozen Ellie. Her stumbling feet crunched pieces of ceramic and each little noise was the knife digging in deeper.

"What on earth is going on in here?!" Mom appeared from the living room in her robe and slippers, her hair rollers creating an evening crown on her head. Her curious stare darted between the floor, Ellie, me, and the floor again. "Is she drunk?"

"Nope," I grabbed Ellie and pulled her in tight beside me, giving her a light pinch in the side in the hopes that she would get the hint and put on the best damn performance of her life. "It was just an accident. A normal, sober accident."

Mom tilted her head, eyes narrow, lips pursed.

The tension while she waited for me to cave was unbearable. The last time I had been challenged this hard was when Noah and I dabbled in pot last summer, ate the entire Fourth of July food preparations, and refused to confess. Mom knew, but she didn't *know*, and we stood solid. Sort of like now, how it was obvious that Ellie was rolled, but I was hoping that she'd mistake it for tiredness and let us be.

"I was drugged!" Ellie suddenly shouted, the quiet snapping like a rubber band. I groaned. "I mean—what?"

"Leroy Lahey," Mom seethed.

"It's not his fault, Mrs. Lahey," Ellie slurred, and I knew we were screwed. "I'm a lightweight, I didn't realize how much I could handle. I only had two!"

"You're holding up four fingers, Ellie," my mom said.

"Oh."

Mom closed her eyes, took a few deep breaths, and pointed at the staircase. "Upstairs. Water, bed. Both of you."

Ellie stepped forward. "I'm so sorr—"

Her sentence was interrupted by an abrupt stream of projectile vomit that coated Mom's slippers, the bottom of her robe, and the floor. My jaw dropped, Mom's jaw dropped, and Ellie slapped a hand over her mouth, bursting into tears.

"Fuck me," I mumbled so quietly that no one heard.

"Upstairs," Mom ordered. There was no hesitation on my part. Ellie didn't protest either when I grabbed her arm and dragged her up the staircase. As soon as we were out of earshot, I laughed—quietly, because if Mom heard me, I might as well ground myself.

"Stop laughing," Ellie blubbered, tears streaming down her face. "What have I done? I'm horrible, Leroy, I'm horrible. I threw up *on* your mom. What the heck?"

I almost doubled over with another burst of laughter as I led her into the bathroom and closed the door behind us. She clearly wasn't coping with the fact that she'd just humiliated herself, but she'd thrown up on my mom and that was not something that I was likely to see again in this lifetime. The situation was a mess, but I had to laugh—it was *also* hilarious.

She sat on the edge of the tub and sobbed while I wet a face-cloth to clean her face. It was a team effort: she pulled her hair into a bun, I wiped her neck, and the mood was quiet while she brushed her teeth, elbows on the counter because she couldn't stand upright. In her bedroom, she had laid out her little sleep set. Keeping herself organized was one of those little things that I loved so much about Ellie: everything in its place, and a place for everything. Somehow, it made how drunk she was even more amusing. There was nothing organized about someone who couldn't dress themselves.

Kneeling in front of her, I pulled her dress over her head. It wasn't until I pulled up the T-shirt underneath that I noticed she wasn't wearing a bra. I inhaled and watched her face while I finished and carefully set her dress aside, never letting my eyes lower, her throat rolled, and her swollen lids fluttered slowly while she let her gaze move over my face. There was no chance that I was going to perv on her at a time like this, so I tugged her sleep shirt and shorts on and kissed her nose.

"Leroy!" Mom's voice came from downstairs and Ellie watched the door, lips parted in concern. "Come here, please."

"Lie down," I told Ellie. She did and I pulled the sheets up and over her. "I'll be right back."

Downstairs, Mom was standing in the living room in a new robe, no slippers, though. It was too hot for slippers anyway— what was she thinking?

She said nothing, just stared, nostrils flared, arms folded. I couldn't even look at her.

"Explain to me," her voice broke the silence. "How did this happen? There were only a few rules, Leroy. Curfew, no sharing a bed, no sex, no drinking. She's been here for about twelve hours. Did I mistake your character judgment?"

I groaned and ran a hand across my face. "No, Mom, no. It's not like that."

"There are different rules for you. I allow you more freedom because you're an adult as far as I'm concerned, and you can make your own choices. But a mother has trusted me with her daughter, and I asked you to respect that."

It was unfair to put her in a position where she had to go against Ellie's mom. "I know," I said. "I'm sorry. She didn't mean to end up like that. She got carried away. She's straight edged, Mom, I swear. She doesn't usually drink but I think it was just a new setting and it went too far. She's a good person. I swear."

It was quiet for a while again.

"Where's Noah?" she asked.

"At Eric's."

"With Cass?"

I nodded and there was definite disappointment in her expression. As much as she loved her son, she knew that the situation between Cass and Noah wasn't the healthiest thing for either of them, but less so for Cass. My mom really liked her. My dad too.

"I'm going to sleep with Els tonight," I told her.

"I do not think so!"

"Mom, come on. She's wrecked. She needs to be watched so that she doesn't choke on her own vomit."

"I told her mom tha—"

"You wanna tell her mom that she died in her sleep?" I challenged, a low blow perhaps but it worked because Mom pinched the bridge of her nose.

"Fine. But don't—"

"She's trashed, Mom. I'm not going to have sex with her. Have a little more faith in me."

Her smile was tired, but it was there, and I thought that the conversation was done, until she pointed at the corridor. "Clean that vomit up. Now."

"Aw, man."

It was just after two in the morning when I slid in behind Ellie and wrapped an arm around her waist so that I was spooning her. There was no better feeling, nothing quite like having her little frame mold so well to mine, tucked in and safe. Her head was under my chin and I kissed the top of it, knowing that I loved every second of tonight. I loved watching her have fun, dance, even drink. I loved introducing her to my friends, calling her mine, having her wear that title with the proudest smile. The way she sought me out throughout the night, waving at me from across the party. Even looking after her made me smile. All

I could do was hope that I got to be the one that was helping her into her PJs after a big night out for a damn long time.

## Ellie

Cottonmouth was real, and this was the worst case of it that I'd ever had. The sun poured in from the bedroom window, heating the room to the point of discomfort, worsening the pounding in my head before I'd even opened my eyes or moved. If there was a way that I could skip this entire day, I would, because it was going to be the worst headache I'd had to date.

A light tickle at the back of my neck startled me into a more alert state and I leaned up on an elbow, peering over my shoulder to find Leroy curled up behind me. I didn't even realize that he had an arm draped across my waist, but my eyes slowly traveled over our tangled state as I smacked my lips together, attempting to moisten my mouth. Worst case of the pasties, *ever*.

As delirious as I felt, I appreciated how handsome he looked behind me. He still wore his T-shirt and jeans, which I assumed was for my benefit. He was a true gentleman, with nothing but respect for me. His hair was a mess and his lips sat parted while he breathed shallow and low. My head thudded even harder, and without warning, the room began to spin, causing me to drop, seeking comfort in the mattress. I must have wobbled as I went down, because my head collided with the side table drawer.

"Darn!" I yelped, grabbing the side of my head as Leroy startled awake behind me. I mumbled an apology about my language, rolling into the pillow and whimpering in pain.

He was fast, because in a split second he had leaped over me and sat on the floor beside the bed, his hands holding my face. As if the headache I'd had before wasn't bad enough. Now it felt like I was going to have to just finish off the job and knock myself out entirely.

"Ellie? You hit your head?"

"You didn't hear that?" I groaned. "I think the neighbors heard it."

"You're bleeding a little," he wrapped a hand around me and helped me sit up. The entire time I kept my face buried in my hands. Maybe it would help with the pain and the unbearable shame at what a tragic mess I'd become.

"Wait here a second."

I leaned against the headboard and breathed through the immense pain that made me feel nauseated. Leroy returned a moment later and I peeked through my fingers to find him holding a first aid kit.

"Can you move your hands for me for a moment?"

I did as he asked and pushed back my hair in an attempt to smooth it out a little before my hands dropped into my lap. My thumbs twiddled with embarrassment as he sat a little closer and dabbed at the warm blood on my face. He was so gentle, wiping it off with a wet wipe before he put a Band-aid on my temple.

"Here," he handed me a fresh wipe. "For your hands."

I noticed the little bit of blood that coated the tips of my fingers. "Thanks."

He leaned over to the side table drawer where a glass of water and an aspirin were waiting. As I reached for it, memories came flooding in and I squealed with shame, slapping a hand to the already sore forehead.

"I threw up on your mother's feet," I whispered, my cheeks suddenly as hot as the sun. All I wanted to do was cease to exist. "I-I . . . what . . . oh my G—"

"Els," he pressed a finger to my lips, silencing the blubbering with a small smile. "It's okay. It was just her slippers. She's got a dozen pairs. And she hated that vase. She kept it there out of respect for Dad; it was a present from him. She'll probably thank you."

"I had forgotten about the vase." I lifted the sheets up to hide my face. "She's going to send me home, right? Tell my mom?"

"No, she—"

"I won't."

Leroy turned around and I peered past him to find his mother standing at the room's threshold. She was dressed in a beautiful coral long-sleeved dress that had a thick belt around its middle. Her feet were bare, but she wore a large sun hat and held a clutch in her hand.

"You can relax, sweetheart," she walked farther into the room. "I've had to deal with Noah and Leroy on a few occasions when they've had too much to drink. But I did assure your mother that you would be safe here."

"I know. I'm so sorry—"

She held up a finger to signal that she wasn't finished, and I gave her an apologetic glance so that she could continue.

"This can be kept between us. *But*. There will be no more drinking. Curfew will not be extended, and if this happens again, I will have to phone your mother and make arrangements for you to be sent home."

I nodded so fast and instantly regretted the enthusiasm as my head pounded. "I swear that it won't happen again."

After the night I'd had, I would gladly never consume a drop of alcohol ever again. I felt terrible, I was sure that I looked terrible, and I'd made a total fool of myself.

"Your father and I are going to church," Eleanor said as she headed back toward the door. "I'll bring lunch home."

She left, leaving the door open. Leroy turned back around to face me and smiled. "That could have been worse. Right?"

"So much worse. Your mom is a godsend."

"She's not bad."

Leroy stretched his hands above his head and yawned. His arms flexed and, *phew*, I might have been lacking brain function at that moment, but I still seemed to be capable of thinking very vivid thoughts.

"I could use a shower," I murmured, still salivating over his toned, taut arms and shoulders.

"Of course. There are a couple of towels in there waiting for you," he stood up and offered me a hand.

"Do you think I'm a mess?" I asked with a small voice as he pulled me up. Being on my feet was harder than I thought it would be, and Leroy kept me upright with his arm around my waist.

"No. I don't think that," he laughed as we went to the bathroom. "You were having fun. Nothing wrong with that."

I felt grateful for his understanding. It would have been fair of him to be embarrassed or disappointed in me for being so ridiculous last night. But without failure, he had been tender and gentle and had taken care of me throughout it all.

He told me that he was going to shower downstairs and would be back in half an hour or so. I could easily have spent that much time in the warm water, washing off the alcohol and regret. But I didn't want to keep him waiting. I washed up as fast as I could, scrubbing with the loofah, hoping it might physically remove the humiliation that I felt over everything that had happened.

After the shower, I stood in front of the mirror, a towel twisted around my hair and my skincare products laid out on the vanity. Each step—the cleanser, the toner, the moisturizer, and sunscreen, each applied in gentle upward motions—aided in feeling clean and relaxed. My soft cotton shorts and camisole smelled like home when I slipped them on, and I went back to the spare bedroom feeling a bit more alive.

Leroy returned to my room in a fresh set of clothes half an hour later, as he said he would. His hair still sat a little damp, the strands sticking to his forehead as he sauntered in wearing a pair of sweats and a muscle shirt.

"Feel better?" he asked.

"Much."

"I figured you wouldn't be up for a lot today," he said, walking toward me, closing the distance as he encircled his arms around my waist. I subtly inhaled his fresh, masculine scent and rested my hands on his shoulders. "But Eric just phoned and asked if I could coach his baby brother's flag football practice this afternoon. He's got a wicked hangover apparently."

"Ooh," I laughed. "Sounds like it's not the first time?"

"It's not. But no sweat. I don't mind helping. Is that cool? You can hang back if you're not up for it?"

"No, no. I'll come."

He pulled me in at the waist, his sights settling on my mouth. "I'd rather we were staying in, though. Just the two of us."

I arched into him. "Me too."

"I can't stop thinking about our night together last month," he murmured, leaning in a little closer. "Your body, your screams, your—"

His words were cut off as he swallowed, and his breathing became deeper. I couldn't handle what happened to me when he spoke like that. His words did wild things to me—it had been bad enough when it was on the phone, but now, pairing it with the lust in his gaze . . . I was a goner.

I didn't wait another moment for him to make the first move I tiptoed up and kissed him. His hand tightened on my back, his fingers dragging inwards as he bunched the camisole in his grip. He pushed his tongue against mine and his hands moved with purpose, traveling the curves of my frame. His touch made me quiver and I moaned into his intoxicating mouth. He was the perfect hangover cure.

He walked us toward the bed and my stomach felt like it was doing backflips as he pushed me down, never disconnecting our kiss, never removing his hands, never faltering. He kept one hand beside my head, kneeling between my legs as his free hand danced over the bare skin of my midriff. He slipped a hand under the material of the cami and dug his fingertips into my waist.

"Are you feeling okay?" he murmured, pecking me between his words so that he could continue kissing me. He dragged his mouth downwards, nipping and sucking at the skin on my neck. I remembered that I was meant to be answering a question, but I could barely remember my own name.

"I'm fine," I answered with a gasp.

"Would you like me to touch you?"

I moaned as his hand grazed my shorts between my legs. "Yes, please."

His mouth was back on mine and he dipped his hand into the band of my shorts just as the sound of the door slamming came from downstairs, Noah's voice hollering loud and obnoxiously. We both stilled and then Leroy cursed as he stood up and moved away from the bed.

I was disappointed, but I reminded myself that we had all summer. Leroy stood with his hands behind his head, biting his lip as he swept me with his hooded gaze.

"I'm going to kill that son of a bitch," he chuckled, without the humor.

I sat up and shrugged a shoulder as I ruffled out my wet hair.

*That's not the only thing that's wet.*

"Okay, should we go downstairs?" I stood and blushed at my own dirty thoughts. It amazed me that in the heat of the moment I felt like doing the wildest things. But I still felt nervous otherwise.

"Yeah," Leroy gestured at the door. "Go ahead. I'll be down in five when this has gone down."

I glanced at where he pointed and giggled.

N

It was about three when we got to the grade school field where a dozen little children were waiting with their parents. There must have been around six or seven boys and girls running around the vast space, tagging each other, throwing footballs, or sitting in the grass. Leroy held a net full of cones and footballs over his shoulder, his free hand intertwined with mine as we made our way toward the group.

"What can I do to help?" I asked.

"If you want to gather the kids and split them into two teams, then I'll set up the cones."

"How about I do the cones, and you look after the kids? You've met them before?"

He laughed, and when we reached the group of children, he dropped the bag and blew the whistle hanging around his neck. The children gathered in one quick swarm, restless with energy and excitement.

"How's it going, team?" he said, nodding to the parents in acknowledgment before he looked back at the children. "Eric is sick, Jordan might have mentioned that. No problem, we'll have a good afternoon, won't we?"

The kids erupted into cheers.

"That's what I like to hear. This is Ellie—she's going to be helping out, so listen to her and be nice. She's going to split you into teams while I sort the cones. Remember, team one puts the flags on. Understood?"

"Yes, Coach," the little ones cheered in unison. Leroy strolled backward and winked, leaving me to organize the teams.

"All right." I felt overwhelmed having a dozen small faces staring up at me. Clearing my throat, I raised my voice. "I'll give you a number and that's your team."

I was about to begin giving them numbers, a simple one, two, one, two, like we did in grade school, when one of the mothers approached me with a kind smile. "It's easier," she whispered beside me. "If you hand out the flags. That way they don't forget their number or attempt to argue so that they can pair up with their friend."

"That makes *so* much sense." I was relieved at her help. "Thank you."

"No sweat." She had thick bangs that fell toward her dark-brown eyes. "I'm Maxi Bryan. Let me know if you need a hand at all."

"I really appreciate that."

The practice was a lot of fun once I was comfortable. Granted, I didn't do much except watch while Leroy directed the kids on how to pass and catch, and gave drills on dodging. Watching the children weave through the cones, sidestep, and their obvious delight when they caught a long-distance pass was so fulfilling. Not to mention how precious it was when Leroy crouched beside someone who was having a hard time and gave them some one-on-one direction. He was so patient and attentive.

Practice was almost over when a little girl tripped as she was running toward her water bottle. Her chin hit the grass and her top tooth must have gone into her bottom lip because there was a drizzle of blood running down her chin when she stood up in tears. One of the mothers informed me that the little girl's mom wasn't here right now, so I ran toward her and scooped her into my arms.

"Aw honey." My heart broke at her distressed whimper. I clutched the bottom of my T-shirt and dabbed at her mouth. "I know, I know, cut lips are the worst. Can I please have a little look? Just to make sure that we don't need to go to the hospital?"

Her gaze widened, her face reddened, and her wail became louder.

"Oh gosh," I panicked. "I'm sure it's fine. Can I have a look? Please."

She didn't raise her head for me and just continued screaming. I was flustered by all the parents watching.

"Carrie!" Leroy jogged toward us. "What's going on, kiddo? You been in a bust-up?"

He kneeled beside me and I transferred Carrie to him, noticing his wince as he looked at my blood-stained shirt, not that it was of much concern to me right now. Leroy set Carrie on her feet and kneeled in front of her, gently cupping her chin.

"Can I have a quick look? I won't touch it, I promise. You know, one time, I slid over and split my knee open and my brother stuck his popsicle stick in it. He was only three, but it *hurt*. So, I know it's super important not to touch people's injuries."

She nodded, tears still streaming down her face. Her gasps for air were heartbreaking. Leroy inspected her lip and gave her a light pat on the arm. "Good news, it's just a little cut. It's almost stopped bleeding. You know, if you get a lemonade popsicle on that, it'll make it feel a whole lot better. I can see Mom coming— let her know Coach Leroy said you need a popsicle."

She wiped her face with the back of her hand, nodded, and ran off toward her mom who was coming in from the parking lot.

After the practice was over, the equipment was cleaned up, and the field had cleared, Leroy and I lay beside each other in the grass. The afternoon sun was warm, but the breeze was refreshing.

"How come you made sure that little girl knew you wouldn't touch her lip?" I asked, still thinking about the exchange and how gentle he was.

"You don't remember being a kid and having an irrational fear that someone was going to assault your injury?"

"Not really," I said. "You obviously have some unresolved trauma from the knee thing, though."

He laughed. The wind carried the sound and gave it notes that had to have come from the heavens. "It's not just me, I swear. Kids have this panic when an adult wants to see their cuts or scrapes or whatever. Watch any child when their mom inspects a cut finger or grazed knee. Their immediate response is, 'Don't touch it! Don't touch it! Don't touch it!'"

My stomach ached from laughing at the high-pitched squeal he put on in place of a child's voice.

"It's true!" he said.

"I guess I wouldn't know," I said, watching a puff of white cloud being pushed across the blue by the wind. "Mom just kept the Band-aids low enough that I could reach them if I needed them."

From my peripheral, I saw Leroy turn his head to look at me. "Your mom didn't help when you got hurt as a child?"

"If it was bad enough, I suppose. She just didn't like to fuss. She said it made me more hysterical when she fussed."

My tone was nonchalant. Factual. But the truth was, it stirred a mild hurt to admit that out loud. I'd never given it much thought before. It was just a norm. Cut knee, grab a Band-aid, get over it, and clean up the mess. Hugs and fuss were just coddling and there was no need for that.

Leroy laced his fingers with mine, the cool grass resting

beneath our hands. "Noah didn't stick a popsicle stick into my knee."

I looked at him.

"I did it to him."

"Leroy!"

He burst into a loud laughter. "I felt so bad."

"You are awful."

"I wanted to see what would happen. I didn't think about the fact that it would hurt."

"You're a monster."

"I was four! He screamed and then I screamed. It was chaotic."

We were both doubled over with laughter, facing each other in the grass, our vision blurred.

## LEROY

After dinner that night, Ellie and I were watching a movie in the living room. Mom and Dad were upstairs, retired to bed to read and catch up on the paper before they popped their sleeping pills. Mom had work in the morning and Dad had decided to give us the living room for the evening. The DVD rack beside the television was stacked from top to bottom, and I told Ellie to take her pick.

"You have a DVD player?" Her mouth fell open as she stared at all the titles. "Our VCR doesn't even work now, it's so old."

DVD players were just over a year old, and as soon as they were on the market, Dad had one under the television. "Dad was like a kid on Christmas when he got that," I explained, settling into the sofa.

"Aw," Els cooed, running her finger down the spines of the DVDs. "Can I put it in the machine? We should watch this—"

She held up *Mrs. Doubtfire* and I nodded, using the remote to switch it all on. Watching her excitement, my heart sped up.

The task was almost mundane to me at this point. Put the DVD into the machine, play, watch. Ellie treated it as though she was delivering the crown jewels, tongue between her lips, focused, a wiggle in her shoulders when she was done. I loved to see it.

"You know what I love about this movie?" she said, sitting beside me.

"Robin Williams in a dress?"

"Ha, Robin Williams is a treasure. But, also, he's literally the best dad ever. He loves his kids so much that he pretends to be an old woman just to spend time with them. How devoted. I can't even imagine what that must feel like!"

I felt for her.

"That's the sort of dad that I'd want for my children."

Then that was the sort of dad that I would be.

I pushed her hair behind her shoulder and drew her into me. "You ever think about your dad? Miss him?"

She tilted her head. "I never knew him, so I miss the idea of him. I'm fine, it doesn't upset me, and I can't miss someone I never knew, but sometimes I think that it would have been nice to have had a dad that I could be close to."

"Yeah."

I couldn't imagine not having mine.

Halfway through the movie, we paused it so that Ellie could run to the bathroom. Which was timed well because I heard the front door open and shut and then Noah came in, dragging his feet. He fell into the sofa beside me and I caught a whiff of his stale odor.

"Dude," I shook my head. "Shower."

"Shut up. What's on?"

"*Mrs. Doubtfire.*"

He scoffed. "Why are you watching this?"

"Ellie chose it."

"Where is she?"

"Bathroom."

He folded his arms and settled farther into the sofa.

"You're in her seat."

His eyes moved to my lap. "You sure?"

"Go and have a shower. You smell like a gym sock. What have you been doing this afternoon?"

"I've been at Natalie's."

Of course he has. Ellie walked back in, her attention moving between Noah and me taking up the entire sofa, leaving only a small gap between us. She was about to head for Dad's recliner beside me, but I gripped her wrist and pulled her into my lap, ignoring Noah's smug expression. It was quiet for a few minutes, the three of us staring at the television, the atmosphere growing awkward. Plus, the smell was intensifying, but I decided not to call him out in front of Ellie.

"How was your night, Noah?" Ellie asked.

He watched her with a curious glare. "I'm wondering how yours was. What happened to your head?"

"Oh, I'd forgotten about that," she touched the Band-aid on her temple and flinched. It was starting to bruise. "I spun out this morning, hit it on the side table."

Noah laughed and I punched him in the thigh.

"It was pretty funny," Ellie said.

It was a relief that Els was making an effort with Noah because I knew that he wouldn't. The fact that she was patient and sweet despite how hostile he was when they first met was gracious of her too.

"Cass was great too," she added, talking to Noah. "She's a lot of fun. Have you guys been together long?"

He wrinkled his nose. "We aren't together."

"Oh . . . I—"

"She's a nightmare. An actual demon derived from the pits of the underworld whose specific purpose is to drive me so insane that I want to put my own dick in a paper shredder."

"Noah, what the hell?" I said.

"Okay, so this morning before I got home," he sat up straight, "we're in bed and she goes, 'I feel like a breakfast burrito from Rocky Ryan's and I'm sitting there with no clothes on thinking, 'Cool, do that then.' And then she said, 'There's a two-for-one on Sunday mornings.' And I'm like, 'Hungry much?' It's quiet for a while and then she starts getting all pissed off and throws the blankets off and I asked what the hell her problem was and she said that I should have offered to go with her and get breakfast together because we just spent the night boning and that's the nice thing to do. Like I'm meant to be a mind reader. Same shit with her all the damn time."

Neither Ellie nor I responded. I heard this sort of thing from him all the time, stupid complaints about stupid arguments that he could avoid if he'd paid attention occasionally. Noah acted as if Cass was difficult to read but all she wanted was for my brother to get his head out of his ass and open the car door once in a while. Metaphorically speaking, of course.

When Noah realized that Ellie and I weren't going to empathize with his complaints, he shrugged. "Good night, though. It's all good when she's not talking. You know?"

Ellie tensed on my lap.

"Don't be a dick, Noah. Stop talking so much smack about her."

He flinched, reddening across the nose. "Whatever," he stood up and left the room.

I didn't care if he felt embarrassed for being called out. His stupid attitude was the embarrassment.

*✎*

It was around midnight, and Ellie and I were at the park at the end of the hill. We'd decided to go for a walk so that we could make the night last longer, neither of us wanting to retire to our separate bedrooms. Our curfew was ten, but Mom and Dad were crashed out. They wouldn't know that we'd left. Streetlights cast a luminous yellow haze on the vast space, hitting the tree-tops and creating leaf-shaped shadows on the grass. It was warm and we sat on the ground beside the playground, throwing a handball back and forth.

"Football practice tomorrow," I said, throwing over arm— she caught it.

"Can I come?"

"Yeah, of course. You wanna help again?"

She threw the ball. "I don't think so."

We both laughed.

"Practice is Monday, Wednesday, and Thursday, right?" she asked, recalling what I'd told her on the phone.

"Yep. It's technically not my practice, but Coach asked me and a couple of the guys to assistant coach the new team. Gives us a chance to keep playing together before we all head off to college."

"That's really sweet to spend so much of your time helping."

"Have to fit the gym in there too."

She tipped her head back and groaned. It echoed in the quiet night air. "I could never. You're so busy. It makes me feel like a lump."

"Sure," I teased, looking at her toned legs stretched out in front of her.

"These are staircase legs," she gestured at them with the ball in her hand. "School and home. I suppose I walk into town a lot too. Question: would you rather exercise every day for the rest of your life or be able to play football for the NFL? You can't do both, though. One or the other."

"Ooh." I caught her throw with one hand. "That's a tough one. They go hand in hand. Have to be fit to play football. But I think I could stay fit enough if I was playing all the time. Can I go to football practice, or does that count as exercise?"

"You can go to practice."

"All right, football for the NFL then," I said. "What about you? You can use skincare for the rest of your life, or you can run a skincare line. But not both."

She gasped. "Oh, wow. Would it be guaranteed that my skincare line would be successful?"

"Yep. The best one in the world."

She palmed her forehead. "The pressure. That's so hard because I love skincare, but if I could guarantee to help millions of people with my products, I mean, I think it'd have to be the successful line."

I was about to throw the ball but paused. "You'd sacrifice your own skin to provide the products to the rest of the world?"

"Yeah," she said, with a *duh* tone. "I'm just one person. Besides, face-lifts aren't technically skincare. I could just invest in that if I was desperate. I'd be earning enough."

She continued to amaze me.

"What skincare do you use?" she asked.

"Nothing. Sunscreen."

She glared. "The injustice. So unfair. I like your mom and dad, by the way," she suddenly said, perking up. "I don't know if I've said that. They're great."

"They like you too."

She ducked her head and grinned. "Does it make a difference that your dad was in the NFL? Does that make your chances of getting scouted better?"

"It means more people know who I am. But nah, if I don't have the skills, I don't have them. No one's going to scout me based on my name alone, but they will be watching."

Moving shadows danced across her thoughtful face and tree leaves rustled when quiet fell upon us, the distant sound of cars humming on the main roads and the occasional bark of a nearby dog echoing in the dark.

"Did your dad always want you to follow in his footsteps?"

"There's never been any pressure," I said. "But he was excited when I joined youth football and developed a passion for the game. He took me to his games and stuff like that from a young age, so I've grown up around the big athletes. I didn't actually spend a lot of time with kids my own age when I was younger. Apart from Noah and my teammates. If I had spare time, I was on the field or at games or getting private coaching sessions in with Dad. Didn't do a lot of the playdates or parties."

"Do you ever feel like you missed out?" Her voice was quiet. "On being a kid?"

"Nah," I said. "Nope. I had a great upbringing. I feel blessed in that sense."

"I used to wish I had a sibling."

"Overrated," I joked, picking at blades of grass.

"I'm sure you don't mean that."

"I loved having a brother when I was growing up. Someone who was just there whenever I needed him or wanted to have some fun or whatever."

Ellie nodded with a distant expression; the ball clutched in her hands. "One thing I know for sure, I will not have fewer than two children."

"I always thought two was a good number."

She smiled; her gaze locked on mine. "Actually, I think so too."

## Ellie

On Monday morning, I changed into a simple sundress, knowing that I would be out in the sweltering sun for hours. Downstairs, Leroy waited in the foyer for me. He cradled a football in one hand, dressed in a pair of white shorts and a T-shirt, his football cleats in his other hand.

"Ready?" He smiled when I stepped onto the tile floor, my sandals slapping with the steps. "You look beautiful."

"Thank you."

He tucked the football under his arm and opened the door for me, following behind as I stepped out into the warm summer air.

We settled into the Mercedes and Leroy slipped a CD into the radio, adjusting the volume button before he sat back and pulled his seat belt on. I sat up straighter with excitement when "I'll Be There for You" began to come through the speakers.

"I love this song," I said. "Do you like *Friends*?"

"For sure," he said. "New season in September. I'm pumped."

"Me too."

Leroy grinned, watching the road but glancing to the side as I bopped in my seat. His hand found mine a moment later. It was such a simple gesture, but it felt like my heart was going to fly out of my chest. He had such an effect on me.

He swung into a parking lot of Archwood High School and we got out. I waited beside the car while he slipped into his cleats and retrieved his football from the backseat. The school's wooden reception doors were locked up. A banner that read *Happy Graduation Class of '98* was falling off the building, attached only by one side. We walked across the parking lot, through a wire fence gate, and onto the large field. Wooden bleachers encircled the entire space and off to the right was a large dark-orange gymnasium where a couple of football players were gathered, chatting amongst themselves.

As soon as we came into view, members of the team gathered and greeted their captain with enthusiasm. I noted how brief Leroy was with his peers. He was polite and smiled and answered questions with what was necessary. But he wasn't the same person that he was with me. He was a hint quieter, more reserved.

He didn't bother introducing me to the entire team individually; instead, he boldly announced me while he had their attention and I blushed at the number of eyes that fell on me with curiosity. I had seen a lot of them on Saturday night during the party, but I hadn't spoken to them. Of course, I knew Eric, so I gave him a small wave and in return he winked. "How's it going, sweetheart?"

"Good," I replied as he walked forward. The rest of the team fell back and began preparing for their practice.

"How was the hangover?"

"It was brutal to begin with, but by the time we got to the flag football practice, I felt better."

"Ah, that's right. Jordan said that he met Leroy's girlfriend," he laughed. "Have fun with that?"

"It was fun. They're cute kids."

He tilted his head to the side and stared at my temple with a furrowed brow.

"What happened there?" he asked, and I realized that he must have been referring to the cut from my careless head banging. "Leroy, you putting hands on this woman?"

He turned and pretended to threaten Leroy, who was sauntering back toward us with a helmet under his arm.

Leroy rolled his eyes with amusement. It was then that he locked eyes with me and cocked a brow. I caught the undertone of his smirk. He sure had been putting hands on me.

"Eric, go and start laps," Leroy instructed. His tone didn't leave room for argument, but it wasn't rude. He seemed to have perfected keeping the lines of friendship and captain in perfect balance.

Eric gave me a friendly nudge in the shoulder and laughed before he took off, falling in beside someone else as they ran around the field. "You'll be bored for a good two hours," Leroy sounded apologetic.

"No, I won't be bored." I stepped closer and wrapped my arms around his neck. "I'll be watching you. That couldn't be boring."

He ducked down and pressed a kiss against my lips. It was gentle and sweet.

"Oh swell, you're here!"

Cass was coming through the wire fence with a bottle of beer in one hand and a pair of shades covering half of her face. She looked effortless in a pair of denim shorts and a striped orange T-shirt that exposed her midriff.

"It's ten in the morning, Cass," Leroy kept his hands rested on my lower back as he scolded the wild curly-headed girl.

She recoiled with confusion but then glanced down at the bottle in her hands with understanding. "It's also summer . . ."

Leroy ignored her and leaned in for a chaste kiss before he headed onto the field. When I turned around, Cass was sprawled out on the grass, the bottle of beer straight up in the air as her throat rolled, swallowing the liquid faster than I could believe I was seeing.

When she was done, she dropped her arm and let the bottle roll across the grass with a sigh. "Want one? I left a box in the shade over there."

I laughed and sat down beside her. "No thanks."

It felt a little bit awkward. We'd been having the time of our lives on Saturday night but without the drunk confidence, she was back to being a perfect stranger. I had a feeling that she didn't have the same problem around other people, though.

"Let's hope that some of these jocks take their tops off, huh?" She sat up and leaned back on her palms, watching the warmups from beside me.

There was only one person that I was interested in seeing topless. And he was still clothed, much to my utter disappointment.

"Can I bitch about something for a sec?" Cass asked after a few minutes of observing. I turned and gave her a quick nod. "Noah is an absolute dick skin. I hate him, I do! But ugh, he's like—addictive. We have great sex. Sometimes we even have great conversations. But then he leaves me in the middle of the night. Or I catch him with some girl in the school hall. I don't know. Like, I can't seem to tell him no, though. I mean, we've never been official, so I can't call him a cheater. But I give in every time. As soon as he kisses me, it's all over. I used to wish I could have liked Leroy. He's so much nicer. But he just doesn't do it for me."

She took a deep breath after the long rant and I glanced at Leroy, glad that he "didn't do it for her." Although I couldn't understand it either. How could he not?

"Tell me how to be strong, Ellie." She flicked her shades up, pushing her ringlets back and staring at me with a pleading gaze.

"I'm not great at the whole advice thing." I winced when she sighed with disappointment. "It kind of sounds like—"

"Do not say love!" She cut me off. "I do not love that moron."

That wasn't what I was going to say, at all. I was more headed in the direction of unhealthy dependence. Especially considering the way that he'd talked about her yesterday. She probably didn't want to hear what I had to tell her, though.

"You got the good one." She sat forward with a defeated slouch.

I couldn't argue with that.

"I need another drink." She burped on cue. "You want one?"

"I'm fine, thanks. How do you get away with drinking in the middle of the day?"

She let out a loud bark of a laugh and adjusted her shades. "Mom hasn't noticed a fucking thing that's gone on around her since James left when I was eleven. James was my dad. If she's not dating someone new, she's at the bottom of a bottle."

"My dad left too," I said. "But I hadn't been born yet. I never knew him."

Cass stared straight out ahead of her. "You're lucky."

It would be an understatement to say that I wasn't the best at offering advice or comfort, no matter how empathetic I felt. I never knew if I should offer a shoulder or an ear. She seemed so sad.

"Were you close with him?" I asked, hoping that she wouldn't find the question invasive.

Cass exhaled a deep breath. "I thought I was. But how close could we have been if he just up and left? Bastard. I know that he and Mom never got along but . . . we did. He could have taken me with him, you know? I'd have preferred to live with him than her. She's a mess."

"Have you ever tried to find him?"

"I wouldn't even know where to start. Besides, why should *I* have to find *him*? He knows where I am. He's the parent. It's his job to act like it."

I'd never thought of it like that before, "That's true."

"Mom dated this one okay dude when I was fourteen. He was pretty nice, and she had her shit semi-together because he was some hot-shot corporate guy. She couldn't act like an alcoholic slutbag when they went to events and all that. But she blew it. Correction: she blew his brother."

I winced.

"That's what Mother Dearest is like. Whatever. It is what it is. I'll be honest, though; I can't wait to get out of this place. Or out of my home. Just a change, you know."

"Are you going to college?"

"When I graduate."

"Oh," I blinked. "You didn't graduate with Leroy?"

"No. I'm a senior this semester. Another whole year at school with Noah and his bullshit buggin' the hell out of me."

"I didn't realize," I pulled my knees to my chest and hugged them, watching Leroy directing his teammates, the passion and dedication in his form. "What will you do at college when the time comes?"

"I'm not sure," she shrugged. "I'll figure it out when I'm there. That's the point, right?"

"Yeah," I said. There was a slightly stronger rush of breeze and it was a refreshing break from the hot sun. The wind made the old bleacher frames groan and the gate rattled. "I guess it is."

We watched the practice for another half hour. Cass sunk three more beers that she'd stashed under the bleachers to keep cool, and we made small talk while we sat in the grass. It became apparent that Cass preferred to keep up conversation rather than sit in silence. There was never more than a beat of quiet, but I appreciated that about her.

"Can I just come with you two, please?" Cass pleaded with Leroy after football practice.

"This is becoming a bad habit," he muttered as we walked back to his car. He was coated with a sheen of sweat—he still hadn't lost his shirt, but it was damp and sticking to his torso.

"What's becoming a bad habit?" Cass dismissed. She stumbled a little and grabbed on to me before she could end up face-first in the concrete.

"Driving your plastered ass around," he answered.

She ignored the jeer and slid into the backseat of the car without further discussion. She could hold her liquor far better than I could, that was for sure. Leroy started the car and put his hand on the passenger seat headrest as he reversed out of the space. The music didn't allow for a lot of conversation as we drove home, but a few minutes in, Cass appeared between us.

She flicked the volume button down and leaned on the center console.

"Are your parents home?"

"No," Leroy said. "Work. Dad's spending the day with Joe."

"Who's Joe?" I asked, casually curious.

"Cool, I'll come to your place. My mom is in," Cass said.

"Joe is an old friend of his. Lives just out of town, so Dad makes a day of it when he visits," Leroy said.

Cass blabbered on about this, that, and the next thing as we all got out of the car and headed toward the house. The windows were wide open, the curtains blowing in the light breeze. As we stepped inside, I could hear Weezer floating from the living room speakers. Cass walked ahead of us, kicking her flip-flops off with ease before she stumbled down the step into the living room.

I had barely toed off my first sandal when Cass's hostile shouting could be heard. Leroy and I exchanged a quick glance and sped up our movements. He was a step ahead of me when we found the cause of her pissed-off shouting; I felt a pang of heartache for her.

Noah was half-naked on the sofa, a beautiful brunet in her bra pinned beneath him.

"You are a sack of shit," Cass shouted, emphasizing each word. The girl pushed at his chest, forcing him off her. He looked like a deer caught in headlights as he glanced between the three of us. "I mean, shit. Did you even have time to shower between the two of us?!"

The girl glowered as she pulled a shirt over her head. "Screw you, Noah." She looked at Cass, apologetic. "I didn't realize—"

"You're fine, Holly," Cass waved the girl off. "*He's* the asshole."

"Noah, go upstairs," Leroy ordered, intervening before the situation could unravel further. Noah seemed more than willing to follow his big brother's orders.

"Excuse me, you little sack," Cass shouted. "We're not done here." She stormed after Noah, following him upstairs despite our warning that it was best if she left him alone. The advice fell on deaf ears and their shouting could be heard from where we stood in the living room.

Holly didn't stick around for long. As soon as she had herself in order, she bolted out of the house.

"This entire situation is fucked," Leroy said as I followed him upstairs. His footsteps were heavy, and he seemed exhausted. I wondered if that was because of practice, or because of his brother and the drama that followed him. "I need to—"

His sentence dropped off as loud moaning and the unmistakable squeak of a bedframe could be heard coming from the end of the upstairs corridor.

Leroy sighed with further frustration, but all I felt was sadness. Cass couldn't see that their situation was so unstable. Or perhaps she could but she didn't want to admit it. Whatever it was, it was clear that some sort of insecurity came into place. And whatever it was, Noah played on it. I mean, seriously. Cass, then Natalie, then Holly, now Cass, it made my head spin, and I had to wonder what was going through his head. Was this a sick game to him? Or was it more? Did he have his own insecurities? Maybe. It didn't make it okay, though.

"It's sad." I wandered into the spare bedroom and sat down. Leroy leaned against the doorframe. "She obviously has some issues over her dad leaving. She told me about that, by the way. Your brother shouldn't take advantage of her like that."

"Trust me, I know," he said remorsefully. "But whenever I try to intervene, both of them tell me to butt out."

I supposed there wasn't a lot that he could do if she didn't want to listen. Leroy let me know that he needed to take a quick shower and he wouldn't be long. I used the spare fifteen minutes to go through luggage and choose tomorrow's outfits, noting that I'd need to do laundry soon. I was watching the street from the bedroom window, not focusing on much in particular, just daydreaming about the beautiful homes and gorgeous lawns outside, when the sound of a door slammed behind me, and Cass screamed and cursed her way down the hallway.

"You just wait, Noah," she threatened with a slurred voice. "I'm telling your mom that I found a girl half-naked on the couch!"

"Fucking hell, Cass, would you shut up for a minute and let me talk?"

Noah's footsteps thudded closer and closer, and when he came into view, he was stark naked. I squealed and averted my gaze.

"What the fu—NOAH! Put some fucking clothes on!"

"Shut up, Leroy!"

"Do what you're told, Noah," Cass shouted from downstairs. "No one wants to see that little piece of flesh flopping around."

"Little? That's not how you usually refer to it."

Leroy shouted again. "Put some clothes on, you fool!

I was still standing in the corner of the room with my hands pressed against my eyes, afraid of what I would see if I were to look. The voices of the brothers came closer and it sounded like a little bit of a scuffle was taking place—very close.

"All right, all right," Noah grunted. "I'm going. Lord, chill *out*."

"Shit, forgive me if I don't want my girl to see you naked."

"She might want a trade-in."

A loud smack against bare skin sounded, followed by Noah's *ouch*. Silence settled after that and I was seeing colorful dots in the black from holding my eyes so darn hard.

A large pair of hands settled over mine and I let them lower my arms. "It's okay now."

"That was, um——"

"Pathetic," Leroy interrupted, and I looked at him, realizing that he was in a towel, still damp from the shower. I had been waiting to see him like this again and it was not disappointing. "He has no shame. Drives me insane."

I swallowed, a little flustered at how hot and bothered he was making me. "I can tell."

The air felt thick as he stepped closer and put an arm on the wall beside my head. "How am I making you feel right now?"

"Breathless."

He dragged his finger down the length of my jaw and took my chin between his index and thumb. "In a good way?"

"The best."

His hold on my jaw tightened as he smashed our mouths together and pressed me against the wall. I would never get enough of this. I loved how equally senseless and overwhelmed I became when our tongues danced together, and his hands roamed over me. He used his knee and pushed my thighs apart, pressing himself against me so that I could feel how much I'd wound him up.

He dragged his mouth lower, down my jaw, tasting me, sucking on the tender spot beneath my ear as his hands rested on my waist. His fingertips dug in, hard, and I gasped, surprised to feel how good it felt. As he kissed his way back up my throat, his hands glided upwards under the tank top. I whimpered with need when his hands grazed beneath my breasts. I was on fire. I didn't want to wait for him another moment longer. I needed him so much.

My hands came to the front of his chest and I dragged them down, feeling his toned, chiseled torso as we kissed with a passion that I didn't believe existed. His masculine groan reverberated right through me and it felt as though I would combust at the simple sound of his arousal.

"I'm hungry!"

We came to an abrupt halt when Cass's shrill voice sounded from downstairs.

"No, no, no," Leroy growled, his hand tucked in the back of my shorts as he cupped my butt. "I thought she'd left."

"Ellie? Leroy? Let's go and get food. I'm starving."

Leroy exhaled a long breath, his disappointment evident as he wrapped his fist in my hair. "When am I going to get to pleasure you, Els?"

His voice was so low, so raspy, and drenched in desire. It felt as though an acrobatic performance was taking place in my stomach and I practically panted as I answered him. "Soon, I hope."

"Soon," he nodded and kissed me again before he pushed away and turned around. I watched his taut back and low-hanging towel, which revealed the plump muscles of his firm butt as he left the room.

We met Cass at the bottom of the staircase, after Leroy got dressed. She was lying on her back, sunglasses on, a halo of curls around her head. "These cold tiles are so refreshing, wanna join?"

"Where are we going to eat?" Leroy asked, sounding on the edge of impatience.

Cass grunted, rolling over and heaving herself off the ground, the back of her shoulders indented with lines from the tile gaps. "Rocky Ryan's," she slurred. "I need a burger, I need a milk shake—"

"If you drink a milk shake," Leroy pointed at her as he held the door handle, "I'll be leaving you there."

She screwed her face into a guilt-ridden smile, lips pursed and cheeks raised. "I'm lactose-intolerant," she told me. "But I love a milk shake. Fries dipped in milk shake."

"My friend Amber likes fries dipped in soft serve."

"Now *that* sounds good," Cass said.

We all headed outside, and Leroy called up to Noah that we were heading out before he closed the door and locked it. He took my hand and glared at Cass with disapproval. "Is it worth the stomach upset after? Think about it."

"It is."

"You never seem to think so when you're locked in a stall ten minutes later."

I laughed but felt bad for her. I don't know what I would do if I couldn't have ice cream or cheese.

Cass ended up ordering a peppermint thick shake.

## Ellie

I'd been in Colorado for a week and it was the Fourth of July. It felt a bit strange to be here, rather than at home with Momma. Not that we ever had big plans. Sometimes we'd go and spend it with her uncle and aunt on their farm. Her cousins were strangers to me—we'd never been the sort of people who were close to the extended family. Most of them were racist, obnoxious assholes, so I didn't envy Mom when she told me over the phone that that was where she would be spending the weekend.

Celebrating with the Laheys sounded far more appealing.

"It's like a community gathering at the lake," Leroy said, holding my hand in the car as he drove. His mom, dad, and Noah had gone separately because we'd had to go into town so I could get a bathing suit first. As organized as I claimed to be, I stupidly hadn't brought swimwear. "Families go down and have barbecues and fireworks and football. It's cool. You'll have a good time."

"Sounds fun," I agreed.

Chatfield State Park was a half-hour drive from where we were, and when we arrived, the afternoon summer sun was at its peak, shining straight down on the lake. It was a beautiful spot—open, surrounded by green rolling land and flat fields. It seemed to stretch on for miles. There were boats and jet skis on the water, campsites set up along the waterfront, and people engaging in various activities around the place.

We drove slowly for a while until we came to a semi-vacant spot where Noah, Eleanor, and Jacob were parked, the trunk open while they unloaded the car. They were on the edge of the grass where it transitioned into sand, and in another six feet, it was water.

"Hello," Eleanor said as Leroy and I got out of the car with our bags. We went straight over and started helping.

"Did you find a swimsuit, honey?" Eleanor asked, and I nodded.

We unloaded the portable barbecue and coolers filled with food and drinks. They had brought foldable chairs, a table, blow-up beds, and a picnic blanket. We left the blankets and bug spray in the car—they wouldn't be needed until later in the evening.

"This place is so nice," I said, standing in front of the lapping water, my toes close to the edge. Leroy and Noah stood beside me. "Is this place a tradition? Do you come every Fourth?"

"Not every Fourth," Leroy said. "Sometimes we hang out at home. It was my idea to come this year. I wanted to show it to you."

My heart melted until Noah snorted.

"We could have gone to Robbie's and got ripped, but we have to hang here with Mom and Dad and pretend we don't want to drink."

"*You* could have gone to Robbie's," Leroy muttered, taking my hand in his.

"No, I couldn't. I'm not invited unless you are."

Leroy was trying not to laugh, but I felt sort of bad for Noah at that moment. "Where's Cass?" I asked. "How come she didn't come?"

Noah gave me a flat stare. "Why would she?"

"Oh . . . I don't—never mind."

"Should we swim?" Leroy pulled my attention from his brooding brother. "Before we start cooking dinner?"

"It's certainly hot enough," I agreed.

We stripped down to our bathing suits, Leroy in his blue-and-white pinstriped trunks and me in the brand-new bikini we'd found at the mall. It was pastel pink with string ties at the hips and a halter-neck bikini top. Leroy watched me while I folded up my T-shirt and set it down with the rest of my clothes, his eyes ravishing me. My heart rate accelerated.

The water was cool but warm enough not to hesitate when submerging our bodies. We walked out until the water came to my chest and then Leroy swept me up, hooking my legs around his waist so that we could keep going without me drowning.

"I really wish my family wasn't twenty feet away from us right now," he said, the light reflecting off the water and shimmering on his sun-kissed skin. "You look so damn good."

"You do too," I said, my arms wrapped behind his neck. "Maybe we could just drift and drift and drift until we got around the corner over there and we'll . . . I don't know . . . never mind, I was thinking we'd find somewhere private but it's kind of open around here."

"I like where your mind is at, though."

"We need a little boat filled with pillows and blankets and we could go way out. Total privacy."

His teeth sunk into his bottom lip and he groaned, tipping his head back. "That sounds so good."

"We could . . . rock the boat."

Leroy burst out laughing at my terrible pun as we dipped and bopped, the water soaking and flattening the ends of my curls. We spent a good hour swimming, splashing at each other, and using a rope swing that extended from a tree not far from our spot. Noah had a swim, too, but he kept to himself despite my offer for him to join us. I couldn't blame him—I wouldn't want to third wheel either—but I still felt bad that he didn't have someone here with him.

When the sun started to set, Leroy volunteered for us to man the barbecue so that his mom and dad could relax. They settled into their beach chairs, facing the sun with a drink each, and Noah lounged on his towel. It wasn't long before the scent of sizzling meat and seafood was floating through the air.

"You wanna skewer that chicken for me, babe?" Leroy asked, still standing shirtless with a pair of tongs in his hand while he flipped steaks. Meanwhile, I'd slipped a pair of overalls over my bikini. He pointed at the container of raw chicken strips that were coated with seasoning. I nodded and got started.

"What's your favorite food?" I asked, sliding chicken onto the skewers.

Leroy watched the grill while he thought about his answer. "Burritos."

"Can I cook those for you while I'm here?"

He looked at me. "You want to cook burritos for me?"

"Yeah. I can't cook at all. But I want to do that, for you. Like as a date-night idea or something. We might need a backup pizza or something."

"How about this," he said, grabbing me at the waist and pulling me in front of him so that my back was to his chest and his chin rested on my shoulder. "Tomorrow night, I'll get mom and dad tickets to a movie, send them off for the evening, and I'll get rid of Noah and we'll have the house to ourselves for a couple of hours?"

"You'll get rid of Noah?" I laughed, taking the tongs from him so that he could wrap his arms around my middle. I flipped the patties. "That sounds menacing."

"Force will be used if necessary."

"I'll leave that to you. Can I put the chicken on now?"

"Yeah," he said, still not moving from his position behind me. "You taking over the grill?"

"I guess I am. Don't leave me, though; I don't want to be responsible for burning and ruining dinner."

He kissed the line of my jaw. "I'm right here."

When the meat was done, we laid out the cold salads and sides and sat around the picnic table—Leroy beside me, Jacob at the head, and Eleanor next to Noah. The food was exquisite and everyone complimented Leroy for it. "Els cooked the skewers," he said.

"Very nice," Eleanor said.

"Oh," I covered my mouth and swallowed before I answered. "I mean, you seasoned them. I just cooked them. Actually, I'm kind of surprised I managed that, though. I can't cook at all."

Eleanor seemed a bit surprised at that. "Your mom never taught you?"

"She tried when I was a kid. But she didn't really have the patience for it. She'd end up doing it herself or getting annoyed if I did something wrong. She's just like that, you know?"

I laughed it off, not all that bothered about the fact that Momma was far too impatient to give lessons in anything practical. She'd explained that some parents were better equipped to teach than others and I understood that, but Eleanor gave me a sad smile, as if I'd been dealt a bad hand and she felt awful for me.

"What about school?" Noah gave me a flat stare. "You didn't think to take cooking as an elective?"

"No, I took chem. I want to develop a skincare line. That felt more practical to me."

"Leroy mentioned something about that," Eleanor said.

"Because starving is practical," Noah quietly muttered.

Jacob shot him a warning glare but even I could see Noah's point of view.

"What's the plan for getting that started, honey?" Eleanor asked, bringing my attention back.

"I've studied chem and biology at home and at school for a long time. I have a lot of knowledge on the skin, how certain elements react to certain people, the cells, the regenerative process, that sort of thing. The next step is a business and accounting course. There's one that they run not too far from home back in Waco. I'll sign up there when I've saved the cash."

"That sounds like a good plan," she said.

"Noah knows a thing or two about business and finances," Jacob said, gesturing his fork at his younger son, who had finished his dinner and was now slouched in his seat with his arms folded. "He took it as an elective last year. Pick his brain if you want."

I smiled but doubted that Noah and I would be gelling over the subject of business anytime soon. Some moments with him were better than others, but for the most part, he didn't seem to want much to do with me.

After dinner, Leroy and his dad threw the football around for a while. Jacob had a great arm, considering his age, but that wasn't surprising. He was fit and obviously taking care of himself. The sun was setting on the horizon, casting a burnt-orange glow across the lake. Dusk was mesmerizing in this open space—everything appeared incandescent and warm, as if warm was an appearance and not a feeling.

"Come and join," Leroy said to Noah, holding the football in one hand.

"Nah," Noah said, leaning back on his palms. "I'm tired."

"Come on, son," Jacob said. "You too, Ellie."

I was helping Eleanor with the dinner clean-up, so I pointed at the paper plates in my hand. "I'm jus—"

"I've got it, honey," Eleanor said, swiping the plates from me. "Go on. You too, Noah. Join in."

Noah made a big show of being exasperated at the idea of getting up, but he did, wiping sand off his hands. The four of us stood in a square, leaving enough room for other people to safely walk along the waterfront without getting a ball to the head. The first thing I noticed was that Noah was a natural, like his brother and dad. It looked like he was barely putting any force behind his throw but the ball traveled so far. After a while, it was obvious he was enjoying himself too—as much as he tried to hide it, the smile that he wore while he cracked jokes with his dad gave him away.

When it was dark, Leroy and I settled down on a rug with a blanket so we could watch the fireworks. We could hear music from other camping sites drifting toward us, we could hear the lap of the water hitting the shore, and stars were glittered across the cobalt-blue night. It was beautiful.

"How's the evening been?" Leroy asked from behind me. He was sitting up and I was between his legs against his chest, his chin resting atop my head.

"The best," I said. "Your family is . . . so warm."

"Warm?"

"Yeah, warm. Inviting. I feel so comfortable and welcome here. It's hard to describe but I feel like I belong."

He held me a little tighter. "I'm glad that you feel that way. Because you do belong here."

The first lot of fireworks were abrupt, and I jolted with fright. Leroy laughed behind me and we watched the bursts of beautiful color exploding above us. Red, blues, and whites, blooming like unfolding flowers. What Leroy said made me feel an inexplicable amount of joy. Because I meant what I said; I felt like I belonged here in a way that I didn't even feel at home sometimes.

Noah was in a better mood the next morning. We were in Leroy's room so that we could talk to him about our plan to have the house to ourselves tonight. As cheerful as he was, that did not translate to cooperative.

"Noah, come on."

Noah leaned against the doorframe while Leroy attempted to coax him into agreement. I watched from the bed, legs crossed and hopes high.

"Let me get this straight," Noah said. "You want me to tell Mom and Dad that I'll be here tonight. But you actually want me to leave so that you two can have some alone time."

"As if I haven't made that clear," Leroy sighed with frustration.

His smug stare darted between the two of us, silence settling while he deliberated his response. If he didn't agree to tell his parents that he would be in for the night, it would be harder to get them out of the house. And then if he did spend the night in, we wouldn't be alone. So, the success of the plan was on his shoulders.

"Nah," he finally grinned. "I think I'll stay in. Perhaps I'll even have a few friends over, since Mom and Dad will be out and all."

"I've been polite," Leroy seethed. "I could just pummel you into submission."

He engaged in a frightening stare-down with Noah. I had a feeling that physical fights weren't all that uncommon between the two brothers. And from the way that Noah's expression became less smug by the second, it was safe to assume that Leroy often won.

"Fine," Noah said. "I'll go and see Cass."

Leroy's nostrils flared. "Leave her alone, Noah."

"Bite me."

Noah left the room with his middle finger raised.

"That's the first part of the plan settled," Leroy said and rested his large hands on the curve of my waist. "I'll talk to Mom; she'll be home from church soon. Dad's easy. He'll just do what Mom tells him to."

I gave him a quick kiss. I was excited to spend some proper time together. It felt like we had been struggling to make it happen since I'd arrived a week ago.

I told Leroy that I needed to shower and change before I went downstairs. I was still in my nightdress. He left me to it and I didn't waste time, getting ready as fast as I could. My hair fell in its natural wave after I had showered, and I changed into a denim spaghetti strap dress and pulled a plaid flannel around my waist. We had plans to go to the grocery store to get tonight's dinner ingredients, so I swiped on a little bit of gloss and mascara as well.

Downstairs it was quiet, save for the hum of the television in the living room. I peeked through the door and spotted Jacob in his recliner chair, a coffee in one hand, the remote in the other. He was watching the football highlights, still dressed in his Sunday best. I was about to continue in search of Leroy when he hollered out.

"Ellie," he smiled. "How are ya this morning, darlin'?"

I skipped down the step and wandered over to the sofa. "I'm good, Jacob. How are you?"

"Not bad," he scratched his head, and I noted what a full head of hair he had for his age. "Leroy's helping his mother with something in the garage."

"Oh, that's fine," I said, sitting down on the sofa.

"He's a good boy," he chuckled, almost more to himself than me. "Good thing about him going to Baylor, you'll be close. Worked out nicely."

He lifted his coffee and guzzled it back, lowering the cup with a content sigh. "Good school that school. I went there."

"How come you moved to Colorado?"

"Eleanor," he answered, his gaze moving between myself and the football. "She always wanted to raise kids in a smaller town, and she got a job offer nearby so it just sort of happened. Good place to retire."

"Of course," I nodded with understanding. I always imagined raising children in a small town myself. "It must be nice to have Leroy attending the same college you did."

He let out a cheerful whistle. "Sure, makes me happy. He didn't have to. He was free to do what he wanted. But I'm proud. Real proud."

I could tell that he meant it in the way he smiled. His tone was bold and enthused. It was such a pure kind of pride and a splitting grin formed on my own face in response.

The sound of the back door opening and closing was followed by the chitchat of Leroy and Eleanor. They appeared at the living room entrance and the room became brighter when he looked at me.

"Honey," Eleanor set down a box of old records and wiped her brow. "Leroy bought us tickets to the cinema tonight and he reserved us a table at Duke's Steakhouse in Castle Pines."

Jacob looked suspicious for a second. But he quickly smiled at his son. "What are the tickets for?"

"*The Truman Show*," Leroy said.

"Oh, that looks good."

"I would have liked to have seen *Out of Sight*," Eleanor mentioned as she sat on the floor, whipping a dish towel out of her dress pants pocket. She wiped down the old records, clearing them of dust.

"You can go and see that next weekend," Leroy suggested.

He and his father locked eye contact as he offered me his hand and pulled me into his side. It would appear as though Jacob could see through our sweet gesture. But he didn't call us out.

"Ready to go to the store?" Leroy asked, taking my hand. I gave him a confirming nod and we started out of the living room. He watched his mother with a curious stare, stopping at the entrance threshold before we rounded into the foyer.

"Mom, what are you doing with those?"

She peered up and waved a record. "I'm donating some of our collection. I've kept the best, of course."

"Let me know if you need me to run them into the thrift store."

"Thank you, sweetheart," Eleanor said.

"We'll be back in an hour or so," Leroy called from beside the front door while he shoved his feet into his Vans. "Need anything from the store?"

"Get me a six-pack," Jacob shouted.

Eleanor frowned. "He isn't twenty-one."

"Never mind then."

I laughed as Leroy held the door open for me. The closer we got to our time alone, the more excited I grew. We slid into the car and wound down the windows as soon as the engine was fired up.

"Steakhouse is always a win," Leroy grinned as he reversed out of the driveway. "I knew that'd get them out of the house."

"Where's Castle Pines?" I asked.

"An hour out of town," he said, leaning across the center console once we were on the road, his hand settling on my thigh. "Finally, a bit of time to our damn selves."

"I can't wait."

There's literally nothing Leroy did that he didn't look gorgeous doing. Somehow, he looked like perfection as he pushed a cart around the store. I wasn't subtle in my admiration, watching as he reached the top shelves to collect various ingredients, his sun-kissed skin pulling taut around his firm muscles.

"What kind of sauces do you want, Els?" he asked as he glanced over a piece of paper in his hand. His lips moved as he murmured to himself and then he shoved the list back in his pocket.

I stared at the shelf that housed a huge selection of sauces and spreads. "Mayo? Peri Peri? Barbecue?"

"What kind of burritos do you eat?" he laughed.

"Peri Peri is good with chicken. We could have chicken burritos?"

Leroy shrugged with a thoughtful look on his face. "Could be good. I usually do ground beef. But that sounds tasty as well."

"We should do a little bit of butter chicken. That could be super tasty in a soft wrap?"

"You're the chef tonight," he swiped a jar of sauce from the shelf. "What else?"

"Mmmm, hummus and sour cream, and we should get some lemon pepper seasoning."

"Are you sure you've never cooked before?" he asked, reaching for the items and dropping them into the cart.

"I'm looking at things that sound like they *might* taste good with chicken," I confessed.

We decided that we'd do a little side of ground beef too, so that we had options. When we got to the end of the aisle, Leroy suggested that I go and pick an ice cream for dessert while he went and got the meat from the fridge. We split off and I went in search of some cookies and cream.

It turned out to be harder than I thought to pick a flavor. I thought I knew what I wanted. But when faced with the ample options, I stared into the freezer and chewed my thumb. Passion fruit sounded good. But, chocolate. Peaches and cream sounds freaking delicious.

"Sorry, excuse me a moment." I jumped a little at the unexpected voice beside me.

A man reached into the freezer and pulled out a tub of vanilla, dropping it into his basket. "Sorry, I didn't mean to scare you," he apologized. "You were off in a daze and I didn't want to be rude."

"Oh, no, that's my fault." I was well aware of my habit to internally drift.

"You're not from here, right?" he said.

"Um—"

"I work here," he shifted his basket to the other hand. "I'm familiar with the regulars, and I'd *definitely* remember a face like yours."

I blushed. Not because I was flattered or wanted to be flirtatious. It was just a reaction to being admired, and while he didn't seem rude or arrogant, I still wasn't that keen on being approached so casually. Of course, I didn't want to seem like a bitch by telling him to shut up, so I stood there with red cheeks while I shifted nervously on the spot.

"I'm David," he filled in the silence and offered me his hand.

"Babe," Leroy's voice pulled my attention to the end of the aisle, where he stood with the cart and a packet of diapers in each hand. "Is Abby in junior- or toddler-sized diapers? I forget. I know, worst dad *ever*."

My jaw dropped and it took every single ounce of self-control that I could muster not to burst into a side-splitting laughter. He just stood there with a dead serious expression. I didn't know how he was doing it because I was about three seconds from snorting like an animal.

"Oh, uh, toddler," I answered and turned back to David, who looked a little disappointed. "Sorry, better get back to it. The baby's waiting with the sitter."

"Of course." He gave me a brief nod and went on his way as Leroy wheeled the cart up beside me with a satisfied smile on his face.

"Who is Abby?" I laughed.

"I have no idea. It was just the first name that I thought of when I saw that slut of a cashier chatting you up."

"Aww, is someone jealous?" I teased.

He stopped the cart and stared at me with an expression that left no room to mistake how serious he was. "That would suggest that I want what isn't mine," he shrugged. "I'd like to think we've established exclusiveness and I will always protect that."

And after he pressed a quick kiss on my lips, he carried on pushing the cart, leaving me reeling with an abundance of emotions. It's an amazing thing when the same man who makes you feel as though the earth is spinning is also the one who can take you by the hand and keep you from falling over.

He made me feel things I'd never felt before—special, protected—because he chose me. He cared enough to make me the center of his world. He was always making sure I felt comfortable and happy. He was showing me what it felt like to fall in love, and I was loving every moment of it.

The stolen kisses while no one was looking. The heated gazes across the room. The excitement when we discovered something new about each other. Because despite the hours of phone conversations, there were still things we had yet to learn, and it was a beautiful thing. I had never been so excited to find out how dark someone liked their toast. Or which side of the bed they preferred. Or if they liked their OJ with or without pulp. Or if they favored sweet or savory. It was all of the small things that made a person who they were, and I wanted to know it all.

We stood at the checkout and started placing our items on the belt while the woman in front of us paid for her groceries. I realized it was one of the moms from the kids' football practice, Maxi Bryan. She hadn't seen us, so we let her continue without bothering her. She chatted with the cashier while her son tossed his football in the air. "Not in the supermarket, Nathan," she playfully scolded. She received her change and the two of them left hand in hand.

We loaded everything onto the belt and then Leroy stood behind me with his arms clasped in front of my stomach. The cashier packed the groceries into the plastic bags.

"That'll be eighty-two dollars and thirty-six cents," she said when she was done.

"Oh, jimmy shoo!" I broke free from Leroy, heading straight for the bags. "We'll put something back. We can just do one meal. Ground meat or chicken? And the ice cream, we don't need—"

"Els," Leroy laughed, and when I glanced at him, my hand still in the bag, he shook his head in dismissal. "I've got it."

"But it's so exp—"

"Ellie," he gave me a sideways glance and ran his card through the machine. "I've got it."

The cashier gave me an amused smile and I stepped back so that he could finish the transaction. I wasn't used to dropping that kind of cash on a whimsical trip to the store. We spent that in a month of groceries at home. The amount of money he spent made me feel a little terrible, made me question whether or not I needed to earn it or do something to deserve such an amount being spent on me.

What if I seemed like a burden? What if he realized I couldn't keep up with his lifestyle? I worked for what I had, and I liked to work hard, but that didn't mean we were in the same league. We weren't even in the same game.

"You're overthinking things," Leroy whispered as his lips brushed my temple. It stirred me from my thoughts and I skipped into step beside him as he pushed the cart full of groceries toward the exit.

"How do you do that?"

"You have a tell," he grinned, staring straight ahead as though he was picturing something. "Your eyebrows pull together and your bottom lip juts out. You do it whenever you're thinking. Usually you follow it up with a question or a statement that bothers you."

"You're very observant," I noted as we wandered through the parking lot, the sweltering sun beaming straight down on us.

"I am when it comes to you," he turned to me with a breathtaking smile. And I do mean *breathtaking*. "You're important to me."

"You're important to me too."

# Ellie

When we got back to the house and headed into the kitchen to unload the groceries, we found Noah sitting just outside of the sliding door on the deck. He was bouncing a handball up and down as music came from the windowsill speaker, and he turned to look at us with a mild frown when he noticed that we'd come back with our ingredients for the meal tonight.

"Is there enough for three?" Noah asked with a robotically loud voice for the sake of their parents outside, "since I will *definitely* be here for dinner and all."

Leroy paused with the fridge door open and gave him a bored stare. He looked as if he wanted to say something, but in the end, he shook his head and carried on putting stuff away. Noah scoffed and picked up a Game Boy from the deck beside him. The little beeps and pings filled the quiet air while Leroy moved around the kitchen, opening and closing cupboards.

Eleanor popped her head through the sliding door wearing a sun hat and gardening gloves. She looked between the three of us before her attention fell on me.

"Can I have a quick chat, sweetheart?"

*Instant panic.* "Ye—sure."

Noah cackled. "Someone's in trouble."

Leroy leaned his palms on the countertop and looked at his mom. "What's wrong?"

"Nothing, for goodness' sake, I want to chat with Ellie for a moment."

Outside, I followed her down the deck, across the grass, and toward a foam mat that was stretched out in front of fresh soil and a couple of colorful flowers that were in plastic pots to be planted. She kneeled on the mat and started digging some little holes.

"Honey, I know that this may be unfair of me to ask because you're here in Castle Rock for Leroy, but I can tell that Noah is itching to spend some time with his big brother. I was wondering if there was something we could do about that?"

"Oh," I turned and looked at Noah sitting on the deck, sulking with his Game Boy. It was sort of awkward because what else was I supposed to do? But he was doing us a favor tonight, so making myself scarce for a few hours was the least I could do. "Yes, I can—"

"Cass popped around here about fifteen minutes ago looking for you. I said that I'd let you know."

"She was looking for me?"

Eleanor set down her garden spade and looked up at me. "I know, it's shocking that she wasn't hounding Noah for attention. But she didn't seem eager to hang around."

"I'll go and see her."

"Thank you, honey."

Inside, Leroy was upstairs in his bedroom putting laundry in his drawers. "Everything okay, babe?"

"Yeah. Your mom wanted to tell me that Cass was here looking for me."

His brows pulled. "She had to tell you that in private?"

"She didn't want to mention it in front Noah for some reason," I lied. "I don't know. But I'm going to go see her. I won't be long."

"I'll come."

"No, no, that's fine." I laughed at his confusion. "I want some girl time."

"Don't you need a ride?"

"If she can walk here, I'm sure I can walk to her house. I'll be back soon." I gave him a kiss. "You could do something with Noah."

He recoiled and then slowly, his expression became knowing and he slid his hands into his pockets.

"Bye, babe," I grinned and slipped out of the room.

N

Cass lived about three blocks from Leroy on a quiet cul-de-sac. The houses weren't quite as elaborate as the ones on Leroy's street, but they were beautiful nonetheless. Cass had a railed front porch with a swing seat and window planter boxes. My hand rapped the front door, and I was waiting for a few moments before it swung open.

She beamed when she saw me, gripped my wrist, and dragged

me inside. "Good bitch for showing up. I have to show you something and I want you to revel in this masterpiece that I've created. Are you a John Stamos fan?"

"Who isn't?" I said as Cass dragged me straight down the corridor by the hand. "Why?"

"You'll see."

We reached a door and Cass swung it open, revealing her bedroom. My jaw fell open. On the same wall as her bed, there was a mural of cut-out magazine pictures and John Stamos posters covering the entire space. Not an inch of wall was untouched.

"Whoa."

"Don't you just love it?" she clasped her hands and bounced, her ringlets were in a bun right on top of her head, a few coils framing her face. "Is that not the best thing in the freaking world? I spent all night doing it. I'm almost tempted to do the rest of the room. Can you imagine? The whole room just John Stamos."

"It's like a shrine."

"Duh. You wanna help me?"

I had nothing else to do. "Okay. How do you have so many posters, though?"

"Did I tell you what my mom does?" Cass asked as she began dragging a box out from under her bed. "I mean, aside from drinking."

"Does she work for a magazine?"

Cass lifted the box lid and there were stacks of *Seventeen*, *Teen People*, *Teen Beat*, and *Cosmo Girl*. "She wishes. No, but she does work for the freight company that oversees and manages the distribution of almost every magazine and newspaper in Colorado. They also have to collect old copies that are left at the end of each month. I get some of them."

"That's pretty cool," I said, sitting down on her neon-orange and pink comforter and folding my legs just as she had. "You've been preparing for this moment, then?"

"You know it. First, we cut out any and every picture of John that we can find. Which isn't hard because he's literally the main feature, like, every single month. I would kill to have his babies."

I took the pair of scissors that she handed me. It was quiet for a minute until she stood up and switched the radio on. Cass's room was cute. Vibrant. There was a lot of neon orange—her set of drawers under the window, her mirror frame on the back of the door. She had bright-pink curtains and a fluffy green rug underneath her inflatable armchair.

"Your room is cute," I said.

"Thanks. Tiff doesn't like it. Says it gives her a headache. Tiff is my best friend. She's in Florida all summer."

"Oh cool. Do you have a big group of girlfriends?"

She pursed her lips and shrugged. "Not really, but kind of. I've always been close to Leroy and Eric, so I hang out with them, and they're, like, popular jocks, so they have a lot of girls hanging around. I get along with the girls at parties and stuff, but I wouldn't invite them for a sleepover. You know?"

"Yeah." I dropped a cutout that I'd finished and moved on to the next one. "I get that. I have a couple of close friends at home. Amber being the closest. Which reminds me that I haven't talked to her in a while. I should call her."

"You can use the phone if you want?"

"What, right now?"

Cass nodded, focused on her careful cutting.

"Oh, no. That's all right. The charges would be huge since it's out of state."

"I don't pay the phone bill. Doesn't bother me," she said. "Better here than at Eleanor's. We like Eleanor, don't charge long-distance calls to her phone bill."

My laugh was amused but dismissive, which Cass must have noticed because she shook her head, stood up, and left the room, returning a few moments later with a handheld. "Call your bestie."

"Okay, fine." I took it and dialed, putting it on speaker so Cass was included in our conversation. That felt rude. Amber answered her own private line in a few short rings.

"Hello?"

"Hey, it's me."

"Hi!" she said, excitement in her tone. "What's going on? How's Colorado?"

"Gooooood," I stretched it out and put the phone on the carpet between Cass and me. "You're on speaker, by the way. Cass is here. She's friends with Leroy and his brother, Noah."

"Hello!" Cass sang.

"Hey, nice to sort of meet you," Amber laughed. "What's going on?"

"Not much," I said. "I've been getting to know Leroy's friends and family, watching his football practices, and I went to a party on my first night here. That's where I met Cass."

"Sounds dope, girl. What's Leroy's family like?"

"His parents are great. Super nice. Noah is—" I looked at Cass, who stuck her tongue out in disgust. "He could be worse."

"Oh no," Amber laughed.

"Wait!" I said, suddenly remembering the fact that she knew Eric. "Remember Eric? The guy that you sort of hooked up with at that frat party where I met Leroy?"

Cass sat up, alert and listening.

"Yeah?" Amber said.

"He's on the team with Leroy. We've hung out too."

"We should call him," Cass said, dropping her scissors and snatching up the phone. "We could put him on a three-way conference call?"

Even I was humming with enthusiasm at the suggestion. "Do you want to, Amber?" I asked.

She paused. "I guess so." Cass quickly switched off the radio. "But if he's not interested, I'm hanging up."

Cass's knees bounced up and down as she started pressing buttons on the phone. "He might not be home. But we'll give it a go."

"Don't tell him I'm here until you ask him what he thinks of me," Amber quickly added.

As it rang, anticipation swelled within the room, our nerves tingling and my heart hammering. I felt as if I was the one who was being connected to the person I had a crush on. Cass bit her nails, and then, after what felt like forever, there was an answer.

"Samuel speaking."

Cass cleared her throat. "Hey, Mr. Washington. It's Cass Summers calling."

"Hang on a minute, Cass," his deep voice became distant. "Eric! Phone."

Cass and I grinned at each other, silent giggles passing between us.

"Hello?"

"Hey. It's Cass and Ellie."

"Hello, ladies," we could hear the smile in his voice. "How's it going?"

Cass quirked a brow, gesturing for me to take the lead. "Eric, do you remember my friend Amber? From Waco."

"Hell, yeah, I do. Couldn't forget a beautiful woman like that."

Eric had this regal, grown-up way of speaking. It wasn't even so much the words, it was his tone and the confidence in his delivery.

"Would you want to talk to her again?" I asked. "If you could."

"I would call her right now if you gave me her number."

Cass slapped a hand over her mouth and fell onto her back, legs in the air, kicking.

"Amber," I prompted.

"Hey, Eric," Amber said sheepishly. "It's me."

"You sneaky little women!" Eric hollered. "Hello, sweetheart. Long time, no talk. How are you?"

"I'm good," Amber sounded as if she was trying to breathe. "Sorry about ambushing you. You don't have to chat if you don't want to."

"I want to," he said. "Cass, Els, leave us to it? I owe you both a big fat kiss on the cheek."

Cass sat up and made a kissing noise. "Look forward to it." She hung up and threw the phone onto her bed. "That was so much fun. Look at us, matchmakers."

"That is pr—"

Cass's bedroom door swung open and a tall, slender woman with dark-blond ringlets and an upturned nose stood in the frame. "Oh," she looked between the two of us. "I thought you were on the phone. That's why I waited outside. Who's this?"

"Ellie," Cass answered with boredom, still cutting out her magazines. I waved. "Ellie, this is my mom, Jessica."

Jessica smiled but her attention fell back to Cass. "You home for dinner?"

"I don't know," Cass said. "I guess."

"I won't be," Jessica said, looking down at her skintight dress. She had an incredible figure, long legs and a thin waist. "That's why I'm asking. I can leave ten on the counter if that helps."

"Whatever."

"Yes or no?"

"Yes," Cass bit back, finally looking over her shoulder behind her. "God, what are you wearing?"

Jessica's cheeks reddened, her hands sweeping her frame. "A dress, Cassidy. Don't be rude."

Cass's face twisted into disgust and she turned from her mom. The atmosphere was tense. There was no way that I could ever have given my momma that sort of attitude. The look on Cass's face alone would be enough to have me grounded for two weeks.

Jessica reached for the door handle when her gaze landed on Cass's wall, then traveled to the floor where we were cutting up magazines. "What have you done to your wall?"

"Covered it in John Stamos photos," Cass mumbled. "What does it look like?"

Jessica muttered something and left, closing the door with a solid thud, it rattled the mirror hanging on the back of it. It was quiet again, neither of us speaking, the sound of paper being cut, slow and careful. The Spice Girls blared from the radio, and Cass bopped her head along to it.

"You wanna stay for pizza tonight?" she finally said.

My heart sped up, feeling terrible about the fact that Leroy and I had plans. "I think Noah said that he wanted to come over tonight," I said.

She looked up at me. "He did?"

"Yeah, he told us this morning."

A flicker of a smile danced on her mouth, but she ducked her head before I could see it. "You don't have to leave for him."

"That's okay. Leroy and I could use some alone time if I'm being honest. His mom and dad are going out, so he's going to teach me how to cook burritos."

Cass winked at me. "You go, girl."

We spent a few more hours cutting out magazines and sticking pictures to the wall before I had to leave, but I promised her that I would come back and help more when I could. The afternoon with her reminded me that no matter how much I loved being with Leroy, girl time was essential. It was nice to know that during my stay here, I could connect with someone other than Leroy.

## LEROY

Mom mentioned that she'd appreciate it if I made some time for Noah this summer. It seemed as if I hadn't acted on that quickly enough and she'd taken matters into her own hands, asking Ellie to leave me alone for a little while so that Noah and I could hang out. My girl didn't elaborate on how the conversation had gone down, but it was obvious that it was Mom's idea.

Downstairs, Noah was still sitting on the deck with his Game Boy. "Hey, man, want to go to the arcade for a few hours?"

He twisted, peering at me over his shoulder. "The arcade?"

No doubt he was surprised because we hadn't been to the arcade together since we were thirteen and fourteen. The arcade was how we killed time on the weekends when we were in middle school—especially in the summer, right before things shifted between us, and I started high school, made the varsity team, and grew up.

"You got something better to do?" I said.

He shrugged and stood up. "Let's do it, then."

✎

We arrived at our local arcade a half hour later, pushing through the glass swing doors to find the place crammed with kids and friends from school. As always, it was dark but there were flashes of bright neon coming from all of the machines lined up together. The sound of coin slots, pings, and the low humming whir of pixelated characters jumping across the screens was loud. The six air hockey and foosball tables were clattering and there were cries of excitement coming from the game of hoops.

"I didn't bring cash," Noah said, standing beside me while we looked around.

"I've got it. Should we get some tokens?"

"I guess."

We went and paid for a bunch of tokens from the front desk and proceeded to walk around in search of something free. I doubted that we'd find a machine that wasn't being used, so we hopped in line for the racing game and waited our turn.

"Where's Ellie?" Noah asked over the noise.

"With Cass."

"I think Cass is still pissed about what happened with Holly. When she came over this morning, she wouldn't even talk to me. Said she only wanted to see Ellie."

"Weird that she'd be mad about you hitting it with another girl."

Noah sensed my sarcasm and frowned. It was our turn to use the racing game, so we slid into the seats and deposited our tokens, gripping the steering wheels while it counted us down.

"She's not my girlfriend," he said. "I can do what I want."

We both put our foot down on the accelerators and steered

through the virtual racetrack, competing to stay ahead of each other. He had an inarguable point. Not that there was ever a point in arguing with him anyway.

"I never said that you can't do what you want. I'm just not surprised that Cass is upset. You know what she's like. You know that she wants more from you."

My car pulled in front of Noah's, cutting him off. He cursed. "Too bad, I told her it's not happening."

"Why not, though? If you're going to keep chilling and sleeping together, why not just go out with the girl?"

Noah's car was gaining speed again and came barreling up toward the tail of my car. "Do I question why you can't just be single and fuck around? No."

"You sort of do."

"Whatever," he sideswiped me and I had to steer through a spinout. "Is it so weird that I like keeping my options open? That I enjoy variety? Sue me if being tied down to one girl doesn't sound appealing to me. I've got my whole life to be a boring sack. Mom was single until she was in her thirties, bro. Worked just fine for her."

"Okay, fine." I steered around a corner and found Noah just around the bend. The finish line was approaching, and I pressed even harder on the accelerator. "That's your business. Cut it off with Cass, then. She doesn't feel the same way, dude. Stop stringing her along and end it so she can move on."

At the last stretch, I pulled ahead, passed Noah, and came in first place. He exhaled and we both quickly vacated the seats so that the next people in line could take their turn.

"I've tried to end it," Noah said. "She's still my friend, though. I don't want to lose that. It just happens. We end up in bed together because . . . I don't know. Everything else is there. I'm not interested in having a girlfriend. Casual sex is fun."

We walked through the arcade, mindful of lines and smaller kids weaving through the crowds. I didn't say anything because there wasn't much that I could say. If that was how he felt, that was his business. How Cass came out of all this was a concern to me, but if she wouldn't listen to Noah when he tried to abstain from her, then she wasn't going to listen to me. She loved him so much and that made me sad for her.

"You've had girlfriends before. What about Anna? You two were dating for like six months in sophomore year."

"Then she slept with Kendrick while I was standing outside of her window in the rain because she'd told me to come over and sneak in."

"What? For real?"

"Yeah. Told me to sneak over and I was waiting for like twenty minutes in the rain and I was like, screw this, and scaled her house. When I looked through the window, there she was with that asshole."

"Shit," I said, slipping my hands into my pockets. "I didn't know about that."

"Nah, I didn't even care, wasn't worth mentioning."

But it was worth mentioning. It had to have hurt him. Maybe that had some part to play in his aversion to settling down. But then again, perhaps he really did just prefer casual arrangements. It was hard to tell with Noah. We saw a couple of kids ditch a foosball table so we took their place and put the tokens into the slot.

"Guess that's why you don't want another relationship, then?" I continued.

Noah shrugged, standing on the other side of the table while he spun his handles around. "Couldn't care less about what Anna did. Like I said, I don't feel like having a girlfriend. Can we drop it?"

"We can."

We didn't talk for the duration of the game, instead staying focused on hitting the small plastic soccer ball with our designated players. Back and forth, back and forth, the table shook, and my palms were aching by the time Noah finally threw his arms up and claimed victory. There were no surprises there—he'd held the championship between us from the time we were kids. There was some sort of calculation involved in the game; at least, that was what he told me. He said that was how he won. Whether that was true or not, I had no idea, but I liked the fact that he won because he never expected to. Me being the athletic sibling, he used to assume his loss would be inevitable, and being who he was, I expected him to be an insufferable winner. He wasn't. We surprised each other, and it was always a subtle but tender moment that neither of us ever spoke on. We just accepted it.

*N*

We were onto our third game of air hockey—we preferred air hockey to foosball, it was smoother—when a couple of girls that I vaguely recognized from school sidled up to the table, zeroing in on Noah.

"Hey, Noah." The first one leaned her elbows on the edge and watched the puck bouncing between us. She had thick black hair with two bright-pink strands in the front and a tongue piercing that she pinched between her lips.

"How's it going, Mel," he winked and looked at the other girl who was wearing thigh-high socks, combats, and had her blue hair in pigtails. "Ernie. This is my brother Leroy."

"We know," they smiled and waved at me. "You didn't come to club the other night. We waited up."

Noah straightened up and abandoned the game. "I told you I wouldn't be there. I had to go to Eric's farewell thing."

Mel seemed amused at the mere thought of it as I made my way over to the three of them. She snorted and folded her arms. "You went to that jock gathering. For real? You and Eric don't even get along."

"We get along," Noah mumbled, but he knew she was right. Eric and Noah were civil and never addressed the obvious distaste for each other. But it was there.

"What club?" I asked.

"Nothing," Noah said.

"It's not a club exactly," Ernie said, twisting a pigtail around her fist. She had an ethereal voice, delicate and dainty as if her octaves floated on air. "It's just a group of us that hang in Mel's basement and green out while we talk about the corrupt and unjust movement of antifeminism in political America."

I raised a brow at Noah.

"We don't always talk about politics," he said.

"That's true," Mel said, winking at him.

"We should go out sometime," Ernie bent over and tugged on the top of her sock. "The four of us. A double date."

"I have a girlfriend," I said.

Ernie didn't seem fazed at the brush-off. She shrugged and linked her arm through Mel's, preparing to leave.

"We're gonna go find the girls," Mel said, sticking her tongue out. She seemed to do that a lot. "See you around, Noah."

We watched them leave, and then I looked at Noah, shaking my head.

"What?" he said.

"You a regular at these feminist meetings in Mel's basement?"

"She's hot. I went once or twice to score. It worked."

"You're literally the opposite of what those girls are about."

"That's not true," he said as we started walking away from the table. The timer had run out and we'd been there long enough. "I'm all for women's rights. I just laid it on a little thick. No harm. You see what I mean, though? I can get all of that and more, and I can do it without guilt if I stay single. You're missing out."

"No, I'm not. I love Ellie. She's my best friend, the most beautiful girl that I've ever met, and losing what I have with her for a bunch of meaningless nights with random girls isn't worth it to me."

He didn't say anything to that, and we beelined for an empty Pac-Man machine. We spent the rest of the afternoon in the arcade, wasting time on game after game until eventually we decided to head home and get ready for our evenings. Ellie was still out when we got back. I thought about going to get her, but there were still hours before it was dark and I didn't want to interrupt her girl time.

"I'm going to make a milk shake," Noah said when we wandered into the kitchen. He opened the fridge. "Do you want one?"

"Sure. Chocolate?"

"Sweet." He paused, turning around to look at me with the fridge still open. "Thanks for today. For the arcade and paying. It was cool."

His sincerity was unexpected, startling me, but I did my best not to show him that. "Yeah, no worries. We should go more often. I forgot how dope the arcade is. Might have to take the girls next time."

He flinched but gave me a small nod. "Yeah. Sure."

## *Ellie*

A warm, low light set an ambient mood in the dining area. The stars added to the magic, twinkling outside in the dark-blue sky. Candles flickered in the middle of the table, the pool lights glowing on the other side of the windows, assisting in the overall atmosphere. I laughed quietly to myself, thinking that the food didn't quite match the romance. But I was excited nonetheless.

Once again, I counted the contents on the table and hoped that I hadn't missed anything. "Lettuce, tomatoes, peppers, onion, cheese, carrot, cucumber, sauces. Seasoned chicken, butter chicken, ground beef—"

I nodded with satisfaction and felt a little bit thrilled that I had been able to follow the instructions that Leroy had written down for me. He'd popped into the kitchen a few times to ask if I needed help, but this was something that I'd wanted to do on my own.

All we needed before we sat down were some glasses and a cold drink. I strolled back over to the fridge and collected the chilled soda and two cups, calling out for Leroy as I set them out on the table. I could hear his footsteps before he appeared at the entrance a moment later. His smile reached his eyes as he took it all in.

"I have never cooked an entire meal without setting something on fire before," I said, standing beside the table. "So I wasn't kidding about calling for a pizza if this tastes terrible."

"It doesn't smell terrible," he wandered in farther and assessed it again before his gaze fell back on me. He stood close and raised his hand, pushing a piece of hair behind my ear. "It smells good. And you . . . you look gorgeous."

My heartbeat sped up at the darkness in his stare. I didn't want to get distracted before we ate. But he made that difficult.

Leroy toyed with the hem of my shirt, his fingertips grazing my midriff and his quiet groan almost inaudible, but I heard it, and it made me weak at the knees. "I would love to see your naked body in this light."

It was like I had been sucker punched in the gut. But in a good way, however the heck *that* worked.

"Food first," he said and gave me a kiss before he pulled the seat out beside us, gesturing for me to sit.

He sat down at the head of the table so that we could face one another, but still be next to each other. We chatted about menial subjects as we filled up the wraps on our plate. There was still a hum of desire in the pit of my stomach, making it hard to focus on the food, but I did my best to calm down and push those thoughts away until later.

I was offered the blessing of a distraction when Leroy finally bit into his burrito. He was unexpressive, a perfect poker face that made it impossible to tell what he was thinking, and the anticipation was almost unbearable.

After what felt like forever, he finally looked at me and smiled the most adorable grin to date. "Best burritos I've ever had."

"You don't have to lie," I teased. "Just as long as they're edible, I'm happy."

"No, I mean it," he said. "I haven't had them like this before and they're great. You did so damn well, babe."

I loved how he directed the word *babe* at me. How he managed to make it sound loving and hot at the same time. "Thank you."

He was right. The food wasn't bad at all, and I was proud of myself. Leroy was helpful when it was time to clean up and we both moved around the kitchen as we conversed, washed the dishes, and tidied up. There was no mistaking the tension in the room, though. It was so thick, the buildup of the evening was coming to its climax—pun intended—and I could feel the desire radiating through me.

It was amazing to me that we didn't have to touch, we didn't even need to look at each other and I was blanketed by sexual tension that was begging to be relieved. My heart hammered at the mere knowledge that he was in the room, an arm's length from my touch.

"Thank you for dinner, Ellie," Leroy said, intertwining our fingers as he leaned his butt against the countertop and pulled me into him. On instinct, my hands clasped behind his neck and I gazed up at his profile.

He looked exquisite in the glow of the candles. A flattering shadow was cast on his sun-kissed cheeks and I had the urge to kiss his sharp jaw and taste his soft lips. His brows pulled together as he stared down at me. It wasn't in frustration or confusion; it was a lust-infused gaze and it made me wobble in his hold.

"Would you like to—play a board game or something?" I asked. Not because I wanted to play a board game. More because I didn't know how to proceed. I wasn't experienced with just coming out with what I wanted.

His strong hands had a tight hold on my waist. It was such a supportive and sensual hold, almost my entire middle was encircled. "No, Els. I don't want to play a board game." His eyes settled on my mouth. "I want to play with you."

I would have gasped, except his lips found mine and his hands wound themselves in the hair at the back of my head. He pushed his tongue into my mouth, not wasting a moment. I leaned farther into him, his arousal pressed hard against my lower abdomen, his hand pulled my hair with tugs that didn't hurt but were libidinous to the core. His other hand squeezed my waist and slid down, gliding over my butt before he squeezed and slammed me against his crotch.

"What do you want me to do to you, Ellie?" he mumbled with a gravelly voice as he pulled my hair so that my head tipped back, and I stared up at the ceiling. He dragged his mouth down, nipping, sucking, licking my throat.

"Touch me," I gasped. I barely recognized myself. I sounded so sultry and seductive, not to mention confident. But his touch was euphoric, and I was losing a sense of self, instead gaining a sexier side that I wanted to embrace.

He pulled my face back to him and kissed me as his hand moved up the length of my torso. He gripped the neck of my tank top, easily pulling the off-the-shoulder garment down so that my chest was exposed to him. His hands were like magic. His fingertips were powerful but articulate and I was coming undone.

I was on the brink, a scream developing, an earth-shattering release begging to be granted. But before I reached that point, he spun us around so that I was leaning against the countertop. The sound of the telephone started ringing, piercing the quiet with an unwanted distraction. "Just ignore it," Leroy ordered when I stiffened at the sound. I thought that it might have been hard to continue with its shrill ring surrounding us, but he was quick to distract me with his hands.

Until it started again. The ringing was relentless. It would pause for a moment before it began again and Leroy paused, resting his head on my shoulder as he took a deep, frustrated breath. He stormed over to the telephone.

"What?!" he snapped, his shoulders rising and falling with his anger. He listened for a few moments, and when his expression became more serious, I straightened up and pulled my tank top up. Whoever was on the phone spoke with panic. He leaned on the wall. "You have got to be fucking kidding me, Noah."

I watched with piqued interest.

"I am so tempted to leave you there and let you deal with it. I was in the middle of something."

It was brief, but I saw the way he flinched with a satisfied look before he was back to big brother mode.

"Fine," he said. "I'm coming. But you'd better believe that I'm about to spend the next month cockblocking the fuck out of you."

Leroy slammed the phone back on its base and immediately moved to the table and began blowing out the candles, descending us into darkness. The glow of the moon and pool lights outside allowed enough luminescence to see his profile as he stretched out and offered me his hand, waiting with little patience. "I'm sorry, Ellie," he said. "I have to go and help Noah. Although it's the last thing that I want to be doing."

"What happened?" I asked. He opened the front door and locked it behind us.

"He's locked in a girl's spare bedroom because her father caught them having sex and now, he's waiting with a baseball bat so that he can kill him."

I waited for him to laugh, or tell me that he was joking. But he remained stone-faced as we got into the car and peeled out of the driveway. I was equal parts confused, scared, and to top it off, sexually frustrated. But more than that, I was disappointed for Cass, who would have been waiting for him to show up tonight.

"How are you going to help him?" I asked. "You might get hurt."

He stared straight out at the road, the streetlights revealing his tense expression. He didn't answer me, instead keeping his hands wound tight around the wheel as he sped up.

"I'll be fine," he murmured after a few minutes of tense silence.

The house was closer than I thought it would be. We swung into the driveway of a single-story home with a porch light illuminating the front path. It didn't look like a lot was going on inside, but as soon as the engine was killed and Leroy pushed his door open, masculine and outraged shouting could be heard inside the house, along with the piercing, shrill voice of a girl.

"Ellie." I glanced at where he stood outside of the car, leaning down with his hand rested on the roof. His expression left me with no room to argue over his next words. "Do *not* get out of this car."

## LEROY

The nerve Noah had. When he first met Ellie, he had accused her of not being good enough for this family. And here he was, at the Weismann house, about to be beaten to death by Natalie's father. The front door was not surprisingly unlocked, and the house stank like old food.

It wasn't hard to find where Noah would be hiding—somewhere close to the unhinged shouting of a madman. As I carefully wandered down the hallway, I noticed the smashed photo frames that had been knocked off the wall and the indents where the end of a bat had met the thin walls. As if the shouting wasn't enough.

I had met Peter once or twice. He had a short temper and a distaste toward the upper class. If Noah got out of this without getting smacked, I would be giving him one just for being such a careless idiot. Natalie was an attractive girl, sure, but he was about to be beaten to death over her.

I cursed when I realized that the bedroom Peter was shouting at was the last one in the hallway and there was only one way out. For a moment, I wondered why Noah hadn't gone out the window, but then I remembered that Peter barred them last time Natalie had been caught sneaking out.

The man stood just a little taller than me and used the baseball bat to bang on the door again, shouting an almost indecipherable threat. I was sure that he wasn't that mad about Natalie being with a guy—it had more to do with *who* she was with. I took a deep breath and cleared my throat, hoping we could get out of this with little to no violence.

He snapped his head toward me and grimaced. "The hell are you doing in my house?"

"I came to get Noah." I held my hands up to proclaim my innocence. "We'll leave and he won't be back. I swear."

He started toward me. "I caught that little asshole in bed with my daughter." I took a step back, but it didn't deter him. He got up in my face as he spat his threats. "The second he comes out of that room, I'm batting his fucking head in."

"Noah!" I shouted as loud as I could. "Call the police."

I wasn't sure why he hadn't done that in the first place. Noah's voice came from the bedroom, but I couldn't hear what he said.

"What's going on?"

I turned around and recoiled when I saw Natalie standing behind me.

She was dressed up, her face made up and a purse in her hand. She glanced between her father and me, becoming more concerned by the minute.

"Wait," I turned back to the bedroom, pointing at it, and then back at Natalie. "Who the hell is Noah in ther—no . . ."

"Noah?" Natalie spluttered as her eyes widened. "Is he in there with Nadia?!"

"Oh fuck." I ran a hand through my hair. No wonder he hadn't called the police. When he told me he was in trouble at the Weissmanns', I'd assumed that he meant with Natalie. I never even considered that it could be with her fifteen-year-old sister. "Shit, Peter, look man, I'm—"

"Don't bother," Peter snarled. "He has to come out at some point and I'm going to put him in a fucking coma!"

He shouted the last part of his threat and I assumed that was for the benefit of the idiot that I was supposedly related to.

"Well, I just came to grab a change of clothes," Natalie said. "See you tomorrow, Dad."

He grumbled some response and then headed back over to the door while Natalie ducked in and out of her bedroom as fast as she could. This was bad. I'd lost all hope that I could talk him down from his rage. In fact, I understood where he was coming from. But unfortunately, I still couldn't let him put Noah six feet under.

"You need to put the bat down and let us go," I said, walking toward him. I wasn't sure how I was going to get us out of this. But I had a feeling that it wasn't going to end well. Peter obviously didn't like being told what to do.

His hand flew out and he gave me a violent shove in the chest, sending me into the wall with a thud. "Leave, or you'll get it too."

I straightened up from the wall. "You're going to want to keep your hands off me."

"Or what?" he hissed.

Before I had time to think about how stupid it was, I lunged forward and grabbed the bat out of his hand. He didn't have time to strengthen his grip, so it slid out of his hold, and I tossed it down the hall before I punched him in the jaw. He stumbled backwards a little, his hands waving to keep himself upright.

Unfortunately, when he did regain himself, he charged like a bull and bowled me up against the wall by the collar. He smacked me across the face, once, twice, three times. The metallic taste of blood filled my mouth and I felt the throb in my cheek immediately. I could hear Noah shouting from inside the bedroom, but before I could make sense of it, the bat appeared out of nowhere and smashed Peter across the back.

Out of reflex, he arched his spine with a pained grunt. His arms flew backwards, and the back of his hand connected with Ellie's face. She dropped the bat and fell backwards with a soft whimper. That was all it took—the simple sight of seeing her harmed. Whether it was an accident or not, his hand had struck her, and I lost it. While he was still grunting with pain, I kicked him in the shin and punched him again so that he landed in a heap on the floor.

"Noah, Noah, run!" Ellie was shouting and banging on the door while I watched Peter and made sure he didn't get up again.

I turned around and saw Noah come barreling out of the room. He ran straight down the corridor and I grabbed Ellie's hand, dragging her toward the door as fast as I could, passing Nadia who stood at her bedroom threshold, staring at her dad with fear. He had a bleeding nose, but he'd be all right. I hadn't done too much damage.

The car was on the road in a matter of moments. But as soon as we were at a safe distance, I pulled over, the tires squealing as I came to an abrupt stop.

"Leroy, wha—"

I turned around and laid a sharp backhand across Noah's cheek, not even stopping to cuss him out before I turned back to Ellie beside me and took her face in my hands.

My chest tightened at the sight of blood on her lip and a small swell around her mouth and cheek. "Babe, you should have stayed in the car."

"Don't worry about me," she cried. "Your face is worse. I'm glad that I came in when I did."

"You could have been badly hurt." I turned around. "She's fifteen, Noah. For fuck's sakes. What is wrong with you?" The main road wasn't alight with traffic, but the odd car sped past and lit up the entire interior for a brief second. "The Weismanns are bad enough. But Nadia? You're a real piece of work. Ellie could have been injured!"

"It's not my fault she ran in!" Noah pouted from the backseat. I was almost tempted to hit him again, just out of sheer need to make him suffer.

"Get out."

"What?"

"Get out of the car, Noah." I looked over my shoulder and fixed him with a glare. "You can walk. I'm not interested in being around you right now."

"Once again," he chuckled without the humor. "She's coming between us. Unbelievable."

"She hasn't done anything, Noah. You're the halfwit that decided to screw a minor and you didn't even help. You did nothing while I was getting punched in the head. You ran. If Ellie hadn't come into the house when she did, you never would have gotten out of there. She has more fucking balls than you do."

I took a deep breath to calm down, knowing how much Ellie hated cursing. But my brother sure knew how to get a reaction from me.

"I didn't know th—"

"Get out!" I cut off his excuse with a shout that caused Ellie to jump in her seat. I found her hand across the center console and squeezed it. "Get out, Noah. I'm going home and you can do whatever the hell you want. But I'm not bailing you out of something like that ever again."

He aggressively swung the door open and grumbled until he slammed it shut again. There was no part of me that felt guilty when I took off, merging back onto the main road without looking back. It wasn't that far. He was more than capable of getting himself home. And considering what he had put us all through tonight, he was getting off lightly.

## Ellie

By the time we arrived back from the Weissmann incident, Eleanor and Jacob were home from their date. Our evening plans had been officially dashed. Leroy had found a hoodie in the backseat of his car and pulled it on, using the fabric to shield his face so that his mom wouldn't ask questions. It did the trick and we went upstairs and hung around in his bedroom for a little while until Eleanor went to bed and sent me to the spare room.

The next morning, I got dressed in a pair of denim shorts and a T-shirt before I went in search of Leroy, finding him in the kitchen. The radio was humming a Shania Twain song, fresh coffee was brewing, and knives and forks pushed against plates.

The first thing that I noticed was the stack of pancakes on the countertop. The second was Leroy and Noah, sitting on opposite ends of the table, glaring at each other. Both showed obvious signs of a fight and I winced, thinking about how I had seen Leroy being punched so hard last night.

"You as well?" Eleanor's voice made me jump, and she stared

at me with disbelief. "That's it! Someone had better start talking. I want to know why the hell it looks like you all got into an altercation last night."

I turned toward Leroy with alarm, but his poker face was in full force. He shrugged and turned back to his food, popping a forkful of pancake into his mouth. Noah shot me a glare, but he did the same, both of them keeping tight lipped on the subject.

Panic rose within me, and I felt all sorts of pressure as Eleanor waited for a response. Sure, it was no problem for the two of them to resist their mother's iron fist. But I couldn't just stand here and lie to her. It felt so wrong.

She tapped her foot and shrugged her shoulders. "Well? What happened."

I stammered until Leroy said, "Mom, leave her alone."

"Okay, here's what happened," Noah stood up with his plate and went to the sink. "I got a little drunk last night and tried to kiss Ellie, because I'm a sack. She has a solid head and used it to fend me off, and then Leroy pissed me off with a long lecture, so I hit him and then he hit me and that's it."

We all stared in silence as he finished rinsing off his plate. He turned, drying his hands on a dish towel. Leroy kept quiet but he almost seemed—grateful? It was hard to tell because he was good at hiding his tells. But from the slight nod that they shared, I guessed that the lie was his form of apologizing. I got the feeling that we weren't going to get much more than that.

"What is the matter with you?" Eleanor finally snapped. "You tried to kiss her? She's your brother's girlfriend!"

He rolled his eyes and left the room, but Eleanor followed along behind him, ranting until we couldn't hear them.

"He knew that would happen." Leroy leaned back in the

dining chair. His hand slipped under his T-shirt and he rubbed his hand across his toned torso, revealing the band of his Calvin Kleins. "He knew Mom would hound the hell out of him. He's forgiven. For now. He's still a dumbass. Breakfast?"

"Oh, sure," I walked over to the table. I was about to take the seat when Leroy gripped me around the waist and pulled me into his lap.

"Here, have these," he pulled his plate closer, which still had two whole pancakes on it, and offered me the syrup.

Leroy wound his arms around my waist and rested his cheek against my shoulder blade while I ate. He hung on to me with such affection that it felt like he was afraid I would be gone if he let me go. I hadn't been listening to the music until his soft voice started murmuring the lyrics to "I Don't Want to Miss a Thing" by Aerosmith from behind me.

I didn't want to react in case he stopped. But I was suffering from some serious heart palpitations. His low, raspy voice was perfect. His tongue caressed the tender words.

His strong jaw was moving against my shoulder as he sang. He was quiet and I could sense that he was just enjoying the song, but my heart felt like it had doubled in size and its beats were so strong that it took my breath away.

He lifted his head as I turned around. My legs hung over the side of the chair and I wrapped my arms around his neck, pushing our lips together in an urgency that I hadn't even realized I was feeling. He wasn't slow to respond. His hand slid up my back and wrapped around the back of my neck, his other hand holding my legs and pulling me closer against him.

Our tongues moved against each other's. His lips were soft and sweet but relentless in their pursuit to taste me. This was the kind of kiss that was dangerous. It heated me in places that screamed for more attention. It was all-consuming and I couldn't even think of where we were as I tried to pull him impossibly close to me.

Eventually, he dropped the kiss, riding it out with soft, chaste pecks and turning me around a mere moment before his mother reentered the kitchen. I hadn't even heard her coming but it didn't surprise me that Leroy did. He didn't like to be caught with his tongue halfway down my throat, so he would have been listening for her.

"When was the last time that you phoned your mother?" Eleanor asked, giving us a subtle once-over. She moved around to the sink and started filling it up with hot water.

"Wednesday," I said. I was supposed to call more often than twice a week, but I had already slacked off and it was only the second Monday that I had been here. "I'll call her after breakfast."

She seemed satisfied with the answer. Leroy stood after a few moments and I took his seat, disappointed at the distance. That was, until he started helping his mom with the dishes. It was so sweet that I turned to watch. I was always taught that a woman should look at how a man treats his mother as an indicator of his character—I was definitely not disappointed.

After I had eaten and the clean-up was done, Leroy left me alone in his room so that I could use his phone to call Momma. I sat down and aimlessly thwacked the chord with a finger while it rang.

"Hello?"

"Hey, Momma."

"Hello Ellie. How are you? It's been a while."

"Momma . . ."

"You said every other day—"

"I know," I tried to keep the impatience out of my tone. "But come on. I'm having fun and it's not free to make these calls."

"As if it matters for those people."

"Don't be like that, Momma," I murmured.

She was quiet for a moment, and I heard her inhale a deep breath. "How are things? Having a good time?"

"I am, I'm having fun, like I said. The Laheys are great, and I've made friends already."

"Staying out of trouble?"

I thought about it and bit down a grin, almost afraid that she'd be able to hear it or sense it in my voice. I couldn't really say that I'd been staying out of trouble. Not truthfully. But I assured her that I was behaving.

"Of course. I've watched Leroy at practice most mornings. We spend time with his mom and dad, and I've been doing some cooking."

"Cooking?" Her voice rose and octave with the shock. "Doesn't sound like the Ellie I know."

"Maybe I'll cook for you when I get home."

"I'll believe it when I see it."

"Well, I'd better get going, Momma. I don't want to rack up the phone bill too high."

"Call me again soon, ya hear?" She wasn't really asking.

"Love you, Momma."

*N*

The sun was merciless later that morning. It shone down on the school football field, burning hot while I sat on the grass and watched the beginning of the warmups. A group of cheerleaders practiced at the other end of the green, being thrown through the air and chanting cheers. It was fun to watch them as well as the football team. There was a lot of team spirit here. It was clear that this school took their game seriously and I understood that—it was the same back in Waco. I'd just never paid as much attention at that time.

A light breeze blew, push the scents of the air around. The smell of fresh-clipped lawns, melting tar from the roads, and the hint of male perspiration from the football players.

The heat must have been getting to them because before a play was made, Leroy straightened up and pulled his T-shirt over his head, leaving him in just his shorts. He clapped his hands together and leaned over again, calling the directions for the play. I watched the sun glisten on his damp, tanned skin. His broad shoulders and biceps flexed as he raised his arms and caught the throw—perfect.

"I knew it," Cass's voice startled me, and I turned to spot her strolling over with her shades on and a pair of overalls over a white tank top. "It's so hot today. I knew the shirts would be coming off."

She sat down and gave me a wide smile. "Love that outfit." She glanced over my spaghetti-strap denim dress that I'd slipped over a black T-shirt. It was nothing special, but I loved how she was always quick to compliment my clothes.

"Damn, just look at him," Cass bit on her lip and sighed. "I would lick the sweat off his abs. And I'd enjoy it."

"Who are you talking about?"

"Robbie," she pointed out a tall guy with shoulder-length brown hair. He did have a nice body. "We used to chat a little here and there, but he's got a girlfriend now." She stuck out her tongue. "As gorgeous as he is, I don't mess with a taken man."

"I'm sure she'd appreciate that."

I watched her and waited for her to ask me why Noah hadn't shown up on Saturday night.

"Wanna go for a walk into town with me?" she asked.

I picked at the grass beneath me and shifted my legs, so they were folded. "What's in town?"

"Soda, shelter, and potentially some bargains," she listed on her fingers before she stood up. "Come on. We'll come back before Leroy leaves. Or he can come and pick us up."

"Should we tell him that we're leaving?" I asked, glancing out to the field where he was in the middle of throwing the ball. Cass thought about it for a moment.

"Leroy!" She shouted with her hands cupped around her mouth. Almost the entire team turned and stared at us. "We're gonna bounce. Get us from Rocky Ryan's!"

He gave us a thumbs-up after Cass was done screaming our plans for the entire state to hear and we headed out through the wire gate and across the school parking lot.

"Town isn't far," she assured me once we were out on the footpath beside the main road. We walked past the large park that was across the road from the school and the closer we got to town, the more business establishments and buildings we passed.

Cass was good at filling in the lull with idle chitchat as we walked. "How was the alone time on Saturday?"

I had an onslaught of different emotions attack me in full force. The first was the happiness that I felt over dinner and how well it had gone. The next was the minor anxiety over how we'd ended up throwing down with someone's dad. And finally, the thought of Cass asking me what Noah had been doing and why he didn't arrive at her place.

"Hello, Earth to Ellie," Cass waved her hand in front of me.

"It was really nice."

"Really nice? Give me some details. Did he like the burritos? Did he eat your burrito for dessert?"

"Chill out, Cass," I blushed and gave her a swat on the arm.

Her singsong laughter was contagious as she shrugged but made no apologies for the crude comment. "Come on. Give me the four-one-one. I don't have a lot of girlfriends to do this with. Tiff is out of town and all boys talk about is how they rock everyone's world with their giant penises."

"That sounds delightful."

"No, it's a load of horseshit," she laughed and skipped ahead of me before she started walking backwards. "Come on, share. Don't be so coy. I'm not going to tell anyone."

"Fine," I threw my hands up. "Things got kinda heated after we cleaned up dinner. We were in the kitchen—"

"The kitchen?" She stepped back into place beside me as we passed a crowded sidewalk of outdoor restaurant patios with chairs and tables. "That's hot."

"Yeah, I guess. So, like, he was in the middle of um, fingering me," I winced as I said the words. Before I met Leroy, I was a virgin and I hadn't partaken in this kind of conversation before. It felt weird. "But then the phone rang, and we had to go out."

I spun around and flailed as she gripped my arm and pulled me to a stop. It was clear that she was not impressed. "That is so anticlimactic! A bit of a finger blast and that's it?"

My eyes widened as I glanced around at the passing patrons on the footpath. "Keep it down, Cass."

She flicked her wrist before we continued our walk. "Okay, so what was so important that the phone couldn't be unplugged so that Leroy could plug you instead?"

"You have a way with words, has anyone ever told you that?"

"Of course," she said. "Now stop dodging the question. What was it?"

My heart was thumping at this point. I either had to come up with a lie—which I didn't feel that she deserved—or I would have to put up with Noah potentially flipping out on me when he found out that I spilled the beans.

It was clear that she should know. The guy that she had been sleeping with was caught in the sack with a minor. Sure, he was only two years older than her. But that wasn't the point. If I were Cass, I'd want to know.

"Can we sit for a sec?"

Cass furrowed her brows, and though she was wearing shades, I could tell that she was confused. We moved over to a bench seat that was outside a tattoo parlor, a bookstore, and a small café. We turned our knees into each other, and I took a deep breath.

"The reason that we couldn't continue our um—finger stuff, was because we had to go and help Noah. He was at the Weismanns, being threatened to be beaten by Peter or whatever his name is."

Cass's shoulders rose with a large inhale. She pursed her lips and I could see that she was aware of where I was going with the story. "Natalie."

"Oh, he wasn't with Natalie."

"Her mom?"

"What? Cass, no."

She gasped and slapped her hand down on mine. "Her dad?"

"Cass! No! I just said her dad was the one who was attempting to kill him." I blanked at how slow she was behaving. She either forgot that Nadia existed, or she was in adamant denial. "Her sister. Nadia. He was with Nadia."

"No, no. Nope." She folded her arms and shook her head, refusing to accept the truth. "He wouldn't. She's a fucking child."

I sat in silence while her leg bounced, and she chewed on her thumb. I felt so bad for her. She had been nothing but sweet since I met her, and I really couldn't understand what possessed Noah to be such an asshole. I also couldn't understand what possessed her to stick around. She could do so much better.

"I feel like some of this is my fault," she said. I couldn't believe what I had just heard. "We're not official. How can I ask him to stop sleeping around if we aren't an actual item? I just need to tell him that I want all or nothing."

"I thought that you hated him and wanted to let him go?" I recalled her speech from last week.

"I think it's obvious that I'm full of shit," she said. "I'm obsessed with that bonehead."

"You shouldn't be. He's thick. He carries his brains in his back pocket if he can't see what a catch you are. You deserve better."

"Honey, I know that." Cass held a hand across her chest. "Trust me, I'm well aware that these curls could be tangled in the fingers of a much more deserving man. But we can't help who we fall in love with."

As inclined as I was to agree, I still had to argue. "Yes, but we can help who we let touch us. You need to be strong. Tell him no. The distance might make it easier to move on."

She sagged with a defeated sigh. "Ellie, I know that he doesn't love me the way that I love him. He's never looked at me the way that Leroy looks at you. And I wish that I didn't care about him so much. But—I do. And I guess I'm just kind of hoping that he'll grow up and love me back."

Her voice hitched and I suspected that underneath her shades, she might have been fighting back tears. It broke my heart that she felt so torn-up over Noah. I couldn't see the attraction; I didn't get it. But she seemed to care about him more than she wanted to and I empathized, unable to imagine how awful it must be, to feel so much for someone who didn't feel it back.

She inhaled a deep breath, let it go, and looked around before her attention stopped on the tattoo parlor in front of us. "Should we go get matching tattoos?"

It was so hard to tell if she was kidding or not, but I had a feeling that she meant it. "I think that would be fun and all, but we could think on it for a bit?"

Her shoulders slouched. "Tattoos are the sort of thing you do on an impulse, chick. Let the moment carry you."

"I don't think I'm in the moment."

She frowned and I almost wished that I was the sort of person who could walk into a parlor with no preparation and get a tattoo. It might have been fun. But the thought of Momma finding out was enough to scare the only shred of consideration right out of me.

"I'll watch you get one."

She waved me off and stood up, regaining the confidence in her posture. Confidence that was admirable and intriguing. Confidence that I wished she had when it came to standing up for herself against Noah. In all other aspects of her life, Cass carried herself as if she were untouchable, in command, sure of herself and her worth. How much of that was an act or a façade? Because I couldn't understand how this was the same woman who let a boy like Noah walk all over her.

We wandered into a nearby pharmacy. I wanted to browse the skincare products, more so when I saw bins full of bargain items.

"This stuff is so cheap," I gasped, turning a bottle of retinol over in my hand to read the ingredients. "And it's the real deal."

Cass dug through the bin too, rummaging through the various cleansers and oils. "I don't know much about this stuff. I never know what I should be using."

"What's your skin like? Problem areas?"

I'd noticed some minor breakouts on her chin and forehead but pointing it out seemed cruel.

"I get pimples on my forehead and chin. Cheeks too sometimes."

"Sounds like you've got an excess oil issue. What about dryness?"

"No, my skin is never dry."

"Definitely an oil issue, then," I said and dug through the bin as a staff member wandered past with intent interest in what we were doing. It wasn't uncommon for teenagers to steal from the pharmacy; it happened all the time at the one I worked at back home. I smiled at her and continued searching. "You'd benefit from using a salicylic acid face wash. Salicylic is good for excess oil. I'd start with a two percent. It's likely to dry your skin out at the beginning, especially if you haven't developed a tolerance to it. Be sure to use a good moisturizer, preferably one with an SPF in it. This is a good brand."

I shoved the moisturizer into her hands, along with the face wash. "Niacinamide is another good product for excess oil. Pure ingredients are so much better than using skincare that has like zero-point-three percent niacinamide and the rest is additives that can sometimes be worse for the skin. Niacinamide goes after the cleanser but before moisturizer. Leave it for about ten minutes to soak. Retinol! Retinol has anti-ageing properties. It speeds up the cell turnover and prevents fine lines, uneven skin texture, and age spots. It also regulates oil production and helps with breakouts. The younger you start using it, the better, but it makes your skin super sensitive to the sun, so, sunscreen every single morning. It can also dry you out so if you start to notice that, leave it for a day or two. I actually use it every second day."

Cass stared at her handful of products. "You might need to write all of that down for me."

I laughed. "Sure."

"Also, are you qualified to be giving out this sort of advice?"

"I'm not giving you medical advice. None of these products are prescription only, so it's safe. And I know what I'm talking about, I promise. I live and breathe this sort of stuff. The worst that'll happen is some inflammation. In that case, you stop using the product and the inflammation will stop. It should be fine, though. Do a patch test on your neck first."

"Okay then," she said, going to the counter. I followed her with a few of my own products. "New skin here I come."

We paid for our items and went back outside with a paper bag each.

"Let's go and get an ice cream," she linked her arm through mine. "It's a furnace out here."

"You sure about that?" I asked. "Ice cream."

"I'm not letting my intolerance tell me how to live. You

know, I didn't eat ice cream, cheese, milk, *nothing* like that until I was eleven. Eleven! Mom cut me off as soon as she found out that I was intolerant. She hated dealing with the aftermath. I was deprived, and then James left, and I ran away when it was dark outside, went to the nearest convenience store, and ate an entire tub while I walked home. *So* worth it."

I laughed as we passed a clothing store. There were racks of scarves on the sidewalk, a stand of hats, and shoes on a table. The little tags with permanent marker prices stapled to the clothes tipped me off to the fact that it was a thrift store.

"We should go in here," I said, stopping to browse the shoes.

"You wanna know why my first instinct was to eat ice cream?"

"Tell me."

"Have you ever seen *Kramer vs. Kramer*?"

"I don't think so," I said as we slipped inside the store and the aroma of musty clothes invaded me. It was so familiar. A little slice of home right here in Colorado.

"I'd watched it with my parents a few months earlier," she explained as we weaved in and out of racks. "Which was totally awkward during a sex scene; I mean, I was eleven. So, anyway, there's this scene with a little kid and his dad, and the dad is telling the kid to eat dinner, but the kid is totally acting out because his mom just left and whatever. So, the kid goes into the freezer, grabs a tub of ice cream, and the whole time his dad is like 'Billy, you better not eat that.' But the kid does eat it and the dad gets mad and sends him to his room, and anyway, at the time I saw ice cream as this prop that'd piss Mom off if she knew. A way to act out, I guess. Now that I look back, I think maybe I was hoping my dad would come back and tell me off for eating ice cream when I knew I wasn't allowed to."

Cass still had her shades on while she flipped through hangers of coats. My heart was aching for her. She'd known her dad and had had a relationship with him—she had someone to miss. I couldn't relate to that because I'd never known mine. Even without him, I had a mom who was there and who, while a bit overbearing, was around when I needed her.

"You wash the clothes before you wear them, right?" Her voice snapped me out of sorrowful thoughts, and I looked to see that she was holding up a cute plaid skirt.

"Of course."

"Great, because this is tight and it's only two dollars."

"It's cute."

She grinned, wide and convincing before she slipped around me toward the counter. Her moments of vulnerability were overwhelming to witness. There was so much I wished that I could do to help her feel more whole.

*⚡*

When Leroy met us outside of Rocky Ryan's an hour later, his brow was damp, all of the car windows were down, and he had a bottle of water between his legs as he held the gear stick. Cass slipped into the backseat, I took the front, and Leroy peeled away from the curb.

"You do some shopping?" he asked.

"There was a skincare sale at the pharmacy," I explained. "I couldn't help myself."

He smiled. "Where to?" He peered in the rearview mirror at Cass, who was going through her bag of clothes, the wind whipping at the paper and her larger-than-life hair.

"Drop me off at Tony's," she said.

Leroy pursed his lips, indicating some sort of internal conflict.

"Who's Tony?" I asked.

"A friend of Noah's," he answered.

Part of me wondered, just for a short second, if Cass was on some sort of revenge mission. Was she going to get even for all the screwing around Noah had been doing? She must have noticed the tension radiating from the front seat, because she scoffed.

"I'm not going to hang out with Tony. I just know Noah will be there. I need to talk to that scrub."

No one else said anything for the rest of the ten-minute ride. The entire time, I was growing increasingly nervous over the fact that I'd told Cass what Noah had done. It worried me to think that Leroy might be pissed off at the fact that I'd snitched on his little brother. Then again, he wasn't a fan of the way that Noah treated Cass either.

We stopped in front of a white brick home with tall pine trees on the front lawn and a tire swing hanging from a thick branch. Turning in my seat, I saw Cass inhale a deep breath and nod with determination. She didn't thank Leroy for the ride or tell us goodbye when she stepped out and shut the door behind her. I concluded that it was probably because she was gearing herself up for a showdown with Noah, and part of me wanted to stand beside her for that. The other part of me knew that she'd be just fine on her own.

Leroy looked over at me as he shifted the car into first. "What was that about?"

"Please don't be upset with me." His brows pulled as I worried on my lip. "I told her about Nadia and Noah. About the whole thing that went down. She was sort of upset."

"Why would I be mad about that?"

"I snitched on your little brother."

He chuckled and settled lower into his seat, one hand on the wheel, the other on the stick. "What you choose to tell Cass is none of my business. No, I wouldn't have told her. But there's no issue if you choose to."

Something about his words bothered me. "Why, though? Why wouldn't you tell her?"

"It's just . . . it's complicated. You don't have a sibling, so you might not understand the dynamic, but the truth is, no matter how much he pisses me off or dicks around, he's my brother."

That wasn't good enough as far as I was concerned. But how could I tell him that he was wrong? He was the one with a sibling. He knew how these things worked; I didn't. But I couldn't fathom that he would be so blindly loyal when Noah was hurting Cass. She didn't deserve that, and he was fine with just . . . keeping quiet?

"Cass knows," Leroy said as if sensing my conflict. His attention moved between me and the road. "She knows what he's like. She's been warned a ton. Her choices are her own."

"I still don't get it, though; you should tell her when you see him doing that sort of stuff. Don't cover for him. You said yourself that he shouldn't take advantage of her."

"I do think that, but I'm not going to snitch on him. That's . . . not how it works."

My breathing grew labored. I was pissed off and it startled me to feel like this toward him. I hated it.

"Ellie—"

"I know I don't understand," I mumbled. "You don't have to protect him when it comes to stuff like this. You're enabling his crusty behavior. Maybe calling him out and getting him into trouble when it comes to stuff like this will help him recognize that he's acting like a fool."

He didn't respond for a while and then when he did, it surprised me. "You're right," he said, I looked at him. "You are. I can have his back without letting him act like an asshole."

"What? I mean, yes, you can."

He leaned over, picked up my hand, and kissed the tips of my fingers. "You're so good, baby," he murmured, watching the road. "You're just good. Good heart, kind heart."

Speaking of my heart, I was a little worried about it at that moment. It was beating fast and hard, and it wasn't just because we'd been on the brink of an argument, but because we'd made it to the other side of one. And the love that he expressed despite my brutal honesty, reminded me of how right we were for each other.

N

Later that evening, Leroy and I were on the couch watching a DVD. His parents had an event of some sort that would give us the house free until around eight p.m. I sat tucked into his side and he used his free hand to create soft circles on my shoulder.

"This is sort of gross," I mentioned, watching Mike Myers on the television screen.

"*Austin Powers* is hilarious," Leroy chuckled, his fingers running through my hair. "We can change it if you want?"

"It's fine. Some parts are funny. It's just super—"

"Crude?" He finished the sentence and I peered up to find him grinning. "You're cute."

I attempted to concentrate but his hands were far too distracting. His firm chest underneath me was arousing on its own accord and I was about to suggest that we make better use of the alone time when the front door slammed and Noah appeared, his eyes scanning the room until they fell on me and pulled me into a harsh stare.

"You had no fucking right," he stormed toward us. "You had no right to tell her!"

Leroy stood up so fast that I fell back into the couch and watched him give Noah a shove, putting distance between us. "Step off, Noah. Cass had the right to know."

"*You* were the one that told her?"

There was only a brief pause before Leroy nodded and shouldered the blame. I stood up to protest but without looking back, he raised his hand behind him to stop me.

"You've never told her what I get up to," Noah growled, his fury obvious, but he appeared more suspicious than anything. "Why now?"

I couldn't handle watching Leroy take the blame for something that I'd done. Not to mention Noah's cowardice was starting to get on my nerves.

"No, I told her," I snapped and stepped into place beside Leroy. "She deserves to know. She deserves to know that the loser that she's in love with is a disgusting pig. I don't know what she sees in you. But she cares. A lot. And the worst part is, she knows that you don't feel the same. But she still cares! She's a great girl and you are a pathetic piece of garbage. She could do so much better and I can't wait until she realizes it."

I was seeing stars. Dots of adrenaline danced in my vision. I was sure that I had red cheeks, but I didn't wait for a response.

The corridor, staircase, and upstairs hall were a blur as I took refuge in the spare bedroom. I was proud of the speech that I had delivered. He deserved to hear it and I didn't regret one word of it.

The bed dipped beside me and I turned to find Leroy watching me. "He needed to hear that," he said, tipping my chin toward him so that I couldn't avert my gaze. "You're an amazing woman, Ellie."

"Do you think it'll make a difference?"

"Honestly, I don't know. I doubt it. But he looked like he had just been slapped across the face when I left the room."

That felt good. I wished I could remember his expression. But it was like a haze when I tried to think about it, as if it was a drunk memory. Adrenaline was a weird thing. I leaned into his hold when he wrapped an arm around my shoulder.

"You seem to care about Cass a lot."

"She's sweet," I said. "I would hate to see her nature get ruined because she wasn't loved in the way she should have been."

He pressed a soft kiss against my forehead. "I'm going to love you so much that you don't know what it's like to experience heartbreak. I promise."

His words were so sincere. I could hear it in his tone, I could feel it, as if the sentence had a physical form that wrapped right around me and instilled a faith and trust that I had never felt before.

"I love you, Leroy."

"I love you too."

N

The sheets were too hot. It didn't seem to matter that the window was cracked, allowing the nighttime breeze to filter through. There was no relief from the summer air. I couldn't sleep. I felt restless as I tossed and turned in the bed.

I had methods for nights when I couldn't drift off to sleep. I had read that breathing slowly was effective. I closed my eyes and inhaled a deep breath for seven seconds, and then let it go, counting to five before I paused and started all over again. On the tenth attempt, it became a real concern that I was going to pass out from a lack of oxygen, and sleep was still nowhere in sight.

The temptation to smother myself with the pillow was about to win when the door handle twisted and I sat up in alarm, watching in a statue-like state as it opened, and Leroy slipped inside.

"You gave me a heart attack," I whispered, clutching my chest. "What are you doing?"

He shut the door and twisted the lock before he quietly walked toward the bed. The moonlight streamed in through the gap in the curtain and captured his mischievous smile as he slid into the bed. "Lie down," he ordered. "I can't sleep."

"Me either," I whispered and snuggled down beside him. We had only slept beside each other once since I had arrived, and I was too drunk to remember it. The craving to sleep in his hold was real. But at the same time, the temperature was horrible already, and body heat was making it worse.

"Ellie," he mumbled and ran his hand across my waist, gliding over my stomach. I was just wearing an oversized T-shirt and underwear and I felt flustered as I thought about his hand dipping lower. "I need you."

I swallowed. "I need you too."

"Can I?" He questioned as his hand met the inside of my thigh and began sliding upwards.

"But your mom?" I quietly gasped, already becoming breathless under his touch.

He shifted so that he hovered above me and stared down with an unmistakable hunger. "I saw her pop a sleeping pill before bed. We're safe."

He didn't let me argue as he kissed me. It didn't begin soft either. It was rough and I wrapped my arms around his neck, pulling him even closer.

Our tongues moved with desperation as he raised his knee and pushed my legs apart. I was a whimpering mess and it just got worse when his hand slid over my arm. He laced our fingers together and pushed my hand into the pillow above my head as he began grinding his length against me.

Though the fabric served as a barrier between us, I was on fire as he rubbed against me. I moaned into his mouth and he shuddered in response, his hand slipping under the shirt so that he could take my breast in his hand. He kissed my neck, chest, and jaw.

He went south but his lips managed to stay on my skin as he went. He pushed the shirt up and let his tongue swirl circles around my hardened nipples. I had to control the urge to moan as loud as I wanted to. The pleasure was driving me wild, but I needed to keep quiet. His kisses continued down my stomach, going lower and lower until he gripped the band of my underwear and started sliding them down.

My chest rose and fell with my erratic breathing as he threw the underwear to the floor and wrapped his arms around my thighs, pulling them apart with an aggressive tug. I had to slap a hand across my mouth as he was suddenly devouring me with so much skill I was seeing stars within seconds.

## Ellie

Leroy must have snuck back to his bedroom after I fell asleep last night. I woke up with a smile in place and I didn't suffer from insomnia again after his late-night snack. I did, however, feel a bit sticky between my legs so I got prepared for a shower and crept down the corridor.

A delectable scent was coming from downstairs and I could hear the radio, which meant that Leroy must have been preparing breakfast. My stomach rumbled as I pushed the bathroom door open.

"Shit," Noah hissed when I walked in on him in a towel. A squeal escaped me, and I tried to pull the door shut but he grabbed it before I could. "I'm done. It's all yours."

He brushed past me while I stood at the threshold clutching my clothes to my chest. The bathroom was still misted, and it smelled of fresh vanilla wash and cologne. Noah paused in the corridor, his back was to me and he twisted, glancing at me over his shoulder.

The atmosphere was tense and I realized that I was holding my breath, waiting for him to verbally lash out. But after a long pause, his mouth twitched into the ghost of a smile, barely there, aside from the faintest lift at the corner of his lips, and then he walked down the hall and shut his bedroom door. It was such a strange moment. Leroy might have been more clued in on the wordless exchanges. But I wasn't sure what had just happened.

⚡

Leroy smiled from where he stood at the countertop when I came downstairs in a cropped T-shirt and some floral shorts. He was dishing bacon onto three plates that had eggs and toast on them. Heat flooded to more than one region when I remembered our night together. The vivid images were on repeat and I moved toward him, remembering his mouth between my legs, remembering his fingertips digging into my thighs, remembering the taste of him. My hand went into my hair, the lingering sensation of the strands in his fist, tugging and moaning my name.

He set the pan down, the noise startling me out of tantalizing thoughts, and he leaned against the lip of the bench with his hands. The muscles in his arms flexed against the action and I pictured how they'd been wrapped around my thighs last night. "Hungry?" I met his knowing gaze. He gestured at the food as if he needed to clarify what he meant and I nodded, attempting to chill out.

"How did you sleep?" he asked as we took our plates to the table. Noah sauntered into the room and thanked Leroy for the food before he sat at the other end, far away from both of us.

"I slept well."

"I was thinking about heading out for the morning." Noah spoke up with his head cast down as he cut up his food. "Give you guys the house for a bit."

Leroy narrowed his eyes in a puzzled glance, his elbows leaning on the table. "Thanks," he said with a little hesitation. I guess he wasn't the only one surprised by the odd behavior.

It looked as though he was about to say more when the doorbell started ringing, continuously, repeatedly. In perfect sync, the brothers sighed and murmured, "Cass."

And as if she was summoned from that word alone, she came barreling into the kitchen, her exquisite ringlets bouncing, her simple pink sundress flowing around her legs.

"Who's up for a road trip?" She clapped her hands together and slipped her shades onto the top of her head. "Don't all look so shocked! I was listening to the after-dark radio station last night while I contemplated the meaning of life, and it happened to be an optimal time. There was a contest for Aerosmith tickets. All I had to do was call in and fill in the blanks to their new song. I just bought their CD like two days ago and all the lyrics are on the sleeve," she took a deep breath and threw her arms in the air with a wide smile. "Easy as."

"Aerosmith?!" I stood up, adrenaline coursing through me. I was on the edge of passing out at the mere thought of going to an Aerosmith concert. "You have Aerosmith tickets?! Shut up! Is that true?"

Cass laughed, watching me from where she sat. "The show's tonight in Colorado Springs."

"Tonight?" I hummed with excitement. "This is the greatest day of my life."

"It was all just total luck," she said.

"And cheating," Leroy added.

"Bite me, Lee," she said. "Who's up for it? I have four tickets. So, even *you* can come," she gave Noah a brief glance. "I guess."

"I would love to go to a concert with you, Cass," Noah leaned back in his seat and gave her a sweet smile. She recoiled and I didn't miss how her expression flittered with a hopeful excitement as I sat down again. "I'll pay for the hotel if Leroy wants to drive?"

It was clear that I wasn't the only person that was dumbfounded at Noah's new and improved attitude. But we all kept tight lipped just in case we spooked the pleasantness right out of him. Leroy nodded. "I can drive. No worries. I'll let Eric know that I won't be at practice tomorrow morning. We'll also need to let Mom know what we're doing. And she'll want you to clear it with your mom first."

It took me a second to realize that he was speaking to me and I looked at him, plummeting with disappointment. "She'll never go for it."

"Don't call her," Noah suggested. "We can just tell Mom that she was—" he gave us a thumbs-up. "I doubt she'll call to confirm it."

"She might," Leroy argued as he grazed his bottom lip with his thumb and adopted a thoughtful expression.

"Just risk it," Noah said. "Better to ask for forgiveness instead of permission."

"I mean, she probably won't call your mom," Cass said, but her tone wasn't confident. "But if she does, we'll already be in Colorado Springs."

Leroy looked conflicted but I couldn't imagine not going. It was worth the risk. Aside from the fact I would get to see

Aerosmith live, we'd be in a hotel, two hours out of town, with no parental supervision. I hated to go against parental authority in most situations, not to mention how much trouble I would be in if I got caught, but it was something I wouldn't get to do again anytime soon.

Noah leaned forward and fixed me with question. "Aren't you eighteen? You're grown. What's your mom's deal?"

"Noah—" Leroy shook his head.

"All right," I said, not wanting to linger on the fact that I don't have the same freedoms as most eighteen-year-olds. "We'll just tell Eleanor that my mom was fine with it."

"Perfect!" Cass slapped her hands on the tabletop with excitement. "We'll leave at lunch. I'm packed and good to go. My stuff is by the door."

"You knew that we would go?" Leroy arched a brow at her.

"No. But I was hopeful. And if you'd said no, I would have just gone to Eric's and asked him. Now hurry up and finish eating," Cass gave me a tap on the back of the hand. "I'll help you pack once you're done."

"Cass," Noah pushed his seat back and stood. "Can we talk for a second?"

She stared up at the boy she adored. I didn't think what they had was love, but I believed she felt it in one of the many forms it came in. Leroy and I watched them leave the room together and when I looked at him, his stare was narrow and calculating. "This is going to go really well or so badly."

Cass hadn't had the chance to tell me what happened after we'd dropped her off at Tony's yesterday. But I was desperate to find out. Which is why, a few hours later, when I heard her come out of his bedroom, I peered out of mine.

"Cass," she looked up from the floor, the biggest smile that I'd ever seen on her cheerful face. "Come," I waved her over, and she skipped into the room, collapsing onto the bed.

Leroy was downstairs on the phone with his mom. He'd asked his dad for permission first, but he'd told us to clear it with Eleanor. He was doing that while Cass caught me up with the details.

"You have such good taste in clothes." She admired a pair of overalls. I was packing up my bag with a couple of outfits so that I'd have options.

"Thanks, but don't keep me waiting. What happened at Tony's? What happened just now?"

She bit on her lip and her chest expanded. "Okay, okay, so after you dropped me off, I stormed straight inside. I'd been hyping myself up for the moment, so I was one hundred percent ready to throw down. Anyway, he was gaming with his friend, and I started shouting 'you slept with Nadia, you are such a hoochie and I hate you.' That sort of thing."

I nodded along.

"He told me that it was none of my business and I had no right to talk to him like that, yadda yadda yadda. So, I said, 'Noah,'" Cass stood up and directed her words at the empty space in the room, reenacting with passion, "'You will not touch me, fuck me, or speak to me ever again unless you commit. Just us. I don't want to share you anymore, and if you can't get on board, we are done.'"

I clapped, fast and loud, but her expression fell, and so did the raise in her shoulders.

"Then he told me he wasn't interested in exclusivity and I was just depriving myself of a good thing because I wanted to have childish labels. That I was the one with hang-ups apparently."

I could have gone into his room and smacked him right across the face. "What did he want to talk about just now?"

That was when she regained her excitement, sitting down on the bed so fast that the mattress bounced, and my bag shook. "He apologized for it all. He said he was scared but he doesn't want to lose me, and he agreed to be exclusive. Noah Lahey is my *boyfriend*."

As far as I was concerned, I still believed that Cass could do so much better. But her happiness was radiant, washing over her in waves that glittered under the sun that was Cass. There was no hiding how much this meant to her. "That's a turnaround! I'm so happy for you."

"I know." She shook her head when I held up a pair of black leather pants. "Those are tight, but it's too hot. We can go on double dates now."

"We sort of are tonight," I said. "A concert could be a date."

"Yes," she gasped. "Double-date night!"

Leroy appeared at the doorway. He folded his arms across his chest with a small smile and leaned on the doorframe. "We've booked a room. It's a double—two queen beds between the four of us."

"Perfect, me and Ellie can share. You and Noah take the other," Cass grinned as she jumped up from the bed. She gave his chest a condescending pat as she walked past him and out of the room.

"I'm not sharing a bed with Noah," Leroy shouted over his shoulder. "I don't even want to share a room with the two of you!"

"Why don't we get our own?" I asked and walked toward him. "I could help with the cost?"

He wrapped an arm around my waist so that he could pull me into him. "It's not about cost, Ellie. I do appreciate the offer, though," he pressed a kiss on my forehead. "The hotels in the area were booked up. The one we did manage to find is almost a half hour from the concert and had a cancellation when we called."

"Oh well, never mind."

"I'm not opposed to locking those two out, though," he leaned his forehead against mine. "Trust me, it'll be the favorable option. Those two will hit it whether we're in the room or not."

I winced and hoped he was joking around. I knew that Cass was a bit looser once she was drunk. But we were going out of town and I didn't think we would have access to alcohol.

"Stop overthinking things." He tucked a piece of hair behind my ear, his knuckle tracing down the edge of my face. "Tonight will be great."

I smiled. "I know."

⚡

The road trip was peaceful for the most part. We stopped for gas and three bathroom breaks for Cass, who had eaten an ice cream sandwich before we left. Besides that, we had fun, listening to music with the windows rolled down. It wasn't until we arrived in Colorado Springs that things took a turn for the tense.

"I'm telling you; it was the street that we passed two minutes ago," Noah shouted from the backseat. Leroy gripped the steering wheel and glowered in the rearview mirror.

"No, it's farther up and around the bend. Like it said on the fucking map!"

Noah lunged forward and appeared between the driver and passenger seats as he waved at the windshield. "The map clearly said that the hotel was off Roderick and you just passed Glensmith and Roderick came before Glensmith!"

"It came after Glensmith!" Leroy shouted back.

"No! Before Glensmith and it comes after Bradley."

Cass snickered in the backseat. "Typical Bradley. Always coming first."

Noah banged his head on the driver's seat. "Cass, not now."

"You come first, too, you selfish prick."

"Damn woman, how much have you had to drink?" Noah shouted.

"She's been drinking?" Leroy twisted in his seat before he peered in the rearview mirror. "What the hell?"

"Focus on the road!" Noah snapped.

"I'm trying but you two won't shut the hell up!"

"She's the one talking shit."

"Whatever you say," she mumbled, and I heard the clink of a bottle from the backseat.

"Did she steal the booze from her mom?"

"Does it matter?" Noah said as he waved his hands about. "She brought enough to share. Except she was supposed to be saving it for the hotel."

"I'm right here," Cass clipped with a sarcastic tone.

"How could we forget?" Noah muttered.

"Excuse me, asshole. That's not how you're meant to talk to your girlfriend."

"I wasn't talking *to* you, I was talking *about* you!"

"You are about to get—"

Noah bit down on his fist and clenched his eyes closed. "I'm sorry, baby. Just . . . just shut up for a second, okay? Thanks, babe."

"There it is!" Leroy interrupted with a loud voice. "I told you it came after Glensmith."

Noah sighed and retreated from between us, falling into the backseat. Leroy pulled into the underground hotel parking lot and gave me a quick glance as he paid the fee. "Sorry about that."

"About what?"

"All the hostile language and shouting."

I laughed at his sincere apology, and he continued past the cars so that he could find a spare space. "It's fine. I'm not offended."

We parked the car and the boys took the luggage for us. Cass was definitely a little bit tipsy, but she managed not to draw too much attention to herself as we took the basement elevator up to the hotel reception. We went through the check-in procedures and all the other requirements. Our room was on the fourth floor and it was nicer than anything I had stayed in before. Momma and I hadn't traveled a lot, apart from the occasional weekends on her brother's farm. We did go on one of the science class trips in junior year—Momma was a chaperone, but we stayed in cabins with stale mattresses and communal bathrooms. That was the extent of my traveling.

The other three didn't seem all that fazed by our accommodation, so I maintained a natural reaction, but quietly admired the large room that was decked out with two comfortable-looking beds, a kitchen/dining space, rich textured curtains, and soft patterned carpet. It was beautifully decorated and vibrant with hues of red and orange in the decor that contrasted with the soft-blue walls.

"Shotgun the bed closest to the window!" Cass pushed past us and dived face-first into the white bedspread.

"You should sleep before we leave," Leroy suggested as he set our bags down beside the other bed where I was sitting. "You'll be denied entrance if you're too wacked."

"I'm fine," she dismissed him and sat up. "You dudes should leave for an hour so that we can get dressed and ready."

"An hour," Noah said sarcastically from where he was leaning on the little round dining table. "It takes that long for you to decide what to wear when we hang out. And the clothes don't even stay on for that long."

"We'll go and get something to eat and bring it back." Leroy leaned down and gave me a quick kiss before he started toward the door. Noah followed him and Cass gave them a sarcastic wave as the door closed behind them.

As soon as we were alone, we dug through our bags, and it wasn't long before there were clothes scattered all over the floor and bed while we decided what to wear. We swapped our clothes and mixed and matched until we created two perfect combinations.

It would be hot in the concert. It was the middle of summer and the arena would be packed. So, I wore a sheer black top over a bra the same color, and pulled it together with a navy-blue, high-waisted skirt. It seemed like the right kind of look for an Aerosmith concert. There was no chance I wanted to end up with broken toes, so I wore a pair of combat boots over some thigh-high socks.

Cass went in a similar direction with a darker look, but she borrowed my KISS shirt and tucked it into a pair of black shorts that she wore over sheer stockings. She was tall enough not to need high heels, so she wore her sneakers and of course her hair sat in its signature tight curls.

I used a wand to add some volume to my hair and teased it out with a comb before I let Cass attack me with more makeup than I had ever worn before. She laid it on thick: foundation, some nude lipstick, and a bit of blush. She gave me a darker eye look with a kohl liner pencil, and of course I added a few coats of mascara because I didn't think that I could ever leave the house without decent lashes.

We were in the bathroom fluffing and adding final touches to our looks when the hotel door opened, and we heard Noah and Leroy coming through. The aroma of hot food came in with them and we shared a look of delight before we ventured out into the main room.

Leroy was busy taking items out of the bag and placing them on the table. Cass skipped straight over to Noah and fell into his lap as he helped himself to a burger. He gripped her thigh and murmured something that made her blush. I had to admit that it was cute to see them being so affectionate.

Leroy glanced toward me and then back to the food before he did a double take and his gaze became awestruck. He stopped what he was doing, and his jaw dropped as his eyes drank me in. "Ellie," he swallowed and walked toward me. "Shit, you look stunning."

"Lee," Cass scolded. "You're sweet. But wrong compliment. Right now, she looks smoking hot. A sex bomb. A straight-up betty."

"I'm trying to eat here," Noah muttered. Leroy shot them a curt glance but didn't pay them a lot of mind as he stopped in front of me and his sights settled on my chest, which was nice and visible through the sheer fabric. Heat crept up my neck and into my face as he stared at me. I was definitely disappointed that we weren't alone.

He inhaled a deep breath after a moment and wound an arm around my back. "Come on, food before we have to leave for the arena," he led me to the table so that we could sit down.

After we'd finished eating, Cass revealed the box of beer that she had brought along. She and Noah were fast to pop the lids and of course offered us a drink as well.

"I'm driving," Leroy declined, pulling his shirt up and over his head so that he could swap it for a black tank top that went under his black, short-sleeve button-up that he left undone. I was practically salivating over his defined chest while he was top-less. A cold bottle being touched to my shoulder gave me a fright and I turned to see Cass waving it at me.

"Oh, no," I said. "I promised Eleanor that I wouldn't drink again while I'm here."

"She won't know," Noah shrugged and guzzled back the entire contents of his bottle in about ten seconds flat.

"I'd rather not."

"Fair enough," Cass said. "Momma Eleanor can be kind of scary when she gets pissed off."

I was glad that she dropped it. Eleanor wasn't the only reason that I declined the offer. We were going to a concert. I wanted to remember the experience, not black out or embarrass myself in front of thousands of people. It was one thing to go to a house party with people that we knew and down a few beers. It was another to go somewhere that was completely unfamiliar while battling the wobbles.

Leroy pulled on his Chucks and buckled the belt on his black jeans before he suggested that we leave. He looked incredible. His arms were glowing from the amount of sun that he'd had, the firm bulge of his biceps making me weak whenever he gestured or unintentionally flexed.

I was unequivocally grateful that Cass had eyes only for the younger brother. But I still couldn't understand it. He was attractive in a sense. But his personality marred whatever physical attributes he had. He would be a total catch if he wasn't such a gross, self-righteous pig.

We piled into the car downstairs and set a tape to play. Leroy turned in his seat. "Ready?"

I was more than ready. The excitement was palpable. Tonight promised to be one of the best nights of my life and I couldn't wait.

## Ellie

Cass and I broke into a loud applause and cheer when "Dream On" finished. We had a decent spot, considering how many people were here. We were off to the left about halfway back from the stage, and we were sandwiched but Leroy and Noah stood behind us so that we had a bit of room to dance.

"We should go and get a water from the concession stand?" Cass shouted when the next song intro started up.

I leaned into Leroy and shouted. "We're going to get a water."

"We'll come?"

"No." I shook my head as Cass tugged on my arm. "Save our spots. We don't want to lose them."

He nodded and gave me a quick peck on the cheek before Cass dragged me away. It took us a little while and a lot of apologies before we broke free at the back of the pit. Security guards gave us polite smiles as we skipped over to the concession stand at the back of the arena.

The fresh air was a blessing. We weren't out in the total open.

But even just being free of the packed-in area was a relief. I fanned at my face as we jumped into the line, still moving to the music while we waited. There was no alcohol being sold since it was a sixteen-plus event, but there were a lot of people picking up chilled bottles of water and snacks.

The line moved at a fast pace. I suppose the fact that there weren't a lot of options to choose from kept it moving. When the man in front of us was finished handing his cash over, he spun around and walked straight into Cass, standing on her feet and almost dropping his bottle of water down her front.

"I am so sorry," he apologized. He looked concerned that he had hurt her.

"It's not a problem," Cass shouted back as she stepped forward with me. I leaned on the bar and peered at her over my shoulder but she was occupied with the man so I purchased a bottle of water each and figured that we could share with the guys.

I stepped back into place beside her and handed the water over. The ground underneath us was sticky from all the beverages spilled on the hard concrete floor.

I guzzled back big mouthfuls of water to rehydrate while Cass talked with the blue-eyed boy. I wasn't listening and it was too loud to pick up on the conversation, so I just stood idle while she had a chat. There was nothing flirtatious in her body language, so I wasn't concerned when I saw Noah making his way toward us through the throng of concertgoers.

He apparently wasn't as placid about the conversation because his gaze narrowed and he stormed forward, all but knocking me out of the way as he gripped Cass's upper arm. "What the hell are you doing?"

"Having a conversation dipshit," Cass ripped her arm out of his hold and glared. "I'm not you, Noah; I can have a chat with the opposite sex without wanting to fuck them."

If I wasn't mistaken, it did appear that guy looked a little bit disappointed, but he regained himself and gave Noah a shove in the chest. "Don't handle her like that, man, it's not cool."

Noah shoved him back and I began to panic at how this was escalating so fast. "Don't tell me what to do with my girlfriend, man."

Cass and I stood behind Noah, who appeared to be growing really agitated. She glanced over at me and winced as though she knew this was on her, but she didn't mean for it to get out of hand. I didn't think it was her fault; Noah was acting like a hothead.

Cass leaned around and gripped Noah's bicep. "Noah, come on—"

"Quiet," he shoved her off again.

"You're an asshole," blue-eye boy shouted and stepped forward. "Stop handling her like that."

"Mind your own fucking business," Noah took a handful of blue-eyed boy's shirt in his fist and punched him in the jaw. My hand flew up and I smothered a loud gasp. That was so uncalled-for.

The boy regained himself and lunged forward, his closed fist connecting with the side of Noah's face. Cass started screaming and attempted to jump between the boys, who were now engaged in a full-on brawl. Dozens of people surrounded us within seconds, and I was getting shoved left and right as they scrambled to get a view of the fight.

I tried to keep my feet planted in a firm stance so that I wouldn't end up on the floor. It was hard considering I was stressing out over Cass, who was now diving on top of Noah while he pummeled the blue-eyed boy. The boy wasn't going down without a fight, though, and he landed some painful-looking blows to Noah's stomach.

Unintentionally, the fight ended up getting closer and closer to me, and I was sure that I was about to get an elbow in the head, when I was pulled back at the arm and drawn into Leroy's chest. He used his strong arms to shove a few people out of the way and stared at his brother with a violent glint.

"Stay here," he ordered, as if I would wander off. He went over and ripped Noah off the stranger, throwing him into the ground and leaning one knee on his chest.

The blue-eyed boy looked as though he wasn't willing to let the fight go, but Leroy held Noah down by his throat and looked up, saying something to the guy that I couldn't hear. My heart was pounding, and the crowd was still pushing and shoving so hard that I kept tripping while I watched. Leroy turned back to Noah. The blue-eyed boy didn't leave, but he wiped the blood on his nose and made no move to attack further.

"Stay the fuck down, Noah," Leroy yelled at his manic brother, who was thrashing under his hold. "Chill out!"

Suddenly the crowd started to dissipate as security broke through, shouting inaudible orders. Cass sprinted toward me and started to pull me along with the rest of the departing onlookers. "Come on, let's go."

"Cass, I'm not leaving." I shrugged her off and waved at the boys, who were still struggling against each other. Noah clearly wanted to get up and continue fighting with the guy, who had disappeared. But Leroy's hold was unwavering as he kept ordering him to get a grip.

Two security guards cleared the crowd before ripping apart Noah and Leroy and shoving them, ordering them to move. They were clearly being led to the exit, so Cass and I joined hands and followed as best we could. It was humiliating: people were watching, whispers of scandal. Noah was a magnet to all things drama, and I was so over it.

By the time we got outside, the security was gone. Noah and Leroy stood about ten feet apart, both looking enraged. Cass dropped my hand, heading straight for her boyfriend. There was seriously something wrong him. The fact that Cass couldn't even talk to another man without him throwing down spoke volumes to his unfaithful nature. He had no trust because he had no loyalty.

"You're such an asshole," Cass shouted, gaining the attention of a few stragglers hanging around on the footpath, smoking cigarettes or climbing into cabs. "You just ruined the concert. We got kicked out because you're a shady little shit who can't miss the chance to start a scene."

Noah got in close to her, intimidatingly so. She didn't seem worried, she stood tall. "You're the one who wanted this exclusive bullshit. Why bother if you're just going to whore it out to the first dude you see?"

She slapped him across the face and I froze. Noah's hand rubbed the bottom of his jaw and he stared at her, furious.

"I was having a conversation with him. About the music, the night," she seethed. "He apologized for bumping into me, and then I ask—" she stopped and shook her head. "You know what, no, I don't have to explain jack to you."

"Could you both grow the fuck up," Leroy snapped, leaning on a bike stand at the edge of the footpath. The three of us watched him. "You're a shit-show. This relationship is a toxic shit-show."

"Lay off," Noah spat. "We all know you're the shining star of Castle Rock. Perfect game, perfect grades, even though you can't submit a damn paper without me looking over it. Everyone knows your relationship is perfect, we've all heard. You're all that, we get it. Just shut the hell up. We can't all be Leroy Lahey."

"Again with this shit? You're the one who makes yourself a victim. No one puts me above you. You do that to yourself. You act like an asshole and wonder why people are fed up with you all the time."

Noah threw his arms wide and shouted, "I'm not imagining this, asshat—just watch Mom and Dad boast about their precious Leroy to everyone and I'm lucky if they even remember that I exist."

Noah was mad, and he was hostile, but there was a hitch in his tone and pain in his expression that I couldn't help but see as heartbreak. He believed what he was saying.

"Do something that makes them proud then," Leroy was calmer, factual. I wondered if he recognized his brother's hurt too.

"I wrote a fucking paper on the subtle privilege of the working-class economy and presented legitimate numbers that could assist in the funding of free education for financially burdened families that was recognized by the state senator! How is *that* not something to be proud of?"

Cass and I looked at each other, sharing a silent 'wow.' That *is* something to be proud of.

"Mom literally threw you a party and you didn't even show up," Leroy countered, and I winced, looking around at the loiterers who were now watching with interest. This was too personal to be said in front of a crowd of strangers.

Noah laughed derisively. "She was just being a shooter—she wanted to brag in front of all of her elite friends."

"Are you fucking serious?" Leroy stepped forward, toe-to-toe with his brother. "You *just* said she didn't mention you enough, but if she does, she's showing off? You are such a wack job. And no, the reason you didn't show up was because you were sticking it in Natalie and that was more important."

Noah averted his stare, red crawling up his neck.

The air was still, the tension pulling at all four of us. Someone had to move; it had to snap sooner or later. And then, it did. Leroy stormed toward me, wrapped his arm around my shoulder, and we started down the sidewalk.

"Where are you going?" Cass called. "You have the car keys."

I was trapped under Leroy's arm. I couldn't see past him when I tried to peer back at her. But he answered for us. "Back to the hotel. Walk."

"That'll take hours!" Noah shouted.

"Good. Cool off. We need some space."

He offered no more explanation as he pulled me tighter against his side and we started toward the car, which was parked in the lot beside the stadium. We climbed in, Leroy started the engine, and we drove away from the pair of them. Streetlights overhead illuminated the interior.

"I'm so sorry that he ruined the concert for you," Leroy said, knuckles white as he gripped the steering wheel.

"Oh, no, it's fine. It's not like I paid for the tickets."

"Doesn't matter," he mumbled. "You love music, you were excited, it—it's just not okay."

He didn't say it out loud, but I had a feeling that he was thinking about the fact that I couldn't afford concert tickets in most cases. That I might not get another chance anytime soon. He was right and it was disappointing. But it was out of his control.

"I heard all of my favorite songs before we got kicked out," I offered, hoping to defuse his frustration. "At least it wasn't at the beginning, right?"

He tried to smile but it was nothing more than a flinch in his lips. There and gone in the blink of an eye. It was sweet that he was so disappointed on my behalf—there was no denying how much my happiness meant to him—but I wanted to lift his spirits so that we could still salvage our evening together. Especially now that we were alone. For the remainder of the drive, we were quiet. Leroy held my hand, kissing my knuckles occasionally, but said nothing. I figured that he needed to process his thoughts and the argument with Noah, so I let him do so without interruption.

When we got back to the hotel room, Leroy switched on the lights and closed the curtains while I sat down on the edge of our bed and unlaced my combat boots.

"Mom and Dad *do* love Noah," Leroy said suddenly, standing beside the benchtop where a little radio was tucked into the corner. He messed around with the buttons and tuning. "Just so we're clear about that."

"I know they do," I said, leaning back on my palms. "When I went to Cass's on Sunday, it was because your momma asked me to give you and Noah some time to hang out."

Leroy looked at me, hand still on the dial as he chuckled. "I know. It was obvious."

"Oh," I laughed. "Well, maybe Noah is . . . I don't know, jealous? Not of the attention but just . . . you and your accomplishments. He probably really admires you."

"I think he was just dropped on his fucking head at birth," Leroy muttered, settling on a station.

The song was "Sex And Candy" by Marcy Playground. I sang along, quiet and without a lot of thought. Leroy was watching me with adoration when I met his stare across the room. He leaned off the lip of the bench and sauntered toward me, offering me his hand when he stopped.

I took it. "What are we doing?"

"Dancing," he wrapped his arm around my lower back and tugged me in close. "I have to admit, this is better than competing for space with a bunch of sweaty strangers."

My head rested on his chest. "I agree."

We moved together, our feet stepping in time to the beat. Leroy spun me out and then dipped me as if it was nothing, his large hand cradling my back. While suspended in air, he leaned in and pressed a kiss against my throat that was so soft it felt like a whisper. It sent a shot of chill right down my spine, and when he pulled me up to stand, I tiptoed to give him a kiss under his ear, right where I knew it would make him shiver. It had the desired effect.

"We should do this more often," he said, his thumb making circles on my lower back, the sheer top so thin it didn't block the sensation of his touch at all.

"Do what more often?"

"Be alone," he said. "Time to ourselves. Quiet. It's peaceful knowing that it's just us."

"I wonder what it'll be like when we're in Waco," I thought aloud. "I wonder how it'll change things."

"It'll be a good change," Leroy said quickly. "I'll have a dorm room and I'll be getting a car. Noah gets the Benz. It'll be just us. All the time."

Fear crept forward and I leaned on his chest. "I'll be at home, though. Momma has . . . old-school rules and values. I have a curfew and I can't just do what I want, whenever I want. What if you—"

"Hey, hey," Leroy pushed me back and cupped my face in his hands. "You sound worried. I know that things are different for us, I get it. That doesn't matter to me. I'll take what I can get, Els. And I'll love you regardless of what time I have to drop you off at home."

"It's embarrassing, though. I'm not a child but I get treated like one."

"Look, it doesn't bother me—"

"It doesn't right now—"

He held a finger to my lips. "Let me finish. But if it bothers you, talk to her. Your mom. Explain that you want the reins loosened. You're a good woman, Ellie. You deserve to be trusted."

"Girl," I muttered.

"What?"

"How can I be a woman when I'm treated like a little girl?"

"I didn't think it bothered you. The rules and all that."

"I didn't know it could be any different," I said. "But I've seen how your family is, and I don't want to keep being told I have to be home at ten. It's barely dark at ten in the summer. Like, Noah has more freedom than I do, and he actually acts like a child."

"You're not wrong."

"That was mean." My hands ran over my face, causing Leroy's to drop their hold. "Sorry."

"Don't be." He pushed my hair behind my ear. "You're definitely not wrong. Like I said, talk to your mom. You have so much respect for her and I love that. But there's nothing wrong with asking for the trust that you deserve."

"Yeah, I should do that." There was more determination in my tone. "Or, I'll tell her that I'm sleeping over at a friend's place and spend the night in your dorm."

Leroy laughed, nodding his head. "Yeah or that. I wouldn't argue."

We continued swaying to the music, feet sinking into the carpet, the night lights of Colorado Springs outside of our window.

"What if you have a roommate, though?"

"Nope, no roommate. Spent a bit extra for the private life. I need it after sharing a roof with Noah for the last eighteen years."

"You'll miss him. You know it."

He shrugged but he didn't deny the claim either. "Enough about my brother. We finally have some peace and quiet." He pulled me in at the waist so that I collided with his chest. "Hop on my feet."

"What?"

"Stand on my feet."

Puzzled, I did what he said and stifled a squeal when he started spinning around the room. He danced, holding me while I clasped my hands behind his neck. We both laughed and I felt the dizzies coming on when he spun me in circles. "Leroy," I groaned, burying my head in his chest. If he wasn't going to let me off this damn ride, I'd jump.

My feet slid off his and then he stood on my toe and we tripped over each other, landing in a heap on the floor, both of us out of breath with laughter. "I'm going to be sick," I groaned, watching as Leroy crawled up and over me.

"For real? I'll take you to the bathroom."

"No. Not for real. But the world is spinning."

"Yeah, it does that. Always has."

"You're hilarious."

He winked and pulled me to my feet in one swift movement. The room was no longer orbiting around me. Slowly, he slid his hands around my waist, his fingertips just a slip from being tucked under the band of my skirt. He was being so soft and gentle, like he wanted to savor the moment as he admired me from head to toe. The atmosphere in the room changed in the space of a breath.

"This outfit has been driving me insane all night," he murmured with a low voice. He pulled me into his front and my hands clasped themselves behind his neck.

I ran my fingers through his soft hair and sunk my teeth into my bottom lip as I gave his strands a subtle tug. He tipped his head back, a soft groan escaping his lips and I quivered, almost short circuiting at what I could do to him. It must have ignited something within him because when he brought his head back down, his expression was dark with lust and he wrapped a hand tightly around the back of my neck, forcing our mouths together in a fierce kiss.

I arched into his hold and our hands moved with erratic need. I was pulsating, moaning as our tongues moved together, and we walked backwards to our bed. He lowered me down onto it, his hand keeping me secure at the lower of my back. All I could feel was him—his scent, his kiss, his touch were a drug that I hoped I'd never get enough of. Our kiss was broken just long enough that he could kneel above me and rip his shirt off before he collapsed on top of me again and I was able to sink my fingertips into the firm surface of his muscular back.

Leroy dragged his mouth down the length of my jaw, kissing and sucking as I tipped my head back and moaned. "Mmhmm, yes," he groaned against me as he pushed my thighs apart with his knee. "I've been waiting to hear those sounds."

He untucked the sheer top from my skirt and pulled it over my head, bringing his mouth back down to my neck as one hand cupped the curve of my chest, massaging it with so much precision that I was startled in the best way when he shifted my underwear to the side. I gasped at the sudden contact, but I was ready for him . . . more than ready.

Leroy leaned up, his free hand on the mattress beside my head and his knees on either side of my frame as he continued working me into a state of euphoria. My hands held on to his taut shoulders, and when I looked at him, he was watching me with a lustful haze, his eyes devouring me. "You're so fucking beautiful," he rasped.

His hand sped up and I could barely breathe. I threw my head back, coming undone. Leroy discarded his pants, rolled on a condom, and stripped me before lowering himself on top of me again. He took my hands in his and put them above my head as he kissed me, rough and fierce in a way that had me begging for more. I wrapped my legs around his waist and pulled him down.

"No more waiting?" he asked, sliding his tip inside of me.

"No more," I gasped as I stretched to accommodate him. "Please just—"

My words turned into a loud gasp as he slammed his hips and

filled me, hitting all the right places in an earth-shattering sensation that could be compared to nothing else. It was even better than the first time. Because this time, we knew each other more. We loved each other. And we had been waiting for what felt like a long time for this to happen again.

I swear that the passion between us, the feelings and desire could start a fire. Our bodies were made for each other—molded to match and fit like two pieces of a destined puzzle. Nothing had ever felt more perfect than when we moved together. Hearing him vocalize his pleasure, knowing that his deep moaning was because of me, sent me over the edge.

His ragged breathing against my neck caused me to shiver, goosebumps forming on my skin as we just lay with satisfaction afterwards. It was one hundred percent worth the wait. Something that I would never tire of was this—not with him. I was glad that I had waited for the right man. He made the entire experience what it was.

## LEROY

Ellie was still sound asleep when I emerged from the bathroom in the morning. Cass and Noah were in the other bed, facedown in their pillows. They must have come back sometime after Els and I had fallen asleep last night, and I was glad that it hadn't been earlier. Not when I thought about Ellie beneath me, writhing, moaning, fingernails dragging down the length of my back. Damn. I ran a hand across my face and exhaled. We were no longer alone, so there would be no morning sex. However, I did need to talk to Noah about last night. It made sense to get it over with before the drive home.

I stood beside his bed and gave his bare back a careless slap. He rolled onto his side and peered through half-closed lids. "What?"

"We need to talk," I said. "Let's go for a walk."

"Later."

"Now."

"What the hell," he threw the comforter back and stood up, scratching himself and stretching.

"You want to keep it down so the girls can sleep?"

"Shut up," he grumbled and stormed off toward the bathroom. "I'll be outside in a minute."

I stood out in the hall and waited for him to get himself together. The hotel staff were pushing carts covered in room service or housekeeping products. Our checkout was in two hours but we didn't have a lot to pack up so it wouldn't be hard to be out on time. Noah appeared ten minutes later, clothed and hair ruffled into a tidier mess than it was before.

He glared at me as he closed the door with no damn care, banging it closed. I threw my arms open in exasperation. "Dude, shut *up*."

"Why should they get to sleep in, and I'm dragged out of bed at eight in the damn morning?"

The conversation was already off to a terrible start. "Come on."

"Where are we going?"

"I dunno. We could go and get some breakfast."

"Fine," he walked beside me, hands in his pockets. "Start talking."

"How are things going between you and Cass?"

"That's what you dragged me out of bed for? To ask how my *toxic* relationship is going?"

It wasn't that I regretted referring to his relationship as toxic. At the time, I meant what I said. But it could have been delivered gentler, I suppose. As hard as it was not to, belittling him wasn't going to help. Neither was enablement. Ellie was right about that.

"No," I said. "That's not the only reason why I dragged you out of bed. But I am curious. Why did you change your mind and make things exclusive?"

He kept his head down, walking beside me. We stepped onto the elevator and he leaned against the wall. "I don't know. I like her, I guess."

It took all I had not to express disappointment in his answer. "You like her enough not to sleep with other girls?"

"I know what exclusive means, Leroy. Thanks for confirming."

The droning tone of elevator music filled the silence while I stared at Noah and he stared at the floor. It was so hard to get a grasp on this kid. We didn't understand each other at all, and it made me mourn the days when he'd been my best friend and we got each other like no one else did. That sort of bond seemed unbreakable back then. But people change with age. We'd clearly grown in different directions and I wondered if we'd ever get back to that place again. All I could do was try.

The elevator doors opened, and we stepped off, crossing the lobby and heading outside. There was no official plan, but I figured we'd walk until we found something.

"It's always her," Noah mumbled, my attention moving between him and the sidewalk in front of me. "She's always there. She's good to me. Your girl had some points, I guess. There was no point in *not* making it official. I didn't want to let her go, but I guess I couldn't keep screwing around. So . . . it made sense."

His answer almost felt . . . cold. But Noah hadn't opened up to me like that in a long time and I wasn't about to make him feel like an idiot for it. He was obviously trying but something told me if Cass was the right girl for him, his answer would have felt warmer, more passionate. Maybe they wouldn't work, but for now, he was doing his best for the girl that cared about him more than he knew.

"Ellie said Cass was happy about the whole thing," I said. "Freaking out about it."

Noah shrugged. We approached a café called Spring Bowl. It was small, not a lot of seating, but it wasn't busy, and it smelled like hot food and coffee. I gave Noah a gentle backhand on the chest to follow me inside. The glass cabinets were full of sandwiches, pastries, and desserts. We ordered for ourselves and decided to get the girls something before we left.

We sat down at a two-person table, a framed photo of the store opening on the wall beside us and menus stacked between condiments. Noah tapped the tabletop and refused to look at me when he said, "Sorry about last night."

Noah rarely apologized in actual words. He preferred to brush things aside or use a gesture of kindness to call a truce. But the word *sorry* rarely left his mouth. I tried not to seem stunned.

"For getting us kicked out," he continued, mumbling as fast as he could. "I got heated when I saw Cass talking to that dude. Pissed me off. I didn't mean to wig out, though."

"You should know that she's not shady, dude."

"Yeah, I do," he said and leaned back in his seat, hands behind his head. It was the first time that I'd had a good look at his face.

"Your eye okay?" I asked. There was a shade of bruising around his socket and a graze on his lip. It could have been worse, though.

"It's fine."

A thought came to me and I pointed at him, failing to hide my amusement. "That's your karma for Nadia. I took the beating that night. What goes around, comes around."

A quick breath of laughter came from his nose and he nodded. "I'll take that."

Our coffee and bacon breakfast was delivered, so we ordered the same for the girls and asked for it to go. We dug in and I thought about how to approach the next topic with Noah. So far, the conversation had been peaceful but all it took was the wrong tone to light a match under the ticking time bomb seated across from me.

"Can we talk about what else you said last night?" I asked. He stiffened and I worried that I'd screwed it. "Dude, Mom and Dad are proud of you, man. You don't need to compete with me for that."

His leg was bouncing under the table.

"I just don't get it," I said when he wouldn't answer me. "Why do you think like that?"

"You have way more in common with them than I do," he stabbed his fork into his food and inhaled a deep breath. "You always did. Football with Dad. Cooking and shit with Mom. I decided that I didn't want to continue football and Dad stopped bothering. You and he practiced together all the time. Watched games and shit. If Mom was making dinner, she'd call for you to help her. You know, I asked her once why she never asked me and she said, 'Leroy enjoys it, darling,' as if I didn't? She never even gave me the chance."

I kept my mouth shut—this was clearly something that had been weighing on him, and if he needed to let it out, I didn't want to interrupt. But I did need to tell him that he was wrong.

"I don't think Mom meant to leave you out, but you preferred playing with your toys when we were little. Or reading picture books and that sort of thing. I think she wanted us to do what made us happy, and those things were different. And when we got older, you kept your interests private. You didn't share them with Mom and Dad."

"Because they weren't the interests that they wanted me to have."

I shook my head. "No, dude. That's not it. You put a barrier up because you assumed they wouldn't care if it wasn't about football or whatever else. But that's not true. Come on, Dad is always telling people how smart you are. Mom misses being close to you. I can tell."

His jaw twitched as he stared at the tabletop.

"I miss you too, man," I said. He was restless and shifting but he didn't tell me to piss off, so I took that as a positive sign. "We're different. We're really different but we don't have to fight so much. It's dumb. Just chill out and stop being so hostile all the time."

He looked up at me and frowned. "Stop being so self-righteous all the time."

"Maturity is self-righteous now, is it?"

He rolled his eyes. "Get over yourself. If you want me to do better, you do better too. Stop treating me like I'm beneath you because I like to sleep around, and you don't."

"That has literally nothing to do with anything. I don't care who you sleep with. You act like a dipshit and make stupid comments all the time."

"I'm funny."

"I guess we'll agree to disagree."

We glared at each other, chewing on our food, and then, slowly, our frowns turned into smiles and then laughter. It was a relief, that was for sure. The tension was lifted, and even though who we were as individuals would never change, this felt like a step forward. One thing that I internally swore to work on was not putting him down. If that was what he felt I was doing, I couldn't tell him he was wrong. His feelings were valid, and I needed to remember that.

N

When we got back to the room, Cass and Ellie were cross-legged on their own beds, facing each other. Their conversation stopped immediately, and the room fell into silence. The girls stared at us, and Cass wore a shit-eating grin.

"What?" I asked.

"Nothing," she said, and I looked at Ellie. Her gaze was moving over me while she chewed on the tip of her thumb. I was obviously missing something here and I wasn't sure I wanted to know what it was.

Noah closed the door behind him and walked past me with the bag of breakfast. He dropped it on the table and headed for the bathroom. "I'm showering. Breakfast is in the bag."

Cass watched him until he was gone and then she looked at me. "Where did you guys go?" I pointed at the food in explanation. "We thought you might have gone to dump Noah's body somewhere."

I sat down beside Ellie and kissed her shoulder. She leaned into me, and Cass watched us with that same stupid look on her face. The three of us sat in silence and I dared her to make some comment that alluded to the fact that she and Ellie were obviously talking about our night. Girls did that. No big deal, but she couldn't hide it for shit.

"Good night last night?" she finally said. I knew it, she couldn't help herself. Ellie stiffened beside me and I looked at her just in time to see the warning glare that she was aiming at Cass.

"Good walk?" I retorted.

"It was awesome," she said, her tone heavily laced with sarcasm.

"You could have taken a cab."

"You had the money."

"Oh," I pretended to be surprised. "That's right. My bad."

She ignored me and stood up, heading toward the breakfast that was getting cold. Ellie joined her after I suggested that she should eat because we'd be on the road soon. The mood was vastly improved by the time we were all in the car. It felt more positive than it had in a while and I was glad that Noah and I had had the chance to clear the air. Even though we'd gotten thrown out of the concert early, it was still the best night that I'd had in a long time.

## Ellie

"How was the concert?" Eleanor asked at dinner that night. We were seated in the dining room, rather than the kitchen table. It was larger and more spacious, which accommodated Cass, who was there as well. She sat on the other side of the table beside Noah, who had been in a better mood than I'd seen him since I'd first arrived ten days ago.

"It was good," Leroy answered as he scooped a forkful of potato salad into his mouth. "Just a concert. The girls had the most fun, I think."

"The girls all swoon over Steven Tyler, don't they?" Eleanor giggled like a schoolgirl as she sipped her wine. Jacob raised his brow but chuckled from his end of the table. To be honest, my love for Steven Tyler had nothing to do with his appearance and everything to do with his voice and music.

"He's not bad for an older dude," Cass said.

Eleanor stared at Cass, likely thinking about the fact that she was older than the 'older dude.' If she was offended, she didn't say anything; instead, she fixed Leroy with a knowing smile. "So what were the sleeping arrangements like last night?"

Cass and I shared an alarmed look.

"Super comfortable," Leroy said, not missing a beat. "How was your night?"

"It was fine, thank you," she seemed mildly amused at her son's attempt to deflect the conversation. "I noticed that there was only one room on the receipt. I could have sworn you said that you were booking two."

"They had a two-beds-for-the-price-of-one deal," Noah jumped in. "Sweet, right?"

It was safe to say that Eleanor did not believe him.

"Oh," Leroy nodded, pointing his fork at his mom. "You meant arrangements as in *where* we slept. My bad. They only had one room left but luckily they had two queen beds. Noah and I shared, and it reminded me why I hated camping with him. He kicks like he's having a fit."

Eleanor narrowed her eyes at him. "Really? You shared with Noah? And Cass and Ellie shared?"

"Of course, Mom."

Then it was my turn to receive her interrogating stare. "Is that tr—"

Her sentence was interrupted when Cass's glass of juice was knocked over and OJ quickly spread toward the edge of the table. "My bad," Cass flailed and tried to catch the liquid with her hands. Eleanor shot up out of her seat and ran to collect a towel while the four of us shared a collective sigh of relief.

Jacob was oblivious. "This lamb is so tender."

Eleanor didn't bring up the conversation again and I wasn't sure if that was because she believed us or if she didn't want to find out that we'd lied. Either way, it made me feel incredibly guilty.

Leroy went to have a shower after dinner, Cass and Noah had gone for a walk to get snacks from the convenience store, and Jacob had gone to bed. It was just me in the living room, watching an episode of *Full House* while I waited for Leroy. That was until Eleanor came wandering in with her PJs on, her hair in rollers, and her makeup gone. She gave me a warm smile and sat down in her armchair.

"Have you been sleeping well in that spare room?"

I nodded. "The bed is comfortable. I really appreciate you letting me stay here for the rest of the summer."

"Not a problem at all, sweetheart. Our door is always open to friends of the boys."

*She was such a kind woman.* "Are you looking forward to going home, though? Missing Mom?"

"Yeah," I felt as if I was lying when I said that. I guess I did miss Momma, but it wasn't a desperate sort of miss. I was quite content here. "I'm looking forward to getting started on my correspondence course too. I have so many plans for effective, affordable skincare."

She straightened up and rested her chin in her hand. "That's nice, honey. It's lovely how much more accepting society is of working women today, isn't it?"

"What do you mean?"

"Well, I was in college in the '50s, and back then, the most common role that women had was a housewife. It was just . . . the way it was and women that were in the workforce were often secretaries. Or nurses. And I didn't want that. I wanted to be a news anchor more than anything. More than I wanted a husband.

More than I wanted children. It was very hard for a long time. I was dismissed a lot, belittled in the workplace, told time and time again that I would never get to where I wanted to be. I knew that if I got married and had children, it would put me behind in my career. So, I didn't until I'd achieved what I wanted to achieve."

"That's really inspiring," I said, in true awe of her determination.

Her gaze was distant as she smiled. "Yes. That's how I met Jacob, actually. I was running a segment on the first ever Superbowl in '67 and I interviewed him. It was quite immediate to be truthful. We fell in love very fast and he had an enormous amount of respect for the fact that I didn't want to begin a family until I was older. And I was thirty-two at that time."

"At least he supported that."

"Oh absolutely," Eleanor nodded and yawned again. "I wouldn't have married him if he hadn't. Mind you, there have been times where I've wondered if perhaps I did myself a disservice waiting so long to have children."

"How come?"

"Well, I'm sixty-four and I've still got a child in high school. How old will I be when Leroy and Noah decide to have children? How long will I have with my grandchildren? Sometimes I wonder if I should have tried to balance motherhood and working earlier than I did."

There was nothing that I could say to that, so I kept quiet. As far as I was concerned, she was an inspiration. She'd worked hard to accomplish a goal that she had for herself in a time that made it very difficult for women to do so.

"Not to mention the fact that I was always so much older than the other mothers. I think that it bothered the boys a little bit. Neither of them said so, but Noah was never that eager for me to do school drop-off or pick-up. Especially as he got older and started to notice that I looked more like his grandmother than his mother. I understood, though. It didn't upset me. Jacob, though, he got away with it—no one bats an eye at older fathers."

We laughed at that. She wasn't wrong but she seemed to take it in stride. The television hummed in the background, audience laughter and clapping crackling between us.

"But," she broke the quiet with a cheerful shrug. "It is what it is. I've had a wonderful career, a great marriage, and good kids. I can't complain."

"There is that," I said, and she smiled.

"I'll head off to bed. These pills are doing their job. See you in the morning, sweetheart."

"Goodnight."

A week later, on Wednesday, the night air was hot. Stars glittered in the black blanket of the sky above us. The sound of the Red Hot Chili Peppers was coming from the kitchen window where the radio sat on the windowsill. The soft glow of the pool lights was enchanting in a subtle but spectacular way, and my feet glided through the water as I sat on the edge of the swimming pool. We'd spent the last week in a comfortable pattern. We spent time with Cass and Noah. We went to football practice, the movies, parks, the arcade. It felt as though I had been here for months rather than weeks.

Eleanor and Jacob had gone to bed, so it was a good night to be out in the yard with the music going, and we didn't have to worry about how loud we spoke. Both of them were down for the count and Cass, Noah, Leroy, and I were in the fenced-in pool area. I adjusted the cup of my bikini and squealed when Leroy jumped in beside me.

"Babe," I laughed as he resurfaced and shook his sopping wet hair off, drenching me while I shielded myself.

Noah stood at the deeper end of the pool and turned around, doing an impressive backflip off the edge. The water was a tepid temperature, which was nice because while the air was hot, it cooled down once we were wet. Cass lounged on a pool chair and gave Noah an encouraging thumbs-up once he appeared again.

"Come in," Leroy didn't give me a chance to argue—he took my hand and pulled me down from the edge. I wrapped around him as we moved through the water. "I want to take you on a date, Els."

I clasped my hands behind his neck and wrapped my legs around his waist as he walked us around the pool. Noah was talking to Cass from the edge, but I was focused solely on the most handsome man that I had ever had the pleasure of knowing. "That'd be cute," I agreed, eager to go on a proper grown-up date with him.

"How about The Chateau?" He stared up at me through his thick lashes, the glow of the pool lights casting a luminous blue hue on his profile.

"Is that the five-star spot that we passed leaving the movies the other night? The one that looks like one in which I couldn't afford to use the toilet, let alone eat?"

"We can go wherever you want, Els. But you deserve to be wined and dined—I would love to treat my girl."

"You treat me every single time you look at me like that."

"Like what?" he asked, beads of water gathering on the tips of his hair.

"Like I'm the only girl in the world."

"You might as well be."

He kissed me and it was a testament to how much he meant what he said. As far as doting boyfriends went, I'd hit the jackpot. He always knew just what to say and there was never any room for doubt.

The sound of hands whipping through the water and Cass's piercing shrieks had both of us glance over at the other side of the pool, where Noah was showering his girlfriend with strong splashes. "Tell her to get in the pool!" Noah shouted, his hand smacking the surface of the water repeatedly.

"I'm not swimming!" Cass replied and retreated farther away so that he couldn't get her. Her curls had become flat from being wet and she used Noah's towel to pat down her front. "I have my period and I hate tampons."

"Thanks for sharing," Leroy sighed with a hint of amusement.

Something occurred to me then, and I did some quick, probably inaccurate equations in my head. I'd never paid a lot of attention to my cycle. As far as I was concerned, my period came when it came and there was no use giving it a lot of attention. But I began to realize I couldn't even remember when I'd last had it.

"You okay?"

I looked at Leroy and realized I had been zoned-out while I thought over the possibility that I could be pregnant. I smiled at him and nodded, not wanting to be dramatic, but the upturn in my stomach was making me nauseated. The mere possibility made me numb with fear.

That night while I washed my face, I went through the motions with a barely-there complex. The reflection didn't look like me—it was pale and twisted with dread. One little match was all it had taken to start a blaze of panicked thoughts, and now I couldn't stop imagining what would happen if it were true. How would my life change? What would Leroy say? What would Momma say? The nausea stirred in my stomach, making me curl over and grip the basin. Momma would be furious; her anger would be unfathomable. I took a few deep breaths and tried to calm down, because if I didn't, I was going to throw up and that was the last thing I needed. All of this worry was probably silly anyway. I'd watched the girls at home fret over late periods a dozen times and it was always just their imaginations running wild.

I hoped that was the case here too.

## Ellie

Thursday morning practice brought overcast weather for a change. It looked as though it might even rain. The football team and the cheerleaders seemed relieved that it was a bit cooler than usual, the clouds offering cover from the harsh summer sun. Cass sat beside me on the grass, no shades this morning, and chattered about celebrity news and gossip. I tried to ask questions and show interest. But I desperately wanted to shift the subject to me for a second.

"Cass," I cut her off and she paused, waiting for me to speak, "I'm late."

"For what?"

"My period."

Her brows shot up as she leaned back and winced. At her expression, I began to panic even harder than I had been before. There was something so daunting about having another person confirm how screwed I was through a single facial movement. After a mere few seconds her face smoothed over, and she lightly laughed.

"You do realize that you've been here for just under three weeks," she stated and spoke at a slow pace. "You can't be pregnant that fast."

"And you do realize that we had sex the first night that we met, almost two months ago," I replied in a tone that matched hers. She leaned back and pursed her lips as she contemplated the information.

"Still," she said. "It was one night. I doubt you're knocked up. The odds are low."

"I don't really want to talk about odds. I would rather just take a test and be sure so that I can stop stressing out about it."

"We could get a test from the pharmacy," she said, "but don't you want to talk to Leroy about this first?"

Cass picked the grass in front of her, the ringlets on her head whipping around her face as she stared expectantly, waiting for a response that I wasn't sure how to give. He would be the first person that I would want to consult and confide in when it came to something so serious. But the last thing I wanted to do was panic him for no good reason.

I shook my head and gazed out at him, where he was giving orders to the team. "I'll just do it and tell him afterwards."

"I dunno. That seems like a bad idea. He'd want to know," Cass argued. I fixed her with a questioning glare.

"Would you tell Noah if you weren't one hundred percent sure what the result was?"

She flinched. It was barely noticeable, but I knew that I had her. She sighed. "Nope. He'd be pissed if I'd gotten him worried for no reason."

"Exactly."

"Come on, then." She stood up and stretched her arms above

her head before she pulled me up as well. "Let's go and do this test."

"What, now?"

"Why not?" She shrugged as we began toward the gate. "He's occupied with practice. I'm here for support. Now is perfect. Might as well just get it over with."

"I suppose," I mumbled, feeling a little more nervous now that I was actually about to do the test. Cass picked up her feet in an excited skip as she gripped my arm.

"It would be kind of cute if you were pregnant," she held up her palm to silence me when I recoiled. "Like, not cool. But sort of. I could be Aunt Cass. I'd be that aunt. The one that drinks too much at events and embarrasses everyone. And of course, I'd be the fun aunt that the kid comes to when it wants to experience weed for the first time or the one it comes to when it runs away from home because Mom and Dad are lame."

"Your imagination is something else," I said. "I'd rather not talk hypothetically, though. None of that's going to happen even if the test is positive."

I looked both ways before I crossed the street and ignored Cass, who I could feel staring at me and not watching where she was walking at all. We weaved through a group of young kids who were trading cards outside the pharmacy and walked through the electric doors, into the cool air-conditioned store.

"You wouldn't keep it?"

"No," I said and scanned the shelves as we walked. "I'm not in a position to have a child right now. I haven't studied. I don't have a lot of money. I'm too young. There are a lot of factors, I suppose."

"Yeah but—"

"Here it is," I snatched the box off the shelf that was surrounded by other related products, such as prenatal vitamins, condoms, and lubricants. How ironic that it was all shelved together. "Come on. I want to get this done before we have to be back at the field."

Cass followed along behind me while I paid for it. She suggested that I might need a bottle of water or something so that I could pee, but I already needed to. We both walked back to the school as fast as we could and as we approached the field, Cass steered me toward the gymnasium so that I could use the girls' locker room toilets.

"Shit, it's locked," she slammed her fist on the wooden door. "The cheerleaders must keep the key on them." She turned around and stared at the other side of the foyer before she looked at me with intent.

When it dawned on me that she was suggesting that I use the boys' locker room toilets, I shook my head and tried the girls' door again. "Gross, no. I am not using the boys' room. The filth."

"We don't have time to be concerned about the labels on the doors. "She gripped my shoulders and pushed me across the wooden floor.

"It's not the labels on the doors! It's the piss on the toilet seats and the stench of body odor that might kill me!"

"I'll come in with you," she said, as if her presence made some sort of difference to the hygiene situation. She ignored my protests and pushed me inside where a wall of potent sweat and dirty laundry hit us and we both screwed our noses up as we shuffled toward the toilets.

I gagged when I pushed the stall door open. "This is feral."

"Don't be dramatic," Cass said. "Don't touch the seat. Just squat and pee."

After I had unboxed the stick and scanned the instructions to make sure that I didn't pee on the wrong end, I did what she said and squatted over the seat. I put the garbage into the box, flushed, and tucked the capped stick under my arm so that I could open the door.

I felt as though I was checked out and not entirely present while I went through the motions. I'd detached myself in order to evade a panic attack. "Where should I put this garbage?" I asked Cass when I opened the stall door. She was fluffing her hair in the mirror above the basin and held her hand out to receive the box.

Before I could stop her, she pulled a lighter out of her overall pocket and lit the box on fire, dropping it into the stainless steel sink. "Cass! Put it out!" I reached out to turn the faucet on, but she stopped me.

"Relax," she ordered, keeping a hold on my wrists. "I do this all the time when I steal my test papers from the teachers."

I gave her a concerned look and she elaborated. "Before they can give it back, I take it and write down what I did wrong. Burn the paper and then I re-sit the test to up my grade."

"Does that work?"

"Every time."

Once the box was charred, she turned the faucet on and soaked the hot bits of black cardboard that were soon washed down the drain. It was all a bit dramatic, but I appreciated her efforts to stop this from getting out. I had a feeling that she might have just enjoyed setting things on fire.

"Okay, let's see that test." She gave an encouraging nod.

But all I could do was begin to feel panicked. I clamped my sweaty palms together and took a few deep breaths that didn't help ease the anxiety at all. "Do you want me to look at it first?"

The stick tucked under my arm began to feel as though it weighed a solid ton. It seemed insane that such a small object had so much power. It could change everything in the snap of a moment, and I knew that I couldn't avoid finding out what it said, but I still wanted to stall for as long as possible.

Reluctantly I nodded and let Cass take the test from me. I remained glued to the spot, my hands came up and rested in front of my chin as I waited with a pounding heart. She'd barely had a chance to look at it when I snatched it from her grasp. "Nope, forget it, I can't risk you playing a prank and telling me the wrong result."

She seemed baffled at the logic, but I ignored her and bit the bullet, reading the result in the little clear window. "Oh no . . ."

Cass stared at me with a dropped jaw, her expression an almost dead ringer for how I felt inside. "Are you sure?"

"It's positive, Cass."

I handed her the stick with trembling hands. I felt shell-shocked. I couldn't believe this was happening. I couldn't under-stand how, after just one night together, we had conceived a child. The longer I stood and let the thoughts weigh me down, the more panicked I became. There was a plan in place for this situation. I knew what I wanted to do. I knew what steps I would take. I had always been efficient. But that didn't stop me from reeling into a downward spiral.

"What now?" Cass questioned, handing the test back. I slipped it into my pocket and shook my head.

Should I tell Leroy? Should I go home and tell Momma? Should I just phone her and have an abortion here?

I felt so overwhelmed that all I could do was sink down into a crouch as I attempted to regulate my breathing. It was all too much, and I didn't know what to do first or how to even make sense and order out of the loud and hostile voices that were screaming at me to start making decisions.

"I am fucked," I said, staring at the concrete floor. "Fucked."

"Did you just swear?"

"Cass," I stood up and gripped her shoulders as she stared at me with alarm. "Tell me what to do. I don't know what to do."

"You should tell Leroy, for starters," she said as she wrapped an arm around my shoulder and led me out of the locker rooms. "I think that he'll be the best help. He's levelheaded, you know?"

When we got outside, I wasn't surprised to see the rain had started to fall. It seemed fitting, to be honest. Gloomy weather for the gloomy mood. The team was already packing up the equipment and heading toward us. Cass and I stood under the shelter of the steps and waited. I was barely aware of the guys that passed us, my thoughts wrapped up in my doom, but I tried hard to detach and remain calm.

"Els?"

I looked up at the sound of Leroy and met his concerned expression. His shirt was clinging to his frame, rain beads cascading down his face. He must have sensed that something was wrong because he handed the cones he was cradling to one of his teammates as he passed.

"What's wrong?"

"I'll leave you to talk," Cass said, touching a supportive hand to my shoulder before she ran down the stairs and sprinted over to the gate.

"Leroy—"

"What's going on?" Leroy closed the distance between us and put his wet hands on my cheeks, forcing me to meet his worried stare. "Els, you're scaring me. What is it?"

"I'm pregnant," I sobbed. Leroy's expression fell, his eyes cast down at my stomach as though he'd be able to confirm it for himself.

He stammered for a moment, his mouth opening but no words coming out as he shook his head. "Ellie, I don—"

"I'm terminating the pregnancy," I interrupted him, raising my voice a little to compete with the rain that had started to pelt down on the iron awning above us. I hoped no one was still hanging around within earshot.

His brows pulled together in question and I nodded, wishing I had been strong enough to do this without telling him. I could have taken care of it without putting a single burden on his shoulders.

"Why?" He dropped his hands from my face and stepped back.

I wasn't sure what to expect from him, but it hadn't been that. "Because . . . Leroy, I'm only eighteen. I don't have a lot of money. I have things that I need to accomplish before I have children. I can't even cook for goodness's sake. It's just—"

"That's it?" he snapped. "You can't cook so you're just going to get rid of our child?"

"*That* was what you got from that?" I shouted. He exhaled a frustrated breath and turned around, heading down the steps and into the thick rain. Of course, I was left to wonder what the heck had just happened. I watched him, flabbergasted for a moment as he stormed across the grass toward the exit gate.

When I was finally able to get a grip, I snapped into it and ran after him. The rain was heavy, but it was almost warm, and I tried to keep my eyes open as I ran across the sopping grass. I caught up to him as he reached the gate and put my full force into shoving his back. I didn't realize how mad I was until I put hands on him, and he turned around with broad shoulders and a pained expression.

"I could use some support right now," I shouted, giving his chest another shove. "You're just gonna make me feel like shit and then leave me? What is wrong with you?"

"Have you even thought about what I want?" He stepped forward. His eyes were narrowed because of the rain and it made him appear even more intimidating. "Did you consider how I would feel, for even a second?"

"Of course, I did! You're going to be playing college football. You'll be going pro. You'll be doing what you've always wanted to, and I'm not going to stand in the way of that. I won't do that!"

"That's not your decision to make!" He stepped closer again. "Maybe I want this baby. Maybe I want that, with you. There's no one else in this world that I would want to have a child with. Maybe I want you to have this child, Ellie."

He looked distraught and it killed me. I couldn't handle hearing the pain in his voice, so I lifted a hand and caressed his wet cheek, my heart pounding as he leaned into it. "That's not your decision to make," I softly repeated his own words. "I'm not ready."

The rain rolled over his defeated expression, the storm in his gaze so much heavier than the one in the sky. He ran a hand through his soaked hair to push it back from his face. "So, what then? What now?"

"I need to go home, Leroy."

"Then I'll come with you."

I shook my head as I pulled on the front of my shirt. My clothes were clinging to me, wet and heavy. "No, Leroy. You won't even be allowed in the house after I tell Momma about this. I need to take care of this on my own."

He stepped forward again and rested his forehead on mine. "Don't do this. Please don't."

"Leroy," I warned with a trembling voice. I hated this. I hated it more than he knew.

He didn't argue again. But I could see how torn he felt, and it broke me. It tore me to pieces to know that he wanted something I couldn't give him. I was so afraid this would change things between us, that he would resent me for what I had to do. And I think that deep down, he knew this would change things between us as well because his hand wrapped around my waist, his other around my neck, and he pulled me in, kissing me as though his life depended on it.

It was desperate. His kiss was clutching on for dear life and I could feel the pain. I could feel the arguments he still wanted to make. I could feel the pleading and heartbreak. His tongue moved against mine, fast and unforgiving, and after a moment, he pulled me up, wrapping my legs around his waist. The rain poured down on us as he walked us out of the gate and over to the car. He fumbled with the door for a moment, and then he pulled it open and pushed me into the backseat.

He was silent as he pulled the door shut behind him. He

hovered over top of me and brought our lips back together as he pushed my soaked skirt up and fumbled with my panties to get them down. The leather underneath me became slippery from our rain-drenched clothes but nothing distracted us as we freed our bottom halves.

The way that he made love to me was as desperate as the kiss had been. Like he knew that we were limited for time. Like he knew that once we left this school and faced having to tell our parents, everything would be different. And it would be. So we gave ourselves this. We had rough, desperate, wordless sex in the backseat of his car and we let it say goodbye for us.

## LEROY

Ellie is the love of my life. I know that because I'm better when I'm with her. And not just in the sense of who I am as a person, but how I feel and look at the world. She reminds me that no matter how impossible a situation feels, there's a way to get through it. She encourages kindness and optimism. She sees the best in people, and she refuses to let the behavior of other people alter how she responds. Ellie is the woman I want beside me when I go through whatever hard times I might face, and she's the woman I want to celebrate our achievements with. Trusting her is like second nature because goodness radiates from her very core.

Which is why I so badly wanted to convince her that despite how helpless this situation seemed, we could move through it together. She was pregnant, and even though the timing wasn't right, there was no one else with whom I could imagine having a child. There was no one else I would ever want to have a family with, and I didn't care how crazy that sounded because we were eighteen and what could we know about forever? But damn it, how could I not know it was forever when I looked at her and I saw her beside me when I graduated. I saw her on the sidelines, waiting for me after I played for the NFL for the first time. I saw her accepting an award for the best new skincare brand. I saw her cutting a tall white cake in a beautiful dress. I saw her sitting in the seats of a school function, exuding pride as she watched her children perform. I saw us sitting in our matching armchairs, old and happy in the life that we had created together. She was beside me through it all and I could see it crystal clear. To me, that was forever.

Maybe this wasn't exactly how I imagined our journey to parent-hood together going, but it was just one of those situations we would get through together. Even if we didn't agree, she was right—I couldn't tell her what to do. It was her body, her decision. It killed me, it did, and I was worried about the impact this would have on her because, even though she'd made up her mind, she hadn't stopped sobbing since she'd told me. Shaking, apologizing. All I wanted was for her to be okay, one hundred percent okay, in whatever choice she made, and that seemed impossible when either choice was going to be life-changing.

Mom was home. We heard her car pull into the drive and Ellie and I sat beside each other on the sofa, waiting with trepidation to tell her what was going on. There was no point in hiding it. Ellie wanted to go home; her flight needed to be changed. Mom would want to know what was going on, and I knew that even though she was going to be disappointed, she'd help.

Ellie twisted her hands together in her lap, her knuckles turning white. Before she could break her own fingers, I took her hand in mine and let her squeeze it as hard as she wanted to.

"She's going to hate me," she mumbled, her mouth barely opening enough to let the words out. "She let me into her home and I—"

"Stop that," I whispered when I heard the front door open. "She won't hate you. Both of us did this. And we did it before she let you into her home."

She looked at me; damn, she could not stop trembling. "Really? That's your loophole?"

"Yea—"

"Afternoon," Mom wandered in and stepped down into the living area, her coat damp from the rain. Her smile started to dissolve as she looked between Ellie and me. "What's the matter?"

"Mom," I started to stand up, but Ellie's grip tightened, refusing to let me leave her side. As much as I wanted to show Mom the respect that she deserved by standing to let her know what was going on, Ellie needed me and that was important. "Mom, Ellie is pregnant."

As if the words had power, she stepped backward, her mouth fell open, and she breathed so visibly hard that I worried she would pass out. For a while, no one said a thing. Silence enveloped us, suffocating to the point that I wanted to open a window. If she didn't speak soon, I was going to have to talk and with the nerves that were coursing through me, I doubted it would be a logical conversation.

"I'm sorry." Ellie was quiet beside me, a tear slipping down her cheek. Mom didn't look at her in anger, but she did turn to me with an expectant stare.

"Oh, me too," I added. "I'm sorry. We weren't as careful as we should have been."

"I don't know what to say," she slowly walked over to her

armchair and sat down. "This is not a great situation. But it's not . . . impossible. It is hard to navigate, though. How long have you two known?"

"I took the test this morning," Ellie sniffed and wiped her face. "I told Leroy straight away."

"Have you called your mother?"

Ellie shook her head and I thought now might be a good time to let Mom know what her plan was. "Mom, Ellie is going to go home and . . . well, she's going to terminate the pregnancy."

If I thought Mom looked disappointed before, that was nothing compared to the expression that she was wearing now. Selfishly, I wanted her to help me change Ellie's mind. But I loved this girl too much to let her feel pressured. That wouldn't be fair. I prepared to defend her but before I could, Mom nodded.

"All right, well, the sooner we can arrange the flight home, the better. I'll organize that and when I have, you can call your mother to let her know you'll be coming home." Mom nodded between the two of us, her eyes beginning to glisten. That hurt. "Ellie, I do not put the blame solely on you. You're a good girl. You're always welcome in my home. That's not to say that I'm not disappointed in both of you. For all your mature ways, this was a very immature mistake that should have been avoided. Especially by you, Leroy. I always made sure that you knew better."

"I know." I couldn't even look at her. "I'm sorry."

"Me too," she said and stood up, leaving the room. It was obvious to me that wasn't the end of the conversation, but a pin was in it for now. All things considered, it could have gone a lot worse.

Ellie let out a quivering breath, more tears too. She shot up out of her seat, so I did too, keeping close as she aggressively wiped at her eyes and cheeks. "I'm going to go upstairs," she whispered. "I need to lie down or pack or something."

"Come on," I told her and took her hand. We walked upstairs, passing Noah as we went. Ellie kept her head down, but it was still painfully obvious that she was upset. By some miracle, Noah didn't question it or make some careless remark, he just watched us until we were out of sight. I closed Ellie's bedroom door behind us, pulled her onto the bed with me, and then we snuggled down, getting comfortable.

"Your mom looked so disappointed," Ellie said, fighting to keep her voice even. It wouldn't have mattered how still she kept her voice; her shoulders were shaking. "This isn't how I wanted the start of our relationship to go, Leroy."

"I know, baby," I murmured, kissing the top of her head. "We'll get through it."

She didn't respond and I wasn't sure how to take that because it scared me to think that she didn't agree. It didn't help that she wouldn't let me go back to Waco with her so that we could be together during this process. It made me ill to think about the fact that I couldn't hold her hand or hug her after the procedure was over. I felt like I should be there for her and it was going to be hard not to be. But respecting her choices seemed more important right now.

After a while of quietly internalizing my thoughts, or trying to understand them, Ellie's breathing became shallow and I carefully peered down to see her lids closed, lips parted. Even in her sleep, she looked distressed. Still, it must have been somewhat more peaceful than being awake and endlessly tearing up over the fact that her life had been turned upside down. As much as I wanted to stay right there with her, I was too restless, and I didn't want to wake her up. Carefully shifting out from under her head, I hopped off the bed and slipped out of the room.

Dad was on the back deck when I wandered outside, hoping to find some sense of calm in the fresh air. It was still raining— not as heavy as it had been this morning but enough that I stayed under the deck awning. Dad had been out most of the morning and I wasn't sure when he got back but it was obvious that Mom had found time to fill him in. He watched me, perplexed, as I slowly approached and sat down on the opposite side of the outdoor table. The worst part was the silence while I waited for him to say something. It wasn't going to be pretty, that was for sure. He'd warned me about this, less than a month ago. *Don't be acting stupid, boy.* He was going to blow a fuse and I couldn't blame him.

"I love you, son," he finally said, and for some reason that I couldn't understand, that sentence alone hit me right in the middle of the chest and I dropped my head into my hands, tears coming on in full force. "It's going to be okay, Leroy. No matter what happens, all right?"

I nodded, still hiding my face. It killed me that I'd let my father down. He'd always been there for me, talked to me, communicated as if I were an equal and not a child because he trusted me and trusted that I was responsible. I'd let him down in the one way that he'd always cautioned me about. Suddenly, I felt his hand under my arm, pulling me up out of the chair. As soon as I stood, he pulled me into a tight hug, and I cried even harder. The shame of his disappointment was ten times worse than the shame I'd felt when mom told me off in the living room, and I didn't think that was possible.

"I'm sorry," my voice was muffled by tears and his shoulder. "I'm sorry, Dad."

"I know," he said, holding the back of my head. "It's not good, son, but it'll be fine. Your mother and I love you and we're here. We're disappointed, but we're here."

We stood like that for a while and the comfort he provided was relief I didn't think I would have when it came to Dad knowing the truth. I'd expected to be reamed out and told what an idiot I was. Not that he'd ever treated me like that before, so I wasn't sure where that fear came from. Perhaps it was a self-reflection of how I felt about myself in that moment.

When we parted, I was calmer, and we sat down in our chairs again. Dad inhaled a deep breath and his gaze went out across the back garden. The lawn was pooling and the flower petals were dotted with raindrops. "I have to ask," he said. "No condom?"

I shook my head.

"Why not?"

There was no good reason. "It was a heat-of-the-moment thing, I guess. We didn't talk about it. We . . . we were stupid."

"You were," he said, shrugging unapologetically when I looked at him. "How often have you done that? And I don't mean with Ellie."

"That was the first time," I mumbled.

He sighed and rubbed his face. "As much as I hate to ask, did you at least . . . you know . . ."

He rolled his arm in a circular motion, brows raised as if I should understand what the hell he was asking. "What?"

"Did you pull out?"

"Ugh. Yeah, Dad. I did."

"Not very effective, told you that before."

"Yeah, I know."

Again, silence descended upon us. We watched the rain pelting down on the pool, creating rippled patterns, listening to the light drum on the tree leaves. Questions kept on forming on the tip of my tongue. Questions about parenthood and fatherhood. But it seemed pointless considering we weren't going to get that far. So, I sat there and said nothing.

"Sometimes I forget that you're only eighteen," Dad suddenly said, folding his arms across his chest. "You're mature and sensible for the most part. It's easy to think you're a hell of a lot older than you are. But the fact is, you're a teenager and teenagers make mistakes. Hell, even adults do. I've met a ton of grown men who don't have the amount of common sense that you do."

I wasn't sure how to respond to that.

He chuckled quietly. "Not sure what my point is, except that you're a good kid who made a dumb decision. We've all been there."

Dad probably had an entire past of choices he wasn't proud of. The man was sixty-five. He'd lived a long life, especially before he had children. But it was hard to imagine him screwing up because he'd always been my hero and I didn't want to ask him about his past because right now, hearing his cock-ups would make me feel better about mine. And I didn't deserve that at the moment.

Mom stepped onto the deck then, her eyes red-rimmed, and I felt so damn awful. "Oh, there you are," she said. "Ellie's flight is at eleven in the morning. She needs to be there two hours earlier than that to check in. You'll need to leave here at about seven. Understood?"

"Yes, Mom."

"The tickets will be waiting at the gate for you, it's all arranged."

"Thank you."

She turned around and left again without another word.

"She'll be okay," Dad said when we could no longer hear her footsteps in the kitchen. "She's just hurting and disappointed. Give her some time."

"I don't blame her. She has every right to be pissed off."

Dad wore a small smile. "That's right. She does."

## Ellie

It was dark when I woke up from a nap, one I hadn't intended to take but must have needed. Even after hours of sleep, I still felt fatigued, my eyes swollen and sore and my head hammering. Crying never did me any favors—it was exhausting, physically and mentally. Instead of getting up to find Leroy, I lay there and stared at the ceiling, thinking about how devastated Eleanor looked when we told her the news. Even worse still when I told her that I wasn't going to keep it.

It was obvious that she wanted to be a grandmother but the fact that she didn't voice that or berate me or attempt to change my mind made me feel even worse. She knew what it meant to be a woman who'd had to fight for her rights. She might have understood me better than anyone. That didn't mean it wasn't hurting her—that thought alone threatened to push me over the edge of the pit I'd just barely climbed out of while I slept.

There was a tap on the door, and I lifted my head to see Leroy hovering at the entrance. I sat up and tried to smile.

"How are you feeling?" he asked, sitting down on the edge of the bed.

"I'm not sure."

That seemed to be an acceptable answer because he didn't press me to elaborate. "Mom arranged the flight home. We have to be out of here at seven in the morning."

"Okay. Thanks."

"You hungry?"

"Not really," I said, sitting up beside him. "I don't have much of an appetite right now. Have you eaten?"

"Yeah. There's a plate for you in the fridge that I can heat up when you get hungry."

"Would it be rude if I hung out in here for the rest of the night?"

Leroy slowly shook his head, as if he was unsure of his own answer. "Everyone is sort of scarce at the moment. No idea where Mom is. Dad is out at a friend's place. Noah went to see Cass. You don't have to hide out if you're worried about bumping into people."

"No, I'm just tired," I lied. "I think I'll sleep some more. After I pack."

"Want a hand?"

"Sure."

Leroy and I went through the drawers and we folded clothes in silence. His hands had a slight tremble that I noticed whenever he lowered something into my suitcase. The tension between us was killing me; it felt so unnatural, like neither of us knew how to behave.

"I haven't even called Momma," I said, an immediate knot of nerves forming in my stomach at the thought of having that conversation. "She's going to want to know what happened, but I don't think I should tell her over the phone."

"It could give her time to swallow the news," he suggested. "You know, give her time to get over that initial reaction before you have to see each other."

"She's going to lose it," I said, feeling nauseated.

"I wish I could be there, Els. I feel like I should be there."

This time when I tried to smile, it was full and genuine. His selflessness never failed to amaze me. He wanted nothing but to ensure that I was okay, and it made it harder knowing that I was leaving him behind to do something that he didn't want for us.

"Trust me," I said, putting the last dress into my suitcase. "You're helping me by not coming. Momma isn't going to handle this well. She'll be awful and I don't want her taking it out on you."

He stepped forward and drew me in at the waist, his gaze full of determination as he stared down at me. "I don't care. I can handle it."

"I know you can. But I couldn't. I couldn't handle her being nasty toward you. She can be . . . brutal when things upset her. I know what she's like and I just couldn't stomach it. It'll be easier for me not to have to witness that."

He chewed the inside of his cheek and nodded. "If that's what you want."

"It is."

"You're going to wait for me, right? Until I get to Waco?"

His expression was concerned, and I felt my chest tighten at how vulnerable he looked. It broke my heart that he believed anything less. "Of course. Leroy, I love you. Of course I'll be waiting for you."

And I meant what I said. I would wait for him because I loved him, more than anything. But things felt . . . different. Something had shifted and I knew he felt it too. He didn't like the decision that I was making, and it scared me. It scared me because I worried that in the future, he would resent me for it. And if he made me keep the baby, then I would resent him for that. It seemed like we were trapped in a lose-lose situation and it broke my heart.

I went to bed after we'd finished packing up the bags. Leroy wanted to stay with me, but I didn't think that would be a good idea after everything. I couldn't sleep, though—I was in overdrive. Different thoughts and scenarios plagued me all night, keeping me tossing and turning repeatedly as I stressed out about what I was going to do. First, I had to tell Momma and then I had to book an appointment. How would this change things between Leroy and me? Would he support me in the future? Would he come to hate me for it?

Would *I* hate me for it?

My hand involuntarily came to rest on my stomach, and I felt my chest tighten in response. It was like I had zero control over the thoughts that were shouting at me.

This baby was a piece of us both.

I had never experienced such an overwhelming concoction of emotions. It was too much to handle and it made me wish that I had some sort of vision into the future so I could see the outcome of each scenario. It would help to know what was in store for me.

It would help me feel secure in my choice.

✦

The next morning, Leroy and I were up and heading out by seven in the morning. There was a solemnness in the air, desperation to change the situation and total devastation because it was impossible to salvage our summer. Eleanor was in the kitchen when I went to use the phone. She was dressed for work and stood in front of the sink, rinsing her coffee cup. I hadn't seen her since Leroy and I had told her about the pregnancy. The hardest part was the awkward tension between us that hadn't existed before. We'd become close in such a short time and all I wanted was to have that back.

"Good morning," she said. It was kind enough, but I could feel the shift in her tone. "You're all sorted then?"

"Yes, thank you."

"Good," she came around the kitchen countertop and stood in front of me. "You have a safe flight, all right? Call Leroy to let him know when you're home."

"Mmhmm," I nodded, fighting tears. "Thank you for having me, and I'm . . . I'm sorry again. About what happened."

Her shoulders fell, an overall softness seeping into her demeanor. "It's forgiven, Ellie. We're going to miss you. Come back soon, okay?"

If I answered her, I'd end up letting the floodgates open and I didn't want to cry again. There had been enough of that last night. She stretched out her arms and wrapped me in a gentle hug, holding me together while fragments of my shattered heart threatened to fall on the floor. When she let me go, she didn't hang around, but left the room before I was able to apologize for the thousandth time. As much as I wanted to say goodbye to Jacob, I knew he would be asleep for a while longer, so I went over to the telephone and dialed Amber's number.

"Hello?" She sounded half asleep, which didn't surprise me. It was only an hour ahead in Texas.

"Hey, it's me," I said.

"Els? What's the matter?"

"I'm coming home a little earlier than planned and I was wondering if you could pick me up from the airport?"

"Is everything okay? Why are you coming home early?"

I clutched the phone in my hand and felt my chin trembling. "I can't talk about it right now. Can you pick me up this morning?"

"Of course," she sounded more awake than she had before. "What time does the flight get in?"

"Twelve," I said.

"I'll be there."

I gave her the flight details and we ended the call. I was immensely grateful to have such a good friend who was willing to show up, no questions asked. Telling Momma the truth over the phone wasn't right—as much as I wanted to take the easy way out, I needed to tell her in person and if I let her know that I was coming home early, she would have pressed to know why. This gave me a little more time to prepare for how I would break the news.

It was warm outside; the rain had stopped overnight and the sun was peeping out from behind early-morning clouds that had been dipped in orange ink and left to dry in the sun. It was a gorgeous morning and I wished I could have been in the right frame of mind to appreciate it. Leroy was leaning against the trunk of the car, arms folded, gaze distant. The sunlight kissed the top of his head and gave him a halo. The thought of missing him made me ache.

We made eye contact just as Cass came running up the footpath with her curls in a bun and her overalls barely buttoned up. "Ellie!" She waved me down and seemed relieved to see that I hadn't left yet. She stopped in front of me and gave Leroy a brief wave.

"I'll wait in the car," he said, and Cass gripped my elbow and pulled me a little farther from the vehicle.

"What happened?"

"Noah didn't fill you in?"

"Well, he did," she said. "But like, I need more intimate details. Share? Are you coming back?"

I shook my head with a sad smile. "I won't be allowed to once Momma finds out. But it is what it is."

"Bitch, I'm gonna miss you," she pouted.

"I'll miss you too."

"I'm coming to visit in Waco, okay?"

"I would love that, Cass."

"Come on, babe," Leroy called from the car. "As much as I don't want you to leave, you're going to miss the flight."

When I turned back to Cass, she was giving him a sympathetic look. I could tell she knew how he felt about the situation. Still, she gave me a warm smile and pulled me in for a hug before I left. During the drive out of town, I couldn't help but watch the views that passed us with sad regret. I'd come to fit in so well in such a short time. I'd made friends and memories that I would keep forever. It was a town that felt just right. I felt like I belonged here, more than at my actual home. I'd never been so sad to leave a place before. And it was for more reasons than just Leroy.

My flight was boarding, and I glanced at the woman who was checking the boarding passes. "Call me when you land?" Leroy said, quiet, defeated, as he had been since we'd left the house. It was obvious that both of us wanted nothing more than to turn back time and do things differently. Whenever I thought about how the rest of this summer should have gone, it winded me. It's hard to accept how wrong a plan can go in the blink of an eye.

"Of course, I will."

His jaw clenched as he stared down at me, a strand of hair falling onto his forehead. "Els," he said, his voice hitching. "There is nothing . . . *nothing* I wouldn't do for you. You need me, call me, and I'll be in Waco in a few hours. You can call me in the middle of the night, whenever. I promise I'll answer. I'll be there."

He was going out of focus, blurring at the moistening of my eyes. "I know," I inhaled a shaken breath. "I know, Leroy."

It wasn't possible to keep a lone tear from falling down my cheek and he took my head in his hands, swiping it with his thumb before he pressed his lips against mine. I took a moment to absorb it all. The feel of his fingertips. The feel of his love. I was sure I couldn't be soothed in such a way by anyone else on earth. He was one of a kind and no part of me wanted to lose him.

"I love you, Leroy," I sobbed, our eyes still fixed on one another.

"I love you too, Ellie."

N

Amber was waiting for me in the airport lounge, just as she'd promised she would be. Her sweet, familiar face was a comfort that I needed after the longest two hours that I'd ever endured. But much to my surprise, she wasn't alone. It was a nice distraction to see that Eric stood beside her, his arm around her waist. Amber had her hair in locs—she'd been wanting them done for a while, but the school wouldn't allow it. She'd graduated now, so she could do what she wanted.

Eric stood a head taller, his golden-brown skin a few shades darker, no doubt thanks to the Texan sun. They made a gorgeous couple and by the time I reached them, I'd had time to realize this must have happened after I had connected with them by phone last week.

"Hello, gorgeous," Eric swept me into a bear hug before I could utter a hello. "What'd he do? Do I need to head home and throw down with that mofo?"

I laughed into his shoulder and shook my head when he set me down. "We haven't broken up."

Amber touched a hand to my arm, concern all over her face. "What happened then, chick?"

"It's just complicated," I told her, staring at the ground. It was hard to lie to Amber. She knew me too well. "I don't want to get into it right now."

"That's okay," Eric gave me a light jab in the shoulder, and I smiled, grateful for their acceptance of my silence. My attention moved between them as we started heading for the exit, me pulling my suitcase behind me.

"So, when did this happen? I thought you were off to college, Eric?"

He threw his arm around Amber, absolute glee on his face as he kissed her temple. "I arrived last night, to be honest. We hit it off over the phone, talked ever since, and then I thought, what the hell, we're going to the same college, might as well spend the rest of summer together before we go. Right, Prez?"

"Prez?" I questioned.

"Oh, I called her princess once," Eric said, and Amber started laughing as we stepped out into the hot afternoon sun. I'd almost forgotten how damn unbearable the weather is here. "But she said she doesn't want to be a princess; she wants to be the president. So I said, I get it babe, and Prez was born."

"That's cute," I said. As beautiful as their blossoming relationship was, beautiful enough to distract me from the grief that I was feeling from my own, I couldn't help but feel a pang of envy. Now might have been a good time to insist that they use birth control. Knowing Amber, though, she was all over it.

The closer that we got to home, to the inevitable truth that I would have to tell Momma, the more I slipped from reality, isolating my mind in order to keep from falling apart in the backseat of the car. Perhaps she would surprise me. Eleanor managed to remain calm when her son's entire future was on the line. Perhaps Momma would tell me that I didn't have to terminate the pregnancy. Perhaps she'd tell me that we should come up with some other plan because being a teen mom wasn't the end of the world. She'd done it. She survived. Perhaps she'd tell me that I would too.

*N*

"You told me nothing had happened with him," Momma snapped, pacing the living room while she chewed on her thumbnail. "You promised me that it wasn't physical. Lord, Ellie! You met the boy once! When did you even find the time to sleep together?"

"I don't think that you need to know that."

"I do," she said with a hostile tone. "My daughter is pregnant by a boy that she'd met *once*."

"Momma," I sobbed because I hadn't stopped bawling from the moment she came home from work and found me in the middle of the living room. "You're making it sound like it was a one-night stand."

"But it *was*!" she threw her hands up. "It would have been. If he hadn't kept in contact."

"Well, he did." I sniffed into a tissue and swiped at my cheeks with the back of my hand. "He loves me, Momma. So, leave it alone. What's done is done and I'm going to deal with it."

"And who is going to pay for this termination?" She stopped pacing and folded her arms. "I sure as hell can't afford it. You need to phone the doctor. You need to go through counseling. You need to have an ultrasound and tests done before you even get to the cost."

I hadn't even thought about that, and as strange as it was, I felt this surge of relief move through me. It confused me because I knew that I wasn't ready to be a mother, but the more time that passed, the harder it was to imagine going through with the termination.

"You have savings, I assume?"

I looked at my mother and couldn't recognize who was looking back at me. Disappointment was nothing new, but this was something else. This was hostile disgust and loathing. She was furious.

"Yeah," I mumbled, standing up so that I could go to my bedroom, but before I could leave, she gripped my elbow to stop me.

"I don't think you should see him again," Momma said. "He's trouble."

"You don't know a thing about him," I bit back and pulled my arm out of her grasp. "He's a good man and I won't be told otherwise."

When I went to leave the second time, she let me go. I knew that Momma would be upset about the pregnancy, but I expected a little more support, a gentler approach perhaps. I hadn't expected her to be so cold and awful, as if I'd done it on purpose. As I stormed up the short corridor and into my bedroom, which was a mess from the haphazard unpacking, I felt tears welling up again. The door slammed when I swung it shut and I collapsed into a heap on the single bed.

Although I was home with my momma and in the place that I'd spent my entire life, I felt so alone, out of place. I already missed Leroy and while I was so distraught, I wanted him with me. Without even thinking about it, my hands moved up and cradled my stomach. I thought about the fact that a part of him was with me, and in some turn of event, it helped me not to feel so alone.

*"Hey, baby," Leroy came in through the back door and set his gear down. "Smells good in here."*

*"I'm making your favorite," I smiled and let him kiss me on the cheek before he leaned over and inhaled the aroma of fresh cooking. "The kids will be excited to see you."*

*"Ooh, where are they?"*

*"Playing upstairs." I arched backward so I could shout in the direction of the staircase. "Abby, Drayton! Daddy is home!"*

*The sound of little footsteps came barreling down the staircase and my two blond darlings appeared with giant smiles and excitement. They bound into Leroy's arms and squealed with delight.*

*"How are you both? Did you watch Dad on television this weekend?"*

*They both nodded with enthusiasm. "You play the best, Daddy," Abby grinned when he gave her a big kiss on the cheek.*

*"I wanna be like you one day, Daddy," Drayton nodded, and I felt my heart flutter. It pounded so hard at the sight of my gorgeous family. My son and daughter were everything to me. The reason I woke in the morning. The reason I tried to be the best that I could be. Leroy looked up at me and his brows pulled together.*

*"Ellie?"*

*I couldn't answer him. No matter how hard I tried. Nothing would come out.*

*"Ellie?"*

*"Ellie?*

I shot up in bed and gasped. My heart was beating as furiously as it had been in the dream. I clutched my chest and took a few deep breaths to calm down. The dream had felt so real that I almost expected to look around and find baby clothes and toys. But there were no signs to indicate that it was anything but fiction.

Before I could forget it, I shot out of bed and ran over to the small desk in the corner of the room. I started writing it down. What had happened, what the cute names of the children were. Abby was the name that Leroy had used when we were grocery shopping in Castle Rock. Doubts had been clouding my mind from the get-go. As much as I wanted to be sure about what I wanted, there had been a niggling battle going on, my heart and head at war. I knew what was sensible, but what I felt was love—love for a child that I'd made with the man I love—and that dream felt like our future. A future that I wanted.

Hope started to swell within my chest as I thought about phoning Leroy. We could do this, right? Together, we could do it.

I was halfway through scrawling down the dream's events when the door swung open and Momma walked in without an invitation. She pulled the curtains open and silently went about picking a few things up from the floor.

"I made an appointment at the clinic for nine on Monday," she said, her tone cold. "It's a consultation but it'll get the process going."

"Momma? I . . . I don't think I want to do it now. The termination. I don't think I want to do it."

I couldn't even look at her, knowing that she would be fixing me with that stare. The one that would weaken my resolve and push me into doing what she said. She had that effect on me.

"Ellie, you don't have to go through with the termination," she said. The weight off my shoulders was enormous, but alas, it was short-lived. "But you will be giving it up for adoption."

"What?"

"You can't raise a child. You are not having a baby under my roof. Are we clear?"

I couldn't think of what to say that would allow me to make a decent argument. She sighed and carried on speaking. "Think about this with some common sense, child. You don't have a dime to your name, apart from the measly savings you have for business classes. Our house is small. You've got your whole life ahead of you. A child isn't a smart idea and think about how immature you still are. You can't cook. You can barely drive. What on earth good would you be to a baby?"

My nose stung and my lip quivered as I slowly sat down on the edge of my bed, looking out into our minuscule back garden, a dry lawn, and the fence just a few feet back from the house. The view had never looked so imprisoning. She was right: I would do no good raising a child. I couldn't expect Leroy to support us through it, even though I knew he wanted to. He didn't understand what a burden it would be and how much of an effect it would have on his career. A dream wasn't enough to go on. That sort of thinking was childish in itself. Getting excited over the idea of a happy ending couldn't secure a happy ending, no matter how we felt right now.

My shoulders shook with violent sobs as I realized that I had to do this alone. I had to give this baby up without involving him because he shouldn't have to bear that burden or endure that hurt. He would believe that I'd terminated and that it was for the best. But it would mean losing him and that hurt more than anything.

## Ellie

The following morning, after Momma had told me I wouldn't raise my own child, I lay in bed and stared at the ceiling, feeling no motivation to leave the confines of my comforter. The phone in the kitchen rang, but I ignored it.

My bedroom was my favorite place in the world. My own space. There was a bookshelf in the corner beside the closet. Old vinyl records made a mural on the wall, there were posters of music legends from floor to ceiling, my bed in the middle of the room was covered in throw pillows, a stack of CDs sat beside my vanity, and my drawers were covered in collectible stickers. The best part: I'd scored almost everything in here from thrift stores. Momma didn't care for room décor. She said a bed and drawers were essential and extras were up to me to provide. So, I had.

But now, looking around, it didn't bring me the same joy that it once had. It was just stuff. Stuff couldn't tell me it loved me or hold me or assure me we'd be okay. I missed Leroy to the point it was painful.

"Ellie, Ellie, Ellie," Amber's friendly voice came from the hall a moment before my bedroom door swung open. She stood at the threshold and folded her arms. "Girl, I've been calling but no one's answering. What's doin'? You know it's beautiful outside, right?"

"Is it?" I sat up, aware that I looked like a creature. "Where's Eric?"

"He's chillin' at the music store. I'm going to meet him later, but first," she came into the room and sat on the edge of the bed, "what's going on? Something happened with Leroy, right? You're a mess."

"I am."

She tilted her head. "What's going on, chick? Talk to me. You didn't come home for no reason. You looked so sad at the airport."

"I'm pregnant, Ambs."

Her brows shot up and her mouth fell open. "No."

"Yes."

"No."

"Maybe if you keep saying no, it'll be true."

"I'm sorry," she said and fell backwards, staring at the ceiling. "I just can't even . . . that's bananas."

I nodded and she twisted her head to look at me.

"What are you going to do? Where's Leroy? Girl," she gasped. "Your mom must've gone postal."

"Yeah, she was pissed," I said and proceeded to explain the events that had occurred since I'd told Leroy about the pregnancy.

"He thinks you've come home for an abortion. But you're just going to avoid him until you've given birth and said 'see ya' to the mini?"

When she said it like that, it sounded awful. It *was* awful, regardless of its wording, but I felt short of breath when I nodded.

"That's not right, girl," she said. "He's coming here for college soon. What's gonna happen when he sees you walking around with a massive bump?"

"Texas is huge. I might not see him at all."

Her expression fell flat, and she sat up. "That's still not cool. You have to tell him something. Break up with him. Closure. Something. You can't just disappear on the boy. That's so mean."

My tears welled over for the millionth time and I buried my head in my hands. "I know, Amber, I know. I'm just c-c-confused and scared and Momma is—"

"Your mom is wrong too. Straight up, that woman is worse than my momma. She'd smack me if I got pregnant but no way she'd kick me out if I wanted to keep it."

I looked at her. "You're using protection, right?"

"We aren't stupid. No offense."

"None taken."

She let out a loud sigh and gave me a light tap on the leg. "Come on. Let's go and do something. You need a distraction. And a shower."

As lifeless as I felt, she was right—I did need a distraction. After I was showered and dressed, Amber drove us into town, and we arrived at a rock-climbing hall, the biggest one in the city. There were dozens of walls for different skill levels and most of them were free at this hour of the morning. I hadn't realized how early it was until I looked at the clock behind the front desk and saw that it was nine.

"Rock climbing is good for the soul," Amber said, while

we waited for the clerk to bring us a harness and helmet each. "Good for releasing tension and giving focus."

"Ambs, we're here. You don't have to sell it."

"I would have suggested that we drink but I didn't think that'd be a viable option right now."

Despite everything, I laughed. "Yeah, no."

After we were harnessed and told the safety procedures by the clerk, we wandered farther into the hall and looked around. There were three separate halls joined by double swing doors. The first hall was toddlers to beginners. There was a colorful area with a foam pit and a little rock wall about two meters tall that kids could jump off and then the walls became a bit bigger, but the rocks were still relatively close together. We wandered through into the second hall, medium difficulty, deciding to start in here and move into the difficult hall if we felt like an extreme challenge.

Because we wanted to climb together, we had to ask a couple of the staff to belay us, which was no problem since it was still quiet. We checked our carabiners, thanked the two belayers, and then started climbing the green walls with multicolored rocks.

"So," Amber said as we climbed, one foot up, the next foot up. "Aside from the situation, how was Colorado?"

"Basically, the happiest I've ever been in my entire life," I said.

"Really?"

My foot slid off the little rock I'd tried to put it on, so I stretched farther for the sturdier one. Amber was right, the focus that this activity required was distracting. "The Laheys are really good people, you know? Super kind and welcoming. I mean, Noah was a bit of a dick but not enough to ruin it."

"What's his problem?"

"It's hard to tell. I think he's sort of jealous of Leroy. Leroy is super athletic and good at football and stuff, which his dad loves. But Noah is book smart, and he thinks his dad doesn't care about that as much. It's kind of sad. He's wrong too. His dad is so proud of him."

We were starting to get tired, that much was obvious. It was a tall climb, so we went the rest of the way in silence, and when we finally got to the top, we hoisted ourselves onto the ledge and sat with our feet hanging over. The belayers at the bottom were chatting and gave us a thumbs-up to let us know that we were good here for a minute.

"It looks so far down from here," Amber said.

"I always forget that we have to go down again afterward," I said, my stomach turning over at the thought of falling, even though I knew that the belayers would lock our carabiners before we could get even halfway down. "How are things going with Eric?"

Amber smiled. "So good, chick. He's so sweet and funny. The boy makes me laugh all the time. I love that."

"He is super nice. I love how he talks."

"Right," she agreed with excitement. "He's so sophisticated and has all the cutest little nicknames. Everyone is 'gorgeous' and 'beautiful' to him."

"I know. You could be having the worst day and he'd say, *how's it going, gorgeous?* and it's a surge of good vibes."

"Totally," Amber was cheesing. "Usually I'd go postal if my man called another woman gorgeous but it's different with him. It's so innocent. It's one of my favorite things about him."

"I don't know what to do, Ambs," I quietly said. "I actually just have no idea how to move forward."

She didn't say anything for a while and then she rested her head on my shoulder. "Want my honest opinion?"

"Sure."

"Tell Leroy that you want to keep the baby, tell your momma to be quiet and be supportive, and go back to Colorado. That family will take care of you."

"I don't know if I do want to keep the baby. I mean, I do. But I know that I want to keep it for the fairy-tale version of this situation. I know the smart thing to do is give it up for adoption. Even if that's not what I want, that's what I *should* do. None of that makes any sense, does it?"

"It does," she said. "It's not wrong to want the fairy tale, though, girl. Even Cinderella struggled before she lived in the castle. It might be hard, but hell, it might be worth it. Only you can decide if you want to take the risk."

"I know," I said, still no closer to having a decision.

N

I spent the entire week debating what to do. There was a long list of possible options that rotated themselves over in my mind. The first being, call Leroy. Or call his mom to ask for help. Running away was starting to sound more and more appealing with every angry look that Momma shot me from across the room too. But no matter how many new options I came up with, the same counter thought came along: It wasn't fair to Leroy.

I would have to depend on him so much. I didn't want to be that person. I didn't want to jeopardize his future or become a burden. When I thought about it with logic, adoption was not only in our best interest, but the child's too. My mind went back and forth, wondering if I should just save myself the turmoil and terminate. It was like a game of ping-pong going on inside my head. But the ball always landed in the adoption court. I'd given this child a face, fallen in love with it. Even if I didn't get to raise it, at least it would have the best upbringing that it could.

Amber was also right, though—I had to tell Leroy something. The radio silence must have been killing him and that hurt to think about.

"Ellie," Momma knocked on the door while I lay in bed and thought about what a mess I had made. "We should think about booking that appointment with the OB-GYN and contacting the adoption agency."

I pulled the covers farther over my head so that she couldn't see me grimace. How was I going to cope when it came time to actually give my baby up when the thought of doing so already made me feel so sick? I was eighteen. I shouldn't have had to feel so submissive.

"Momma, we've got time," I mumbled from the dark of my comforter. "Can we just . . . not?"

"You can't put it off for long, Ellie." The mattress dipped as she sat down beside me. "And you need to see an OB-GYN sooner rather than later."

I could call Leroy, tell him that I want to have a child with him. His mom could help. I could try to get my old job at the pharmacy back. But what if she doesn't want me to keep the child either? Leroy would struggle juggling college football and a baby. It could ruin his chances of a career. I couldn't be responsible for that.

The thoughts screamed at me, my chest tightened, and I felt

sick with confusion the longer I thought about it. No matter what I chose, someone was going to be disappointed in me. A relationship would be ruined on either side of the spectrum. I had never been so conflicted, ever. And just when I thought I was content with a choice, my mind went into overdrive again. Ping-pong. Back and forth, back and forth. It was draining.

"I think that I'm going to go down to the community college and look at the business course sign-ups," I said, flicking the blanket back and swinging my legs over the side of the bed. "It'd be best to get in and get it sorted. I might need a job or something as well. My savings have dwindled a little."

Momma stood up and followed me around the room while I organized an outfit for the morning. "That's what you're going to do with your day? You have more important things to concern yourself with, Ellie."

I turned around and stared at her with disbelief. "Isn't that the point in this decision that you've made for me? That it's to benefit my future? Well, that's what I'm doing, Momma."

"Drop the attitude," she warned. "This isn't a choice that I've made for you—you made it when you decided to be foolish and irresponsible. I really thought you'd have been smarter after knowing what I went through when I was a teenager. Is this the life you want to end up with? A shoebox of a house and no damn career? You made this choice, Ellie. You want that baby, you go ahead and get out of this house. I'm not living through the consequences of stupidity ever again."

It was true that she had always been vocal about the importance of abstinence and the fact that she didn't want me to go through what she had. But she'd never said it in such a vicious way. In a way that made it sound as if I was at fault for the life that she'd led. I didn't know how to respond. So I didn't say anything at all. I clutched the shirt in my hand and resisted the urge to scream and demand some damn space. I'd just end up grounded and I needed out of this house.

"Fine, go to the college," she said. "I've got work."

"Can I get a ride into town?" I asked as she began to leave the room.

"No. Take a bus."

N

The weather was ridiculously hot when I stepped off the bus about two blocks from the college in the mid-afternoon. I fanned myself as I looked from left to right before crossing the road. My cute little red floral sundress did little to relieve the heat. All I wanted to do was lie in a bath of cold water. But I needed a distraction, something to take my mind off things. I figured that sorting my business course was a good use of time.

The walk to the college wasn't long, but I was sweating by the time I got there, and it felt disgusting. The office was air-conditioned, and surprisingly there were a lot of people hanging around the photocopiers and desks. I thought for sure that because of the summer break, it would be mostly empty. I suppose even the staff still had things that needed to be done before the new semester commenced.

The conversation with the receptionist was brief. She handed me some information booklets and applications to fill out. I stuffed the papers into my bag and left, feeling grateful for a distraction in the form of reading material and applications.

I'd planned for that to take a lot longer than it did, so as I walked back to the bus stop, I wondered if there was anything else that I could do in town. And then the aroma of a café hit me, making my mouth water—the smell of fresh bread, the hot savories, the coffee. I stared through the windows with longing, feeling resentment toward the people who could consume caffeine without guilt.

Realizing that I had enough cash for a bus home and that was it, I kept walking and had gone about four feet when a masculine voice called out for me.

"Ellie!"

Turning around, I saw Amber and Eric walking hand in hand. They waved when I stopped, waiting for them to catch up. "Hey," I said. "What's going on?"

Eric beamed as he pointed over his shoulder. "You want to grab some lunch with us?"

"Oh . . . I don't have any cash right now."

"My treat," he held up his hand when I tried to argue. "I got it, girl. Come on, Amber told me that she wants hot fries and soft serve. As in . . . together. Is that normal?"

Amber and I looked at each other and laughed as we headed back to the café that I had been lingering outside of just a few minutes earlier. "I don't think it's normal," I said. "But it's more popular than you'd expect."

"Sounds awful," he held the door open and we headed inside. My stomach rumbled and I hadn't realized how starved I was until the aroma of hot food was all around me.

"You're going to try fries dipped in soft serve," Amber pointed at Eric. "And you're going to love it, I promise."

His narrow stare was disbelieving as we stood in line. "We'll see, Prez."

We ordered our food and sat down at a free table with the number card. As hungry as I was, I didn't want to order too much, considering I wasn't paying for it. A bowl of fries and a soda would do for now. I was just grateful to be with friends after the week that I'd had. Isolation was draining. It took a huge toll on a person and I hadn't realized how desperate I was to be with familiar people until we were sitting across from one another.

We made small talk while we waited for our food. What we'd been up to for the last week, what our plans were for the rest of summer. Amber was kindly acting as though nothing was out of the ordinary in front of Eric too. The food came to our table after a long ten-minute wait.

"All right," Amber said, pushing her locs behind her shoulder as she twisted in her seat to face Eric. She ran a fry through her soft serve and held it out to him, disgust twisting his mouth. "You promised that you would taste it. It's good. You'll be surprised."

He was reluctant but he finally let her pop it into his mouth, and after he'd made a big show of chewing and tasting, he shook his head. "Nope, not a fan. I don't dig the sweet and savory thing. It's weird."

"I agree," I said.

"You two are so plain," Amber dismissed and helped herself, enjoying her combination.

"So," Eric said and looked at me. "Heard Cass and Noah made it official. Yikes. How's that going?"

"Oh . . . it's going fine, I suppose. The dysfunction is still the same but I can tell that Noah is trying. I think that's what counts." I hadn't talked to any of them in a week, so I didn't even know if they were still a thing, but I suspected Eric didn't know what was going on and didn't want him to wonder why I hadn't called Leroy.

"Cass is the one that was on the call with you, right?" Amber asked and I nodded.

"That girl has been a good friend since I was a kid, but damn, she has never known how to pick them." Eric wistfully shook his head.

"Aren't you and Noah friends too?"

"Ha," Eric basically shouted. "No. I put up with him because he's Leroy's brother, but that fool does my head in. Arrogant little shit. Plus, the way that he treats Cass."

That wasn't entirely surprising. I could see how Noah and Eric would clash but Eric did well at hiding how he felt. Although, I'd only seen them in the same setting once so that might have been the reason that I'd been oblivious to the animosity.

I didn't want the afternoon to end when we'd finished eating and stood up to leave. Outside on the pavement, I asked Eric for the time and he lifted his wrist to check his watch.

"Just after two."

"You should come and hang out with us." Amber gave me a nudge. "We're going to the hotel that Eric is staying at and having some drinks. A few more friends will be coming over later tonight for a little party, I guess. It'll be tame, though, I promise."

"It's fine," I said, knowing that she was assuring me it would be safe for my pregnant condition. "You're staying at a hotel?"

"As if Mom would let him stay with us," Amber mumbled. "I told her that we met a few months ago and kept in contact over the phone, which she was chill about. But you know Mom. There was no chance she'd let me have a boy sleeping in the house. I can't wait for college."

She had a point. Our mothers were almost on par with how

rigid their rules were. Amber was so lucky, having an escape, college, freedom.

"I'll need to call Momma from the hotel if that's okay. Just to let her know that I'll be out."

"Yeah, of course," Eric said as we climbed into a rental car. I took the backseat.

During the drive, I let the lovebirds converse and attempted not to sob over the fact that I missed Leroy so much. What was he doing right now? How is he? He was probably upset and confused about why he hadn't heard from me since I left. Stress and panic rose at a rapid pace. Like it was going to simmer over, and I'd need to be physically sick.

Eric was staying in a small one-level motel. The single room was basic with a bed, chest of drawers, and a little kitchenette. Amber used the phone first to call her mom and let her know that she'd be out for the evening. She was given permission but had to return home for dinner first. Eric let her borrow the car and I phoned Momma while they stepped out to say goodbye.

I knew that she wouldn't be home, so I left a message on the answering machine and told her that I was catching up with Amber at her house. It meant that I didn't have to have an actual conversation with her. It meant that I didn't have to hear the resentment in her voice when she spoke to me.

I was hanging up the phone when Eric ducked back inside with a genuine grin etched into his features. I knew that feeling well and I felt so happy for my best friend to know that she had a decent man. Especially considering they would be at the same college.

"She won't be long," he said as he strolled toward the kitchenette and retrieved a couple of glasses from the cabinet. When he pulled open the mini fridge, there was a selection of alcohol in miniature bottles. "Want one?"

"Oh, just a water will be fine, I suppose."

He grabbed a bottle of vodka and let the fridge swing shut. He handed me the water and mixed his drink with some apple juice before switching on the radio, an all-too-familiar song was on. "Don't Want to Miss a Thing."

My chest tightened at the memory of Leroy singing this song to me in his kitchen just a couple of weeks ago. I could almost feel his hands on me again, hear his voice whispering beside me, smell his intoxicating cologne and natural musk.

"Hey, what's wrong, honey?" Eric wrapped his arm around my shoulder and let me lean into his hold as I fell apart. I wanted to blame the hormones, but I knew that it was just me. "Is this about Leroy?"

I nodded, taking a deep breath and attempting to dry my cheeks.

"What'd he do? I'll hit him if he's acting up."

I laughed. An ugly choked sob of a laugh. "No, he's perfect. It's me. I fucked everything up."

"You just cursed. Must be bad."

I nodded again as he rubbed my shoulder and let me lean on him. As much as I didn't want to drag him into the middle of such a shit-show, I had the desperate urge to vent. So, I told Eric everything and cried while he comforted me through the erratic rambling.

"Please don't say anything to Leroy," I blubbered after I was done offloading. Eric pursed his lips like he didn't want to agree to keeping such a secret from him. "Eric, please. Please don't tell him."

"I just don't think giving up your baby for adoption without telling him is the right thing to do," he gently said. "I would want to know. So would he. Plus, he'd support you if that's what you need. I know him, and I know that he would do anything for you."

"That's why I want to keep him out of it. I don't want him to jeopardize his future for me. Or feel burdened. Plus, my mom—"

"Yeah, that's the other thing," he cut me off and stood up. "You're letting your mom decide something so major. It's messed up, girl."

I didn't expect him to understand. Most teenagers didn't give a shit what their parents thought. But that's not how I was raised. I was raised to respect, be truthful, and do what I was told or face consequences. My momma had always known what was best for me and I wanted to believe that she still did. Even if it was tearing me apart.

"I know that I have things to figure out," I said with a quiet voice. "Please just let me figure them out before you say anything to Leroy."

He rested his hands on his hips and stood in front of me with a warring expression. He didn't like it. But he eventually nodded in agreement and sat back down beside me. "Sure. This is your business. I won't tell him."

I exhaled a sigh of relief. "Thanks, Eric."

## Ellie

I spent the next couple of days hanging around with Eric and Amber. Mom was at work a lot, and when she was home, I avoided her so I wouldn't have to talk about topics that I didn't want to discuss. I knew that I couldn't put it off forever. Soon I would need to see an OB-GYN and have health checkups and contact the adoption agency. Every time that thought surfaced, I squashed it before I ended up a nauseated wreck. It was procrastination at its finest but right now it felt like the only thing I had control over.

Eric and Amber were wonderful at pretending that I wasn't pregnant. A week with the two of them was just what I needed. Fun, distraction, the chance to forget. We caught up with the rest of our friend group from high school. We spent time at the river. We saw movies at the theatre. It was a blessing. But it didn't heal the hurt. It just set a nice little Band-aid on the open wound.

But Friday came around and Eric was leaving for Georgia, where he had family that he would be staying with for the rest of summer. Amber planned on joining him before college started, if she could manage to convince her mother to let her leave early. Apparently, her mom was just as smitten with Eric as Amber was, so I assumed it wouldn't be hard. He was impossible not to love.

The airport was air-conditioned and we stood beside the gate with Eric, who was obviously disappointed to be leaving.

"I had a great week," he smiled as he pulled me in for a hug. "Talk to Leroy, okay?"

I stepped back and gave him a tight smile. I couldn't pretend that I wanted to do that, but his heart was in the right place. I felt bad for letting him harbor such a big secret from his friend. If I hadn't been so unstable in that hotel room, I probably would have realized that he was the last person I should confide in about something like that. He just had such a laid-back but inviting vibe about him. Someone that you could share anything with.

I said goodbye to both him and Amber and left them to have a more intimate farewell without me hanging around. We'd come in Eric's rental but that had to be left behind so I decided to take the bus home. Amber was getting picked up by her mother, but I didn't want to ask for a ride. The short walk from the bus stop to home would be good anyway. I'd felt a little nauseated this morning, which surprised me. So far, I hadn't had any signs of morning sickness.

The bus didn't have decent cooling. It was cramped and stuffy, but I endured it until it came time for me to get off the bus and I inhaled a deep breath of fresh air the minute I hit the sidewalk.

My neighborhood offered a quiet walk. Some of the elderly

homeowners were in their gardens, pulling weeds or watering their flowerbeds. Small children played on their trampolines, rode their bikes, or played hopscotch on the footpath. I couldn't help but feel a pang of heartache when I watched the little ones laughing and playing with their bright, innocent smiles. Life is so much simpler as a child. Why the hell are we always in such a rush to grow up?

My hand ran along the top of my picket fence as I whistled and approached the little latch gate that led toward the front door of my home. My gaze flickered up and I startled at a woman standing on the doorstep. She turned around and I realized that it was Eleanor.

I just stood there while she smiled and waved with no hesitation. She glanced from side to side before she came down the steps and walked toward me. I met her halfway, not quite feeling the ground beneath my feet, not sure what to say. It had been two weeks since I'd left Colorado, but it had felt like a lifetime.

"Hello, Ellie," she held her purse close to her side. "You must be wondering what I'm doing here."

I wasn't sure how to respond to that.

"Can we talk inside?"

Momma was still at work for a few hours, so I nodded and stepped around her. She followed me inside and took a seat at the kitchen table while I pushed all the windows open. "Would you like a drink?"

"No, darling," she tapped the table space beside her. "Come and sit down so that we can talk."

My heart sped up as I did what she asked and sat down at the table. My fingers twisted together on the surface. It was hard to feel calm with Leroy's mother sitting in my dining room after what had happened two weeks ago. Part of me wanted to ask her how Leroy was. I wanted to bombard her with a million questions. But I kept quiet and waited for her to begin.

"I won't beat around the bush," she said. "Eric phoned and told me . . . everything. The adoption. Your mother. All of it."

I began to shift with discomfort. Heat crept up my chest and neck and all I could think about was how I had asked Eric not to tell Leroy. He said he wouldn't. But Eleanor was never discussed. He'd found a loophole and I wasn't sure if I was pissed off or relieved. That would depend on how this conversation went.

"Please don't be upset with him," she said. "He really felt like he was doing the right thing."

"Of course," I murmured. "I'm not mad. I shouldn't have put that on him in the first place."

"I'm glad you did, though." She ducked her head so that she could meet my eyes. "I imagine that you're feeling quite alone at the moment."

I gave her a small but confirming shrug.

"Leroy doesn't know, Ellie," she said. "I thought that you should be the one to tell him that you're giving the baby up for adoption. I'm not sure why you felt that you couldn't tell him in the first place."

"Because I didn't want to put him through that," I said. "I know that he wanted to keep the baby. I didn't want to put him through the pregnancy only to hand the child over in the end. That would hurt him so much and I didn't want to put that on him."

"And that's very sweet of you, darling," Eleanor said. "But you're talking as if he's the only one who's going to hurt. Won't it hurt you as well?"

I took a deep breath and felt the familiar tingle of my tear ducts. "Of course it will."

"Exactly. I know my son, Ellie. He would be more hurt that you kept this from him. He would be more hurt if he didn't get to support you through this. He's a good man. He does the right thing. No matter if he likes it or not."

I quickly swiped at a tear that slid down my cheek. She was right, of course. I wanted to protect him so much I hadn't even considered how badly I could hurt him in the process. But no matter how I went about my next steps, someone was going to get hurt.

"Now, let me tell you this," she straightened up and her tone was authoritative, her expression stern but her eyes were full of kindness and comfort. "You have options, sweetheart. You do not have to give this child or your future up. You don't. I want you to know that Jacob and I will support you if you want to keep him or her. We can provide financial support. We could help with babysitting, living costs, even your education. You wouldn't have to struggle. But I don't want you to feel pressure, or swayed into a decision. This choice can't be mine, and it can't be Leroy's or your mother's. It needs to be yours. But I want you to know that I am here to help if you want it. I want you to have options."

I felt my heart speed up as I realized what she was offering. It was something that I had imagined but never believed she would do. "Why?" was all I could murmur.

She looked thoughtful for a moment. "I'll admit, I was disappointed when I found out that you were pregnant. Leroy has his future set up. He has goals and plans. You both do. But he loves you. He loves you so much and I would never want to stand between him and having a family. We're blessed enough to have the resources so that he could have both a child *and* his career. A lot of people aren't that fortunate."

I swallowed and took a few deep breaths while I processed the information. It was a lot to think about. I assumed that having her support would solve all of my problems. But there were still a lot of details to figure out.

"This isn't a decision that you need to make right at this moment." She picked her purse up from the floor and retrieved an airline ticket. She slid it across the table as she spoke. "There is no pressure from me. But there are options. So, think about it. For you. You are welcome back with us whenever you like. And honey, you don't need to give up your relationship with Leroy. No matter what you choose."

I stared at the ticket on the table and nodded, not able to get a word out. I was vaguely aware when Eleanor stood up and took her leave. It was such a whirlwind. I couldn't believe what had just happened. But what I did know was that she meant it. She wasn't pushing me in one direction. She was letting me know that whatever I chose, I had support. And that was more than what I'd been given by my own mother.

*N*

I spent the rest of that afternoon thinking. Seriously thinking. I sat in the empty bathtub with a pen and paper—not to write pros and cons, but just to have something in my hands that I could focus on. Lately there had been a lot of avoiding thoughts and refusal to face the truth. Now, I was one hundred percent dedicated to facing this and making a decision. It was time to stop pretending like the situation would sort itself out.

The house was still hot at eight o'clock that night. The windows were open, the curtains ruffled in the breeze, the aroma of spaghetti and meatballs made me feel a little ill as Momma and I sat at the table. The food wasn't entirely to blame, though, I was wound up over the conversation that I needed to have with Mom.

"Momma," I said as I twisted the strands of spaghetti around my fork. She glanced up and I flinched at her expression. I don't even think she realized she was doing it, but she didn't look at me the same way anymore. There was a constant disappointment in her gaze, and it hurt so much.

"What is it, Ellie?" she asked.

"Oh," I dropped my fork and began scratching my neck, which was feeling hot and flushed. "I just. I need to say something, and I want you to keep an open mind because, well, it's—"

"Spit it out."

"What if I wanted to keep the baby?" I blurted and felt my heart rate speed up as her stare hardened.

"How many times do we have to go over this?" she said. "No."

"But what if I could support myself. Financially?"

"It's not just about finances, Ellie. It's about the rest of your life. It's about being held back from opportunities because you've got a child. It's about being tied down to one man. Because this is about Leroy, correct? That's what this is about. Being with Leroy because you're in love and it all seems so easy right now."

"This decision isn't about being with him, Momma. It's about the fact that I've bonded with this child and I want to raise him or her. And yes. I love Leroy. He's a wonderful man. What's wrong with that?"

"What's wrong is that it's unrealistic. Men like that don't stick around. Not at that age. You'll end up alone with no room to move left or right because you trusted some boy that offered the world to you and he made promises that he clearly never intended to keep."

"You're making this about yourself!" I shouted, my blood pressure rising. "You had a bad experience. That doesn't mean it's going to end like that for me."

"You'd like to think so," she snapped. "Your father was a wealthy man. Handsome. Sweet. All of those things and as soon as he was faced with impending fatherhood, he left. He wanted no part of it. If I was smart, I would have seen it coming and perhaps if I hadn't been so young and stupid, I wouldn't have made so many mistakes."

"Oh." I slammed my hand on the tabletop. "I'm guessing that I'm the mistake?!"

She didn't answer, instead keeping her gaze downcast as she drank her water. I could feel myself becoming more wound up by the minute.

"Well, I'm sorry that you're stuck with me and a dead-end job and no love life, but Leroy and I aren't you."

"That's the naivety that lands you in hot water. You think that you're untouchable." She laughed as though I was a stupid little kid that knew nothing at all. "You're like every other young couple who wants to believe their love is different."

I stood up and leaned across the table. "It *is* different!"

"You're being stupid!"

My whole body was humming with tension and anger. I couldn't believe that this was the woman who had raised me. She had always been a bit pessimistic and on the controlling side. But this was different. This wasn't my momma.

"They want to support me. No matter what I choose. They want to help me. I don't have to struggle."

"If you believe that there isn't a catch, you're being extremely dense." She leaned back in her seat and folded her arms. "You can't trust people like that."

"You're wrong." I attempted to regulate my breathing. "You don't know them. They're good people. You're just being selfish."

"I'm looking out for you!"

"No, you're not!" I tugged on my hair and held in a piercing scream. "You're stopping me from having what you never could: happiness and the chance to succeed. You don't like the fact that they have money and you don't want me to be a part of that kind of family."

"Of course I don't," she scoffed. "Money changes people. Ruins them. I don't want you to be like that."

"If it's the money that ruins them," I hissed, "then what the hell is your excuse?"

She stood up, fast, and slapped me across the face so hard that my head snapped to the side. I didn't even register what had happened until I felt the painful throb and sting. I turned back to her, clutching my cheek, tears welling. "How could you?"

"You will have some respect for me!"

I never would, ever again.

"I'm going to bed," I murmured, still clutching my cheek, which was now oozing a little bit of blood. Her ring must have split the skin. "Did you block Leroy's phone number?"

"Hardly seems important, but yes, I did."

"Jealousy is an ugly disease," I said before I ran up the corridor and slammed my bedroom door shut.

My decision was made. Although it hurt to think about how

damaged my relationship with my mother was, I couldn't stay or respect her after what she'd said and done tonight. I quietly sobbed as I packed up my belongings into a travel bag. I folded and stuffed things in so that I could utilize the space efficiently. I wasn't sure when I would be back, so I grabbed a couple of picture frames, documents, course-related papers. Whatever I needed to start over, including some of my most treasured CDs and skincare—those things I couldn't leave without.

The entire time my eyes were clouded with pools of tears. If I had just been more careful on that first night with Leroy, none of this would have been happening. But it was, and I had to be brave because Eleanor was right. Only I could make this choice. I sat on the floor and zipped up the suitcase before I placed a hand across my stomach and felt my heart speed up.

"I've got you, little one. Always."

When I opened my bedroom door, I took a deep breath, trembling. There were no words. There was nothing that could articulate how devastated I was. How deep the betrayal ran. I was aware that by getting pregnant I had let down my momma, but I was still her daughter and this felt wrong. This wasn't how people should treat their children. I went down the hall and made it to the front door when I heard Momma behind me.

"If you leave, do not come back."

My hand tightened around the door handle. There was so much that I wanted to say. The urge to stand here and convince her that Leroy loved me and would never hurt me was tempting but, in the end, it would get me nowhere. Her mind was made up: Leroy and I were naïve children, about to flush our futures down the toilet, and no one could tell her otherwise. I pulled the door open and stepped out into the warm dark night, slamming it shut behind me.

## LEROY

"The number that you are trying to reach is unavailab—"

"Dammit!" I slammed the phone down on its base and leaned against the countertop, inhaling a deep breath. My head hung as I stared at the floor and tried to calm down.

It didn't work.

Two weeks I had been phoning Ellie's house, always getting that same fucking message. I hadn't heard a single word, and no matter how much deep breathing I did, I couldn't clear the red dots that danced in front of me.

I straightened up and gripped the phone, throwing it with so much force that it flew across the room, hitting the wall.

"Dramatic," Noah mocked from the table with a mouthful of food. The thought of smacking him in the face was enticing. But I settled for sending him a harsh scowl instead. It wasn't his fault that Ellie had disappeared from the face of the earth.

It better not have been anyway. "Have you spoken to her?"

He glanced up, his eyes darting from left to right with confusion. "No? Why the hell would she talk to me?"

"I don't know," I dropped into the seat at the head of the table. "What about Cass?"

Noah shook his head as he bit into his sandwich. "Nah." He gave me a disgusting view of his chewed food as he spoke. "She hasn't heard from her either."

My head fell into my hands, elbows resting on the table as I groaned with frustration. The lack of contact was driving me insane.

"Maybe she's on a new dick."

"Would you shut up!"

Noah sniggered and I picked up the closest item to me—which happened to be a bottle of water—and threw it at him so hard that his sandwich flew out of his hand when he tried to cover his face. Salad and meats covered the tabletop and himself.

"My lunch!"

"What is going on in here?" Mom's voice had both of us turning our attention to the entryway where she stood with her travel bag behind her and an ·unimpressed frown as she took in the mess we'd just made. "I spend one night out of town and the phone is across the room and there's salad all over the floor."

"Both are his fault," Noah declared as he started picking bits of food up and putting them back on his plate. He did a piss-poor job of cleaning up before he started toward the corridor, calling over his shoulder as he left. "He's out of control."

"Sorry, Mom," I said, not bothering to deny it. "I'll clean it up. How was the conference thing?"

"It was fine," she said. "Just the usual. Where's Dad?"

"He went to help Joe with his new deck or something," I

shrugged, recalling what Dad had told us about helping his friend earlier this morning. I stood to clean up the food.

Mom intercepted me before I could crouch down and begin cleaning up. "Sweetheart, I know that you miss her but—"

"I don't just miss her, Mom." I sighed with frustration because I felt like no one understood. "I'm worried. I'm worried about her. I don't know how she is. I don't know how she's coping. I fucking hate this. I want to go there."

"I know," she said, "But I don't think that it's a good idea to just show up. Give her some time. She'll get in touch."

"She might not," I snapped with immediate regret when Mom flinched. "I'm sorry. It's just . . . She might not get in touch. What if she's unwell? Or she never made it home? What if something terrible happened?"

Mom tilted her head, empathy in her stare. "I think that her mother would have been in touch with us if she hadn't made it home. Perhaps they just need some time alone to get through what's happened. Relax, okay?"

It was easy for her to tell me to relax. She didn't understand how hard it was to not hear a single word from the woman that I loved. Things had been perfect one minute and the next she was on a plane and she was gone. It was hard to accept. It was hard to be okay with her sudden departure. I wanted her back with me. I wanted to know that she was safe.

Mom left me alone to clean up the mess, letting me know that she would be lying down if I needed her. What I needed was to clear my head. A walk or a run. I needed an outlet, and no one would practice football on a Saturday. So a solo jog would have to do. I finished sweeping up the bits of broken plastic when the door rattled open and closed, Cass calling out a greeting soon after.

"Hey," she smiled and leaned against the doorframe with folded arms as I closed the trash can lid. "Noah around?"

"Upstairs," I said.

She looked as though she was going to spin around and take off. But she paused and fixed me with a stare that was full of sympathy. "Are you okay?"

"I'm fine, Cass. Thanks."

She pursed her lips, not looking convinced. "Noah and I are going to the movies tonight. Want to come?"

"No," I said without hesitation. The last thing that I would want to do is third wheel a date with those two. It sounded like a nightmare.

She laughed but seemed to understand as she nodded and twisted on her heel, leaving me alone again. Which is what I'd wanted—a bit of space to get my thoughts together. Truthfully, I wouldn't have minded forgetting altogether. I hadn't been this torn up over something in a long time and I hated it. But I hated getting blackout drunk more. So, substance wasn't an option.

Sorrowful thoughts and a depressive mood lingered and wrapped around me while I pulled my shoes on at the door. It had been a long two weeks. A hard two weeks that were miserable in comparison to the time that I'd spent with the beautiful girl who had done a disappearing act on me. Despite not wanting her to get rid of the child, I supported her and was going to do whatever she needed of me. Things were right when she left. It just . . . it didn't make sense.

I pulled the door open and felt my stomach flip. There she stood in front of me. A sundress flowing from her figure, her soft blond waves loose around her shoulders. She looked tired, perhaps upset, but she looked beautiful. "Ellie?"

"Hi, L—"

Her words were cut off when I pulled her into my arms and held her, hoping that this was real. The scent of her fruity shampoo filled me with relief, giving me affirmation that she was really back and I wasn't imagining it. When I cupped her face and leaned back so that I could get a good look at her, I stilled, my thumb pausing mid-stroke against her freckled cheek.

"What the hell happened to your face?" I took her chin in my hand, turning her head to the side so that I could get a better view of the red abrasion that had swelled her cheek. She became flustered and I felt immediate aggression toward whoever the fuck put their hands on her. "Who did that?"

"Can I come in?"

I reached down and took her suitcase before ushering her inside. Her sweet scent fanned me as she brushed past and my chest tightened, my need to be near her was stronger than ever.

Before she could move even a mere few feet, I gripped her waist and pulled her toward me again, taking a handful of those soft curls as I cradled her head and kissed her. It was like being able to breathe again. The weight lifted from me, my head felt clearer, and I sighed in relief as she kissed me back with equal need. I was scared that something had changed between us. But she ran her fingers into my hair and pushed her entire frame against me, her tongue moving fast with mine.

I could have stayed like that for the longest time. I could have kept kissing her, holding her, feeling her, never letting her go again. But her soft sob and damp cheeks caused me to break apart and I became alarmed to see that she was crying, tears running down her face.

"Ellie," I cupped either side of her neck, my thumbs stroking circles on her jaw. "Baby, what's wrong?"

"I don't deserve you," she stared up at me. "I don't. Leroy, I'm so sorry—"

"Stop, Ellie, stop." I attempted to calm her down as I swung the door shut. We didn't need an audience, so I quickly led her upstairs and closed my bedroom door. She was still shaking with sobs and my heart ached at how distraught she looked. "Talk to me, baby, what's going on?"

She inhaled a shaking breath and wiped under her eyes. "You don't even seem mad that I disappeared for two weeks."

"I'm just relieved to see that you're okay." I caught her hand before she could drop it. "Except for that bruise. Who did that? What happened?"

"I don't even know where to start."

She stared at the floor and nibbled on her lip, so I led her toward the bed and sat down, pulling her into my lap. "Start wherever you want, beautiful. I'm listening."

She lifted a hand and caressed my jaw as she smiled with appreciation. Tears had given a glow to her green gaze. They shone brighter than usual. However beautiful they were, I would take their previous color in exchange for knowing that she wasn't hurting.

"Well, I'll put it simply," she said. "I decided to keep the baby. And Momma wasn't pleased," she added, pointing to her bruised and scratched cheek. "That about covers it all."

There was nothing casual about what she said but she'd delivered it almost flippantly. I stilled, staring at her as my heartbeat sped up a little. I didn't know how to respond. She . . . she was still pregnant. That was the last thing that I had expected. But her mother had done that to her. Her mother had hit her. It made me sick.

"I've rendered you speechless," she laughed. "I'd be proud of that but you're not that vocal to begin with."

"You're still pregnant?"

She nodded and picked up my hand, placing it on her stomach. Her fingertips caressed the top of mine as she spoke. "I couldn't do it. We made this baby with love. I fell in love with him or her whether I wanted to or not."

There was more that I wanted to know. More questions to ask. But instead I gripped her waist and threw her down on the bed, hovering above her as I kissed her. Her soft hands clasped the back of my neck, her grip rough and urgent, and her legs wound themselves around my waist. She was back. Back here with me. Carrying our child who we would love and raise together because no matter what, I would stand by her and protect her and never let her down.

The door swung open. "Leroy I ha—"

Mom's voice came to a stop as I peered behind me and felt Ellie still. She became so still that she didn't even try to correct her position. It was like she was hoping she wouldn't be seen if she just stopped moving.

I was about to move off Ellie when Mom sighed and gripped the door handle, leaving as she spoke. "Guess she can't get more pregnant than she already is."

When she was gone, I glanced down at Ellie, who had turned a bright red. We both laughed and the sound of her elated melody made me soar. Our mouths met again, tongues colliding. There were so many emotions that I wanted to express but couldn't find the words, so I hoped that she understood how I felt through our kiss because our love had a language of its own and our bodies never failed to say what our mouths couldn't.

## Ellie

The outdoor furniture had been set for dinner that night. It was a beautiful evening, not too hot, not too cold. Noah, Eleanor, and Jacob were seated and waiting when Leroy and I stepped onto the back deck, hand in hand. It would be a lie to claim that I wasn't nervous, but even so, I was comfortable back in this familiar setting. To be honest, I might have grown up in a two-bedroom home in Waco, but it was here where my heart rate was steadiest, where my walls were right down, where I felt I belonged.

Jacob smiled from the head of the table as we sat down. "Good to have you back, darlin'."

His warm welcome rendered me speechless. It was still hard to comprehend the kindness that these people had shown me.

Noah gave me a subtle chin nod, but his attention, as well as Eleanor's, was fixated on the small gash in my cheek. It didn't hurt but it was blatant.

"You all right, sweetheart?"

"Actually, I'm great. Because of you. I seriously don't know what I would have done if you hadn't shown up. I'm—thank you. I don't know how I'll ever be able to make it up to you."

"You don't have to," she said, sliding a bowl of salad toward us. "You're family. We love you and we want you to be happy and safe and healthy. You hear?"

More tears stung my eyes. I'd lost count of how often I'd cried in the last two weeks, but it was getting ridiculous. Hormones had to be the blame—there was no other reason for it. Well, aside from the copious amount of support I'd been shown here. Her words would have made me sob even if I hadn't been pregnant.

"I was never going to say anything," she continued. "Because it would have come across as pressure, but wow am I thrilled to be a grandmother soon. It's hard being sixty-three and not even having the privilege of grandchildren."

We both laughed and when I looked at Leroy, his face was so full of emotion that it almost winded me. He looked proud, in love, grateful. Eleanor wasn't the reason that I'd changed my mind about keeping the baby, but it was a bonus to see how excited she was. There was no mistaking how blessed I was to have this level of love around me at a time like this. Women my age and older struggle with parenthood all the time and I knew that it would come with challenges, but I was in a place of privilege and I wouldn't take that for granted. Not ever.

"So, I know an OB-GYN that could see you here in Castle Rock?" She offered. "She's the best of the best. I can make the phone call if you'd like?"

Noah screwed up his face. "Do we have to talk about vagina doctors at dinnertime?"

Jacob lowered the fork that he'd been directing into his mouth and gave Noah a flat stare.

"Have you had a dating scan?" she continued, ignoring Noah, and I shook my head. "We'll get one of those booked in at the radiologist as well. They do a few different things at the dating scan. Check the baby's organs and that sort of thing."

"I think I'm about eleven weeks along," I told her, feeling a warmth in my cheeks. "I know when . . . it . . . you know . . . happened. So, I counted from my last period."

"Oh, right," Eleanor said. Leroy dished pasta onto my plate; his mother gave me a thoughtful look. "You didn't notice how late your period was?"

"Fuck sakes," Noah threw his hands up, speaking with a mouthful of food.

Jacob clipped him across the head. "Language."

"I'm trying to eat and you're talking about pissing blood. It's disgusting."

"Dude!" Leroy said. "Grow up."

"No, I didn't notice," I tried to navigate the conversation back into a calmer state before it spiraled. "But I'd never paid it much attention before. Oblivious, I know."

"You might not need a dating scan, then, if you're quite sure of the date and that sort of thing. You could wait for the twelve-week scan instead."

"Oh . . . what do you think I should do?"

Leroy leaned in a little closer. "It's up to you, baby."

"We can just wait and do the twelve-week scan," I said.

"Do you have any allergies?" Eleanor asked.

"Nope."

"I'll get some prenatal vitamins from the pharmacy tomorrow then."

My head was a mess of thoughts and words that I wanted to express but somehow, nothing seemed adequate. "Thank you." I settled on simple and hoped she knew how much I meant it. "Thank you so much."

The sun was still a few hours from setting, but it was darkening into that burnt-orange dusk shade that casts a blinding light the lower it goes. The back garden was illuminated, flecks of evening sun touching the pool surface, the plants, and behind the fence palings so that it shone through the gaps.

"You been sick at all, darlin'?" Jacob asked.

"Not so far."

"That's good. Don't want to be stressing out about Eleanor's slippers, do we?"

There was a collective laugh around the table and my face ignited, hot and humiliated at the reminder of my first night here. His teasing was harmless, though. That was just Jacob, so I joined in and felt lighter than I had in a long time.

Noah's laughter subsided and he fixed Leroy and me with a sarcastic smile. Something told me that we were about to hear something that we didn't want to. "I love how we're all laughing over the fact that Leroy got a girl pregnant but if it was me, I'd be getting the life beaten out of me."

Eleanor tilted her head in disappointment. "Honey, you've been wonderfully sensible and wise not to get a girl pregnant. You have our permission to hold this over your brother's head for the rest of his life."

Leroy's jaw dropped. "What?"

Jacob raised a palm. "You messed up, no offense, son, but he can have this one."

Noah looked proud of himself—I couldn't blame him.

After dinner and wash-up, Leroy and I disappeared back upstairs so that we could lock ourselves up, appreciate our aloneness, and make up for the two weeks we'd spent apart.

※

Leroy slept so peacefully. His expression was relaxed, his features smooth. Even the edges of his lips curled up a little. I didn't know if that was because of me or not. But it was a nice thought. Our bodies were tangled under the sheets of his double bed. Now that I was already pregnant, the rules about separate rooms were unnecessary. His dark-blue walls kept it from getting too bright, despite the sun streaming through the large window that stretched the length of his wall. The heat was awful and our limbs were damp with sweat. But I wouldn't have traded it for anything. Being beside him again, it was perfect.

I reached out and ran a finger down the length of his exposed chest, biting down on my lip as I felt the grooves and dips of his muscles. He was so beautiful, so sweet and caring. I couldn't imagine getting sick of being beside him. This felt like home. It was comforting, soothing. The sadness that I'd felt over what happened with Momma was dull. My heart was full of love that I knew he returned.

He started to stir; a soft yawn followed by lip smacking before his hand found mine on top of his chest. His eyes remained closed, but he held my hand and squeezed. "Morning, baby." His rasp was heart-clenching. Everything about him drove me wild and I couldn't believe that I'd gone an entire two weeks without him. I never wanted to do that again.

When I didn't answer, he tilted his head and peered at me with one eye open. "You okay?"

"Yeah," I leaned up on an elbow. "I just missed you. A lot. I'm glad that your mom is fine with us sharing a bed."

"You wanna do something today?"

I looked up at Leroy while he waited for an answer to his question. His arm was wrapped around me, his hand rubbing soft circles on my shoulder while I rested on his chest. There was no feeling better than being held in his incredibly strong arms.

"Yeah, what should we do?"

"It's a surprise."

It didn't matter that I pleaded for him to fill me in—he didn't budge. It wasn't until we were in a furniture store full of brand-new sofas, tables, desks, and beds that he told me what we were doing.

"A sofa?"

"Yeah," Leroy nodded. He rested his hands on his hips and glanced around the furniture store before his gaze fell back on me. "You're coming to Baylor with me, right? We'll have our own place. We should get a sofa."

He was so sweet. His blue, collared T-shirt looked perfect against his skin tone. I watched him with a ridiculous smile, letting his plans sink in. He spoke as though there wasn't a thing to be worried about. Like no matter what happened, it would be him and me. And we'd be fine. The only furniture stores that I'd ever bothered setting foot in were secondhand ones. They all had the distinctive scent of mothballs and must. There was none of that here. It smelled like clean material: brand new leather, fabric cleaners, and wood stain.

"So, which one should we get?" he asked. "It can be our first purchase together toward our apartment."

"Leroy, I can't afford this. I'm running low on savings and I'm going to need something to put toward the baby things."

He shook his head from side to side with an amused smile and sighed. "Baby, you need to stop stressing out," he wrapped his arm around my waist. "I'm going to take care of you. Always."

It was so hard to believe that he wanted to look after me so much. But at the same time, I knew that he meant what he said. "I wonder if I can get a job for the rest of the summer?"

"Els, summer is over in a couple of weeks," he laughed. "Wait until we get back to Waco if you want to work that badly. But you don't have to."

"I want to," I said, dropping into a plush corner sofa with an intricate pattern and detailing. It was a rich blue with tones of black weaved throughout the patterns on it. And it was comfortable. "I'm sure I can find something for a few months until I can't work anymore. I love this one, by the way."

Leroy smiled and sat down beside me. "This one it is, then."

"Where are we going to put it until we move?"

"I'll get the store manager to ship it to us on a set date. He knows our family. It'll be no problem."

There was still a lot that we had to figure out before we went back to Waco in a few weeks. We had to decide where we'd live. It had to be close enough to school that Leroy could get to and from without hassle. He was planning on living on campus in student housing, but that plan wasn't going to work with a girlfriend and child.

"What are you thinking about?" Leroy interrupted my internal churning as he wrapped an arm around me and I realized that I had been gnawing on my lip.

"Where we'll live. Rent. Furniture." My stomach started to feel like it was in knots, twisting and making me nauseous. "There's just so much—"

"Listen." He pulled me tighter against him and I rested my head on his shoulder, letting his presence calm me. "I know things haven't come easy to you. But my parents are sitting on a comfortable fortune. Dad was in the NFL for years and they don't splash their funds about. I know it sounds like a rich kid thing to say, but they can help us, and it won't make a dent in their account. Just let them help. All right? It's okay."

It made sense. I knew they did well for themselves. But money was something I had stressed over since I was young. We could never have gone out and spent it without saving for what we wanted first. Momma had taught me to be cautious and attentive to what I was doing with my allowances. It was odd to have this list of things that we needed and not have to worry because it would just be made available to us.

Leroy made arrangements for the sofa. He paid for it and said he'd be in touch with a date and location drop-off. We also decided to do the rest of our furniture shopping in Waco once we had an apartment, which was on our list of to-dos. We needed to spend a weekend viewing places so that we could apply. I felt a little nervous about being back in Waco so soon after the dispute with Momma. Some irrational part of me was afraid that I would bump into her.

But I knew where she worked and spent most of her time. So, I was sure that I could avoid those particular places. When we arrived home from furniture shopping, Eleanor was in the living room, sitting on the floor with boxes surrounding her. Jacob was reclined in his chair with a beer, as usual. Both of them greeted us when we strolled in and sat on the sofa.

"Good day?" Jacob asked.

"We bought a sofa," Leroy said as his mother paused what she was doing and stared at us. "It's for when we move. I'm having it sent to Waco."

She raised her brows but made no further comment as she reached back into her boxes. "You got it from Furniture Tree, I hope?"

"Yeah, we did," Leroy said. "What's all this?"

"It's old baby things." Eleanor's expression brightened as she held up an adorable onesie and waved it about. "We kept sentimental things from when you and Noah were babies. You two can go through and have a look. See if there are bits that you'd like to keep. There are a lot of gender-neutral items. But you can have the blue outfits as well if you have a boy."

I was almost bouncing out of the seat at the thought of looking through Leroy's old baby items. He gestured for me to go ahead. My heart couldn't handle the excitement. I stood up as Noah came strolling down the step and into the living room.

"Damn, girl," he hollered as I held an outfit in front of me. "Filling out there a little, huh, Ellie? Maybe lay off the donuts."

"Noah, shut the hell up," Leroy snapped.

He leaned on the wall and sniggered. "I'm kidding. I know it's the baby. Shit, man. I'm teasing."

I stared down in front of me and after a moment I noticed what he meant. I *was* protruding a little, which seemed odd for how far along I was. It couldn't have been a matter of getting the dates wrong, considering I'd been a virgin before Leroy.

"Oops," Noah laughed. "Leroy didn't tell you that you can't wear crop tops anymore, huh?"

"Buzz off," Jacob snapped at his son and waved his hand toward the corridor. "Stop being a pain in the ass."

"Honey," Eleanor captured my attention. "Don't listen to him. You still look wonderful. You're just starting to show. It's normal. And beautiful."

"But I'm only eleven weeks," I said. "I shouldn't be showing this soon."

"Nonsense," she said and stood up, grunting a little from sitting on her legs. "We all carry differently. And you're so little. I'm not surprised at all. There's not a lot of room in that belly of yours."

Leroy sauntered over to my side and let his large palm slide across my stomach, the touch sending a chill right up my spine. He kissed my forehead and his lips remained against my skin when he whispered, "You look perfect."

*✴*

On Thursday, my leg bounced up and down. The plastic chairs squeaking because I couldn't stop fidgeting. Leroy placed his hand on my knee, and I looked up to find him regarding me with a small but knowing smile. Saying that I was nervous was an understatement. But how could I not have been? We were about to see our baby on screen.

It was a good kind of nervous.

"Relax, Els," Leroy whispered, leaning in a little closer. "It's going to be fine."

"I know. I'm good. I'm fine."

"Makes it all real, huh?"

His hand gave mine another squeeze and the fact that he understood me so well was comforting in a form all of its own. This did make it all real. This was the beginning of the rest of our lives. Seeing our baby would make it official in such a concrete manner. But with Leroy, I was ready for this. I could do anything with him beside me.

"Ellie Livingston?"

We both snapped our heads in the direction of the woman who waited at the threshold at a set of double doors. Leroy stood up, took my hand, and we wandered over to where she was waiting for us.

"Hi, Ellie." Her smile was warm, her narrow nose was pierced, and she extended her hand for me to shake. "I'm Pira. I'll be your technician this morning. Are you Dad?"

Leroy nodded and shook her hand before we followed her down a corridor with harsh artificial lighting, clinic awards on the walls, and the overwhelming scent of sanitizer and latex gloves. We reached door number six and Pira let us go ahead.

"Just hop up on the bed, Ellie. Lift your top to beneath the breasts and unbutton your jeans. We have to get the wand quite low on the abdomen because the baby is still very hidden at this stage. The notes said you're aware of conception date?"

Leroy stood behind me on the other side of the narrow bed, his hand resting on my shoulder while I adjusted my clothes to expose my stomach like she'd asked. Pira fell into a roller chair before she slid toward me with a clipboard and pen.

"It was the twenty-eighth of May," I said and Pira smiled as she scrawled something down on her clipboard.

She went over a few basic questions about my health, how I had been since discovering that I was pregnant, etc. Basic medical questions.

Before much longer we were watching the computer screen that Pira was organizing. She switched it on and squirted some blue gel onto my tummy, which made me wince with the cold. Also, because I'd had to drink about twenty gallons of water right before this, I felt like I was going to burst. She placed the handheld device on my stomach and the computer screen became bright with a black-and-white image. My name was in the top corner, next to the date: Thursday, August 6, 1998.

I had no idea what I was looking at while Pira continued moving the wand over my stomach.

"Well," she turned toward us and looked at Leroy, nodding. "That is a set of twins in there." Leroy's hand became tighter and he stared at the screen with a dropped jaw.

"What?!"

Twins.

What?

"These two little blobs are the babies—if I pause the image, you can see both of the hearts," Pira pointed at the screen. "And these here are the outlines of their separate sacs. Which means that they're not identical. Of course, we couldn't determine their gender this soon. But congratulations. You get two for the price of one!"

"Take it back!" I said, terrified.

"Els," Leroy murmured and tucked his finger under my chin so that I had to meet his irrationally calm expression. "It's going to be fine. Calm down."

"There are two babies growing inside of me. Don't tell me to calm down. I want a refund."

He took a deep breath and gave the doctor an apologetic smile. I was aware that I was going off the deep end. But I couldn't breathe. I'd had a hard time accepting that I was pregnant with one child. Now I would be giving birth to two. It was a lot more than I'd signed up for and the reality felt like it was going to suffocate me.

"Do you two want a minute alone?" Pira gently asked. "Or should I continue?"

"Continue what?" I threw my arms up. "Are there more tiny humans to be discovered in there?"

"No," she nervously laughed. "But we haven't determined the due date."

Leroy gave my hand a squeeze, and when I met his soft expression, I was able to relax. Well, relax enough to let the doctor perform the rest of the ultrasound. It turned out that I was bang-on with my calculations.

After we left, there was still a flare of nausea keeping me worked up over the fact that we were expecting twins. It was double the work. Double the diapers. Double the cries. What was I supposed to do when Leroy was occupied with college and practice? I'd be alone, in an apartment with two babies. I knew nothing about babies, and I had to keep two of them alive!

"Pull the car over," I said. Leroy looked over at me with panic but must have seen how pale I was because he veered the car up beside the sidewalk.

It was almost a miss, but I managed to get out of the car before I vomited in a shrub beside the sidewalk. It was humiliating and I hoped that no one was watching. After a few moments, Leroy was behind me, rubbing my back in slow but firm circular motions, soothing me with his gentle but reassuring voice. This wasn't the first time that I had been ill in front of him. But it was still embarrassing.

"I'm sorry." I kept one hand on my knee, slouched over as I wiped my mouth. Leroy tugged on my arm so that I had to straighten up. Despite my attempts to keep a distance, he pulled me into his hold.

"You're scared?" he said, his hand tucked at the back of my head where his fingertips gently massaged the base of my neck in order to soothe me.

I felt horrible. Having vomited, I probably stank, and I didn't want to gross him out. But I felt so much better when he held me. "Of course I'm scared, Leroy. We're having twins and I don't know how I'm supposed to handle that. It's a huge responsibility."

"I know it is, Els. I know." He pressed a kiss on my forehead. "I don't have all the answers right now. I know it'll be hard. But I promise you won't do it alone. Not ever."

Of course, his words were a comfort. There was something so sincere about his tone. He meant what he said, and I didn't need to question his commitment. I could only hope that later on, he didn't regret his decision. Leroy saw something in me. Something that he loved and believed was worth whatever hardship was thrown at him. I never wanted that to change.

# *Ellie*

The next morning, Leroy told me that we were going to the roller-skating rink with Noah and Cass so that we could have a bit of a time-out and fun amid all the drama that filled our lives right now. The rink was busy but not overcrowded. The lighting was low and spotlights circled the smooth, maple-wood floor where people were skating to the pop music blasting overhead. Surrounding the rink were chairs, tables, and places to eat from the canteen as well as a few pool tables and dartboards.

"Wait," Cass paused lacing up her roller skates. "Twins? As in two?"

"No, twins as in seven," Noah said mockingly, sitting on the bench seat beside her.

"That's—I'm like, my mind is blown."

"Me too," I said from where I was leaning against the clear windowpane and walls that surrounded the rink, Leroy standing beside me. We were going to be heading to Waco in a few days to search for an apartment, and Noah and Cass started school next week, so I was glad to have some fun with them before things changed and we had less time together.

"How did Eleanor take it?" Cass asked.

"She seemed pretty shocked as well." I turned to Leroy and he nodded in agreement. "But she has that can-do attitude. I don't think she's worried that we can't do it."

"She left a box of one hundred condoms on my dresser," Noah added, and we all turned to him. "They'll last a week."

"You wish," Cass spat and turned back to me. "Will you name one of the babies after me?"

It was hard to tell if she was being serious or not. "We don't know what the genders are right now," I said. It wasn't that I didn't love Cass. I just didn't think that I'd be naming a child after her.

"Okay, well, if it's a girl, call her Cass. Or Cassie." She snapped her fingers. "Either is cute."

Leroy gave Cass a blank stare. "No."

"Why not?"

"Because I've heard my brother shouting your name during sex before. It's never going to happen."

Noah hollered with laughter.

"That seems fair," Cass said.

"Come on," Leroy took my hand and we skated over to the rink entrance. Noah and Cass weren't far behind us as we circled the floor, careful of others. The music was loud and Leroy and I held hands, gliding along to the sound of "I Wanna Dance with Somebody" by Whitney Houston.

The spotlights flashed with the beat of the music, illuminating the place with colorful lights.

"I feel like I'm in an '80s music video," I said to Leroy.

"You need some fluro spandex, some leg warmers, and a perm and you'd be good to go."

"Fluro will make a comeback—it's iconic. Just watch."

He winced. "I hope not."

We both laughed and did another lap of the rink, our hands still intertwined. With a quick peep behind me, I saw Cass and Noah doing the same thing. Cass had never looked happier and Noah was watching her with tender affection that I wasn't used to seeing on him. Hope moved through me, hope that he could be the sort of man that Cass deserved.

The song switched to a slow one. Groups left the floor so that it was down to couples and Leroy slowed down, tugging on my hand so that I had to as well, and then he turned me to face him and drew us close together. My hands clasped behind his neck.

"I know we talked about how many children we wanted to have," Leroy said as our wheels slid slowly, our bodies close. "Still two, right?"

"Yes," I said. "Still two. Even if they arrive at the same time."

"Okay, good. We didn't talk about the sort of parents we want to be, though. Have you ever thought about that?"

"Hmm," I hummed. "No, I don't think so. I feel like I know the answer, though. I think I'd like to be the sort of mom that my kids can relate to really well, you know? And feel super comfortable telling me anything. And I'd want to do lots of baking and host all the cool parties and be the house that the kids and their friends want to hang out in. I want to be their friend, but also firm. Does that make sense? So that they respect me and don't turn into little shits."

"I think all parents want that," Leroy said, his hand resting on my lower back.

"I'm being hopeful. I don't want to be like my mom. Now that I think about it, I feared her. I don't want my kids to fear me. Your mom and dad are a perfect example of how it should be done."

Leroy smiled. "They're great but Noah is an example of kids-with-good-parents-gone-wrong."

"No, no, no," I shushed him, looking behind me to see that he and Cass were leaning on the wall, no longer skating but kissing and laughing. "He's making an effort to do better. We're not going to speak negatively about that."

He laughed. "You're going to be an amazing mom, Els."

"You never told me what sort of dad you want to be."

"I want to be the sort of dad whose children watch how he treats their mother and loves and respects her. I want my example to set their standards high. If the twins are boys, I want them to know how to treat a partner. I want them to be sensitive and strong and know that you can definitely be both. And if I have girls, I want them to have high standards for who their partner will be. I want them to be anything they want to be and do whatever they want to do. Of course, it might be one of each."

His answer could not have been more perfect. It was impossible to know how our lives would map out from here. We probably wouldn't always have all of the answers: surely we'd mess up from time to time, and no doubt we would find ourselves questioning our own sanity. But we had the best intentions and we had each other, that had to count for something. Besides, thinking about how beautiful our family could be was a nice respite from all of the fear that I had been feeling since we'd discovered this news.

We took a small break from the rink and went back to the seating area for something to eat. Cass went to the bathroom and Leroy went to get food, leaving Noah and me alone at the four-seater table beside a jukebox and pool table. It was awkward for a few moments, terse silence that seemed too obvious for such a busy place. Finally, he swept a hand through his hair and clacked his tongue.

"Must be feeling weird, huh? Having twins and all that."

"Yeah." *Maybe I could actually have a normal conversation with Noah.* "It's . . . well, it's life-changing. Kind of hard to even wrap my head around."

"Yeah, I bet."

"I'm really happy for you and Cass, by the way," I said. "It's nice that things worked out."

He gave a slow nod. "Yeah. You like music, right?"

"Uh, duh," I laughed and then cringed. *Duh?* "Yeah. I do. How come?"

"Are you into the Spice Girls and all that girl stuff, or do you like decent bands? I assume you must have good taste if you like Aerosmith. Which reminds me, I feel kind of bad about ruining that concert for you and wanted to apologize."

"Oh," I said, trying to hide the surprise in my tone. "It's forgiven. Also, the Spice Girls are awesome. I don't have a favorite genre, though. If it's a good song, it's a good song."

Noah gave a greeting nod at a couple of girls heading into the rink with their skates on, I assumed they were school friends. "Yeah, I think I'm a rock person. Pearl Jam is sick. Red Hot Chili Peppers."

"I love them! What about Nine Inch Nails?"

"Yep," he said. "Pantera?"

"I like some of their songs. Some of them are a bit too aggressive for my taste but I like 'Walk.'"

"Yeah, that's a good one," he said and seemed more relaxed than I'd ever seen him around me. It was nice to have a common ground. He leaned in like he was going to tell me a secret. "All right, don't tell anyone, but I kind of like No Doubt too."

I laughed. "I love No Doubt. Gwen Stefani is a babe too, right?"

"Yeah, she is," he grinned.

"I hate periods," Cass said as she approached the table. A couple of guys on the pool table gave her a look, but Cass couldn't have cared less. She sat down and pouted. "You're so lucky that you won't have a period for ages, Els."

"Would you rather be pregnant?" I asked.

She recoiled. "No! No, I would not."

I might have had the same answer as her a few months ago, but now this was my reality and I wouldn't change it.

※

Two days later, Leroy and I had just arrived home from Waco after spending the weekend house-hunting near the college campus. Eleanor and Jacob wanted to help with rent and whatever we needed but that didn't mean that I would sit back and get something for nothing. I wanted to get a job, even if it was part time. Leroy of course had a trust fund that kept him comfortable.

I still wanted to pursue a college diploma. It was always going to be correspondence so I was confident that once the babies were a little bit older, I could go ahead with the courses while the children were at home.

The apartments that we looked at while we were in Waco were all great, but there was one in particular that we applied for that we were hoping to get. It was a two-bedroom apartment on the bottom floor of the building. It was so close to Baylor that Leroy could walk if he really wanted to and the bottom floor was ideal, considering we wouldn't have to lug babies, diaper bags, strollers, and car seats onto the elevator.

There was nothing spectacular about the actual apartment. It had been recently renovated with new hunter-green wallpaper and a white carpet that offered a brighter component to the rather dark room. I'd already envisioned how perfect some white wicker side tables and shelves would look in the living area.

The kitchen and bathroom were a soft pastel yellow and the curtains throughout the apartment were patterned with floral designs. I sort of hated them and would have preferred something more subtle. But it didn't bother me enough to not hope and pray that our application was accepted. We were told that we would hear by tomorrow at the latest.

"Els." Leroy strolled into his bedroom as he pulled a dark blue-and-black dress shirt over his head. His hair was still damp from his shower and he wore a nice pair of slacks. I arched a brow from the bed as he picked up his watch to check the time. "Can you shower and put on something nice. We're going out."

"Wait . . . what?"

"You'll look beautiful in whatever you wear," he added with speed, as if he thought that I was upset about how he'd worded his request. "Just . . . well—"

"Since when did we have plans to go out?"

"Since I made them so that I could surprise you and take you out," he grinned and sauntered toward the bed. He picked up the magazine that was in my lap and tossed it to the side, grasping my hand so that I had to stand up. "I don't want to be late. So if you could?"

I giggled as he gave me a playful swat on the butt. Leroy and I had been together constantly since I'd returned a week ago, but we hadn't done a lot in the way of romance. It had been about getting ourselves organized to move and arranging things for the babies. We deserved a little time to enjoy each other's company.

The dress that I changed into was a white sleeveless turtleneck that hugged me in the top half and flowed from the hips down. It stopped mid-thigh and while I had a definite bump, it still looked nice. I snatched a denim jacket and met Leroy downstairs, where he was sitting in the living room with his mom and dad, chatting and watching the football reruns.

"Wow." Leroy stood up and swept me from head to toe with an adoring expression. He cleared his throat as his gaze darted toward his parents and back to me again. "You look beautiful, Els."

"Have fun, you two," Jacob waved as Leroy put his hand on my lower back to steer us out of the room. "Have her home by nine and no making bab—"

"Jacob," Eleanor gave him a swat as I peered over my shoulder, blushing while the two of them laughed. "Don't tease the kids."

Leroy held my hand as we drove into town, his thumb making circles on my skin. We arrived at a quaint little restaurant on the corner of a central street that wasn't quiet, but it wasn't packed. The windows were illuminated with fairy lights. Vines with sweet little flowers wound around the posts on either side of the door, which rang when Leroy pulled it open. The small space was enchanting, the low lighting creating ambience. The walls were a soft yellow with what appeared to be hand-painted flowers tastefully scattered. Tablecloths covered the round tables, an identical shade to the walls, and candles flickered in the middle of couples and friends who were dining. It was magical.

"My, my, Leroy Lahey, what do we have here?" An older woman with thick dark waves and a pair of thin-rimmed glasses wandered toward us with a couple of menus in hand. "Is this the Ellie that I've been hearing about?"

"Hi, Helen." Leroy's greeting was warm and familiar. "This is Ellie. Els, this is Helen. A friend of Mom's."

"It's nice to meet you," I shook her hand before she handed us a menu each.

"You too, sugar." She wiggled her finger and gestured for us to follow her. "She's a pretty one, Leroy. You tell that mother of yours to give me a call. We need to get together."

She stopped when she'd led us to a private booth with a window. It was intimate and we grinned at each other across the table as we slid into our seats. Helen gave Leroy a pat on the shoulder and smiled. "Congratulations, by the way."

"Thanks, Helen," Leroy smiled up at her. "I'll get Mom to phone."

"Good boy. I'll be back to get your order in a few."

Once she was gone, Leroy reached across the table and picked up my hand, pressing a soft kiss on the top of it. "How's this?"

"Perfect," I said. "This place is gorgeous."

"Yeah, we've been coming for a while," Leroy said and read

his menu. "Helen likes to let us eat for free, so we leave her an extra-large tip."

The food was exquisite; I would have paid for that meal *and* left a big tip. It was a bit of a shame that the taste of meat had been off-putting for the last couple of weeks, otherwise I would have ordered the steak like Leroy. Instead, I had fries and a salad, which was still delectable. After we'd eaten, he told me that our night wasn't over and there was another surprise in store for me.

"A drive-in movie?" I almost squealed with excitement as Leroy drove the car down the designated road, past all of the idle vehicles that were stopped and waiting for the movie to begin. "What are we seeing?"

"*Armageddon*," he said, turning the wheel into the very last row of vehicles. "You mentioned that you hadn't seen it before, and I knew it would be on tonight."

Leroy stopped and switched off the car beside a pickup truck that didn't appear to be occupied. The truck bed faced the projector and on the back of it was a mattress and a couple of thick warm blankets. We were right at the back and tucked away from the view of others. My stomach turned over on itself.

"Is this where we're watching from?" I asked.

Leroy jumped up on the tray and held a hand out for me. "It sure is. This is Robbie's." I remembered that he was the one Cass had salivated over during practice. Leroy hoisted me onto the pickup and we both snuggled into the makeshift bed, covering ourselves with the comforters.

"This is so nice," I said. I hadn't been to a drive-in for quite some time. There was something authentic about watching a movie like this.

Leroy reached down beside him as the shorts before the film

began. He revealed a few bags of sour candies and cola bottle candies as well as a bottle of water each and a bag of potato chips. "I know that you said you were full from dinner but—"

"Stop," I interrupted and grabbed the sour candies. "There's this second stomach that we have for after-dinner treats. It's starving."

I opened the packet and popped a few in my mouth, immediately wincing as the sourness hit me in full force. My eyes began to water, and I took a few deep breaths, willing myself not to cave and spit them out.

"You okay there?" Leroy laughed as I battled through the pain, rolling onto my side and burying my face in his chest. "I should have warned you just how sour these are."

It took me a moment, but I recovered, leaning back so that I could exhale and wipe my watering eyes.

"You good, babe?"

"Yep," I smacked my lips. "I'm good."

"Can I have a taste?"

Before I could reach into the bag and hand him a sour candy, he cupped my jaw, angled my face upward, and kissed me, not hesitating to meet his tongue with mine.

"Oh shit," he pulled back, still holding my face while his eyes watered. "Whoa, those are *so* damn sour! You do taste delicious, though."

He dipped his head again and pried my mouth open, sucking my bottom lip in between his teeth. My stomach immediately turned over; my thighs clenched at how erotic it felt. It started off slow and sensual, tasting each other, licking, nipping, pushing our tongues together and panting as the feeling became overwhelming. Leroy shifted, throwing his legs over mine so that

I was encased beneath him and then our kiss picked up pace, becoming frantic. We grabbed at each other, his hands sliding up underneath my thighs so that he could hook them around his waist while my fingers slid into the strands of his hair and pulled.

I threw my head back and gasped when Leroy thrust his hips down, grinding against me. My dress had slid up around my hips and only my underwear served as a barrier against the strain on his jeans. A low groan erupted from the back of his throat whenever I whimpered, so he kept doing it, lowering his hips to mine, thrusting, causing a friction that was leaving me breathless while he grabbed my hair in his fist and kissed my throat.

We were alone for the most part, but that didn't mean I wanted to be loud enough for the nearest cars to hear my cries. It was hard to contain, though; I was thrashing, desperate for the release that was building in my core. Leroy leaned up on one arm, his hair a mess from my fingers clutching and pulling it. He slipped his other hand between us and unbuttoned his jeans, lowering them just enough so that he was freed.

"Are you okay?" he panted, kissing me again. "Is this okay?"

"Yeah," I gripped his shoulders, pulling him back in with my feet against his butt. "I just want you inside of me."

"Mmm," his growl was guttural and animalistic, and he tugged on my panties, pushing them aside. "I've got you, my beautiful girl."

He pushed inside of me, swallowing my cry with his mouth, his tongue tasting me and moaning with pleasure as our bodies connected.

After, we lay beside each other, my head on his chest, euphoric and relaxed under the comforter. Leroy's thumb made circles on my shoulder and he kept on kissing the top of my head. I could have fallen asleep right then and there, the release having sent waves of pleasure and satisfaction throughout my body.

"Comfortable?" Leroy asked, his voice heavy with tiredness.

"Yeah."

"Warm enough?"

"Yep."

"I love you, baby."

I nuzzled his chest. "I love you too."

In the morning, Leroy was sleeping as soundly as he always does and I wanted to leave him to it. He didn't have long until college started, and his sleep-ins would become a thing of the past. I thought it was best to let him make the most of it.

I pulled on a sundress and a sweater before I crept out of the room and tiptoed downstairs. I'd never been one to spend all morning in bed. It felt like a waste of daylight. When I walked into the kitchen, Eleanor was at the countertop with a blender full of different ingredients. "Oh, good morning. I thought that you'd be up soon."

She switched on the blender. The entire kitchen echoed with the loud noise and I winced as I glanced toward the entrance, almost expecting the entire household to stumble through and demand that we keep the noise down. "Don't worry!" Eleanor shouted. "The men in this family could sleep through a wrecking ball splitting the house right down the middle."

Laughing, I leaned against the other side of the countertop while she got a couple of glasses out and filled them up. "I noticed that you haven't been eating a lot of red meat. But you really need to keep those iron levels up. This has some supplements and kale and a few other bits and pieces in it."

"Oh, thank you."

"Don't thank me, sweetheart. We need to keep those little Laheys in good health."

I caressed my stomach while she stuck a straw in the smoothie and pushed it across the countertop. It was a rich reddish purple and it smelled delicious. The taste was even better. We both sat at the table and talked while we drank. There was something about Eleanor that made it so easy to open up. I found that I could ask her anything without the need to feel embarrassed or ashamed. She was empathetic and answered my questions no matter what they were.

Some of the medical-related queries that I had could be kind of TMI, but it didn't bother her. She had a vast range of knowledge and insisted that I came to her and she would do her best to help.

When Eleanor and I talked like this, a small part of me missed Momma and wished that these were the things she and I could be doing together. But whenever I spared her a minute of thought, I remembered how she'd hit me. That slap was horrific, hateful, and vehement with rage. If things were ever to repair between us, she would need to be the one to extend the olive branch first.

"There you are." Leroy wandered into the kitchen, still in his boxer shorts but he'd pulled a T-shirt on. His hair was fluffed in all directions and I grinned as he stifled a yawn. He always made my heart flutter in the mornings. Just the state of him was adorable, sexy, and cute all at the same time.

I stood up and gathered the now-empty glasses, giving Leroy a quick peck on the cheek as I passed. It didn't matter that we were having twins together, he still didn't like being overly affectionate in front of his mother, and I respected that.

Eleanor cleared her throat and I glanced up from rinsing the dishes. "Now that you're up, Leroy," she said, wearing a knowing smile, "guess who called at seven this morning?"

We exchanged a curious look and shrugged, not sure who could have been calling at such an hour that would incite so much excitement from Eleanor. She clapped her hands together. "The owner of the apartment that you two were so set on. You got it! He wants a call back as soon as possible to arrange the details. But it's all yours."

Leroy jogged toward me and wrapped his arms around my waist, spinning me in a circle that threatened to make me ill. But I laughed with delight because things were falling into place. It had all seemed impossible less than a month ago, each morning beginning with a sensation of absolute dread over the unknown. Now, even the unknown didn't seem so bad because waking up beside Leroy reminded me that whatever we faced, he was there.

"We did it, Els. We got the apartment."

"We should celebrate."

He agreed with enough volume that his mother heard but then he leaned in and with a hushed whisper, his voice raspy and seductive beside my ear, said, "We will, baby."

I almost choked as he set me down. It was typical that he kept a straight face as though he hadn't said a thing at all and left me to blush and feel flustered.

"You'll both need to do some furniture shopping before Ellie gets too big to decorate," Eleanor said from where she sat at the table. "You can't put the bed and drawers on a plane."

"It'd be best to do it as soon as possible," Leroy agreed, his arm was still rested around my waist. "Before classes start on the twenty-fourth. That's only two weeks from now."

I felt a bit overwhelmed at the sudden bout of plans that were being made. But it was a good overwhelming. We had a lot to do—we needed to arrange a moving date, go furniture shopping, and get comfortable before Leroy became swamped with college classes and football. Not to mention that I needed to mentally prepare to be a full-time mother to twins.

"I'm going to redecorate that spare room and put the old cribs in there. For when those grandbabies come and stay with me," Eleanor stood and laughed with excitement as she strolled out of the kitchen.

Leroy looked down at me when we were alone again, his elation evident in the softness of his stare. He really did look at me as though I were a prize.

"How do you do it?" he murmured, his fingertips grazing my forehead as he slowly traced my face and tucked my hair behind my ear.

"Do what?"

"I swear, Els, I look at you and I feel my heart expanding in my chest. I have never felt anything like it before."

Then it was my turn to wonder how he did it to me. He delivered these words without flinching. He didn't seem shy or nervous. He was bold and declared his love for me with so much sincerity that he didn't even need to use the word *love*—I still felt it.

My mother was wrong about him. He wasn't trouble. He was

the best thing that had ever happened to me. And although our circumstances weren't complication-free, I wouldn't change a thing. We were forever. I knew it.

## *Ellie*

"—and then we—"

"Leroy, stop!"

"What? I'm telling them about the first night that we met. Every child should hear their parents' love story."

"First of all, they're not even born. Second, I think that we can skip the finer details."

Leroy laughed and nodded with agreement. We were lying beside each other in our new bed, in our new apartment. We had been here for two weeks and this was his first weekend as an official college student. He'd done well during his first few classes. He worried about me a lot and kept calling throughout the day, interrupting me trying to settle us into our new home. But it was safe to say that we adored living together in our little apartment.

It was still early, so we hadn't left our bed yet. He'd proceeded to tell my stomach the tale about the night that we'd met. He believed it was good to talk to the babies. And what better story to tell them than our one-night stand? Personally, I think that he just liked to reminisce. As did I. It was an exquisite memory.

Because I hadn't been able to bring any of my old bedroom décor from Momma's house, I'd had to start from scratch in our new bedroom. There were a few things from Leroy's house— sentimental items such as trophies, framed football jerseys, and some childhood memorabilia that lived on his desk. A piggy bank, figurines, and toy cars. As soon as we'd arrived, I'd gone to the thrift store and found several band posters, a CD rack, some plastic plants, and a couple of vinyl records. It was an updated version of the room that I loved at home. It was more minimal but still full of the things that I loved, including Leroy's contribution. It was representative of both of our interests, which made it more special.

"Everyone will be here soon," I reminded Leroy as he rolled me onto my side and spooned me.

The family was coming to see our new place for the first time and to go watch Leroy's football game that night. They'd arrived last night and stayed in a hotel because we didn't have the room to put them up. Eleanor, Jacob, Noah, and even Cass were coming for lunch, and I couldn't wait to see them all and show them what we'd done with the apartment.

"How are you feeling about the game tonight?" I asked.

His breath tickled my neck as he spoke from behind me. "Confident, for the most part. Nervous for the other."

"You've been training so hard, I'm sure it'll go well."

"Mmmm."

I rolled over so that I could see him, and even though he smiled, there was this hint of concern hidden deep within the features that I was so familiar with. "What's wrong?"

"No, nothing. I just want to do well, you know. Especially when my dad will be there watching. He's been preparing me for this my entire life. Not in a forceful way or anything."

"I know what you mean."

"Even if I feel like I'm prepared and my plays are solid and everything is perfect, it's impossible to know what the other team is going to bring. I just want to do as well as my dad believes I can."

There was something sincerely beautiful about his vulnerability, something inspiring. "He already knows how much the game means to you and how much of your heart goes into it. Win or lose, he'll still believe you're the best."

He looked down at me, his eyes scrunched up because his smile was so big.

"What?"

"You're going to be the sweetest mom," he said and pulled us even closer together. "Can't wait to hear you give our kids cute little motivational speeches."

My excitement grew. I'd never thought about it like that before. "I can literally not wait for that! But what if I screw it up? What if I give terrible advice?"

"Stop," he groaned with amusement; meanwhile, my excitement had turned into panic. "You're not going to give terrible advice. You're already too good at it. And besides, moms have instincts. You'll know what to tell them when the time comes."

"Ooh. You're pretty good at it too," I said.

He kissed my forehead. "We make a good team, don't we?"

"The best."

*N*

We pulled ourselves out of bed not long after that. We'd showered, changed, and had just vacuumed when the doorbell rang. It hadn't been long since we'd seen everyone, but the greetings commenced as if it had been a decade.

"The apartment looks beautiful," Eleanor said, sweeping inside after she'd crushed me in a vice-like hug. The front door opened into the kitchen/dining area. We had enough room for a small round table and a shelf where I kept a few houseplants for decoration. A wide arched entryway gave a generous view of the living area. It was almost an open plan design aside from the half wall cutting between the rooms.

"Cozy, isn't it?" Jacob closed the door behind him while Cass and I hugged.

Leroy laughed. "Cozy is code word for *small*."

"You're eighteen, darling," Eleanor said. "Anything of your own is wonderful."

"Hey," Leroy raised his hands. "I'm not complaining. We love it here."

"We do," I said.

"It's not bad," Noah mumbled, looking around. The kitchen seemed to have shrunk with all the extra people standing in it. "Sort of plain. Hang some art up or something, maybe."

"I'm getting there," I defended as Cass slipped her arm through mine.

"Ignore him and give us a tour. This place is adorable. I'm totally jealous."

There wasn't a whole lot to show them, but I led the way, taking a few short steps into the living area where our lovely blue sofa that Leroy and I had chosen together was against the wall, and beside it was a single armchair. We had a small television on a wooden cabinet, a matching coffee table, and some framed photos of Leroy and me above the gas heater.

We moved into the corridor and paused briefly at our bedroom. There was something strange about showing a group of people where I slept every night. Or . . . did other things.

"And this is the twins' room," I said as I swung the door open on the last stop of our small tour. Eleanor, Jacob, Cass, and Noah shuffled over the threshold and glanced around at the new furniture that I had put together.

Okay, that's a lie.

Leroy had put it together, but I put it where I wanted it and added all the little bits of décor. The fluffy rug on the floor. The adorable colorful canvases. The trinkets on the shelves and the wall stickers of enchanting animals and Winnie-the-Pooh. Of course. I loved Winnie-the-Pooh in kids' bedrooms. This is the room that I'd given the most attention to, which is probably why Noah had commented on the lack of décor elsewhere.

Our landlord told us that we weren't allowed to paint the walls, which was a bummer, but it wasn't the worst thing. The neutral cream color with indented pattern was suitable just the way it was. I was certain that our time would come to purchase our own home and then we could decorate as we pleased.

"You've done so well," Eleanor said as she ran a hand along the top of the new pine cribs.

We were well prepared, considering I was only fifteen weeks along. We still had a while until the twins arrived, but that couldn't stop me from setting up now. I loved having things organized.

Jacob pointed at the recliner Leroy and I had chosen. He smiled and wandered toward it before he sat down and sighed. "This is a good chair." He gave us a thumbs-up.

"You'd know what a good recliner is, wouldn't you?" Eleanor teased her husband.

Noah and Cass were in the corner having an argument about something that had been ongoing for the duration of the tour. I smiled at Leroy and he nodded with understanding before I strolled toward Cass, who had her back to me and startled with a jump when I touched her shoulder. She turned around and smiled, ignoring Noah, who was pouting.

"Look at this bump," she sang and bent over, almost hugging my stomach. "I can't wait to cuddle them!"

I put a hand over hers and laughed. "Come and help me with lunch?"

"Sure."

We left Noah and the others to chat, their voices becoming quieter as we entered the kitchen. Despite being in another part of the house, we still had to keep our volume down if we didn't want to be heard. The walls were thin, and unlike the Laheys' home, we didn't have a lot of space to create distance.

"Cass, what's going on with Noah?" I interrogated her as I opened the fridge and began to retrieve different produce for sandwiches.

She lifted her slim frame onto the lip of the countertop and sighed. "We're just . . . arguing."

"I can see that," I said. "About what?"

"Coming here from Castle Rock, I've seen how far I'm going to be from Noah when he starts college at Baylor. I dunno. I felt a little . . . upset about it?"

I mulled over her words as I sliced a tomato into small cubes and threw them into a serving dish. "I mean, it's his college choice. You can't get mad at him for going to college, Cass."

She pressed her lips into a tight line. She knew that I was right.

"Come with him?" I suggested. "Or do long distance. It wouldn't be the end of the world."

"I couldn't do long distance." She shook her head as she stared down at her fingers twiddling in her lap. "Not with him."

"How come?"

"It's *him*," she said. "He's devious and college girls would be all over him."

"You don't trust him?"

"Would you?"

"No," I said. "But I wouldn't date someone that I don't trust either."

Her shoulders slumped in obvious disappointment. I hated to be the bearer of bad news. But she needed to hear it. I wasn't going to coddle her and support a relationship she wasn't comfortable in. If she was happy and had no second thoughts about the commitment, then I would be thrilled for her. But that wasn't the case—that much was obvious.

"I can't go to Baylor anyway," she said and tucked a leg under her bum. "I'm not smart enough. Senior year is already way hard, and it's only just started."

"It's all about your attitude." I gave her a bop on the nose with a cucumber. "You have to work with your circumstances, and any situation is as good as you make it."

She tilted her head to the side and fixed me with a bored expression. "You do remember having a full-blown meltdown when you found out that you were pregnant, right?"

I laughed and handed her a carrot and the grater. My kitchen skills hadn't improved much, but I could prepare vegetables.

"Yes, I remember having a meltdown. But I'm making lemonade with lemons. I'm choosing to embrace and be grateful."

"That's easy for you to say," she mumbled and hopped off the countertop. "Your boyfriend worships you and his mother can't wait to be a grandma. It's easy for you."

"Cass," I turned to her with a soft sigh. "I haven't spoken to my mom in a month. She hit me and wants nothing to do with me. I mean, I'm so fortunate to have the support that I do, I'm not taking any of that for granted. But it's still been hard."

"I'm sorry," she said, her cheeks a shade darker than her natural blush. "That was insensitive. I think I'm projecting. It's not your fault."

My heart hurt for her. As it did when it came to Noah—she deserved more. But unless she was willing to make a change, then I couldn't help her. Those choices were her own.

"How are things with *your* mom?" I changed the subject, though it might not have been a less painful one.

"The same. She wasn't even home on the first morning of school. Senior year and she was out. Not that I'm surprised."

"Where was she?"

"At her new boyfriend's."

"Another new one?"

Cass gave a small exhausted nod. "He's okay. He's nice, I guess. I've learned not to take my frustration out on them. It's not their fault my mom is a deadbeat."

"That's gracious of you."

"Tiff told me that I should sleep with him to get back at my mom." I stared at Cass with alarm. "I'm not going to," she said. "But I probably would if I was single. It's kind of a good idea. It'd be funny too."

My next words surprised me. "Tell Tiff to do it."

Cass and I burst into a bout of giggles. "She probably would if she wasn't dating some college dude that she met in Florida over the summer."

"Bummer."

Cass's amusement subsided and she sighed. "It wouldn't even matter if I did do that to Mom. She'd just move on to the next man in five minutes. She hasn't lasted with one of them for more than three months since Jamie left."

"Maybe she's never recovered after losing him. She might be trying to recreate what she had with him, but it doesn't work because the way she loved your dad was so intense. It's kind of awful if you think about it. Momma's never dated again, either. Well, not that I know of. I doubt she'd tell me anyway, but people cope with grief in different ways."

Cass stared at nothing; her gaze was distant as if she was contemplating what I had said. Perhaps she was realizing that she had more in common with her mom than she realized. It certainly seemed like they'd both given their hearts to undeserving men and didn't know how to get them back.

Having said all of that, it made me think of Momma in a similar sense. Perhaps she was stuck in her grief too. She'd fallen in love and had been left behind to clean up the mess, raise the child, sacrifice everything just so that she could raise me. I'd accused her of being jealous, but maybe, she really was just scared that I'd be left in the same way that she'd been: heartbroken by the father of my child.

*N*

We set lunch out on our small table. Unfortunately, there wasn't enough room for us all to sit. So we piled our plates up with food and wandered into the living area to sit on the sofa or floor. This wasn't how Eleanor and Jacob were used to dining, but there were no complaints from either of them as they huddled on the couch and ate.

I had barely had a mouthful of food when the doorbell started ringing and I paused, glancing around with confusion as Leroy jumped up and strolled toward the door with a knowing smile. I watched him with puzzlement from where I sat on the love seat, and when he swung the door open and revealed Eric and Amber, I gasped with excitement.

"What?"

"Surprise!" Amber shouted as the two of them wandered in and gave brief waves to the family. I started to stand up, but she waved in dismissal. "Stay there, Momma. Look at that bump. It's adorable."

Despite her protests, I stood up and beelined straight for Eric, embracing him in a crushing hug. He seemed startled for a moment, but being Eric, he didn't hesitate for long and he squeezed me back. "Thank you for calling Eleanor," I leaned back. If he hadn't snitched on me, I might still have been miserable at home, scanning adoption catalogs and sobbing over heartbreak.

"Of course, sweetheart," he winked. "Someone had to save these ones," he gave me a light poke in the stomach. Amber shuffled Eric to the side so that we could have a quick cuddle.

Eric and Amber were doing well at Emory together. Both of them lived on campus and had made a small group of friends. I realized that I needed to phone Amber more often so that I could keep up with the finer details of her life. She was my best friend, and I'd been so wrapped up in the pregnancy and having my life turned upside-down that I hadn't seen any of the girls from school in a while. I needed to do better.

Amber sat on the floor beside my chair and cradled a sandwich in her hands. "Noah doesn't seem so bad," she whispered. "He's kind of funny."

"He has his moments," I said and looked over at where he and Leroy were talking to Eric and Cass.

"You seem really happy with this family," she smiled. "Happier than I've seen you in a long time."

"I am happy. It does suck that you and Cass live so far away though."

Amber swallowed her mouthful. "She's cool. I like her. Yeah, I know what you mean. We all live so far apart now. It's weird how much has changed in such a short time."

"Tell me about it."

After a half hour of eating, talking, and catching up, Leroy came and stood beside me. Cass was sitting on Noah's lap, and Amber and Eric were on the floor beside them so that Eleanor and Jacob could have the other end of the sofa. Of course, the love seat was my throne and no one dared to steal it from a pregnant woman.

"One sec, everyone." He cleared his throat and gathered the attention of the room. "I need to ask Ellie something. And I know how much the people in her life mean to her. Because I did consider asking her this question when it was just us. Perhaps during dinner. Or during a drive-in," he grinned, and I could feel how utterly breathless I was becoming. This was happening. "But then I realized that this is the sort of moment that she would want to share with the people she loves. She's generous like that. Loving and caring. Full of an untamable energy. Full of light and hope. The brightest star in the sky wouldn't hold a flame to this woman. She's going to make an incredible mother . . . and wife—" he fell to his knee in front of me and revealed a small box that popped open and held a beautiful diamond "—if she'll have me. Ellie Livingston, would you be mine? Forever?"

I wasn't sure what made him think that I would want everyone to see me losing it. Tears blurred my vision, my nose stung, my chin quivered. No one should witness that. But it didn't matter. Because Leroy had just asked me to marry him and I was on top of the world.

"Of course," I stammered and swiped under my eyes before I stretched out my trembling hand for the ring.

It was a beautiful ring, a teardrop diamond with micro-sized encrusted jewels in the frame. It was classic and enchanting.

"That was my mother's." Eleanor's voice pulled my attention to her tearful gaze. She sat beside Jacob and their emotions were obvious. It made me blubber all that much harder. Leroy's gentle fingers slid the ring into place, and I raised my hand out in front of me, marveling at how it glimmered and shone, almost appearing as though it belonged with the stars.

"I love you." I threw my arms around Leroy and we both stood, embracing in a hold that was safe, sweet, and secure. There was nowhere else that I would rather be.

He whispered his words into the crook of my neck. "I'm sorry that your mom couldn't be here. But I'm here Ellie, I'll always be here."

It might have been bittersweet that Momma wasn't here for this moment. But the people who deserved to experience my happiness were. "Can we please wait until I can fit into a cute dress again?" I sobbed as he leaned back and swept my hair behind my ear, the front strands having become damp with tears.

Leroy laughed—along with the others in the room—and nodded as he pressed a kiss on my forehead. "We can wait. This is a promise to make you my wife, Els. Whether it's this week or next year. I'm not going anywhere."

We accepted the congratulations of our friends and family, and it meant so much to me that Leroy made sure Amber and Eric could be around for the celebration.

I never wanted to live without him.

⚡

That night, at Leroy's first football game as a college student, I sat in the first row on the bleachers as the fiancé of the home team's quarterback. They were leading, and whenever I wasn't watching him rule the hell out of this game, I was staring at the diamond on my finger, pride swelling within my chest. It was hard to believe that this was my life now. Eleanor, Jacob, Noah, Cass, Eric, and Amber were beside me, all equally as excited about how well he was doing.

The pride in Jacob's expression was about the sweetest thing that I had ever seen. Whenever Leroy made a play that was particularly impressive, he'd ask us all if we'd seen it. He'd say, "Look at that arm, the boy is brilliant." It made me wish that Leroy could be in the stands to witness it as well as on the field. However, Noah kindly used a camcorder to film the game and that excited me because all of the proud commentary would be watchable later. It was a miracle that he wasn't sulking about all of the attention that Jacob was giving to Leroy. In fact, he seemed rather proud of his brother and it was lovely to witness.

The time on the clock was almost over when everyone got into formation in the middle of the field. Leroy stood in his position at the back of the lineup, his name and the number twenty-one across the shoulders. The scoreboard read 46–32, Baylor leading against Mississippi. It seemed that Leroy was doing an incredible job leading his team and calling the shots. Considering the fact that there was a constant hum of chatter in the stands, the place was quiet while we waited for the snap. Leroy leaned over, rolled his left shoulder, and then shouted "Hut!"

He caught the ball and the rest of the players collided, their protective wear crunching at the impact as Baylor's defense tried to prevent Mississippi from getting near the ball. Leroy stepped backward and threw the ball to a wide receiver, who caught it and threw it back to Leroy right before he was thrown to the ground. Leroy threw it to another wide receiver as he ran toward the end zone. Once again, the wide receiver threw it back before he, too, was tackled. It zigzagged between them and it looked like Leroy was going to get it back again, but Mississippi must have caught on because the players honed in on Leroy so that he couldn't catch it. However, the Baylor running back appeared beside him and caught it while the attention was elsewhere. Mississippi weren't fast enough to get hold of the running back and he took off toward the end zone, weaving through the offense with ease until he scored a touchdown right as the buzzer sounded the end of the game.

We all got to our feet and screamed with excitement, clapping and cheering as Leroy and his teammates huddled into an enormous group hug. It almost looked violent, people throwing themselves at each other, chest bumps, and slaps on the back. Jacob and Eleanor were beaming from ear to ear.

We met Leroy on the edge of the field after that. His smile was full of relief that his hard work and training had paid off. Winning his first game as a college student was a brilliant first impression, and I knew how glad he would be that he'd done well in front of his dad.

"You were so good," I said as he gave me a hug and kiss. "I'm so proud.

He winked. "Thanks, baby."

"Excellent, son," Jacob said, patting him on the shoulder as Eleanor nodded in agreement. "Brought back a lot of memories watching that. Same field I was on as a student. Same colors. Felt like old times."

"I'm glad you didn't tell me that before I went on," Leroy joked. "That would have been a lot of pressure."

"We should get a photo," Eleanor suggested. "Who has the camera?"

"I'll take it," Cass said and held her hand out to Noah, asking for the camera. He handed it over and she gestured that he stand next to his mom, dad, and brother.

"I think it's just the three of them," Noah said.

"Get in here, man," Leroy flicked his head while Eleanor and Jacob stood on either side of him, positioning themselves into a picture-perfect pose, the field in the background. Noah sighed but I could tell he was glad to be included. He stood next to his mom and dropped an arm around her shoulder.

"Shuffle over a little bit," I said. "That way you'll have the scoreboard behind you."

Cass nodded with enthusiasm and raised the camera so

she could peep through the viewfinder. "Little bit more," she instructed, and everyone went a few steps left. "Stop! That's perfect. Okay, smile!"

We took a few more with different combinations. Leroy and me. Cass and Noah. Cass and me. Jacob and Eleanor. The parking lot was still congested when we finally left, cars in a line, waiting for their turn to leave. We'd all agreed to go and get something to eat so we could make the most of the family visit. Leroy and Jacob couldn't stop discussing the game, dissecting it and analyzing it in more detail than I thought possible. The part that I loved most was how obvious it was that Leroy loved his father's approval. He'd ask what Jacob thought of a certain play and when Jacob told him how well he'd done, Leroy's expression would light up, thrilled. Nothing made me happier than seeing those two in their element. It was a bond like I'd never seen, and it was beautiful.

# FIVE MONTHS LATER

## *Ellie*

Leroy sat at our kitchen table and started toeing his shoes off. It was dark out and I longed for a fireplace rather than gas heating. I missed the lick of flames on a cold night, casting ambient light and offering a comforting warmth.

"Els, you don't need to make dinner. I've told you. I'll come home and do it."

I waddled the burritos over to the table so that he could eat.

"That doesn't seem fair. You spend the entire day at school. I want you to have hot food when you get home."

He chewed on his lip as he stared down at the plate. "You're amazing and this means so much to me. I just—"

"What's wrong?" I sat down, needing to take the massive thirty-five-week weight off my feet.

"Els, I don't think I can eat another burrito." He gave me a perplexed expression and took my hands in his. "I'm sorry. Baby, please don't be upset. It's just, I've had so, *so* many burritos over the last few months."

"Well, it's chicken tonight. It was beef on Wednesday and we had grilled cheese last night?"

"Please, baby," he pleaded with concern. "Just let me cook when I come home. I swear it's no big deal. And I do love how you make these. I just need something different."

"I get it. Even *I'm* kind of sick of them."

He seemed relieved that he hadn't upset me. But there was no use in getting worked up over the fact that he wanted a bit of variety. When I thought about it, it made sense why he volunteered to keep all of the Christmas leftovers and bring them home from Castle Rock. He'd been working so hard at college, and I wanted to help however I could. No one wanted to hire me on the grounds that I would be leaving soon to have twins, so I wasn't working. The most I could do was cook, clean, and keep the home comfortable for Leroy so that he had less to stress over.

We were making it work. But there were still nerves that lingered over the fact that things were going to be a lot harder once the kids were born. Football season would be done once they were here, which would make life just a fraction simpler. But Leroy would still be swamped with his studies.

"How about we go out to eat?" I suggested as I glanced out at the cold night with a wince. "We could go and get a burger or something?"

"I can go and get them?" He stood and took our plates over to the sink, seeming super eager at that suggestion. "You don't have to go out in the cold."

"No, I'll come," I said and stood, using the table to lean on while I adjusted to shifting. The babies started moving around and I breathed through the acrobatics. It was breathtaking. Literally.

Leroy rushed toward me and wrapped his arm around my back. "Are you all right?"

"Yeah, I'm good." I exhaled, taking his hand and placing it across my stomach so that he could feel the kicks of our son and daughter.

He smiled and crouched down, placing both hands on my belly. "Never gets old," he murmured.

We were thrilled to be having one of each. When the doctor told us that it was a boy and girl, we had the same response. It was perfect. A brother and sister. A protector and a princess.

After I told Leroy about the dream I'd had, he agreed that it was a sign, a vision of our future, and we had decided on their names with little discussion. He loved Abigail, Abby for short, as he had used in the grocery store back in Castle Rock. And I never was able to figure out where Drayton came from. It was just the name of our dream child and we both thought it was perfect. A strong name.

"Come on, then." Leroy stood after he pressed a quick kiss on my stomach. He snatched the oversized hoodie from the coat rack and my rain boots, helping me to get sorted before we headed for the front door. "What do you feel like eating?"

"Nuggets," I responded as he held my hand and helped me down the front step. "Ooh, with barbecue sauce. And a mint shake. With whipped cream on top."

He laughed as we reached the car. We drove the short distance to the burger joint that we'd become familiar with. I'd gained a fair bit of weight so far—I tried to control the excess with clean eating, but I liked to have a treat occasionally. Cravings are cravings, after all.

We pulled into the drive-thru and Leroy started speaking to the woman in the window while I bopped along to the Creed song on the radio. He paid for the food and drove to the next window to collect the order when I felt an abrupt rush of liquid between my thighs, followed by a tight cramp pain in my stomach.

"Shit!"

Leroy whipped his head toward me with a startled gaze. "Wha—"

"I either just wet myself, or my waters broke," I shouted, barely aware of the woman in the drive-thru window watching with bewilderment as she held out the bag of food. "I think it's my waters. Yeah, it has to be—"

I was cut off by another sharp jolt of pain. It lasted a few seconds, and I was aware from the dozens of birthing tapes that I had been watching that these were contractions. "It's too soon!" I snapped, waving my hands in panic. "I'm only thirty-five weeks!"

"Should I call an ambulance?" the woman in the window asked, leaning out.

"I'm in a car!" Leroy turned to them and grabbed the food, tossing it to me before he slammed the car into gear and tore out of the drive-thru.

"You didn't need to yell at her," I panted as I held on to my stomach. "She just wanted to help."

"I didn't yell at her!"

"You're yelling now!"

"I'm freaking out!"

"Get it together! Someone needs to be fucking stable right now!"

Another contraction began to disable me. He reached across

and held my hand. "It's okay. I'm here. We're not far from the hospital."

All I focused on was breathing through the pain and ignoring the saturated mess beneath me. But Leroy was right. We arrived at the hospital in good time. Not that I was fully aware of much else going on around me. There was so much fear—the fear of pushing two babies out, the fact that they weren't meant to be here for another five weeks.

Leroy left me in the car so that he could find a wheelchair. But when he returned, he was followed by nurses and a stretcher. I would have been embarrassed at all the fuss if I wasn't whimpering through another contraction. The nurses let me know that a doctor was waiting inside and that it would all be okay.

I felt Leroy's hand squeezing mine as he ran alongside the stretcher, the bright lights blinding me as we pushed through the double doors. There was nothing slow about the process, which didn't seem to comfort me. There was a definite panic as the nurses spoke over me in jargon that I couldn't understand. The jolts of the stretcher, the bumps and bangs as we turned corners and went over dips in the doorways, just added to the discomfort of each contraction. This was not how it had gone in the birthing videos. They had attempted to dispel all of those birthing myths about the panic and the rush and the speed of having a baby. According to the videos, during the early stages of labor, you should be reasonably calm, but there was nothing relaxed about these nurses right now.

When we arrived at the delivery suite, a couple of scrubbed doctors greeted me with calming voices. "Right, first things first," said the first doctor, an older man who spoke to me through his mask. "We're going to help you change into a gown and then I need to do an internal and find out how those babies are doing. This needs to happen quickly because you're not full term and we want to get the situation under control as quickly as possible. The good news is, it's not uncommon for twins to arrive early; as long as they're good, it'll all be fine. Good?"

I nodded and let the nurses do most of the hard work, getting me out of the clothes that I was wearing. Leroy stayed beside me but changed into his own pair of scrubs as well. I was offered modesty for the most part, but I was past caring. I just wanted to know that my babies were okay.

Once I was changed, strapped up to a monitor that allowed the doctor to hear the babies' heartbeats, and given an internal examination, the panic seemed to slow. The doctor draped the gown back over me and removed his gloves as he walked toward me. "All right, the babies' heartbeats are wonderful. There's no stress and, yes, they are early, but like I said, that's not uncommon."

"They're coming now?"

He nodded and rested his hand on my shoulder. "We're going to keep a very close eye on that monitor and if anything changes, we've got a surgery room on standby. All right? We can do this. How's Dad feeling?"

I peered up at Leroy who was beside the head of the bed, his fingers laced with mine. He was pale—his usual golden skin had become a lot whiter. But he swallowed and nodded. "Yep. Good. I'm good. As long as she's good. I'm good. Are you good?"

I met his concerned stare and smiled. "I'm good."

*N*

I was in labor for three hours. I couldn't move from the bed. The contractions became worse and worse, longer and far more painful, before I was eventually instructed to push. The nurses stood at the foot of the bed, where the doctor was seated and waiting. He peered up at me, but I couldn't see straight. I was exhausted. "Push Ellie," he shouted with encouragement. "Push for me."

Leroy leaned down and ran his fingers through my damp hair as he murmured with a loving tone. "You can do this, Els. I'm here. I'm right here. You can do this."

I gripped his hand and sat up, putting as much as I could behind a push. I took a deep breath and started again, repeating the action until the doctor told me to stop. "We have a head! Just hang on while I check for a cord, okay? Don't push again until I give the go."

It was almost impossible, but I resisted the urge to push for a few moments before he shouted for me to go again. So, I did, pushing with all that I had until I felt the pressure relieve and the most precious noise filled the entire room. The piercing cries of our baby.

"Come and cut the cord, Leroy," the doctor said. "We have a little man here."

I felt tears falling down my cheeks as I listened to the sweet cries of our little Drayton. Leroy rushed over and cut the cord before the nurse carried him over to the little station in the corner of the room to do their checkups. I wasn't offered a lot of downtime before the doctor told me that the next one was on her way out. The entire process began all over again and when she came out, piercing screams and all, I was a mess. I couldn't stop crying with the most overwhelming sense of joy and exhaustion that I had ever felt.

"Mark down 9:33 p.m. and 9:47 p.m. on the twelfth of January," the doctor called out, "nineteen ninety-nine."

Plump pink lips, skin softer than silk, innocence exuding from their small bodies. After their arrival, the doctors needed to put the twins on a machine to ensure that their lungs were working. They both needed a little bit of help as they weren't fully developed yet. And we would be here for a while before we could go home. But we were allowed to cuddle, so we were making the most of it.

Leroy sat beside me on the edge of the bed and held Abigail in his arms, her five-pound frame wrapped in pink swaddle while I held Drayton, the little blue bundle of perfection. I couldn't get over how beautiful they both were. How something so delicate and fragile could hold so much power. I'd never felt this sort of sense of protection or determination before.

Leroy never stopped watching Abigail. He talked to her, his hushed voice telling her what a sweet little angel she was.

Their lips moved, their little tongues peeping out as they yawned and squeaked. I giggled at the way Drayton opened his eyes, slowly blinking and staring up at me. My heart had never been so full.

"I'm so proud of you," Leroy said, watching me with a sincere gaze. "You did an outstanding job and I will never be able to express with words how proud and how in love with you I am."

My lip quivered as he leaned across and kissed me, stealing the air in my lungs and giving me life, all at the same time.

*N*

Childbirth is exhausting. You hear about it, the toll that it takes on your body and the fatigue that lingers afterward. Still, I wasn't prepared for how hard it would be to wake up again once I fell asleep. Leroy was a huge help overnight. The nurses were so impressed with how attentive he was. He jumped as soon as the twins cried; he helped me latch them onto the breast since I could barely open my eyes. He changed their diapers. He cuddled them back to sleep. Apparently, they didn't do much of anything anyway, just eating and sleeping. The nurses liked to remind us that regardless of what people said about newborns, this was the easiest part.

Eleanor and Jacob arrived sometime after lunch the next day, I was in the middle of pulling my hair into a new bun. It didn't seem to matter how many times I redid it, my hair felt all wrong. I needed a shower more than anything and I'd been hoping to have had one before they arrived. All my worry disappeared when I saw Eleanor with an armful of extravagant gifts with big bows and satin wrapping. Of course she would go right overboard.

"Oh sweetheart," she stopped at the foot of the bed, Jacob close behind her, beaming. "You look beautiful. Glowing."

That had to be a lie, but I appreciated it nonetheless.

"Leroy," she demanded her son's attention, looking at the side-by-side bassinets where Drayton and Abigail were sleeping. "Come and take these gifts so I can get those beautiful babies in my arms."

He grabbed them from her and set them on my lap as Jacob and Eleanor went for the babies. Leroy sat on the bed beside me and we made quick work of tearing wrapping paper open.

"Ooh," Jacob chuckled as he scooped Drayton up. The five-pound bundle looked microscopic in his hold. "Look at that. Most newborns look like wrinkled toes. These ones are beautiful."

Leroy laughed. "Wrinkled toes?"

"This is lovely," I held a box, the picture on the front was of a mobile, one with baby animals on it, glowing animals with dozens of different tune options. "Thank you."

"How is the feeding going?" Eleanor asked, rocking from side to side, her enthralled stare on Abigail. "They latching okay?"

"Yeah," I said. "It's going great, actually. Leroy was amazing last night. He helped get them on and he got them back to sleep and I think he's had less sleep than I have."

Her expression was one of absolute pride when she looked at Leroy. It was a look that I'd become familiar with. In fact, that smile might have been my favorite of hers because it mirrored how I felt about him and how I felt about the sort of man and father he was shaping up to be.

"Oh," she gasped. "What are their names? I can't believe we haven't asked that."

Leroy and I shared a look of excitement because we'd been waiting for them to ask. "That's Drayton Jacob Lahey," he said, and we watched his father's lips press together, emotion evident, "and that's Abigail Eleanor Lahey."

The room fell quiet; both Eleanor and Jacob seemed overwhelmed. "Well, that is . . . that's a big honor." Eleanor sucked in a sharp breath and smiled, teeth baring and all. "Beautiful names. Drayton and Abigail. Just beautiful."

Leroy draped his arm across the pillow behind me. "Where's Noah?"

"He's at school, honey. He wanted to come but he had an important exam that he couldn't miss. He did want us to pass on some good news, though."

"He got accepted to Baylor?" Leroy guessed and Jacob lit up, nodding with excitement. "Good for him. That's . . . good. He must be pleased."

"He is," Eleanor was oblivious to the strain in Leroy's tone. Leroy didn't want to come across as though he didn't want Noah near him, but the space had definitely helped their relationship. There were more phone calls, and when we did see Noah, the get-togethers were generally pleasant. Leroy was nervous that being together again would push them back into old habits, but it wasn't as if they were going to be under the same roof. I wasn't as worried as he was.

"What about Cass?" I asked. "Has she heard back?"

Eleanor's smile slipped. "She wasn't accepted. Quite an unfortunate thing, but I've tried to tell them that it might not be so bad. There are other colleges, and besides, I don't think them being apart would be so terrible. I think they've both got a lot of growing to do, and it might be best done alone."

"You didn't actually say that to them?" Leroy said, bewildered. "It's not as if they would listen."

"No, I didn't say that part out loud," she said and ran her finger down Abigail's soft cheek. "I was just thinking it. I love them both, but I don't know that I love them together. Still, it's their relationship. I won't be the one telling Noah how to navigate it."

"He'll get there," Jacob murmured. I could hear the smile in his voice as he kept his stare directed on Drayton. "He'll no doubt get to college, get focused, and realize that there are some priorities to get in order. He's a smart kid. He'll be fine."

"Speaking of priorities," Eleanor cooed as Abigail began to get restless in her hold, "I think we should consider moving back to Waco so that we can see these little darlings every day."

Jacob chuckled. "Leroy and Ellie don't want us in their faces every day. We'll come and visit every other weekend."

"Every other weekend?" Leroy said, but there was no chance that I would turn that sort of offer down right now. Having helping hands around the house while the twins were brand new would be incredible. Not to mention, I loved his parents as if they were my own. I could never tire of their company and I know Leroy couldn't either, which is why he smiled and said, "That sounds perfect."

## Ellie

Fitting a single stroller through the aisles in Target would be a challenge—even shopping cart jams happened from time to time—so when I tried to move the double stroller through the baby clothes aisle and bumped the wheel into a stand of pacifiers, causing them to spill all over the floor, I wasn't surprised. Embarrassed, but not surprised.

"Sorry," I said to a store assistant who came jogging over to help me clean up.

"Don't be," she said. Her name tag read Yuke. "These aisles are not practical for strollers at all. Which is ridiculous considering this is the baby department."

We made quick work of picking up the pacifiers and Yuke told me that she would organize them properly herself. "Twins," she whispered with awe, peeping into the stroller at my two swaddled bundles, a beanie on each head. "How old are they?"

"Three weeks," I pulled the awning back to make sure they

were still sleeping. Yep, snoozing, oblivious to the rest of the world. It made shopping a lot easier when they were out to it.

Yuke stood up straight, lips parted. "So young. You should be at home, sleeping when they do."

Unsolicited advice was a given at this point. This was the third time I had left the house with them since they'd been born but I'd been told what I should be doing as a parent far more than three times.

"I had to get some thermals," I said. "It's hard to find preemie-size clothing, though. They're too small for most of the outfits that I bought before they were born."

"Oh," Yuke gestured for me to follow her. "We have a small range, you're right, it's hard to find little clothes. How big are they?"

"Just over six pounds."

She looked at me over her shoulder as I tried to keep up with her, being careful not to crash the stroller again. "So little!"

"They were five weeks early."

She stopped beside a rack of clothes that were hidden in the back corner of the Newborn section. She wasn't kidding when she said the selection was small—there wasn't much to it at all—but I did manage to get them a button-up thermal each and some microsized socks. The weather was cold outside, so I threw the rain cover over the stroller and walked back to the car as quickly as I could. Leroy was at classes this morning, I'd dropped him off so that I could use the car and he'd get a ride home with a friend later. Loading the twins into the car was a marathon of its own. Untangling them from their swaddles, strapping them into the rear-facing seats, tucking the blankets over them, collapsing the stroller and hoisting it into the trunk. I was exhausted when I finally dropped into the driver's seat.

When we got home, the process began all over again, in reverse. The parking lot was behind the apartment building, so I couldn't take them in one at a time. I had to put them in the stroller, blankets, rain cover, inside, unload.

"Momma is so tired," I huffed, setting them down on the living-room floor at a safe distance from the heater. Drayton was waking up, gurgling, kicking his strong little legs. It would be time for a feed any minute, but I quickly raced over to the stereo and switched on the CD player so that there was some background noise.

Before I could grab the tri pillow that I used to rest them on during feeding, there was a solid knock on the door, which was strange because the only people who visited were back in Colorado until next weekend. I wasn't sure who to expect but it certainly wasn't the woman standing on the other side of the door when I opened it.

"Mom?"

"Hi," she said, clutching her purse tightly against her side.

Shock rendered me frozen. I stared at her, noticing how different she looked. Her hair was short now, chopped into a pixie cut. She was thinner and overall looked more vibrant. Younger. Which shouldn't have disappointed me, but whenever I thought about Momma without me, after all that had happened, I imagined her miserable, drowning in guilt for how things had been left between us.

"What are you doing here?"

She seemed nervous, pointing over her shoulder. "I saw you at Target and I . . . well . . . I was hoping that we could talk?"

"Did you follow me here?"

"Yes, I'm sorry. I wanted to approach you in the store but I was—well, I was nervous. I can go if this isn't a good time."

The twins started fussing from the living room, little cries and gurgles, and Mom's curious stare went over my shoulder. As stubborn as I wanted to be about the situation, as much as I wanted to stand my ground and let her know that I was still upset, the need to hear what she had to say outweighed all else. The truth was, I'd missed her and I hoped that she was here with something positive to say.

"Come in," I stood aside. "I have to feed the twins before I can offer you a coffee. Go straight through to the living room."

All of her movements were slow and cautious. She looked around, head twisting and turning as she moved into the living room, and then her focus fell to the twins on the floor and she wore an expression that I'd never seen before. Awe, admiration, regret. It was hard to tell which one she was feeling the most.

"Take a seat if you want," I said, gesturing at the sofa.

She was still clutching her purse as she lowered herself into the sofa, watching as I tucked the tri pillow around my waist. One at a time, I picked the twins up off the floor, put them on the sofa a few feet apart and then I sat down between them. Drayton went on first, his torso and legs tucked around my waist—he was the most impatient and made a lot of noise if he didn't get fed as quickly as possible. Abby went on next, in the same position on the other side. They latched on and I listened to their guzzling and quick breathing through their noses.

"You're doing well," Mom said after a few minutes of deafening silence. She watched the twins, their tiny fists balled up on my chest. "It's just you here?"

I wasn't sure if she was questioning my relationship status but I felt defensive nonetheless. "Leroy is in class right now. He has—"

As if he'd been summoned, the front door swung open. "Els? I'm home. Have the twins been fed yet? Sorry, I tried to get back on time to help but our professor had some riddle that he wanted us to think about overnight. You might be able to—"

His sentence dropped off as he walked into the living room, his gaze moving between Mom and me.

"Hey," I smiled, the awkward tension in the room was magnified. "This is my mom, Sandra. Mom, this is my fiancé, Leroy."

"Fiancé?" Mom quietly said to herself while Leroy stared at me as if to say, *what the hell?* I shrugged, equally as confused. "It's nice to meet you, Leroy."

"You too," he rested his hands on his hips. "Have they had enough to eat?"

The twins had fallen into a milk coma, their lips detached from the nipple while little drizzles of white ran down their cheeks. "Yeah. They need to be changed, though."

"I've got it," he said and darted forward so that I could put a twin on either of his big strong forearms. He could carry them both at the same time with no issue at all. After he gave me a quick kiss, he disappeared to our bedroom and shut the door.

Silence ensued again and it was making me somewhat restless. Every time I opened my mouth to initiate conversation, the words got caught in my throat, or a blank wave washed over my mind and thinking of any words at all seemed impossible. Surely, she hadn't shown up here just to sit there and say nothing at all.

"He seems like a very young nice man," Mom said so suddenly that it startled me. "Very involved."

"He is," I said, playing with the frill on the edge of the tri pillow. "He's at college but he's still really hands-on around here. He comes home during his breaks and he helps at night."

"And you're engaged."

"He proposed last summer. He's pretty eager to get married but we're waiting for the right time."

Her stare drifted, it became distant and sad.

"Mom, what are you doing here?"

"Your father came into the store a couple of weeks ago," she said and the ground fell out from beneath me. "He was asking after you."

"What? My . . . father. He was asking after me?"

She inhaled a deep breath and nodded. "He claimed it had taken him far too long but it was about time he had some involvement. He wanted to know where you were and how he could contact you."

"What did you say?"

"I told him that you were out of town and I'd talk to you," she dropped her gaze and her voice took on a slight tremor. "I was embarrassed to admit that I didn't know where my daughter was or how to contact her."

She sniffled and swiped at her cheek, leaving me with this sinking feeling in my stomach. Seeing Momma cry was something I hadn't witnessed a lot in my lifetime, but it was hard no matter the occasion.

"Seeing him," she said. "Reminded me of a decision that I'd made a long time ago. The decision to raise my daughter the best I could, despite being left in the lurch by that man. He walked away, he chose not to love you, and I knew it was up to me to do better."

Her crying got heavier. "And then I did the same thing that he did. I walked away when you needed me the most and I am so sorry, Ellie," she buried her face in her hands. "It felt like I was watching history repeat itself. Young love, a wealthy man, a pregnancy. I'd done it all and I was so terrified that it was going to end the same way. I didn't want that for you. I didn't want you to go through that heartbreak and end up struggling for the rest of your life."

The fact that I had no idea what to say was starting to frustrate me. Whenever I came close to a response, she continued speaking.

"I know I haven't always been the most affectionate woman. I had a lot of rules and I had a short temper, but I do love you, Ellie, and I only wanted the best for you. I can see now, you were right. You're doing very well for yourself and that boy loves you."

"He does," I finally said, my throat feeling thick. "I don't think you were wrong to be worried, Momma. It's normal to be worried about the unknown, especially when it comes to something so major. All I wanted was for you to have a little bit of faith in my judgment."

"I should have," she agreed. "You've always been a smart and sensible girl. I should have trusted your choices and I handled it all wrong. Ellie, I really am so sorry for how I behaved."

"I forgive you, Momma."

Her lip quivered again, her face crumpling as she stood up and opened her arms. Being pulled into her hug felt like a new beginning, a chance to start over. In all of my life, I'd never felt as comforted by a hug from her as I did in that moment. All of her anguish and regret was obvious in the way she held me—she truly was apologetic.

"Your children are beautiful," she mumbled into my hair. "Just beautiful."

I leaned back and swiped at a tear that slid down my cheek. "They are pretty great."

Leroy came back out with the twins and Momma sat down with the tri pillow so that we could rest them on it, and she could enjoy a cuddle. It was an odd sight to see—I wasn't sure if I would ever witness Momma looking longingly at her grandchildren, but the smile that she wore made my heart swell.

"Would you like to stay for dinner, Sandra?" Leroy asked.

"Oh," Momma looked at me for permission and I nodded. "That would be lovely."

Leroy tilted his head for me to follow him and when we were out of sight in the kitchen, he leaned against the countertop and pulled me between his spread legs. "You okay?" he whispered.

"Yeah," I whispered back; Momma was just in the next room, after all. "That was nice of you to ask her for dinner."

"I realized about zero-point-two seconds after I said that, I should have asked you first."

"It's fine," I assured him, caressing his stubbled jaw. "I'm happy she's here. I mean, I haven't felt like I'm incomplete or anything without her, but it's still really nice that she wants to try."

He leaned in and kissed my forehead, his lips lingering for a few sweet seconds. "I'm happy for you, baby."

"Oh, what was the riddle that your professor gave you guys. Is it in English class?"

"Yeah," his brows pulled with thought. "*I may only be given, but never bought, sinners seek me, but saints do not.*"

"Wow," I winced. "Blank."

"Me too," he laughed. "I'll have to have a think about it."

We kissed and then I went back out into the living area where Momma was still staring at the twins with contentment.

"Have you seen my . . . father again since he came into the store?" I asked, sitting down beside her.

"No," she said. "He left his phone number, but I haven't contacted him. It's totally up to you what you do with that information, Ellie. I won't try to control things like I've been guilty of in the past."

I smiled at her and tucked my legs up under my bum. "I appreciate that. I'm not sure I'll do anything, though. He's a complete stranger, you know? Too little, too late."

She didn't say anything.

"I don't know. I'll need some time to think about it."

"Of course."

"It's my birthday next weekend."

Momma looked at me with an amused grin that felt so foreign on her features. "I know that."

"Leroy's family are flying in for a small birthday party. It won't be much. Dinner, cake. That sort of thing. Do you want to come?"

"I'd like that very much, Ellie."

We sat around our small dining room table that night, the twins swaddled in their bouncers. Leroy never let the conversation dwindle. He talked to Momma, asked her questions about the store, exchanged life stories and talk of the future. My heart felt full and suddenly Leroy's riddle came back to me. *I may only be given, but never bought, sinners seek me, but saints do not.*

Forgiveness. The answer was forgiveness.

# EPILOGUE

## LEROY

*Six months later*

Ellie and I brought the twins home for the summer. It was their first time in Colorado and Mom and Dad were thriving, ecstatic at the attention they were able to bestow upon Drayton and Abby. Mom decorated the spare bedroom, turning it into a nursery with the cribs that Noah and I used as babies.

Out in the back garden, there was a large picnic blanket spread out on the grass. The twins were wriggling around, picking up toys that were scattered and gurgling with excitement. Both of them had wispy blond hair and eyes that were becoming greener the older they got. Green like their mother's. I didn't think that I could love anyone more than I loved Ellie, but these two had unlocked a part of my heart that I didn't even know existed and I had never felt fuller.

"Ooh, isn't he quick?" Mom said, watching Drayton commando

crawl off the blanket, using just his arms and a wormlike shuffle. Ellie had dressed him in a sleeveless one-piece that morning—the weather was sweltering and he and Abby both had bucket hats tied to their heads. Abby was currently sprawled out on her back, tugging hers with frustration.

"Careful, Mom," I said, pointing at Drayton. "That one is unpredictable."

I was about to go get Drayton when Abby started sulking, frustrated that her hat wouldn't come off. I pulled her into my lap.

"She's such a daddy's girl," Ellie said, standing up. "I'll grab Drayton."

Mom watched Abby cuddling into me, yawning. We did have a special little bond happening, her and me. When she was unsettled, she wanted me to rock her to sleep, and when she was excited, her gaze fixed on me while she babbled and cooed. Of course, she loved Ellie too. Ellie was her mom who breastfed her and that connection with a mother was unique. But I felt sort of special knowing that my little girl often came to me when she needed some cuddles and comfort. Ellie came and sat back down, putting Drayton between her outstretched legs.

"These two will need their afternoon nap soon," she said, shoving a bunch of toys in front of Drayton in an attempt to distract him from zooming off again. He was so adventurous and could move very well for someone who wasn't yet crawling properly. It was a challenge, but I loved that about our son. I loved that he was so curious.

Dad rolled the little plastic football toy to Drayton, who picked it up and started gumming it. Everything went straight into his mouth these days.

"How many quarterbacks can we get in a row before the future generations break the cycle? Hmm?"

"Might even go to Baylor too," I added, lightly jostling from side to side so that Abby could drift off. Her lids were hooded, and she was relaxed in my arms. "Could be a cool tradition."

"Ah, imagine that," Dad said, smiling. "A long line of Baylor graduates. That'd be a delight. Don't suppose we'll be around to see it, though."

My chest tightened. Mom and Dad joked about their age a lot, but I hated hearing anything to do with the fact that they wouldn't be here one day. I knew that they wouldn't be here forever but that didn't mean that I wanted to dwell on it.

"You'll be fine," I said, meeting Ellie's eyes, who mirrored my expression. She loved them, too, and couldn't imagine our lives without them.

"We'll be in our eighties," Mom gasped, clutching her chest. "That's a frightening thought. But who knows, perhaps we'll still be kicking it."

"No doubt," I said just as Noah and Cass came through the back gate hand in hand.

"Who's up for mini golf?!" Cass hollered. She had shades on, but I could tell the moment that she saw Abby asleep in my arms because her mouth fell open and she came to a standstill. "That is the cutest shit I have ever seen."

"Mini golf sounds like a wonderful idea," Mom said. "Leave the twins here and go and have some time out."

"Are you sure?" Ellie asked. "That does sound fun."

"Of course," Dad said. "Go and have a break. We'll manage with these two."

"I'll put them down for their nap first." Ellie smiled at Cass who had plonked herself down beside Drayton so that she could coo at him. Noah sat and stretched his legs on the grass. "Is it just us four for mini golf?"

"Eric and Amber too," Cass said, tickling Drayton. Amber and Eric had returned to their homes for the summer as well. From what I knew, they were splitting time together between his parents and hers.

Ellie stood up and hauled our son onto her hip. He was a chonk, lots of rolls and chub, but Els never complained about having to haul him around. As it was, I tried to take that task off her hands as often as possible, especially if we were out at the store or park and we had to put them in the double sling. After Drayton had tried to climb out of the pram while we were on a scenic stroll, we'd decided to retire it and attempt a more secure method.

Mom offered to help Ellie with the twins, and I carefully transferred a dozing Abby into Mom's arms. She, Cass, and Ellie disappeared inside, leaving me with Noah and Dad out under the hot summer sun. Not a cloud in sight.

"I put the payment through for the campus housing," Dad said to Noah.

"Thanks, Dad," he said.

"Not a problem. I'm very proud of how hard you've worked to get into this program at college. You applied yourself and it paid off. You've done well, son."

Noah swallowed and I could tell that he wasn't expecting the praise. It wasn't the first time Dad had told Noah that he was proud of him, but Noah rarely chose to hear it, instead focusing on the things that he wasn't being told.

"Thanks," Noah said, a small nod aimed at Dad.

"Both my boys at Baylor," Dad grinned. "Wonderful, isn't it? And you'll be close together again. That'll be nice."

Noah and I shared a brief glance. We'd been getting along better since I'd moved to Waco, but it was hard to know what our relationship would be like when we were living close together again. Ellie told me to be more positive, as she often did. She assured me that we'd be fine considering we weren't under the same roof and we could still hang out as little or often as we liked. Something told me that college would be what Noah needed. He'd find his people. He'd find groups and clubs, and it might be exactly what he needed.

"Right," Dad said. "I'm going to go and make a cup of tea. Want one?"

Noah and I both declined and watched our old father move across the lawn much faster than a man his age should be capable. It made me hopeful that he'd be around for a lot longer than he seemed to think.

"Your kids are cool," Noah said, lying in the grass with an arm across his face. He'd been giving the twins attention here and there since we'd arrived in Castle Rock, but he wasn't affectionate in any sense of the word. "The little dude is funny. Seems like he's going to be hard work."

"For sure," I laughed. "You gonna babysit for me when you get to Waco? Watch the kids so that Ellie and I can go out once a week."

"You wish," Noah scoffed but there was a small smile on his mouth. "You'd trust me to watch the kids?"

I plucked at the grass and laughed. "Probably not. Ellie won't even let me hire from the babysitter directory."

"Fair enough. Too many weirdos."

"Yeah," I said and looked at the upstairs window to see my girl walking back and forth with Drayton over her shoulder. He was stubborn—he didn't like to be told when to sleep. "Has Cass decided what to do this semester?"

Noah let out a sound of exasperation. "She wants to come to Waco, but she can't live with me on campus and she's not going to college. I don't know. She's stressing out all the time. She said she wanted to find a job there and talk to you and Els about boarding with you for a while."

That was definitely not happening. Our apartment was tiny, we didn't have a spare bedroom, and Cass was a bit of a whirl-wind. Of course, if it was an urgent matter, we'd take her in without question. But her wanting to live in Waco because she doesn't trust Noah at college didn't seem urgent to me. Sure, Els could always use the extra hands when I was at classes, but that was what her mom had been popping around a few times a week for. She'd watch the twins while Ellie had a nap or showered or cleaned. She was a great help. Cass would be more like a third child to look after.

"Have you done a lot to convince her that she's got nothing to stress over?"

Noah shrugged a shoulder. "I guess."

In other words, no.

"How are things going between you guys at the moment?"

"Fine."

"Dude," I said, nudging him with my foot. "Maybe now is the time to think about . . . calling it quits? If you're not truly invested in the relationship, go to college with a clean break. It'll get messy otherwise."

He was quiet for so long that I thought he'd fallen asleep.

Eventually, he grumbled and sat up, rubbing his face with his hands.

"I don't—I'm not really sure that I love the same way that you do," he said quietly. "She's my best friend and I trust her, I care about her, but . . . I still think about other girls. I see someone and I'm thinking about how to approach them and then I remember that . . . I remember that Cass would be hurt and so I don't. I don't do anything, but the fact that I think about it . . . that shouldn't happen, right?"

"Attraction is normal. It does happen. Acting on the attraction is . . . not okay. But you don't act on it. So, that's good."

"You been attracted to other women since Ellie?"

"Sure, I can appreciate when a woman is beautiful."

"But do you think about going over to them and asking them for a phone number and taking them out and . . . do you think about having sex with them? Do you think about all of that when you see a beautiful woman? Is it hard to be faithful?"

He was waiting for my answer, hope in his desperate stare. He so badly wanted me to tell him that I knew exactly what he was going through. Sure, appreciating someone's beauty was a natural thing, but the fact that he struggled so hard to be faithful, and the only reason he chose to be was because he knew it was the right thing to do, told me that he didn't love Cass in the way that he should. It shouldn't be hard to remain faithful when it's real.

"No, it's not hard for me to be faithful, Noah," I said, honestly. "It's the easiest thing in the world. For starters, appreciating that a woman is beautiful doesn't immediately transpire into animalistic attraction for me. It just doesn't. Ellie is the only woman I feel like that about. Second, no part of me would ever want to be the reason that she hurts. I don't ever want to lose her, and I won't ever put myself in a position that would cost us our relationship. It's easy to avoid. I honestly don't get how people have such a hard time just not . . . cheating."

His shoulder's sagged, he exhaled with defeat. "Why can't I feel like that?"

"Maybe she's just not the right woman for you."

"But you like Cass."

"I love Cass," I told him. "That's not my point. She's not wrong as a person. She just might not be right for you."

He slowly shook his head, watching the road. "If she's not the right woman, I don't know who could be. I love her more than any other girl I've ever been with."

"You can fall in love with her," I told him and gave him a nudge in the arm. "Proper in love. You know? It takes time and effort and all of that. But you can get there if that's what you want."

"I have to get there. I care about her too much to lose her."

"Well, then you're already heading in the right direction," I said, proud of the fact that at least he was trying. He knew what was right and he wanted to do it. Some people knew what was right and still followed wrong. For now, I'd support him however I could.

*✗*

Ellie, Cass, Noah, and I arrived at the mini-golf course and saw Amber and Eric waiting on the brick wall that circled the parking lot. As soon as we'd hopped out of the car, I went over to Eric and we grinned at each other before we hugged. It'd been a while since we'd caught up.

"How's it, bro?" He slapped me on the back. "Or should I say Dad?! Man, what a trip. How are the little ones?"

I stepped back and saw Amber, Ellie, and Cass giggling and greeting each other with excitement. Noah sidled up beside me, hands in his pockets. "The kids are good," I said. "Keeping us busy."

"Yeah, I bet. How do you manage that and college? All I have is a girlfriend and I'm like, shit, this is rough. Studies and exams and papers and football. How do you do it?"

"Ellie," I said as an explanation. "For real. She does the meals, she does the housework, she takes care of the kids. She's a straight-up legend. During the week, I go to classes, come home and study until seven, and then we have dinner, and then I do bath time, bedtime, and help her clean up the house. It's not a bad routine at the moment."

"Aw man," Eric said, "that's so cool, bro. You've nailed it. Els!"

Ellie turned her attention to the sound of Eric calling out for her and made her way over to us.

"Hello, beautiful Momma." Eric pulled her into a bear hug, and I said hello to Amber. "Leroy was just telling me about what a superwoman you are. Got shit locked down, huh?"

"I do try," Ellie said, modest as ever. "Leroy is a huge help, though. I couldn't do it without him."

She gave me more credit than I deserved. Watching Ellie raise our children gave me an entirely new level of understanding toward what women sacrifice for their kids. Her body had changed—not that I minded at all; she was still perfect as far as I was concerned. Her life now revolved around our twins. She couldn't act on impulse and meet up with girlfriends or go to the thrift store without first loading the car up with the diaper bags and strollers. Showers had to be scheduled events. Her sleep was broken, and she was exhausted all the time. But she was happiest when she was with the three of us and I'd never loved her more. I would give her the world if I could and it still wouldn't be enough.

We held hands and the six of us went inside to pay for our turn on the course. Ellie and I walked behind everyone else and I kissed her cheek, grazing the side of her mouth. "When are we getting married?"

She bit down on a grin. "After you've graduated."

"That just seems so far away. I think we should bring it forward."

"We talked about this," she said, angling her face up to look at me, a light dusting of summer freckles across her button nose and rounded cheeks. "Graduation first, house second, wedding third."

"We could be traditional. We could get married first."

"You sound so impatient," she teased. I stopped walking and tugged on her hand so that she spun around and collided with my front.

"I *am* impatient," I said, tucking her hair behind her ear. "But I'll do whatever you want. Always."

She threw her arms around my neck. "I guess being traditional wouldn't be the worst thing. I'd be a Lahey. That would be nice."

"Mrs. Lahey." I stared into the distance and smacked my lips as if I was tasting something delicious. "I love the sound of that."

She gave me a quick kiss. "Can we do something before we go back to your parents' house this afternoon?"

"Sure, what is it?"

"Find somewhere private and quiet where we won't be disturbed for an hour?"

My blood rushed south, and I swallowed. "We should absolutely do that. We could do that now. Should we bounce?"

"Come on, you two!" Eric waved us over, holding our putters in his hand. The group was wandering toward the double swing doors where the course waited on the other side. "Let's go."

"Come on," Ellie took my hand again and winked. "We'll have our time alone later, promise."

"Yeah," I said. "We will."

Besides, this girl was my forever. We had all the time in the world.

**THE END.**

# ACKNOWLEDGMENTS

Book number two would not have happened without the beautiful people who were so supportive of *The QB Bad Boy and Me*. Every private message of appreciation, every Instagram post and story that I was tagged in, photos of the book and the reviews on Goodreads—it all made a world of difference.

Thank you to the team at Wattpad for taking a chance on me and working alongside me to bring this book to life. Deanna for her excellent notes and editing help. Jen for her incredible advice when it came to tying the book into a nice little parcel with a ribbon on top. Monica for answering every question and email that I sent, and the marketing team that sent me emails on how to promote the book on social media. The staff at Wattpad are an incredible group of people that strive to help hundreds of writers reach their dreams. It's incredible to see what has been done for so many people like myself.

Thank you to God who answered my prayers and gave me strength when I was struggling over late nights and sore eyes.

Thank you to my friends and family and husband for helping with the kids when I was rushing to meet a deadline or needed a bit of a break. I have an incredible support system around me. A wonderful mum and sister, grandparents, best friends.

Thank you to my three children who, while stuck in quarantine with me, had to deal with the fact that there were days when Mummy absolutely had to work on edits, and were gracious enough to be patient when I couldn't play all the time. It wasn't easy to balance the children being at home 24/7 and working at the same time. They discovered just how much time I spend on my work and some days they struggled with it, but they never complained. They're wonderful kids and I feel blessed.

A list of people from Instagram I want to mention because of the friendships we've developed: Ashley Marie, Alyssia May, Taylor Hale, Cathron, Alexandra Marie, Danya, Tayler, Krissy Dunnigan, and Lauran J.

Trust me, I know there are a hundred more names that I could add to this list. If you've ever sent me words of encouragement or support, you have a special place in my heart. Thank you. I could never say it enough.

# ABOUT THE AUTHOR

Tay Marley wears many hats: bibliophile, entrepreneur, wife, mother, and featured Wattpad author. Her whirlwind journey on Wattpad began in 2017 and led to one hundred thousand dedicated followers, a five-part series, and three stand-alone books—including her breakout story, *The QB Bad Boy and Me*—which have amassed over forty-one million reads. She resides in New Zealand with her husband. When she isn't writing about confident women and their love interests, she's teaching her three small children how to be the leads of their own epic tales.

# Where stories live.

Discover millions of stories created by diverse writers from around the globe.

Download the app or visit www.wattpad.com today.

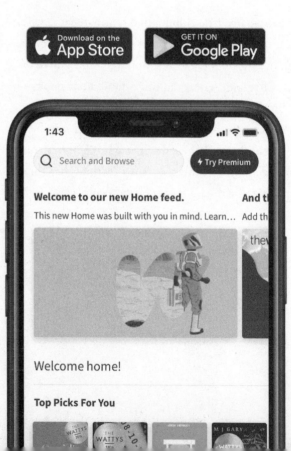

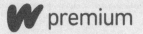

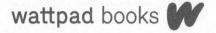